GALAXY OF FOOTBALL

To The F2 Family across the galaxy...

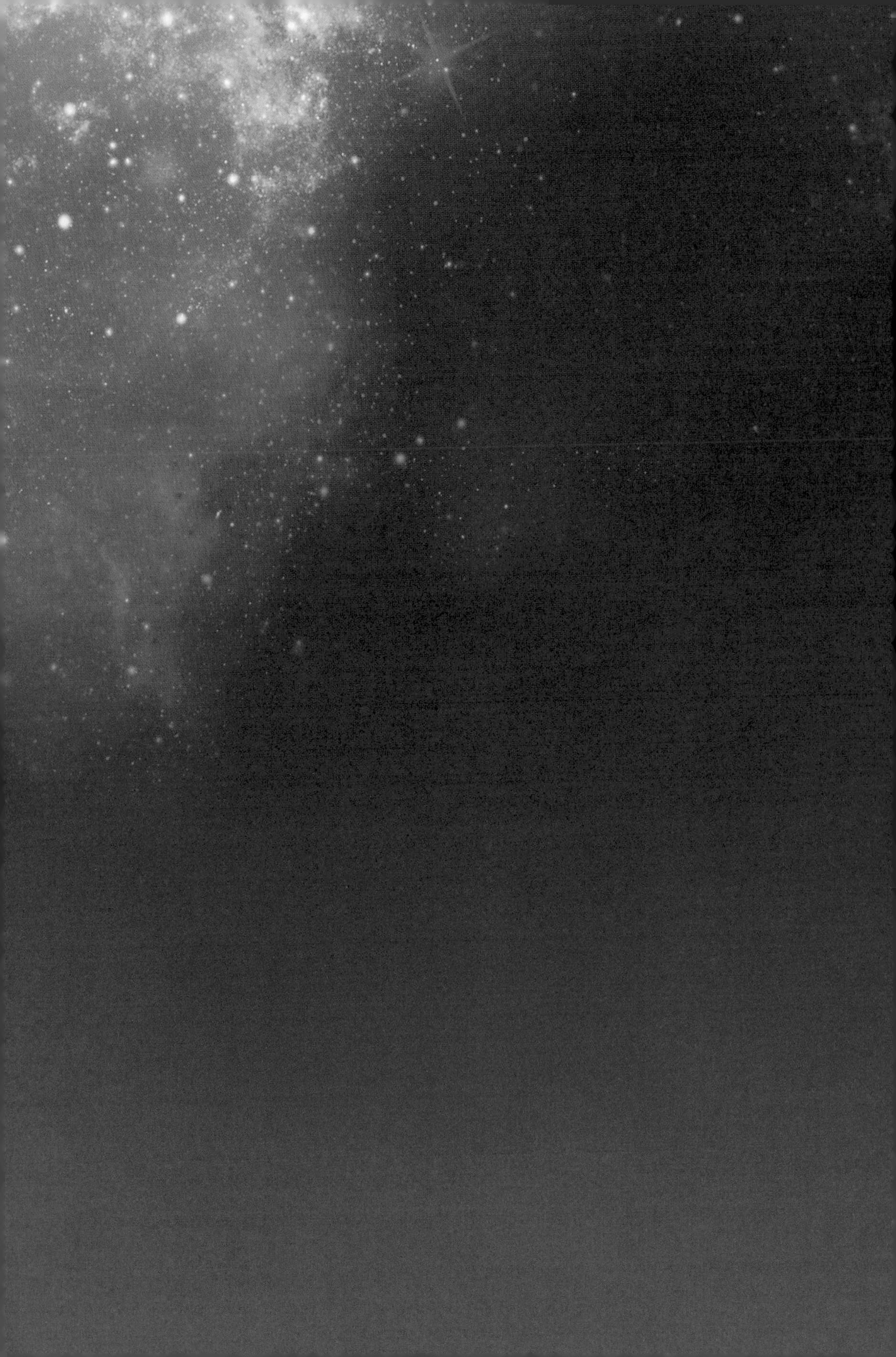

GALAXY OF FOOTBALL

ATTACK OF THE FOOTBALL CYBORGS

BLINK

bringing you closer

Published by Blink Publishing
3.08, The Plaza,
535 Kings Road,
Chelsea Harbour,
London, SW10 0SZ

www.blinkpublishing.co.uk

facebook.com/blinkpublishing
twitter.com/blinkpublishing

Hardback – 978-1-911-60000-8
Ebook – 978-1-911-60011-4

A CIP catalogue of this book is available from the British Library.

Artwork by Amrit Birdi
Printed and bound by Stige Arti Grafiche

1 3 5 7 9 10 8 6 4 2

Artwork produced by Amrit Birdi & Co
Pencils: Amrit Birdi
Inks: Renzo Rodriguez
Colours: Joaquin Pereyra
Colour flats: Riley Jones
Letters: Mindy Lopkin
Writers: Dan Watters and Alex Paknadel

Blink Publishing is an imprint of the Bonnier Publishing Group
www.bonnierpublishing.co.uk

YES GUYS!

JEZ: Welcome to The F2's first ever graphic novel. Actually, no, let's do that again... Welcome to the *OUT-OF-THIS-WORLD, TOTALLY AWESOME, OUTRAGEOUSLY SICK, F2 GALAXY OF FOOTBALL*, where worlds collide, aliens play football, robo-Tekkers come alive and I invent a time machine!

BILLY: You mean we invent a time machine, Jez?

JEZ: Oh yeah, I meant we. Sorry, I'm just so excited to introduce to The F2 family our brand-new graphic novel, which --

BILLY: -- which is probably the best football book you're ever likely to read.

JEZ: Exactly!

BILLY: And not only that, a football book that includes some of the coolest Tekkers you'll ever see and is packed to the rafters with cameos from the game's greatest players...

JEZ: Like who, Billy?

BILLY: That would be giving it away on the first page. Let's just say some of the game's most legendary characters turn out to help us defeat the Galaxicos and save the world from their evil plans.

JEZ: Sounds awesome. In fact, it's more than that: it's probably the greatest adventure story ever told, right Billy?

BILLY: Right. Good vs. evil; human vs. cyborg; Team F2 vs. an alien life form intent on taking over the galaxy... It's got it all!

JEZ: Don't forget the love interest too. Gotta have a love interest to make it a truly great story!

BILLY: Exactly. It also has a story that we hold close to our hearts - a tale of how a bit of belief in yourself can see you do anything, no matter what the odds. Just work hard and you can overcome anything! And don't listen to the naysayers - you'll see that those guys never come out on top!

JEZ: But wait, Bill; we're nearly at the end of this Introduction. Shouldn't we get ourselves into position? I think our first appearance is on page 4, right?

BILLY: You mean your first appearance. I need to find my time-bike before I blast on to the page...

JEZ: Easy mate - don't want to give the game away!

BILLY: Sorry, guys. But don't worry, this book is so full of awesome things, revealing that I have a time-bike that allows me to travel through a time vortex and into a galaxy far, far away, really isn't revealing much.

JEZ: Too true, too true. Well, let's get this book started, shall we?

BILLY: Let's do it! Enjoy the book, guys. Settle down, buckle up and join us on a journey through time and space...

JEZ: Love, Peace...

BILLY: ...And Tekkers!

THE F2

ACROSS THE NIGHT IT COMES, DANCING TO THE LOW, WISTFUL CHANTS OF DYING STARS.

IT COMES IN SEARCH OF NEW PLEASURES, STRANGE DESIRES STIRRING IN ITS FLUID DEPTHS.

WITH CHILDLIKE JOY IT SEEKS STIMULATION, IT SEEKS GAMES, AND PAYS NO MIND TO THE RUINED WORLDS IT LEAVES IN ITS WAKE.

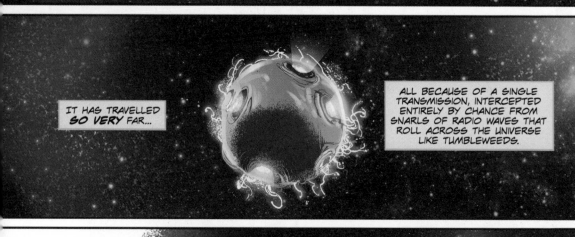

IT HAS TRAVELLED *SO VERY* FAR...

ALL BECAUSE OF A SINGLE TRANSMISSION, INTERCEPTED ENTIRELY BY CHANCE FROM SNARLS OF RADIO WAVES THAT ROLL ACROSS THE UNIVERSE LIKE TUMBLEWEEDS.

BUT IT WOULD TRAVEL FARTHER, TO SEEK WHAT THE SIGNAL SPOKE OF...

... IT WOULD CROSS THE UNIVERSE IN PURSUIT OF THIS SO-CALLED "BEAUTIFUL GAME."

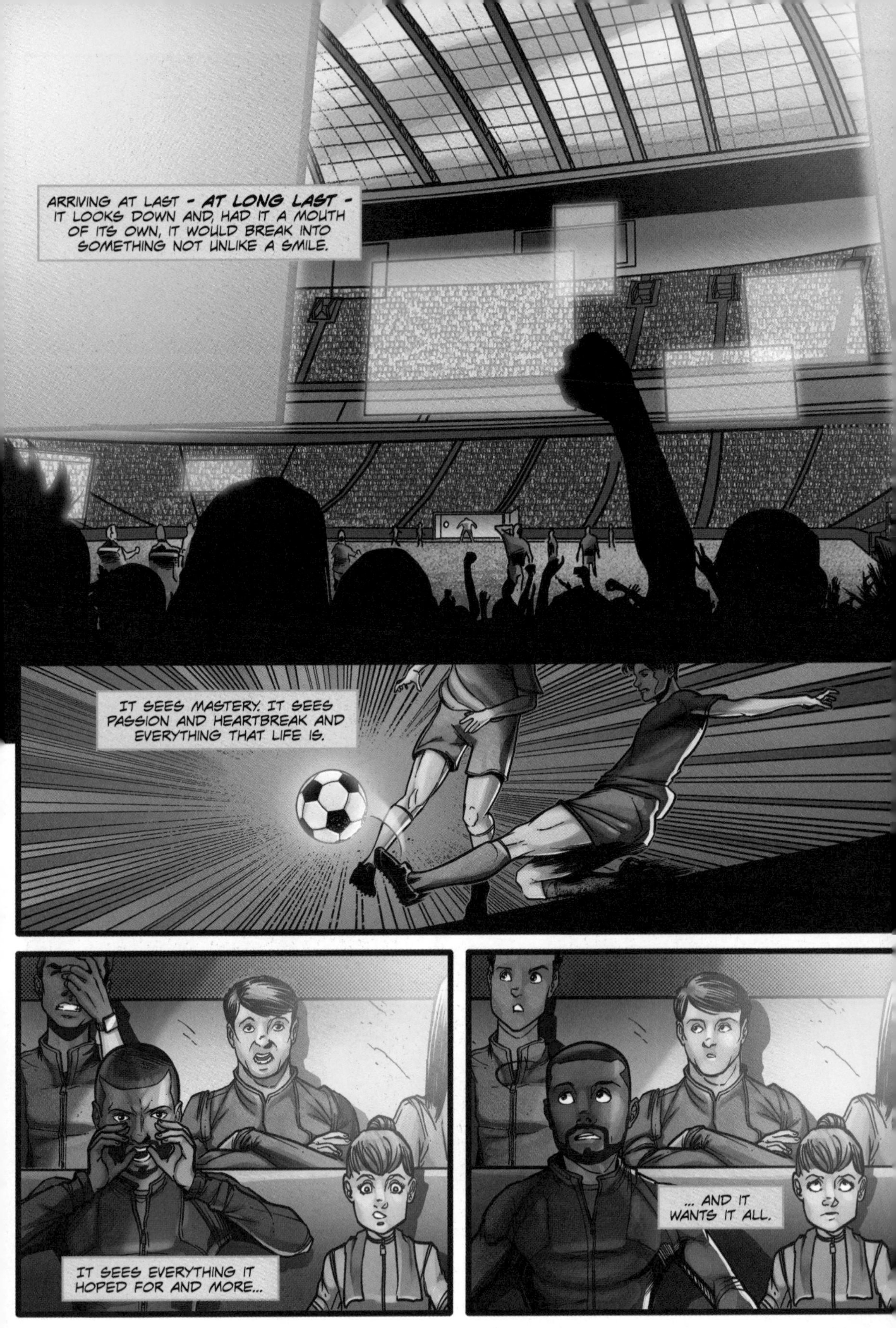
ARRIVING AT LAST - AT LONG LAST - IT LOOKS DOWN AND, HAD IT A MOUTH OF ITS OWN, IT WOULD BREAK INTO SOMETHING NOT UNLIKE A SMILE.
IT SEES MASTERY. IT SEES PASSION AND HEARTBREAK AND EVERYTHING THAT LIFE IS.
IT SEES EVERYTHING IT HOPED FOR AND MORE...
... AND IT WANTS IT ALL.

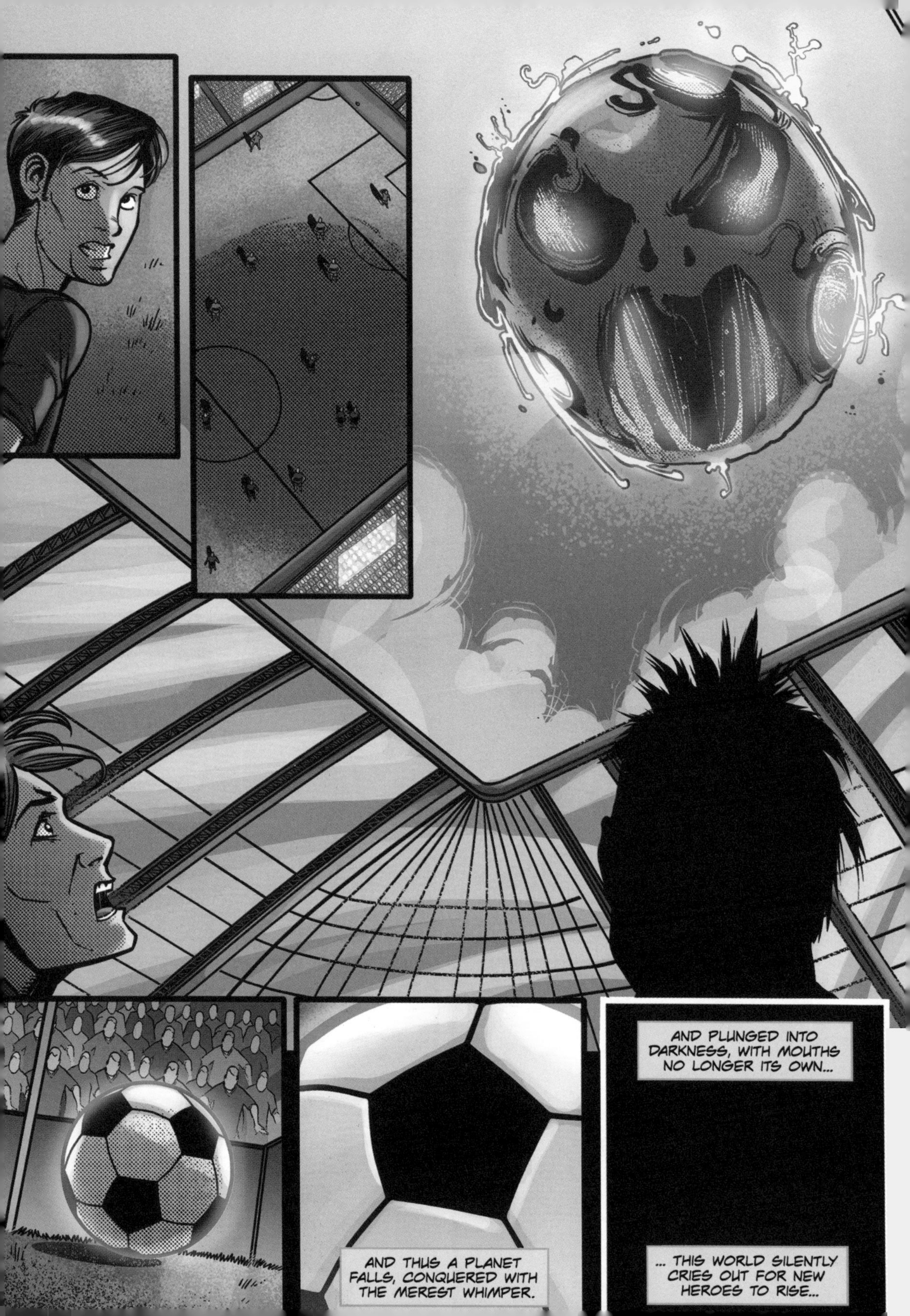
AND THUS A PLANET FALLS, CONQUERED WITH THE MEREST WHIMPER.
AND PLUNGED INTO DARKNESS, WITH MOUTHS NO LONGER ITS OWN...
... THIS WORLD SILENTLY CRIES OUT FOR NEW HEROES TO RISE...

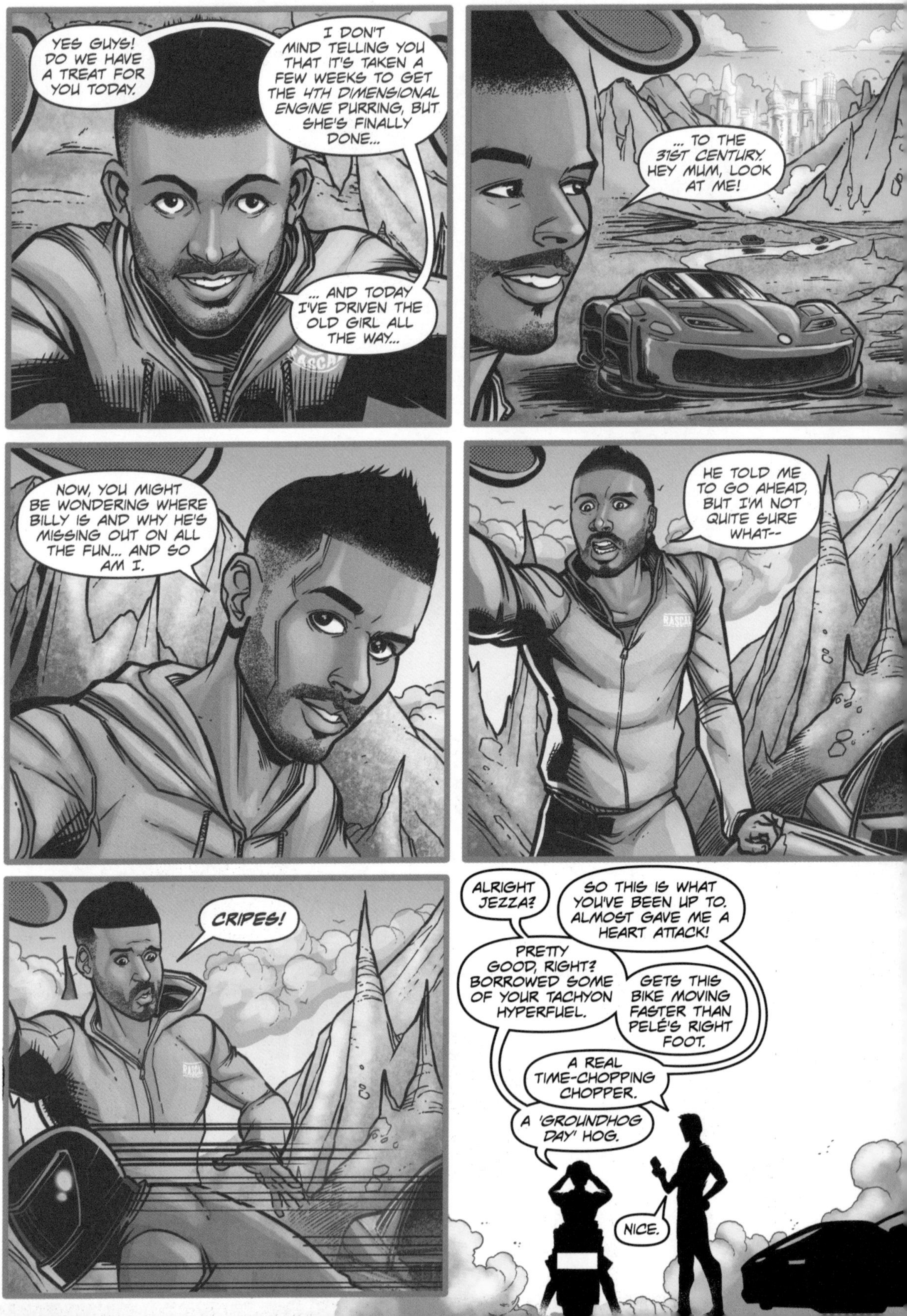
YES GUYS! DO WE HAVE A TREAT FOR YOU TODAY.
I DON'T MIND TELLING YOU THAT IT'S TAKEN A FEW WEEKS TO GET THE 4TH DIMENSIONAL ENGINE PURRING, BUT SHE'S FINALLY DONE...
... AND TODAY I'VE DRIVEN THE OLD GIRL ALL THE WAY...
RASCAL
... TO THE 31ST CENTURY. HEY MUM, LOOK AT ME!
NOW, YOU MIGHT BE WONDERING WHERE BILLY IS AND WHY HE'S MISSING OUT ON ALL THE FUN... AND SO AM I.
HE TOLD ME TO GO AHEAD, BUT I'M NOT QUITE SURE WHAT--
RASCAL
CRIPES!
RASCAL
ALRIGHT JEZZA?
SO THIS IS WHAT YOU'VE BEEN UP TO. ALMOST GAVE ME A HEART ATTACK!
PRETTY GOOD, RIGHT? BORROWED SOME OF YOUR TACHYON HYPERFUEL.
GETS THIS BIKE MOVING FASTER THAN PELÉ'S RIGHT FOOT.
A REAL TIME-CHOPPING CHOPPER.
A 'GROUNDHOG DAY' HOG.
NICE.

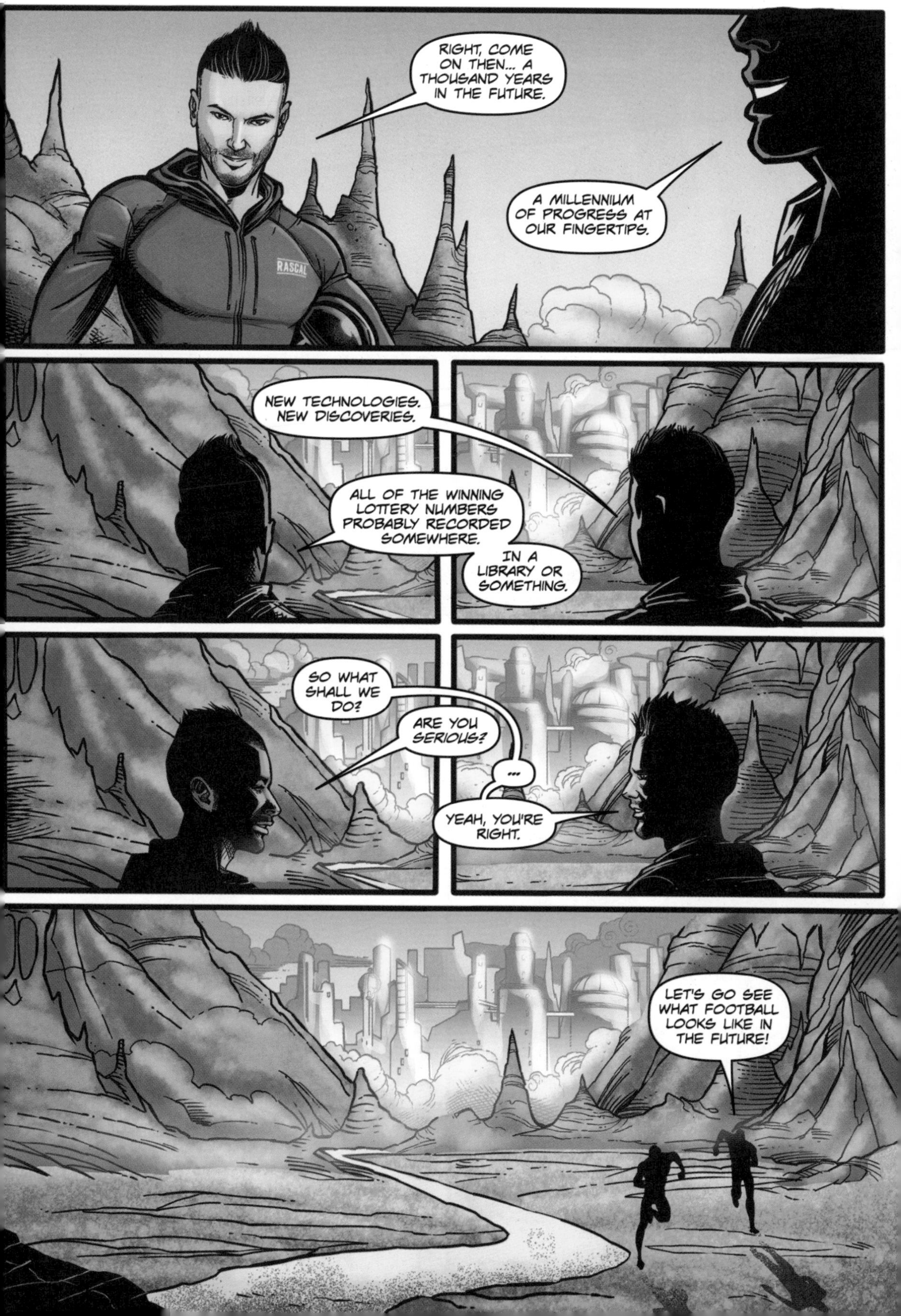
RIGHT, COME ON THEN... A THOUSAND YEARS IN THE FUTURE.
A MILLENNIUM OF PROGRESS AT OUR FINGERTIPS.
RASCAL
NEW TECHNOLOGIES. NEW DISCOVERIES.
ALL OF THE WINNING LOTTERY NUMBERS PROBABLY RECORDED SOMEWHERE.
IN A LIBRARY OR SOMETHING.
SO WHAT SHALL WE DO?
ARE YOU SERIOUS?
...
YEAH, YOU'RE RIGHT.
LET'S GO SEE WHAT FOOTBALL LOOKS LIKE IN THE FUTURE!

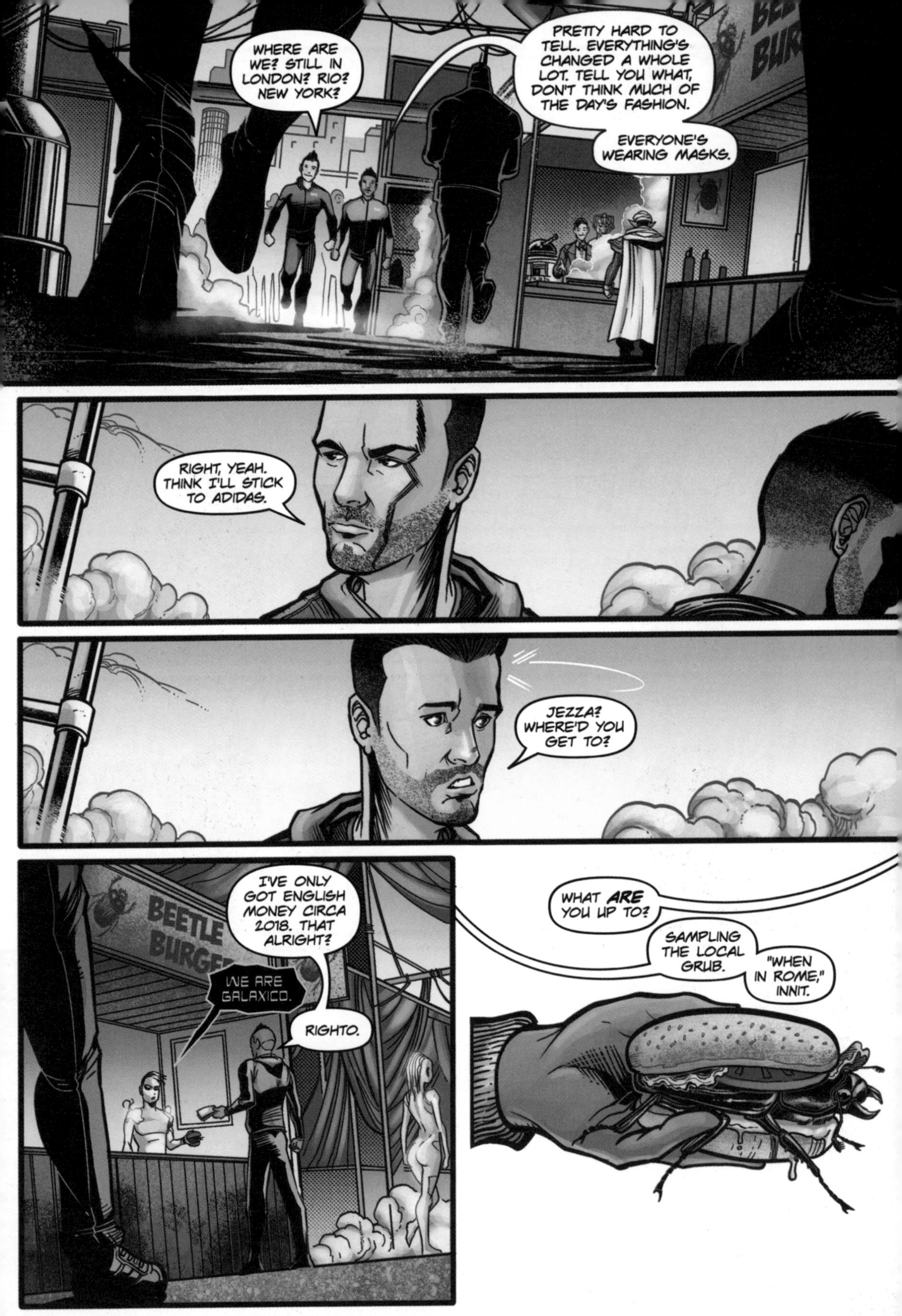
WHERE ARE WE? STILL IN LONDON? RIO? NEW YORK?
PRETTY HARD TO TELL. EVERYTHING'S CHANGED A WHOLE LOT. TELL YOU WHAT, DON'T THINK MUCH OF THE DAY'S FASHION.
EVERYONE'S WEARING MASKS.
RIGHT, YEAH. THINK I'LL STICK TO ADIDAS.
JEZZA? WHERE'D YOU GET TO?
BEETLE BURGE
I'VE ONLY GOT ENGLISH MONEY CIRCA 2018. THAT ALRIGHT?
WE ARE GALAXICO.
RIGHTO.
WHAT **ARE** YOU UP TO?
SAMPLING THE LOCAL GRUB.
"WHEN IN ROME," INNIT.

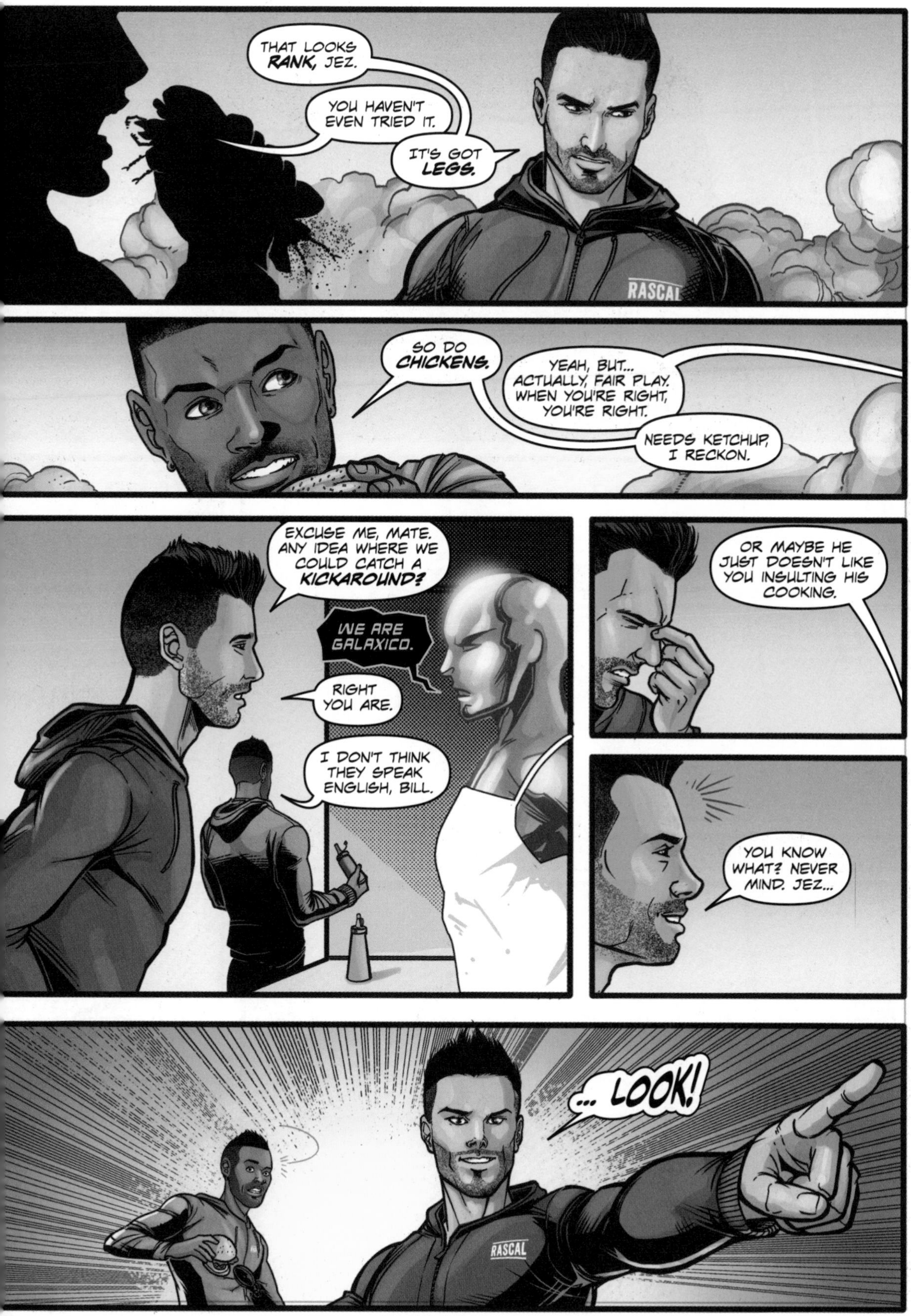
THAT LOOKS **RANK,** JEZ.
YOU HAVEN'T EVEN TRIED IT.
IT'S GOT **LEGS.**
RASCAL
SO DO **CHICKENS.**
YEAH, BUT... ACTUALLY, FAIR PLAY. WHEN YOU'RE RIGHT, YOU'RE RIGHT.
NEEDS KETCHUP, I RECKON.
EXCUSE ME, MATE. ANY IDEA WHERE WE COULD CATCH A **KICKAROUND?**
WE ARE GALAXICO.
RIGHT YOU ARE.
I DON'T THINK THEY SPEAK ENGLISH, BILL.
OR MAYBE HE JUST DOESN'T LIKE YOU INSULTING HIS COOKING.
YOU KNOW WHAT? NEVER MIND. JEZ...
... LOOK!
RASCAL

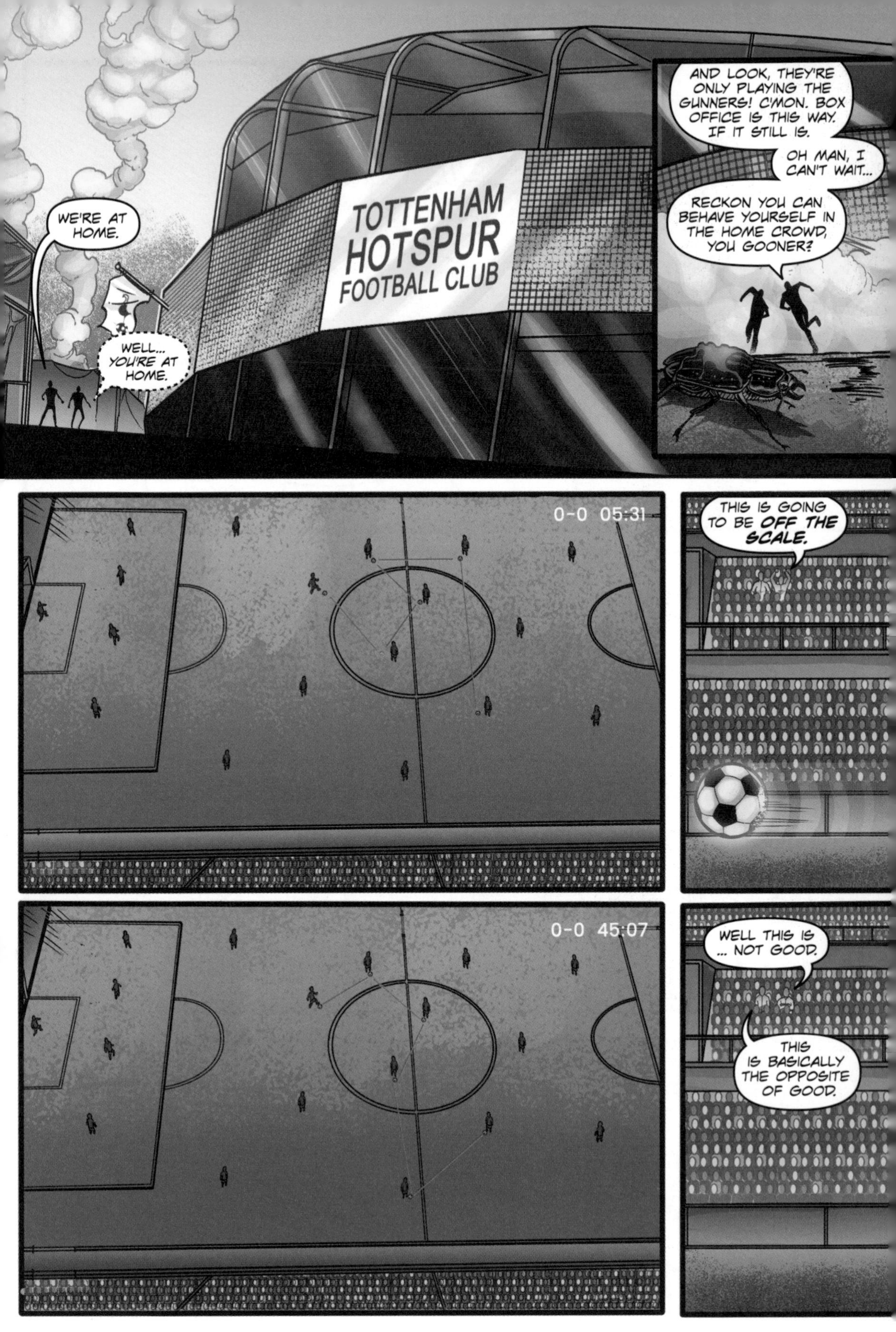
WE'RE AT HOME.
WELL... YOU'RE AT HOME.
TOTTENHAM HOTSPUR FOOTBALL CLUB
AND LOOK, THEY'RE ONLY PLAYING THE GUNNERS! C'MON. BOX OFFICE IS THIS WAY. IF IT STILL IS.
OH MAN, I CAN'T WAIT...
RECKON YOU CAN BEHAVE YOURSELF IN THE HOME CROWD, YOU GOONER?
0-0 05:31
THIS IS GOING TO BE OFF THE SCALE.
0-0 45:07
WELL THIS IS ... NOT GOOD.
THIS IS BASICALLY THE OPPOSITE OF GOOD.

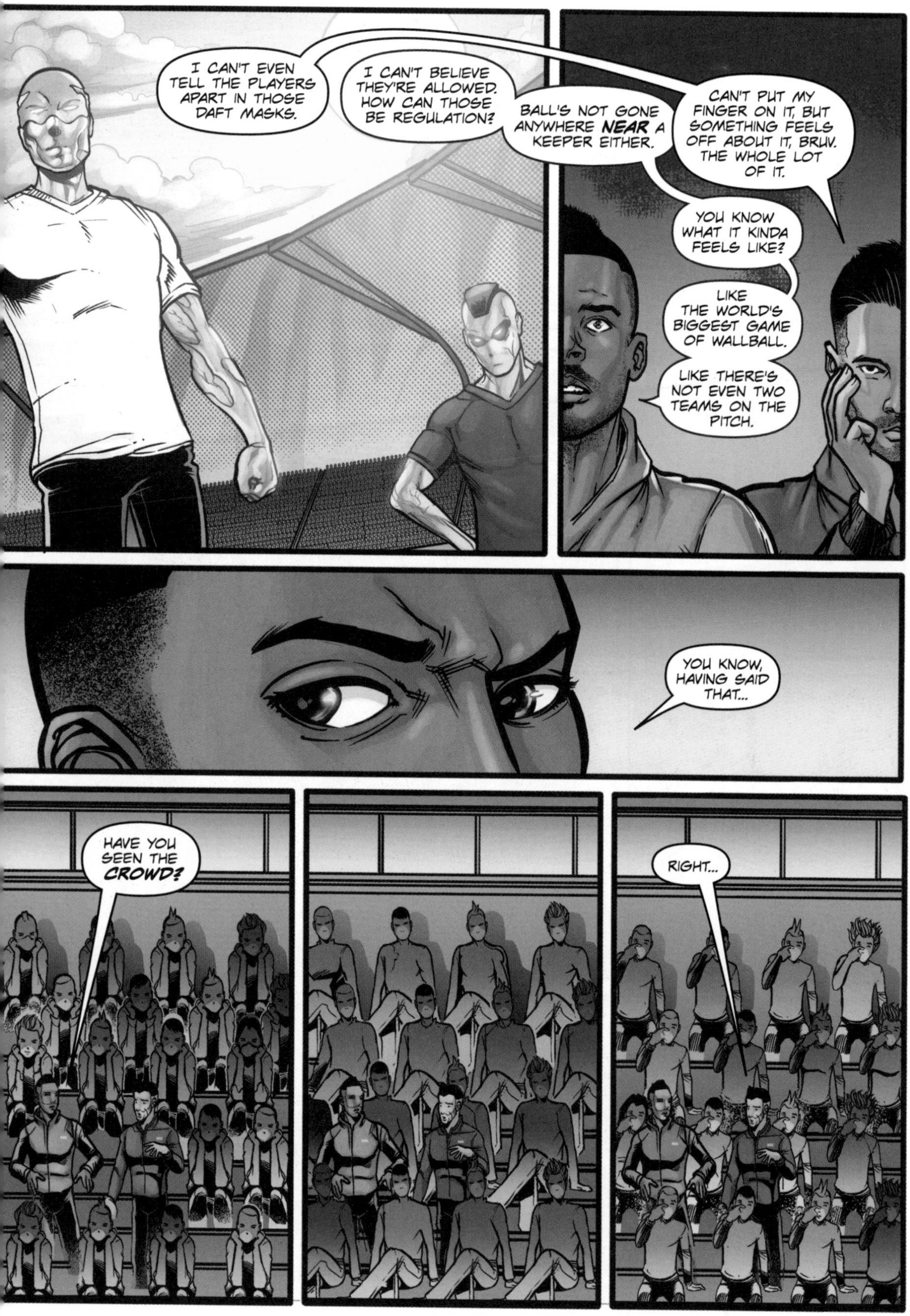
I CAN'T EVEN TELL THE PLAYERS APART IN THOSE DAFT MASKS.
I CAN'T BELIEVE THEY'RE ALLOWED. HOW CAN THOSE BE REGULATION?
BALL'S NOT GONE ANYWHERE NEAR A KEEPER EITHER.
CAN'T PUT MY FINGER ON IT, BUT SOMETHING FEELS OFF ABOUT IT, BRUV. THE WHOLE LOT OF IT.
YOU KNOW WHAT IT KINDA FEELS LIKE?
LIKE THE WORLD'S BIGGEST GAME OF WALLBALL.
LIKE THERE'S NOT EVEN TWO TEAMS ON THE PITCH.
YOU KNOW, HAVING SAID THAT...
HAVE YOU SEEN THE CROWD?
RIGHT...

THEY LOOK A BIT WRONG, DON'T THEY?
I'D EVEN CALL THAT AN UNDERSTATEMENT.
SHOULD WE MAYBE SORT OF... DO ONE?
THAT MIGHT BE AN IDEA, YEAH.
RIGHT.
EXCUSE US.
COMING THROUGH.
SORRY. CHEERS.

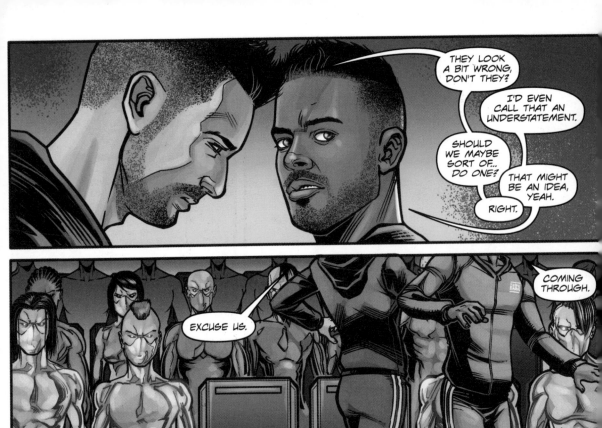

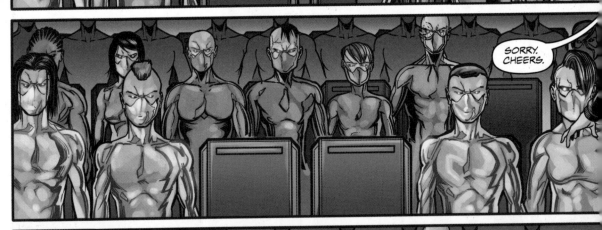

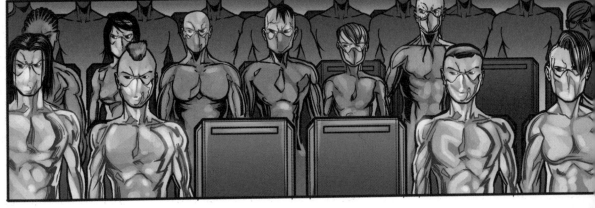

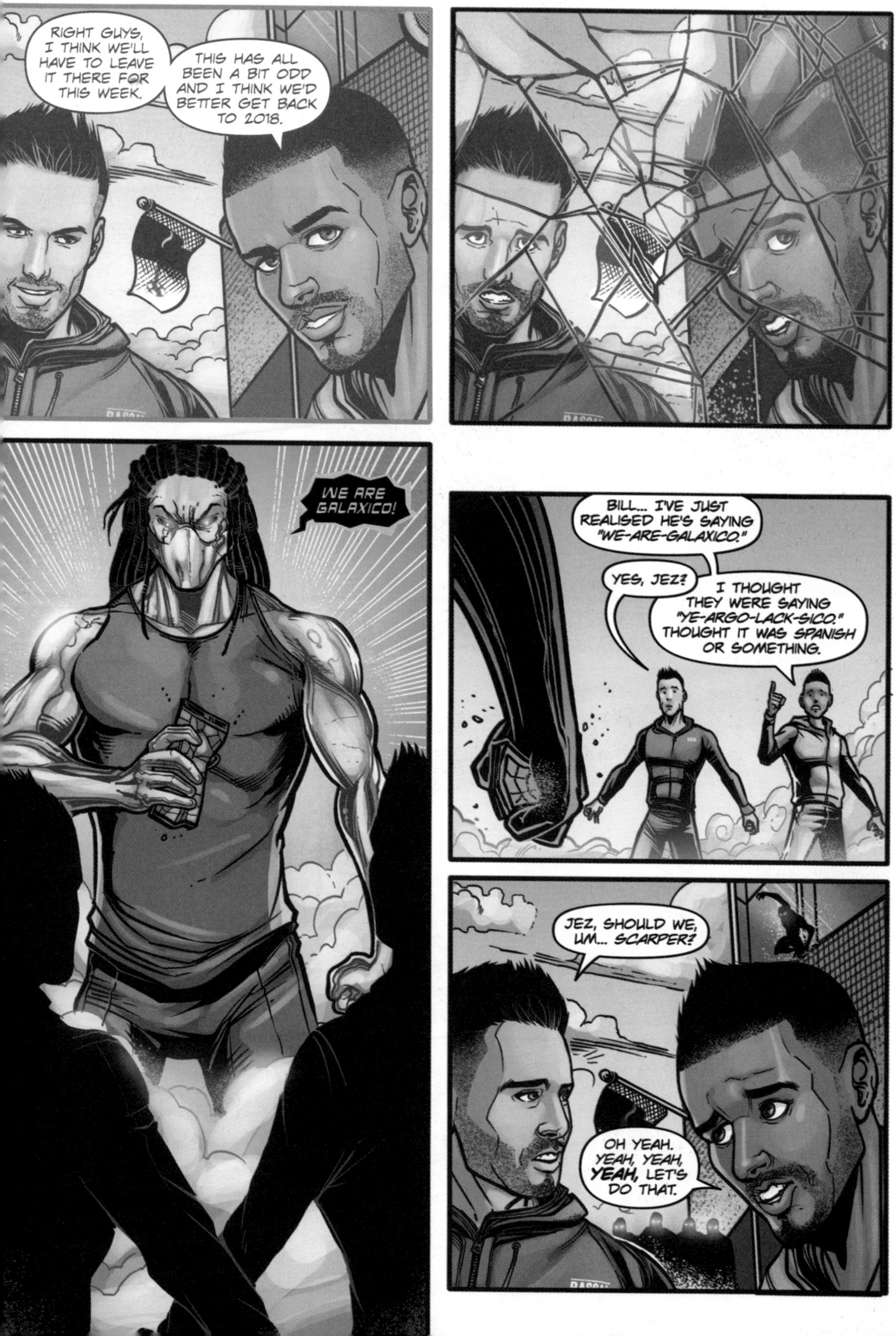
RIGHT GUYS, I THINK WE'LL HAVE TO LEAVE IT THERE FOR THIS WEEK.
THIS HAS ALL BEEN A BIT ODD AND I THINK WE'D BETTER GET BACK TO 2018.
WE ARE GALAXICO!
BILL... I'VE JUST REALISED HE'S SAYING "WE-ARE-GALAXICO."
YES, JEZ?
I THOUGHT THEY WERE SAYING "YE-ARGO-LACK-SICO." THOUGHT IT WAS SPANISH OR SOMETHING.
JEZ, SHOULD WE, UM... SCARPER?
OH YEAH. YEAH, YEAH, YEAH, LET'S DO THAT.

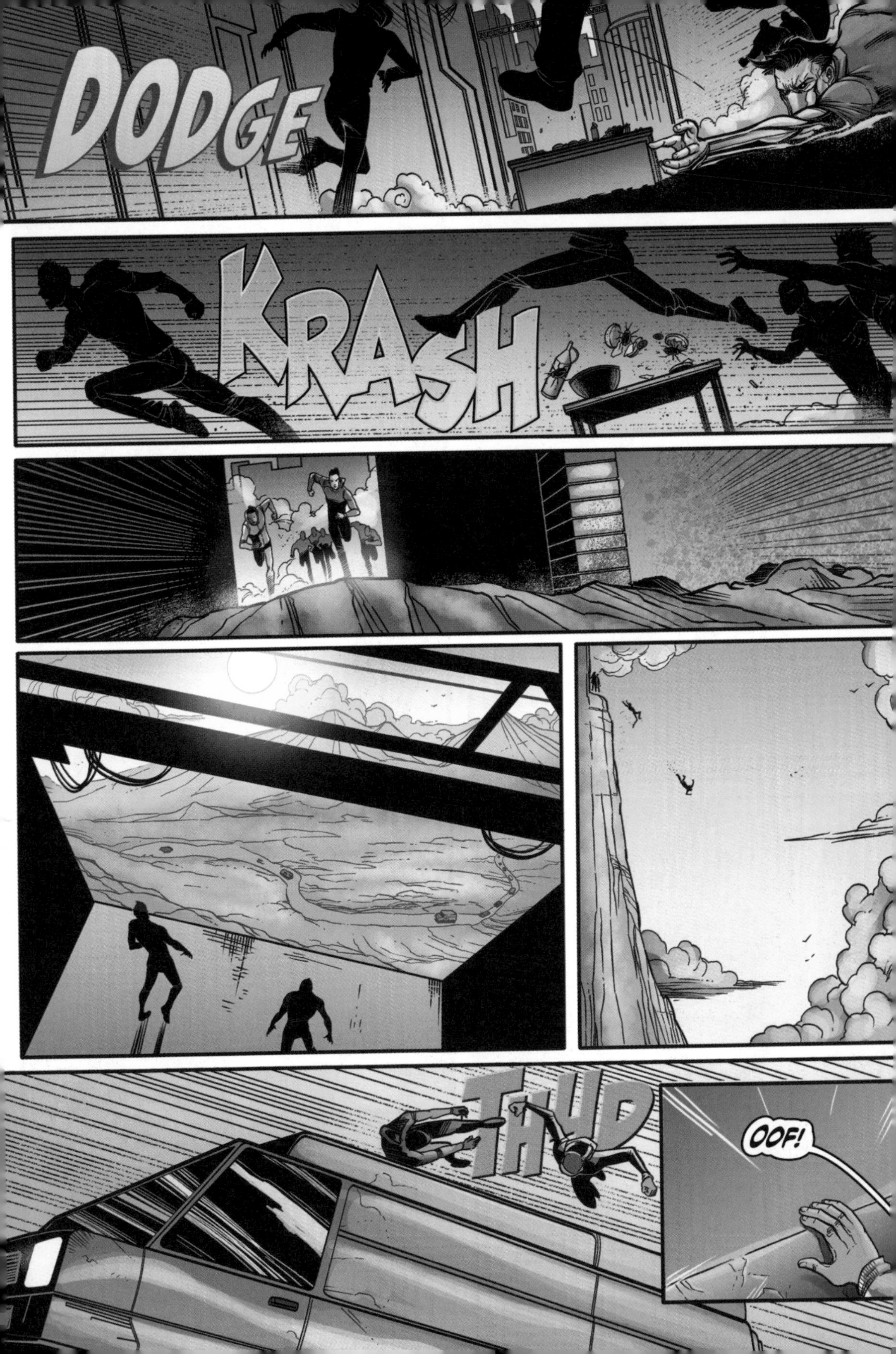
DODGE
KRASH
THUD
OOF!

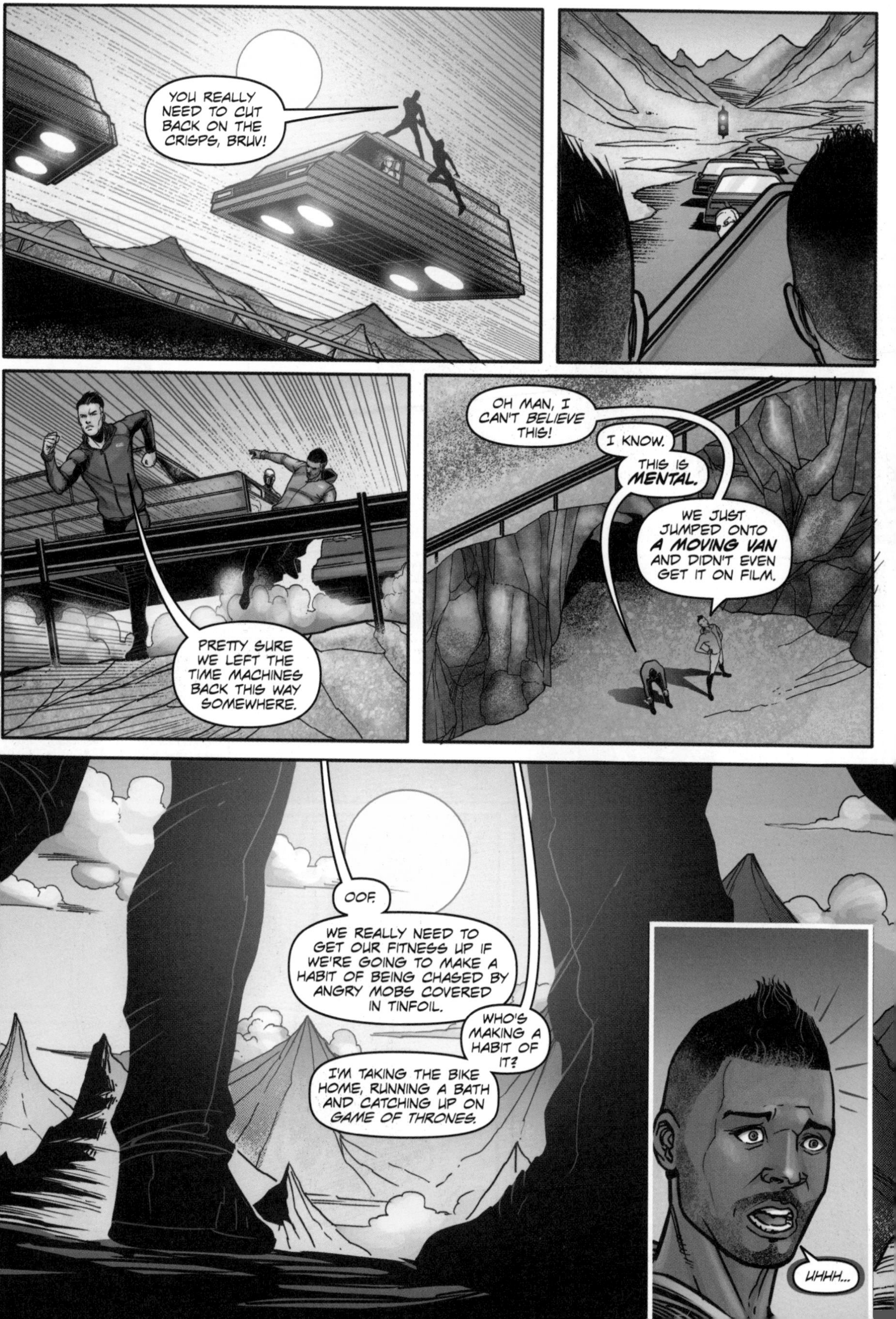
YOU REALLY NEED TO CUT BACK ON THE CRISPS, BRUV!
PRETTY SURE WE LEFT THE TIME MACHINES BACK THIS WAY SOMEWHERE.
OH MAN, I CAN'T *BELIEVE* THIS!
I KNOW.
THIS IS ***MENTAL.***
WE JUST JUMPED ONTO ***A MOVING VAN*** AND DIDN'T EVEN GET IT ON FILM.
OOF.
WE REALLY NEED TO GET OUR FITNESS UP IF WE'RE GOING TO MAKE A HABIT OF BEING CHASED BY ANGRY MOBS COVERED IN TINFOIL.
WHO'S MAKING A HABIT OF IT?
I'M TAKING THE BIKE HOME, RUNNING A BATH AND CATCHING UP ON *GAME OF THRONES.*
UHHH...

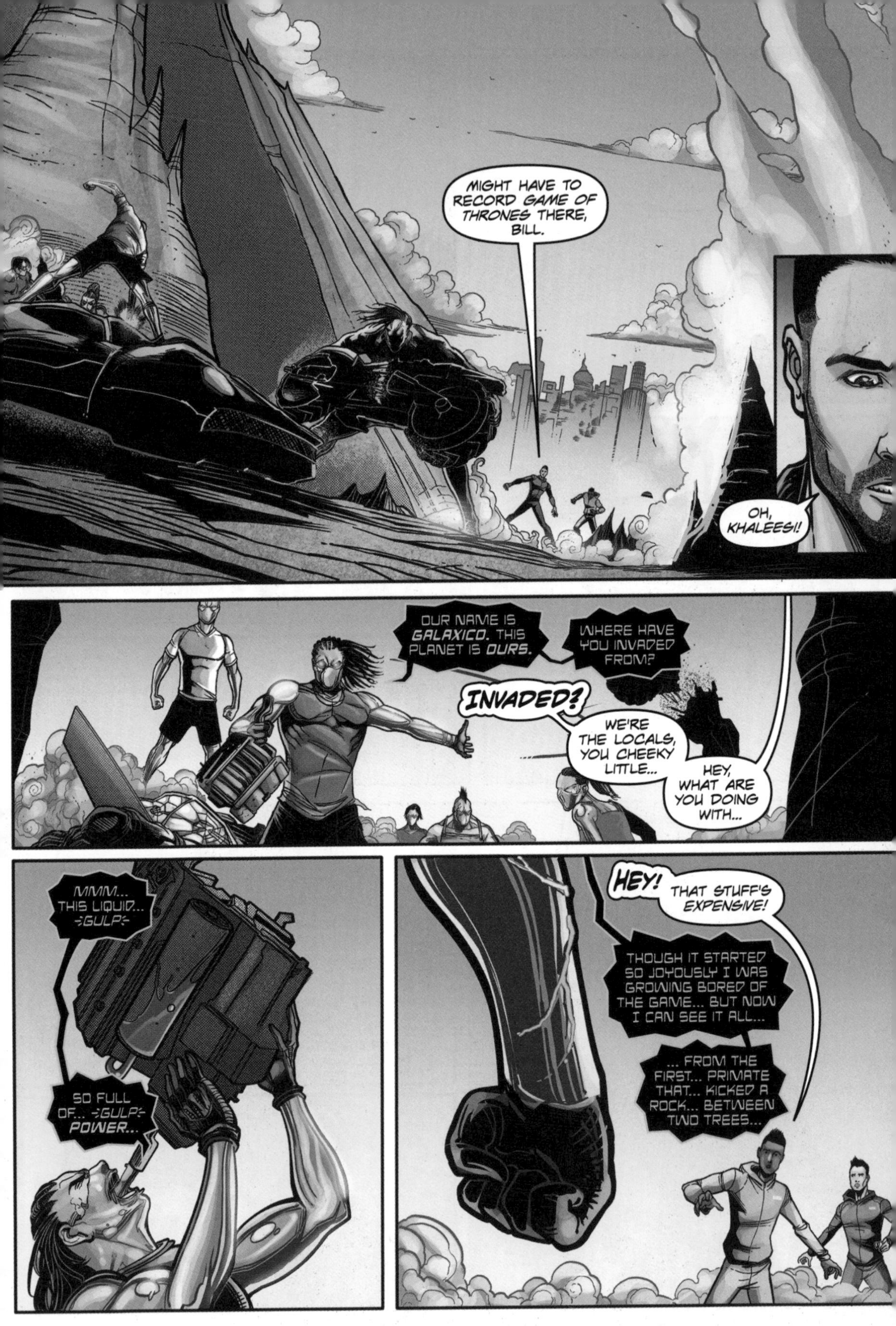
MIGHT HAVE TO RECORD GAME OF THRONES THERE, BILL.
OH, KHALEESI!
OUR NAME IS GALAXICO. THIS PLANET IS OURS.
WHERE HAVE YOU INVADED FROM?
INVADED?
WE'RE THE LOCALS, YOU CHEEKY LITTLE...
HEY, WHAT ARE YOU DOING WITH...
MMM... THIS LIQUID... -GULP-
SO FULL OF... -GULP- POWER...
HEY!
THAT STUFF'S EXPENSIVE!
THOUGH IT STARTED SO JOYOUSLY I WAS GROWING BORED OF THE GAME... BUT NOW I CAN SEE IT ALL...
... FROM THE FIRST... PRIMATE THAT... KICKED A ROCK... BETWEEN TWO TREES...

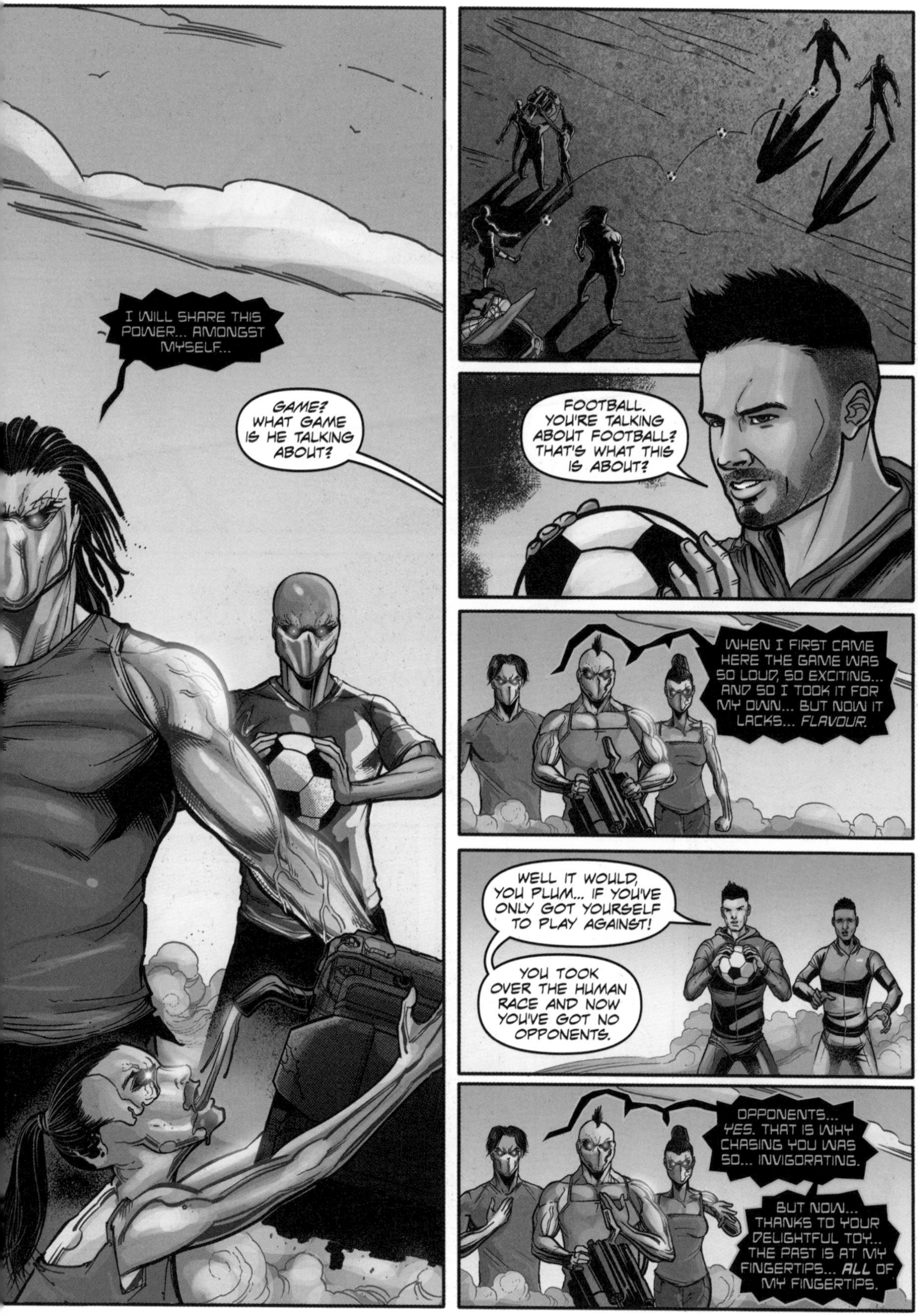
I WILL SHARE THIS POWER... AMONGST MYSELF...
GAME? WHAT GAME IS HE TALKING ABOUT?
FOOTBALL. YOU'RE TALKING ABOUT FOOTBALL? THAT'S WHAT THIS IS ABOUT?
WHEN I FIRST CAME HERE THE GAME WAS SO LOUD, SO EXCITING... AND SO I TOOK IT FOR MY OWN... BUT NOW IT LACKS... *FLAVOUR.*
WELL IT WOULD, YOU PLUM... IF YOU'VE ONLY GOT YOURSELF TO PLAY AGAINST!
YOU TOOK OVER THE HUMAN RACE AND NOW YOU'VE GOT NO OPPONENTS.
OPPONENTS... *YES.* THAT IS WHY CHASING YOU WAS SO... INVIGORATING.
BUT NOW... THANKS TO YOUR DELIGHTFUL TOY... THE PAST IS AT MY FINGERTIPS... ***ALL*** OF MY FINGERTIPS.

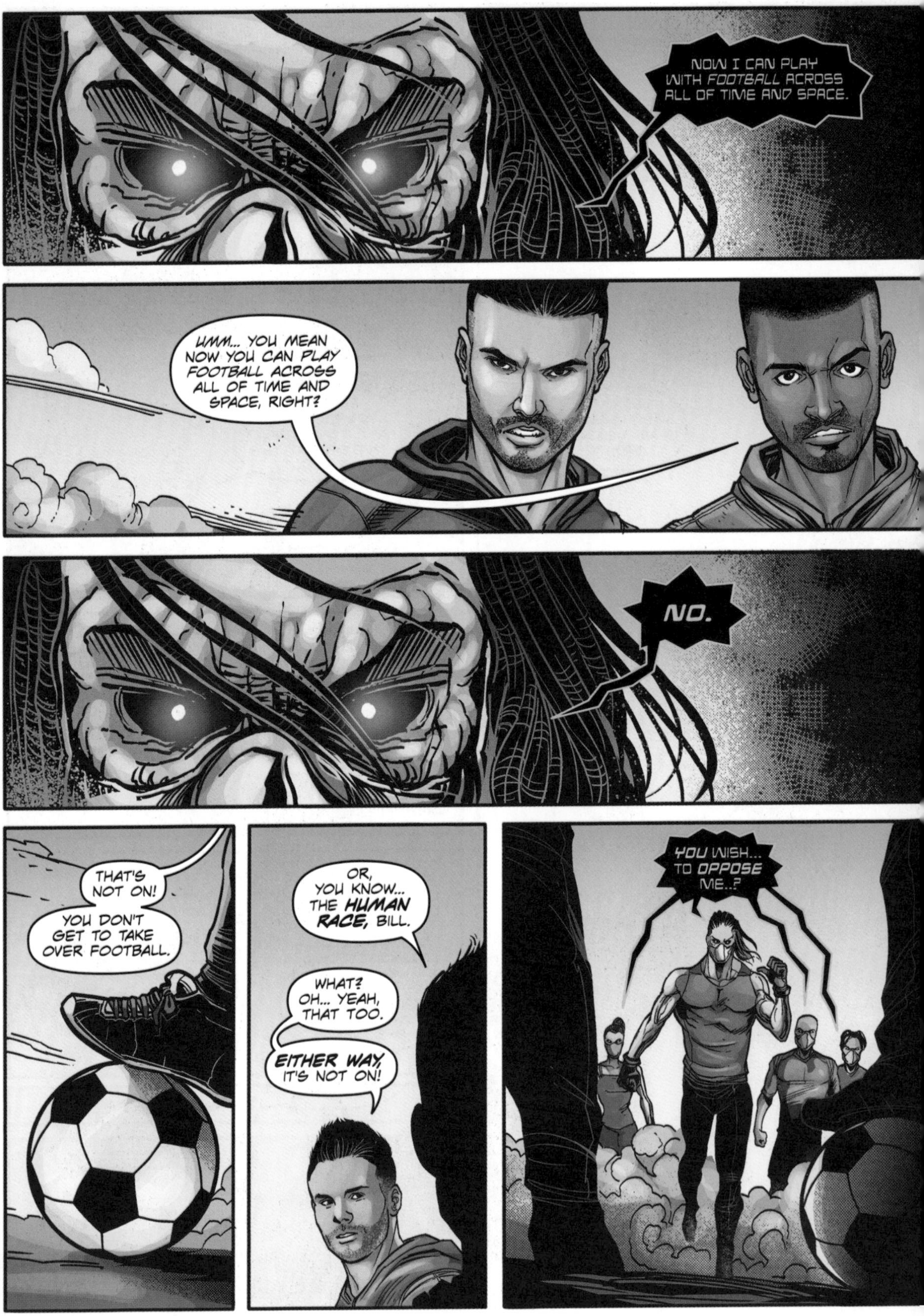
NOW I CAN PLAY WITH FOOTBALL ACROSS ALL OF TIME AND SPACE.
UMM... YOU MEAN NOW YOU CAN PLAY FOOTBALL ACROSS ALL OF TIME AND SPACE, RIGHT?
NO.
THAT'S NOT ON!
YOU DON'T GET TO TAKE OVER FOOTBALL.
OR, YOU KNOW... THE HUMAN RACE, BILL.
WHAT? OH... YEAH, THAT TOO.
EITHER WAY, IT'S NOT ON!
YOU WISH... TO OPPOSE ME..?

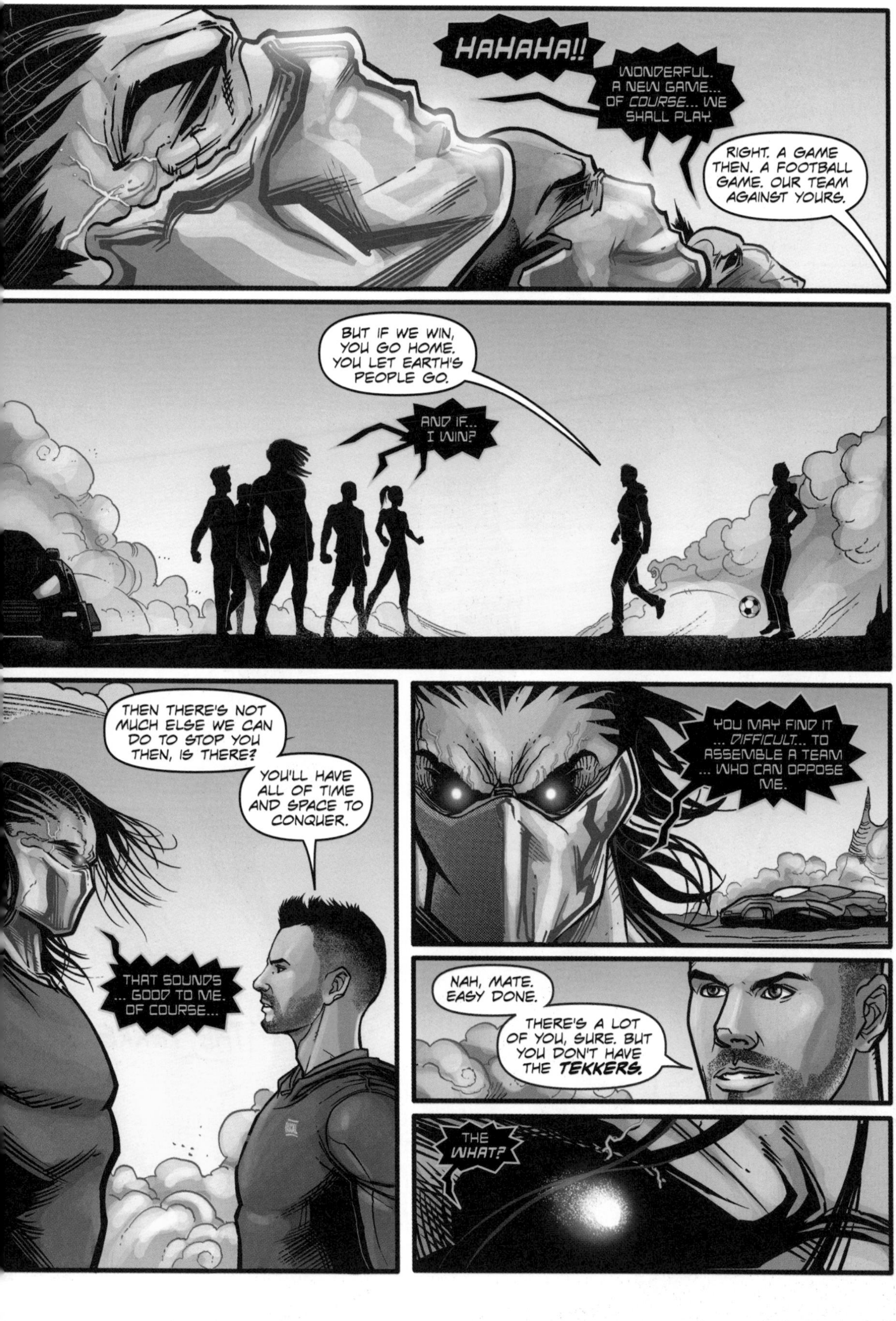
HAHAHA!!
WONDERFUL. A NEW GAME... OF COURSE... WE SHALL PLAY.
RIGHT. A GAME THEN. A FOOTBALL GAME. OUR TEAM AGAINST YOURS.
BUT IF WE WIN, YOU GO HOME. YOU LET EARTH'S PEOPLE GO.
AND IF... I WIN?
THEN THERE'S NOT MUCH ELSE WE CAN DO TO STOP YOU THEN, IS THERE?
YOU'LL HAVE ALL OF TIME AND SPACE TO CONQUER.
THAT SOUNDS ... GOOD TO ME. OF COURSE...
YOU MAY FIND IT ... DIFFICULT... TO ASSEMBLE A TEAM ... WHO CAN OPPOSE ME.
NAH, MATE. EASY DONE.
THERE'S A LOT OF YOU, SURE. BUT YOU DON'T HAVE THE TEKKERS.
THE WHAT?

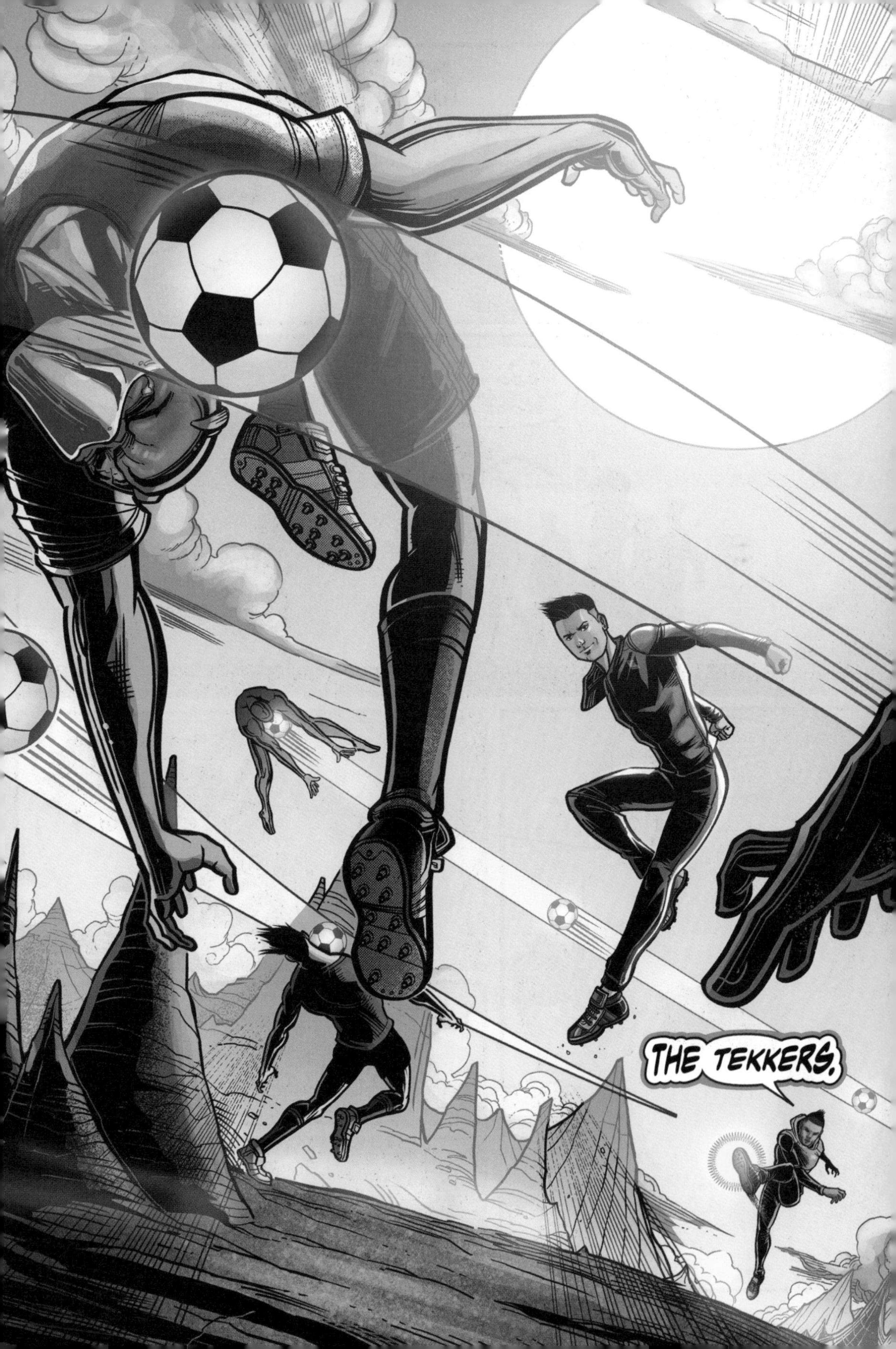
THE TEKKERS.

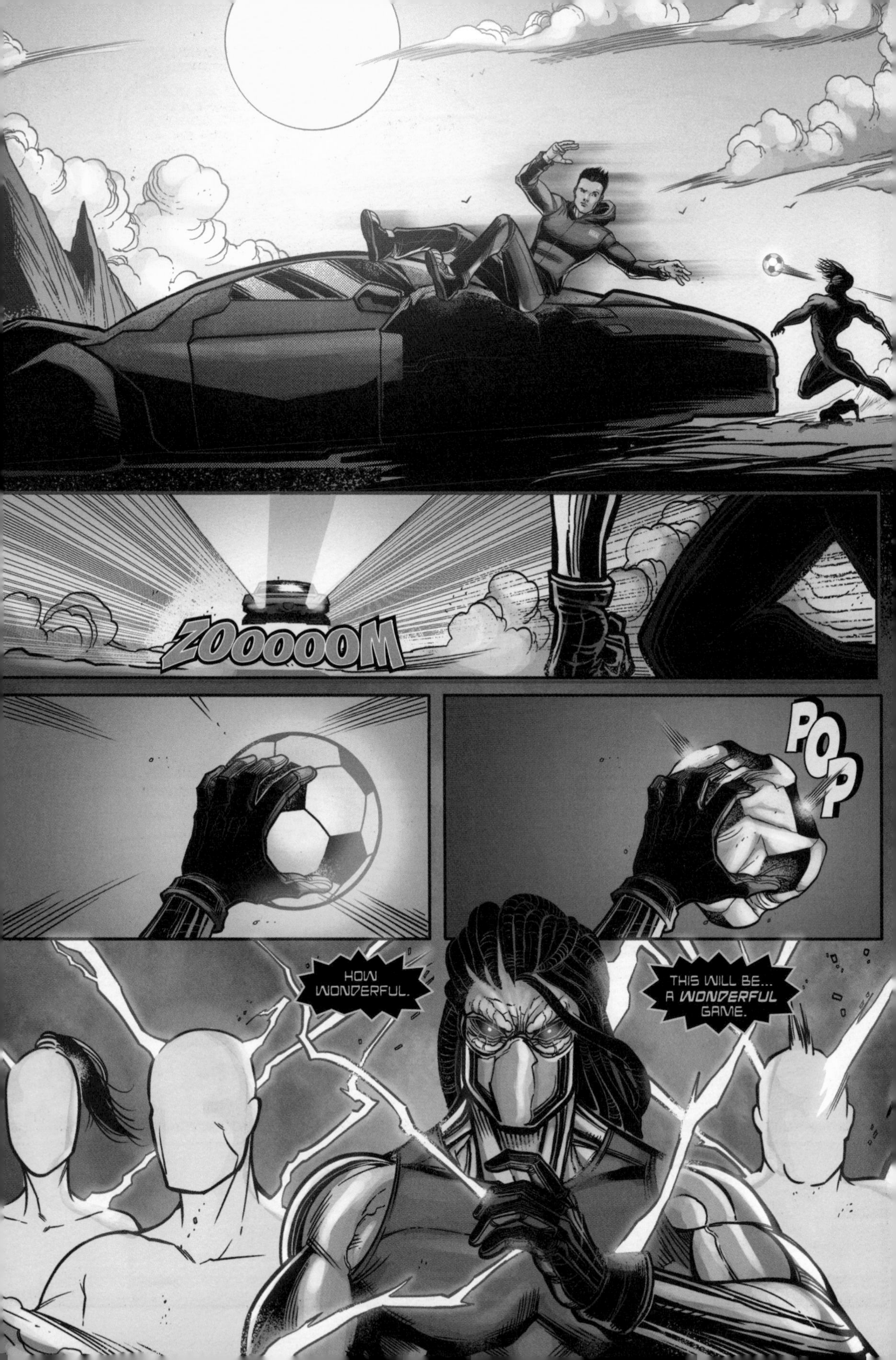
ZOOOOOM
POP
HOW WONDERFUL.
THIS WILL BE... A WONDERFUL GAME.

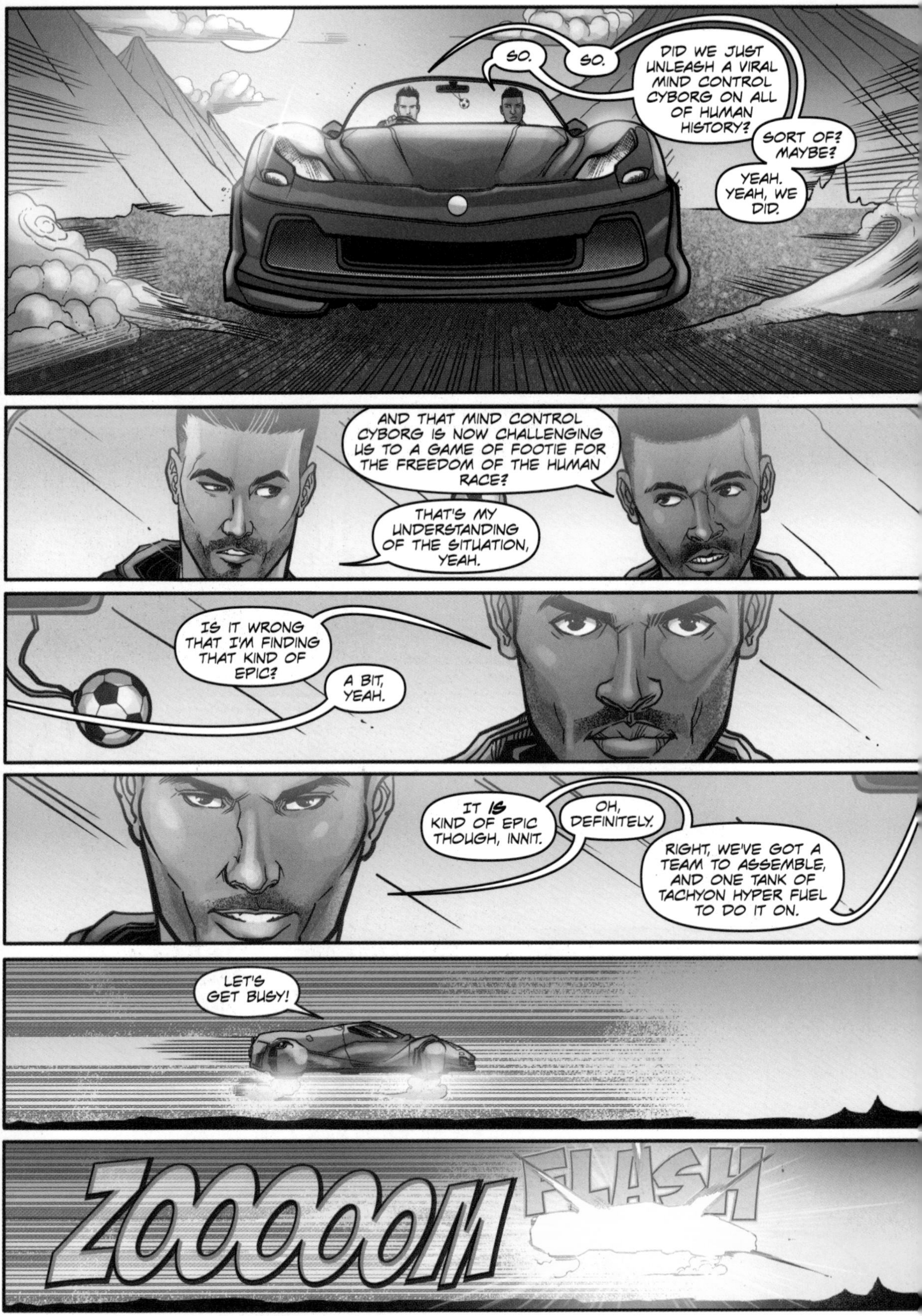
SO.
SO.
DID WE JUST UNLEASH A VIRAL MIND CONTROL CYBORG ON ALL OF HUMAN HISTORY?
SORT OF? MAYBE?
YEAH. YEAH, WE DID.
AND THAT MIND CONTROL CYBORG IS NOW CHALLENGING US TO A GAME OF FOOTIE FOR THE FREEDOM OF THE HUMAN RACE?
THAT'S MY UNDERSTANDING OF THE SITUATION, YEAH.
IS IT WRONG THAT I'M FINDING THAT KIND OF EPIC?
A BIT, YEAH.
IT *IS* KIND OF EPIC THOUGH, INNIT.
OH, DEFINITELY.
RIGHT, WE'VE GOT A TEAM TO ASSEMBLE, AND ONE TANK OF TACHYON HYPER FUEL TO DO IT ON.
LET'S GET BUSY!
ZOOOOOM
FLASH

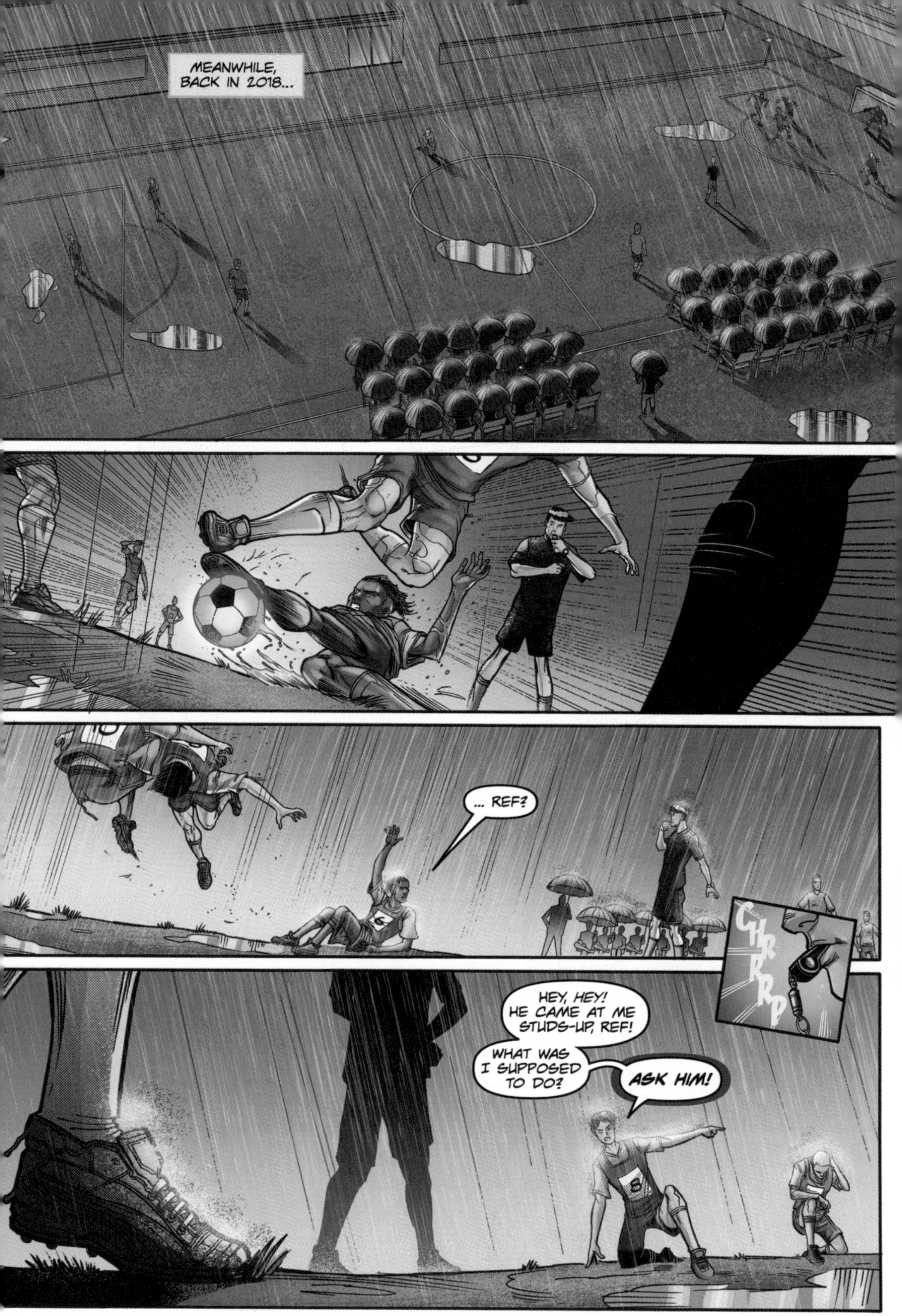
MEANWHILE, BACK IN 2018...
... REF?
CHRRRP
HEY, HEY! HE CAME AT ME STUDS-UP, REF!
WHAT WAS I SUPPOSED TO DO?
ASK HIM!

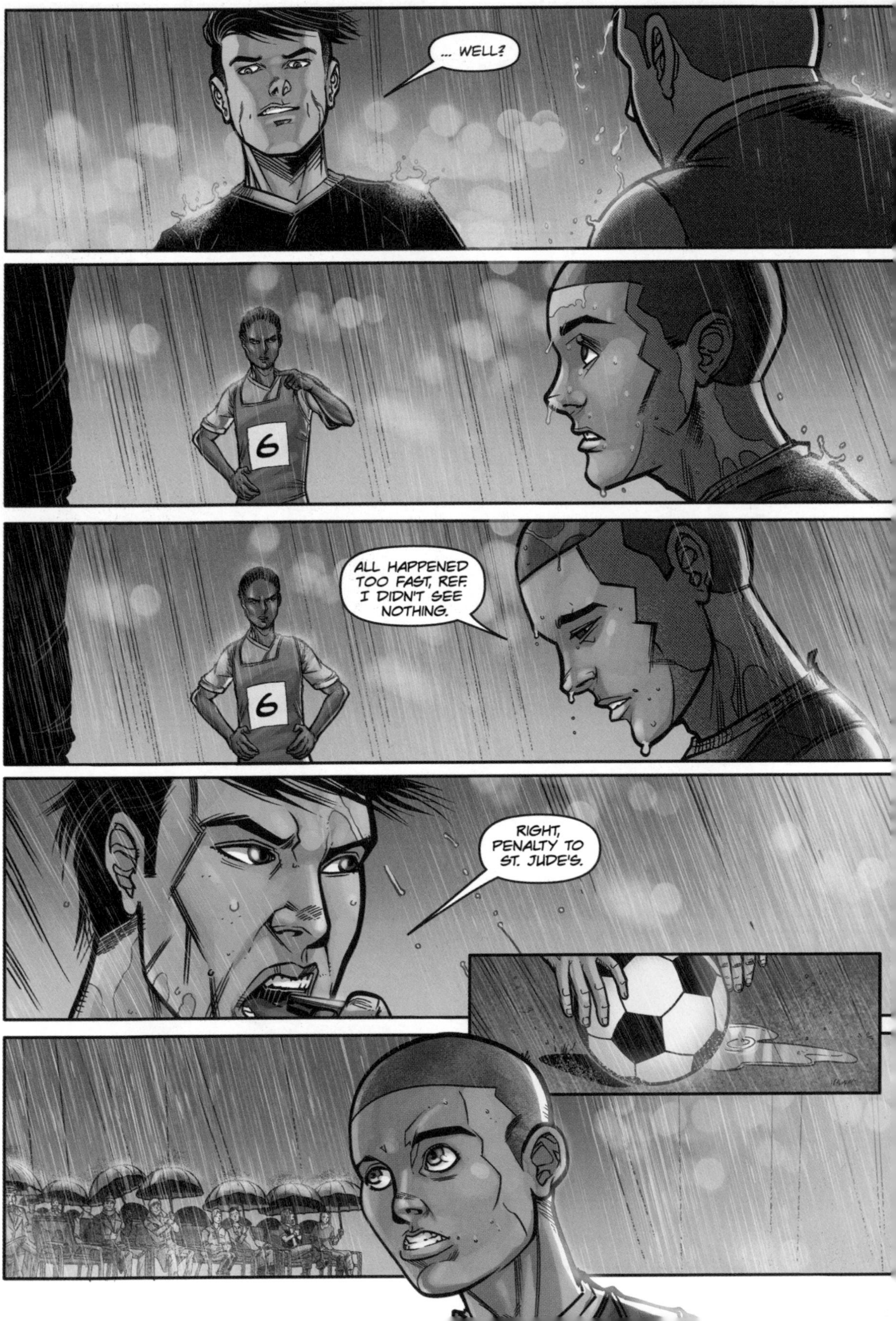
... WELL?
6
ALL HAPPENED TOO FAST, REF. I DIDN'T SEE NOTHING.
6
RIGHT, PENALTY TO ST. JUDE'S.

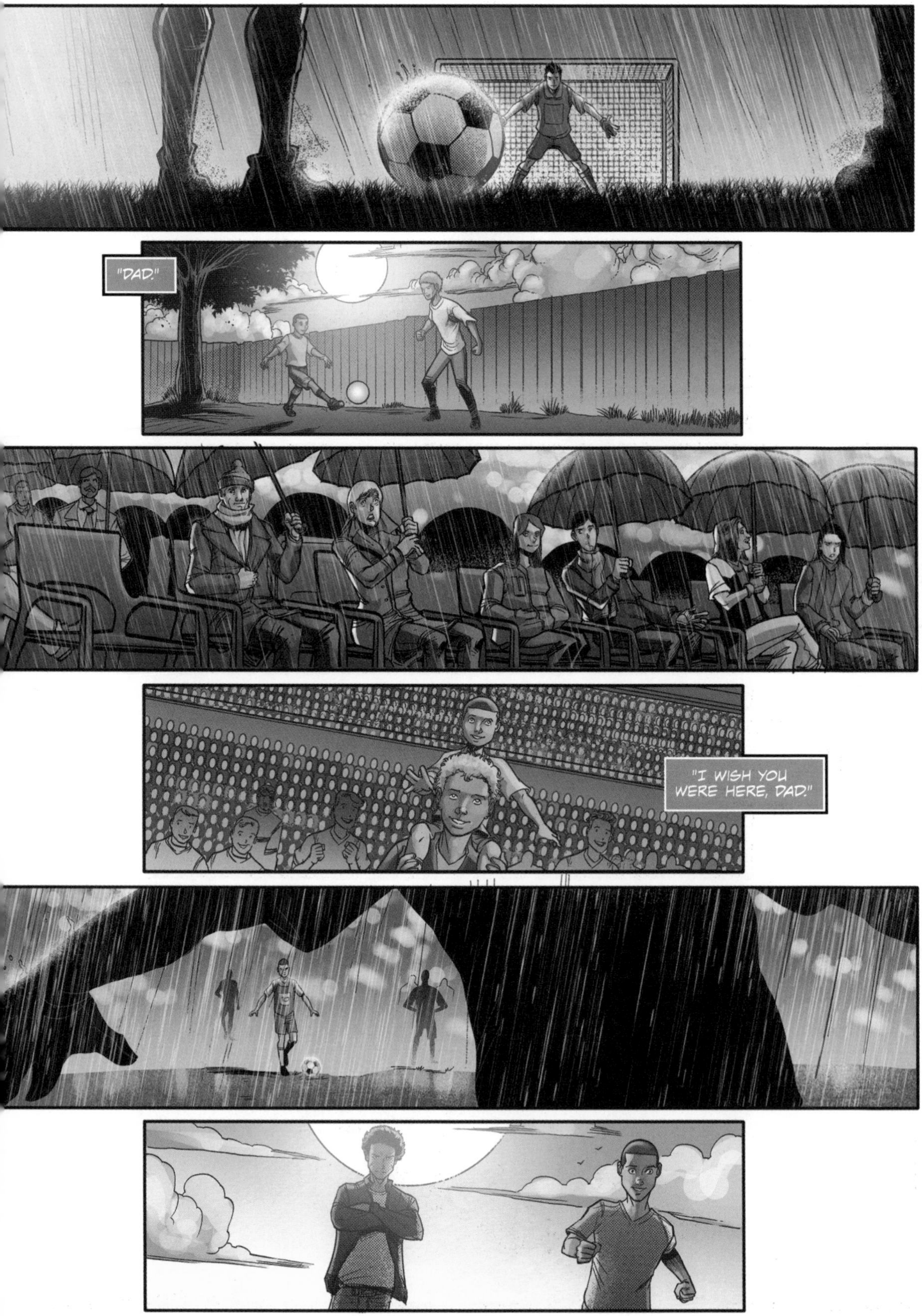
"DAD."
"I WISH YOU WERE HERE, DAD."

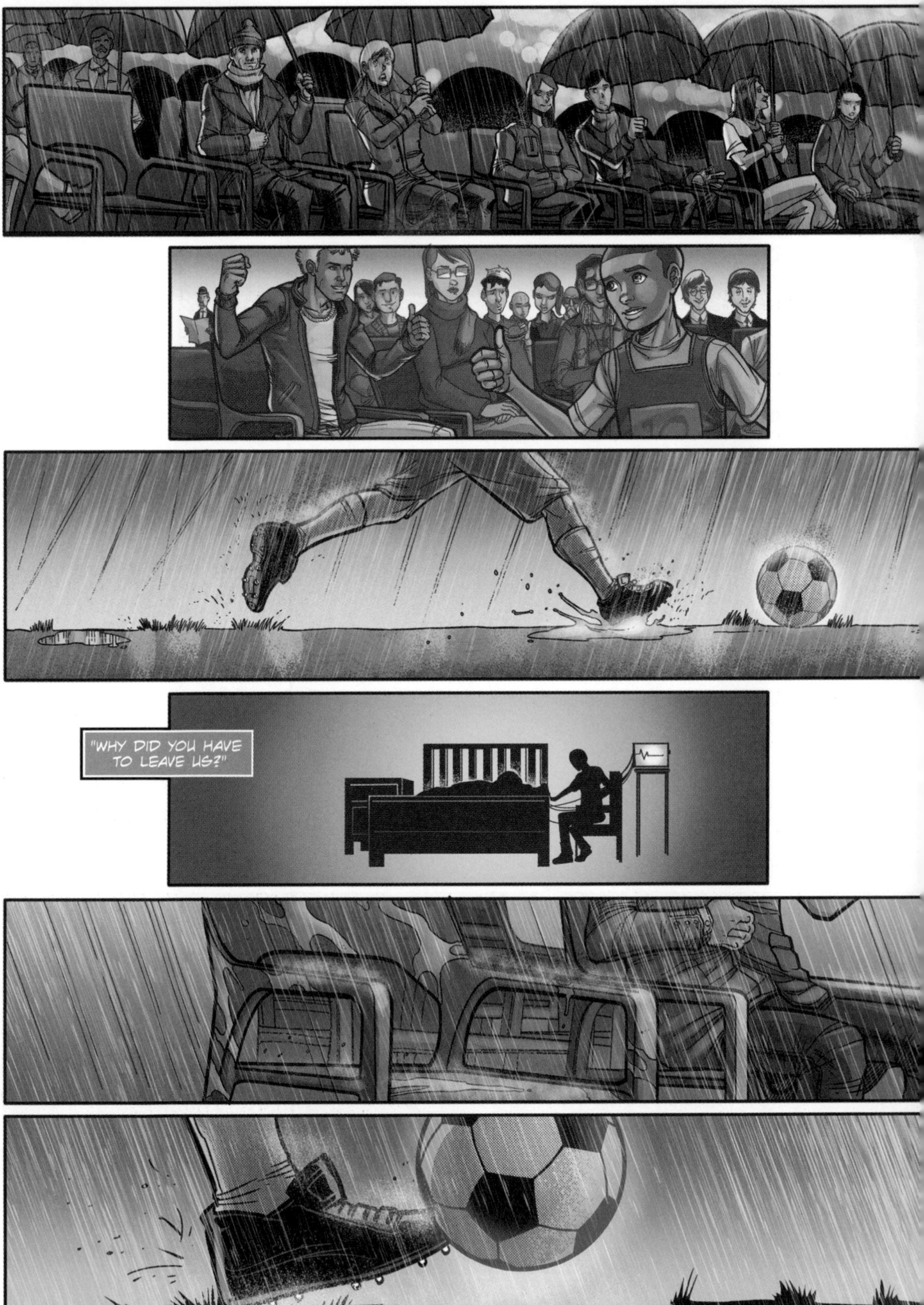
"WHY DID YOU HAVE TO LEAVE US?"

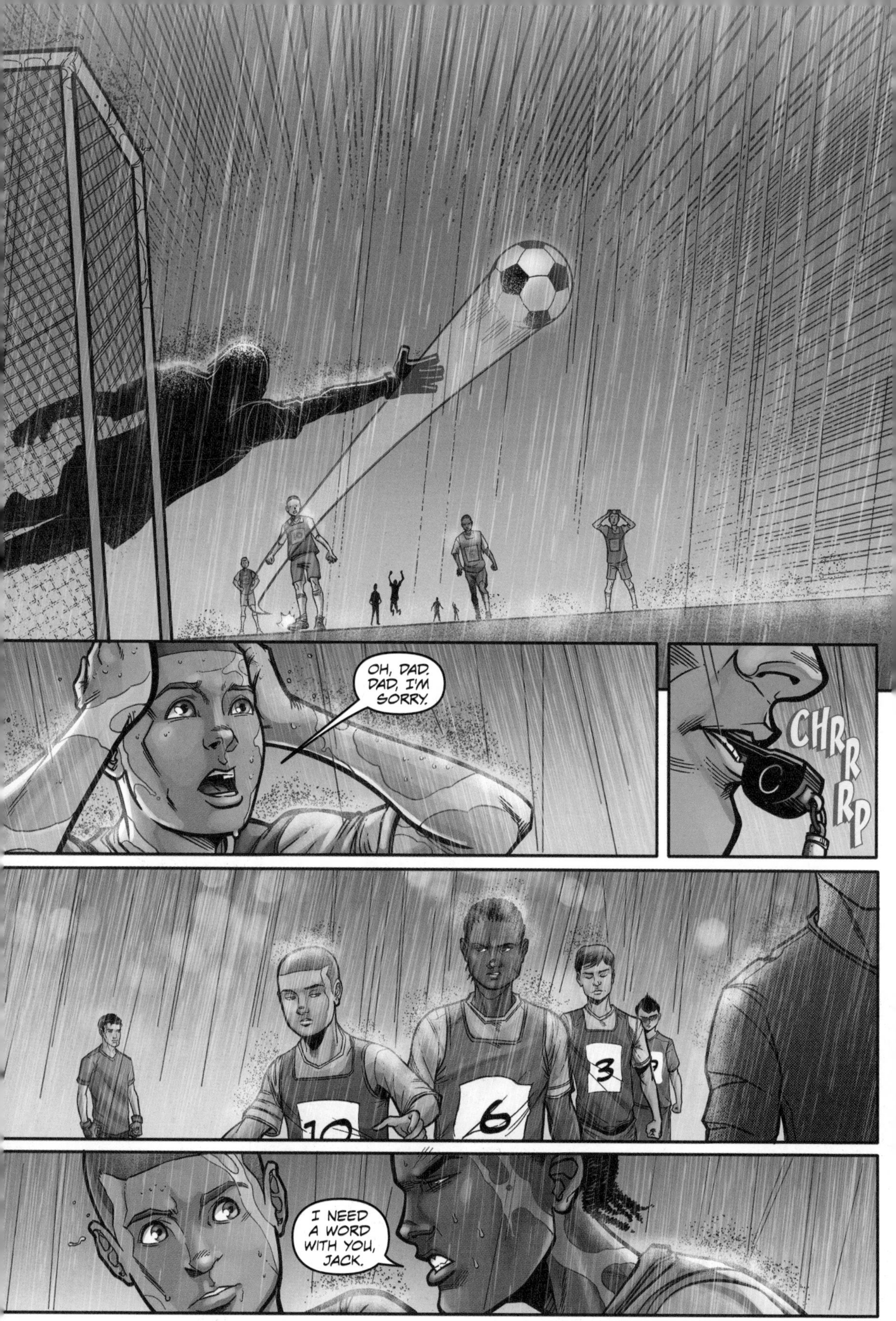
OH, DAD. DAD, I'M SORRY.
CHRRRRP
I NEED A WORD WITH YOU, JACK.

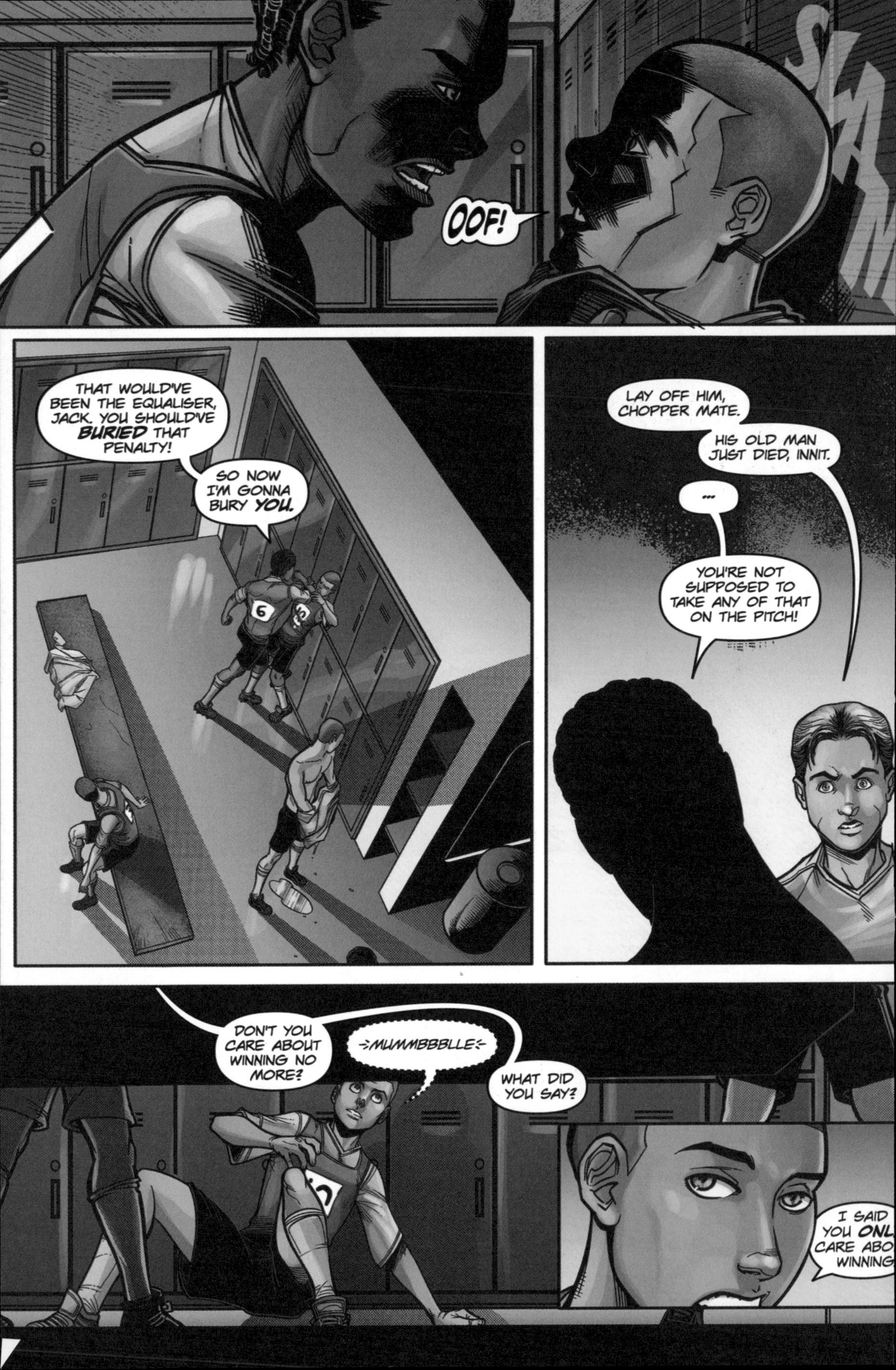
OOF!
THAT WOULD'VE BEEN THE EQUALISER, JACK. YOU SHOULD'VE BURIED THAT PENALTY!
SO NOW I'M GONNA BURY YOU.
LAY OFF HIM, CHOPPER MATE.
HIS OLD MAN JUST DIED, INNIT.
...
YOU'RE NOT SUPPOSED TO TAKE ANY OF THAT ON THE PITCH!
DON'T YOU CARE ABOUT WINNING NO MORE?
MUMMBBBLLE
WHAT DID YOU SAY?
I SAID YOU ONL CARE ABO WINNING

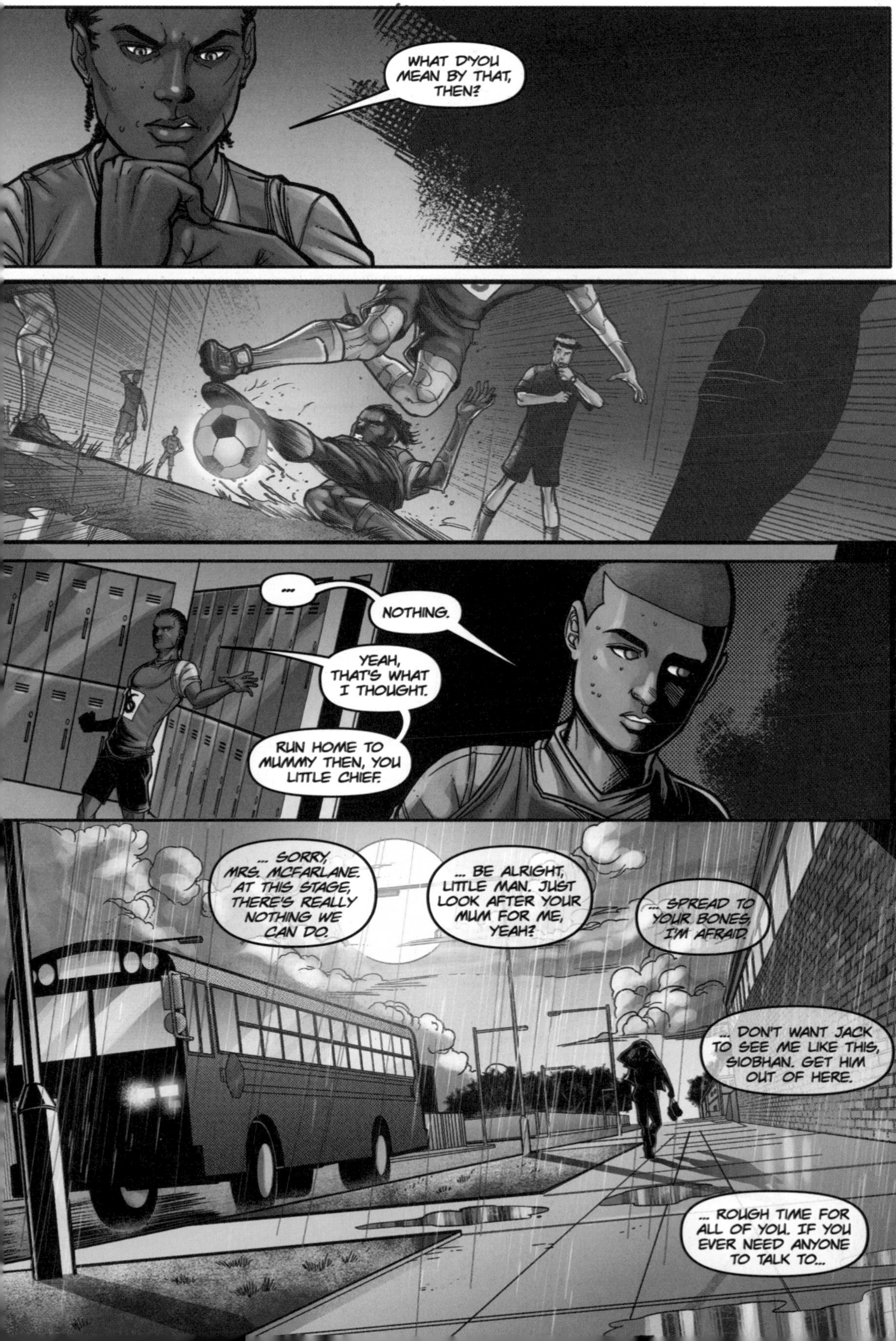
WHAT D'YOU MEAN BY THAT, THEN?
...
NOTHING.
YEAH, THAT'S WHAT I THOUGHT.
RUN HOME TO MUMMY THEN, YOU LITTLE CHIEF.
... SORRY, MRS. MCFARLANE. AT THIS STAGE, THERE'S REALLY NOTHING WE CAN DO.
... BE ALRIGHT, LITTLE MAN. JUST LOOK AFTER YOUR MUM FOR ME, YEAH?
... SPREAD TO YOUR BONES, I'M AFRAID.
... DON'T WANT JACK TO SEE ME LIKE THIS, SIOBHAN. GET HIM OUT OF HERE.
... ROUGH TIME FOR ALL OF YOU. IF YOU EVER NEED ANYONE TO TALK TO...

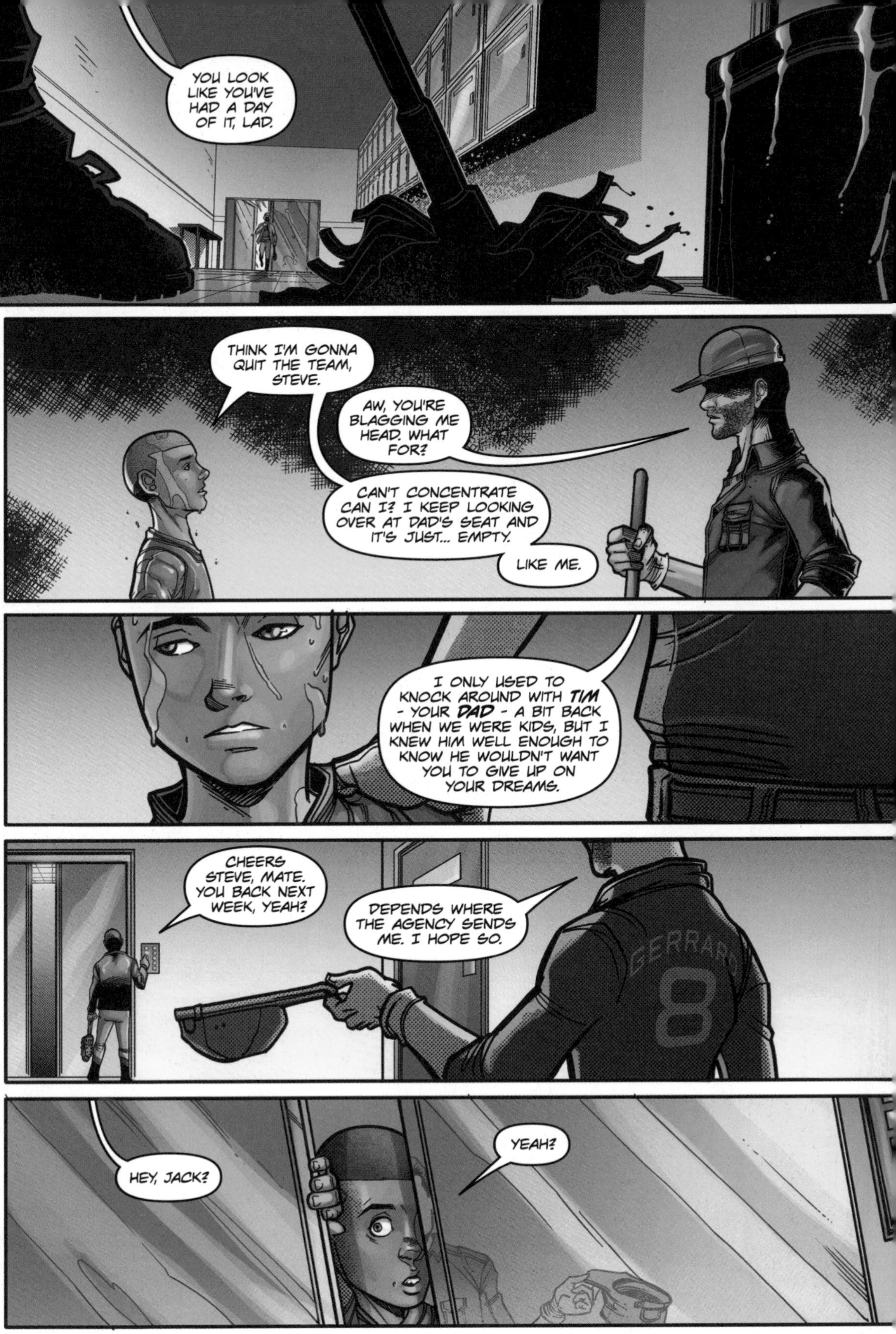
YOU LOOK LIKE YOU'VE HAD A DAY OF IT, LAD.
THINK I'M GONNA QUIT THE TEAM, STEVE.
AW, YOU'RE BLAGGING ME HEAD. WHAT FOR?
CAN'T CONCENTRATE CAN I? I KEEP LOOKING OVER AT DAD'S SEAT AND IT'S JUST... EMPTY.
LIKE ME.
I ONLY USED TO KNOCK AROUND WITH TIM - YOUR DAD - A BIT BACK WHEN WE WERE KIDS, BUT I KNEW HIM WELL ENOUGH TO KNOW HE WOULDN'T WANT YOU TO GIVE UP ON YOUR DREAMS.
CHEERS STEVE, MATE. YOU BACK NEXT WEEK, YEAH?
DEPENDS WHERE THE AGENCY SENDS ME. I HOPE SO.
8
HEY, JACK?
YEAH?

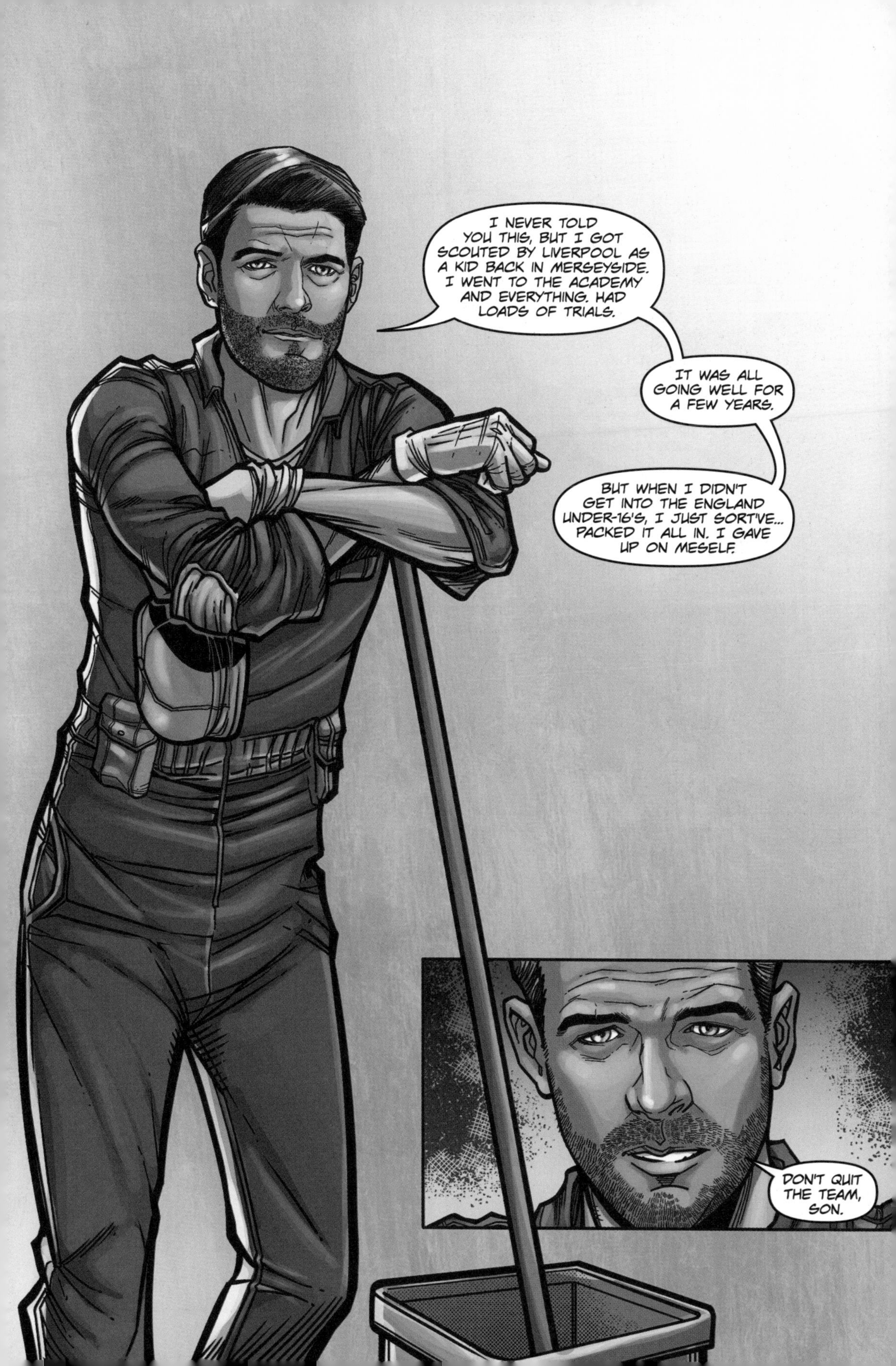
I NEVER TOLD YOU THIS, BUT I GOT SCOUTED BY LIVERPOOL AS A KID BACK IN MERSEYSIDE. I WENT TO THE ACADEMY AND EVERYTHING. HAD LOADS OF TRIALS.
IT WAS ALL GOING WELL FOR A FEW YEARS.
BUT WHEN I DIDN'T GET INTO THE ENGLAND UNDER-16'S, I JUST SORT'VE... PACKED IT ALL IN. I GAVE UP ON MESELF.
DON'T QUIT THE TEAM, SON.

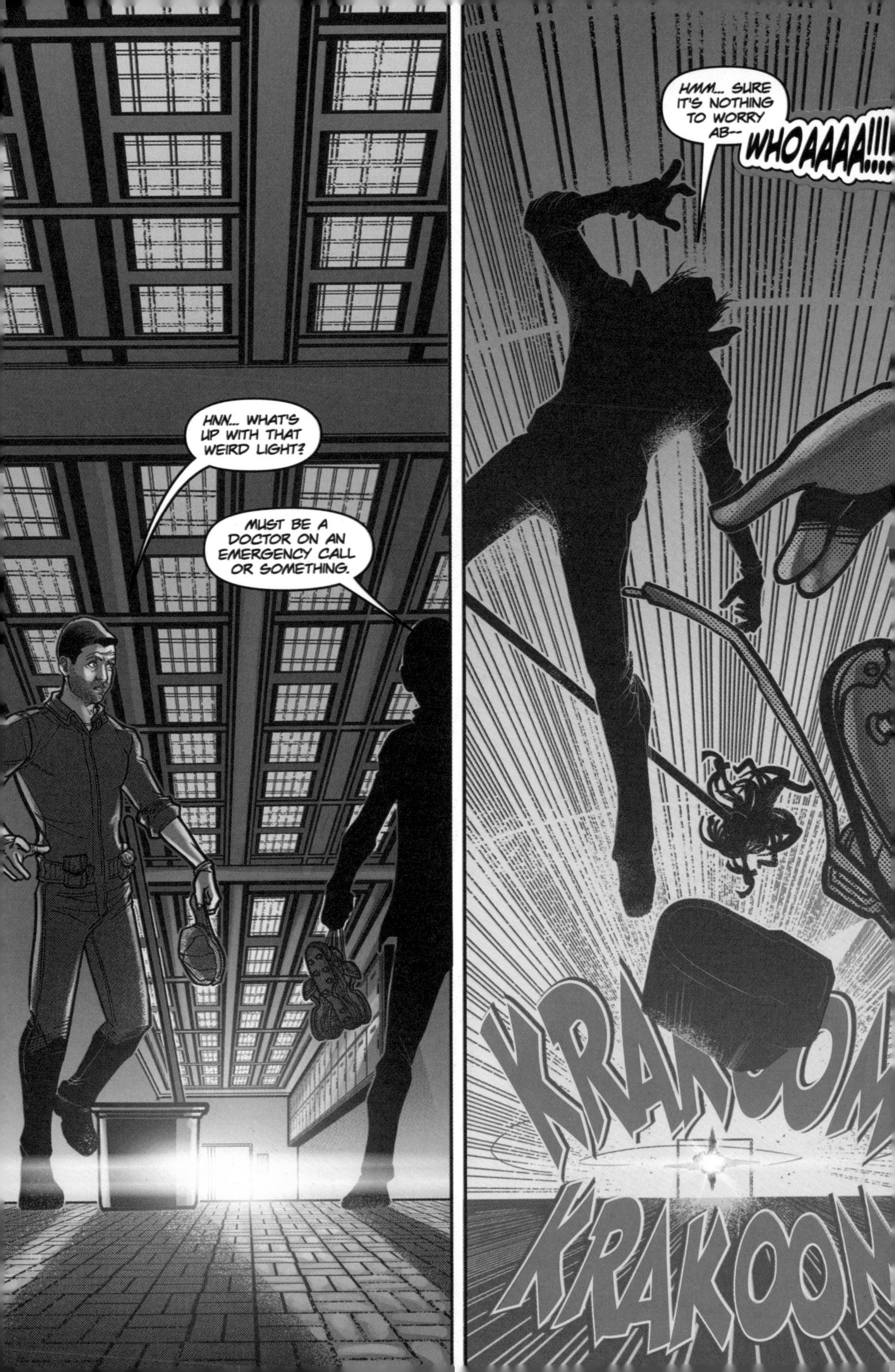

HNN... WHAT'S UP WITH THAT WEIRD LIGHT?
MUST BE A DOCTOR ON AN EMERGENCY CALL OR SOMETHING.
HMM... SURE IT'S NOTHING TO WORRY AB--
WHOAAAA!!!!
KRAKOOM
KRAKOOM

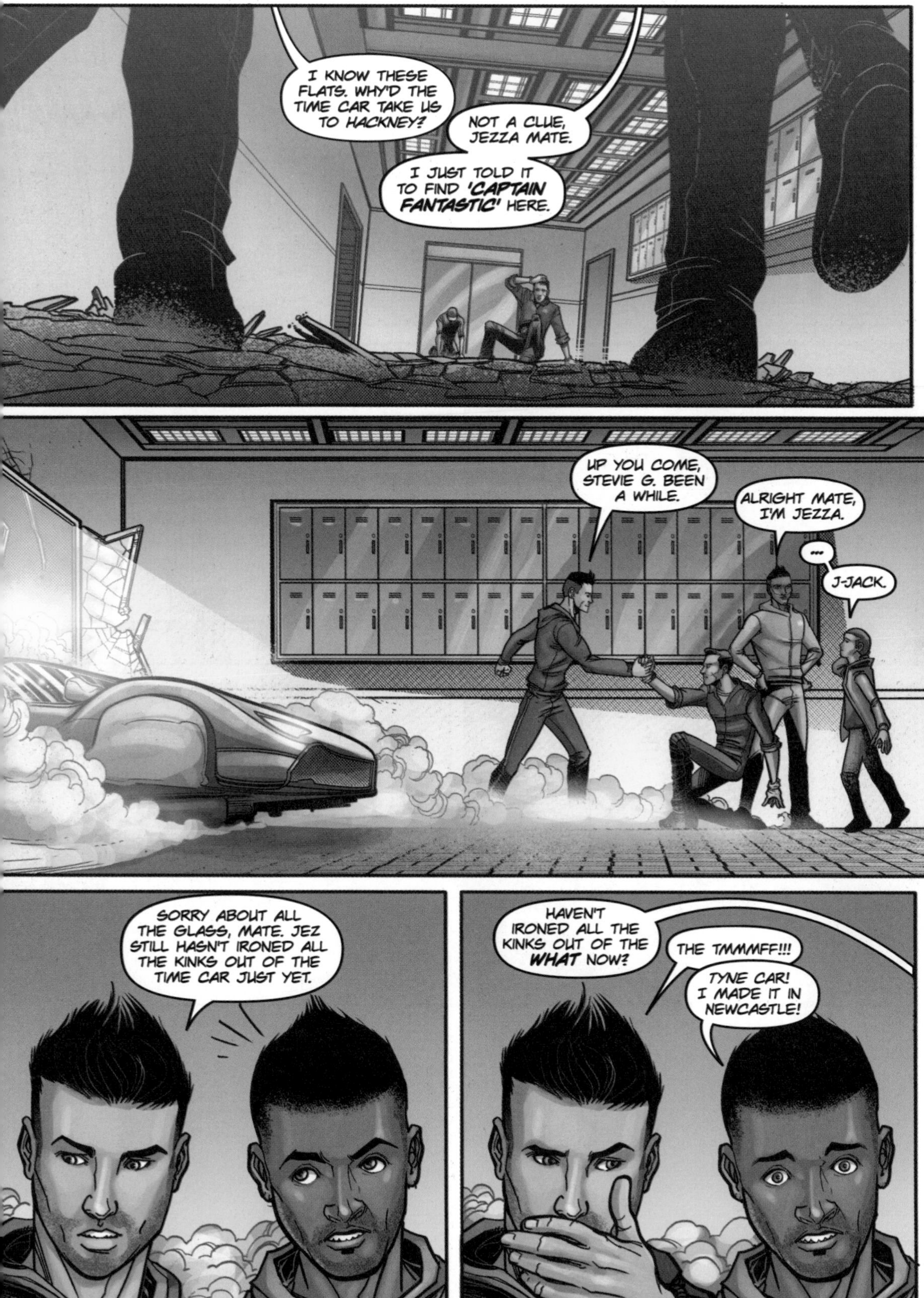
I KNOW THESE FLATS. WHY'D THE TIME CAR TAKE US TO HACKNEY?
NOT A CLUE, JEZZA MATE.
I JUST TOLD IT TO FIND 'CAPTAIN FANTASTIC' HERE.
UP YOU COME, STEVIE G. BEEN A WHILE.
ALRIGHT MATE, I'M JEZZA.
...
J-JACK.
SORRY ABOUT ALL THE GLASS, MATE. JEZ STILL HASN'T IRONED ALL THE KINKS OUT OF THE TIME CAR JUST YET.
HAVEN'T IRONED ALL THE KINKS OUT OF THE WHAT NOW?
THE TMMMFF!!!
TYNE CAR! I MADE IT IN NEWCASTLE!

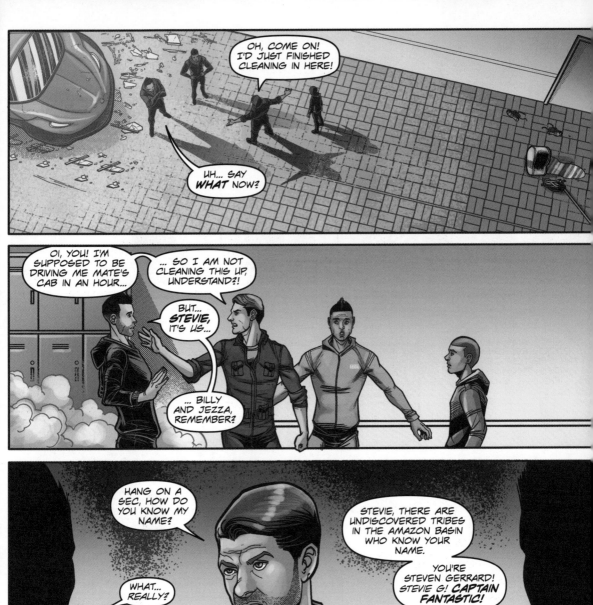

OH, COME ON! I'D JUST FINISHED CLEANING IN HERE!

UH... SAY *WHAT* NOW?

OI, YOU! I'M SUPPOSED TO BE DRIVING ME MATE'S CAB IN AN HOUR...

... SO I AM NOT CLEANING THIS UP, UNDERSTAND?!

BUT... *STEVIE,* IT'S US...

... BILLY AND JEZZA, REMEMBER?

HANG ON A SEC, HOW DO YOU KNOW MY NAME?

STEVIE, THERE ARE UNDISCOVERED TRIBES IN THE AMAZON BASIN WHO KNOW YOUR NAME.

WHAT... REALLY?

YOU'RE STEVEN GERRARD! STEVIE G! *CAPTAIN FANTASTIC!*

OKAY, IS THIS A WIND UP? DID HAZEL AT THE OFFICE PUT YOU UP TO THIS?

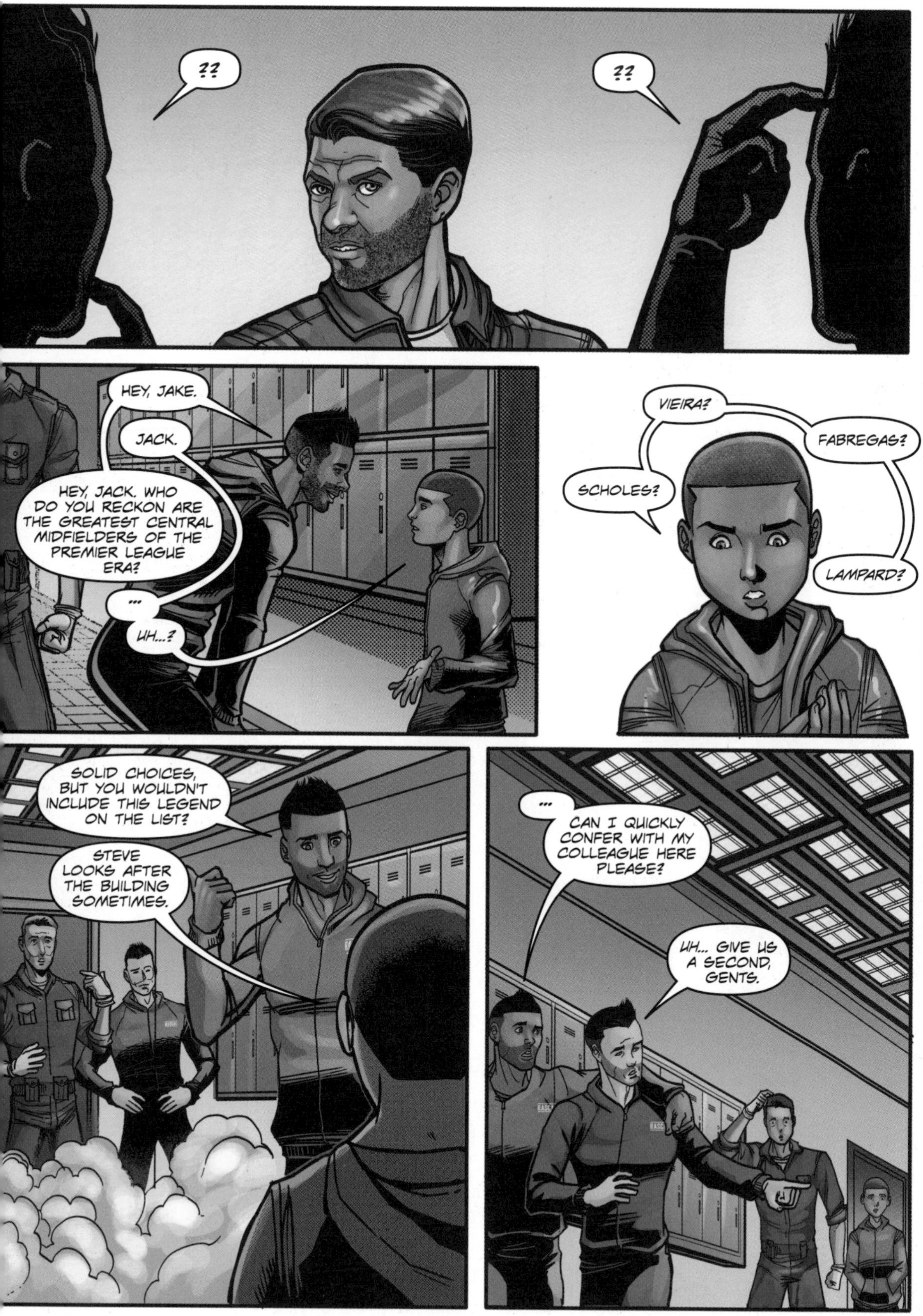
??
??
HEY, JAKE.
JACK.
HEY, JACK. WHO DO YOU RECKON ARE THE GREATEST CENTRAL MIDFIELDERS OF THE PREMIER LEAGUE ERA?
...
UH...?
VIEIRA?
FABREGAS?
SCHOLES?
LAMPARD?
SOLID CHOICES, BUT YOU WOULDN'T INCLUDE THIS LEGEND ON THE LIST?
STEVE LOOKS AFTER THE BUILDING SOMETIMES.
...
CAN I QUICKLY CONFER WITH MY COLLEAGUE HERE PLEASE?
UH... GIVE US A SECOND, GENTS.

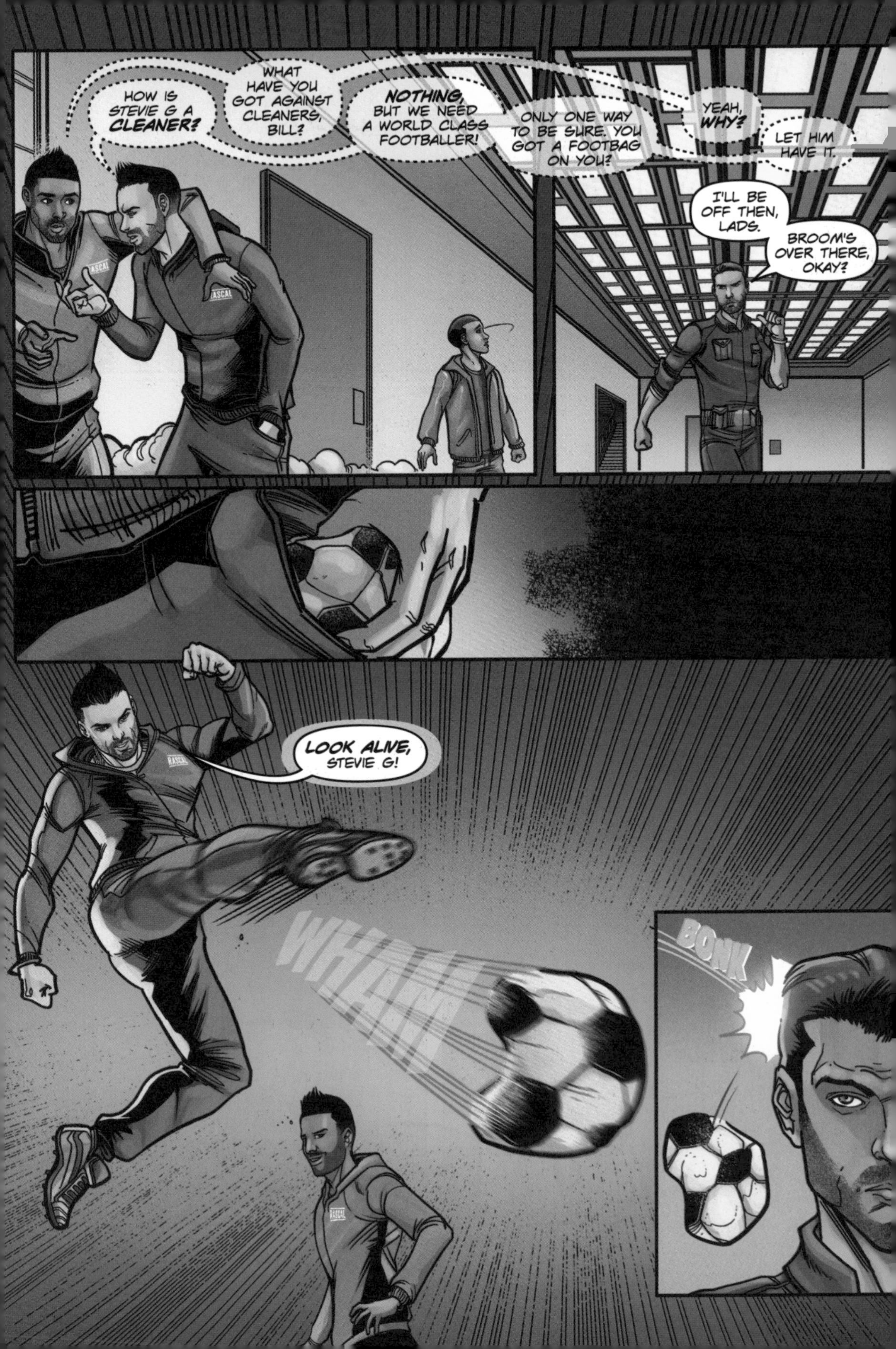
HOW IS STEVIE G A CLEANER?
WHAT HAVE YOU GOT AGAINST CLEANERS, BILL?
NOTHING, BUT WE NEED A WORLD CLASS FOOTBALLER!
ONLY ONE WAY TO BE SURE. YOU GOT A FOOTBAG ON YOU?
YEAH, WHY?
LET HIM HAVE IT.
I'LL BE OFF THEN, LADS.
BROOM'S OVER THERE, OKAY?
LOOK ALIVE, STEVIE G!
WHAM
BONK

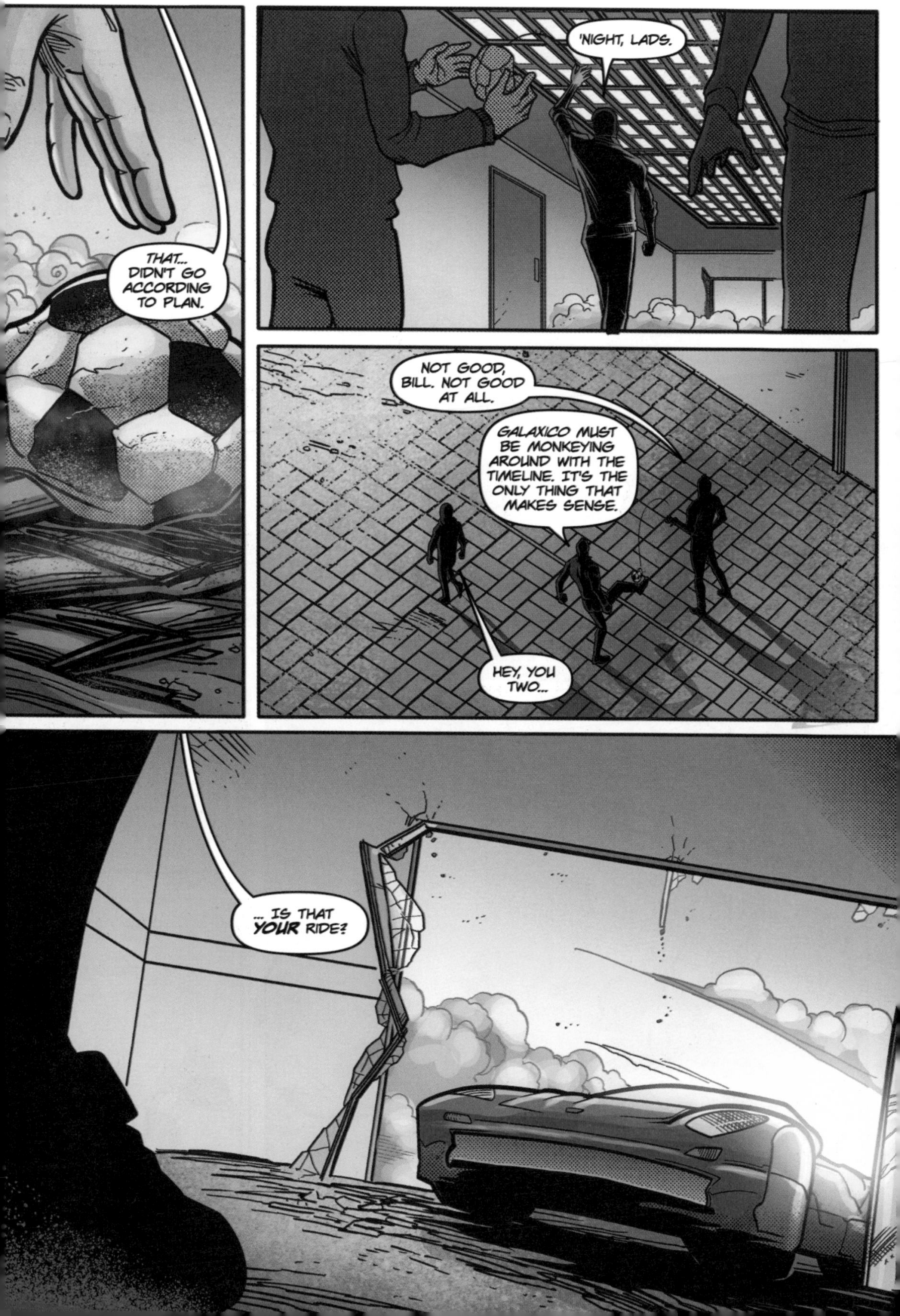
THAT... DIDN'T GO ACCORDING TO PLAN.
'NIGHT, LADS.
NOT GOOD, BILL. NOT GOOD AT ALL.
GALAXICO MUST BE MONKEYING AROUND WITH THE TIMELINE. IT'S THE ONLY THING THAT MAKES SENSE.
HEY, YOU TWO...
... IS THAT YOUR RIDE?

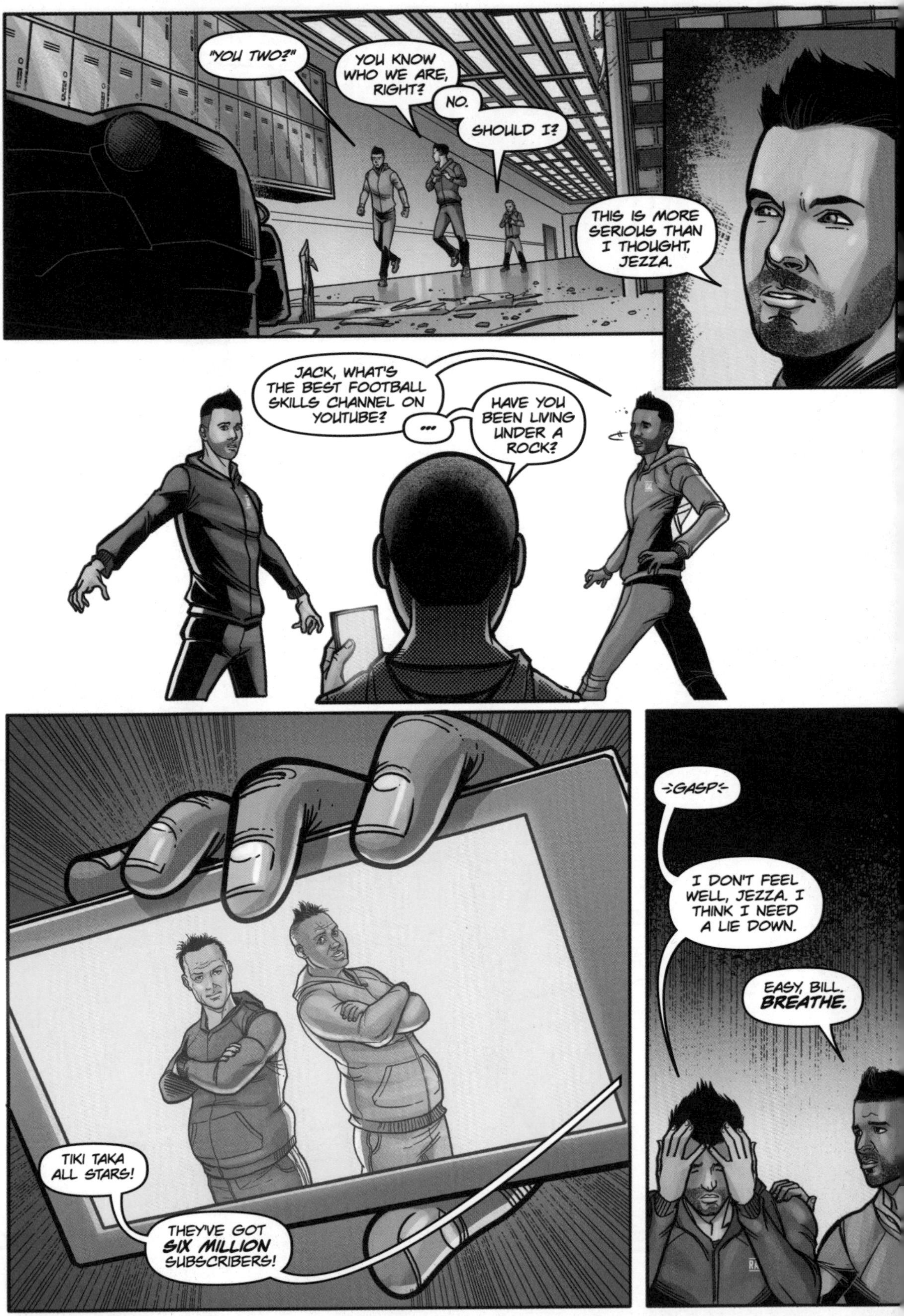
"YOU TWO?"
YOU KNOW WHO WE ARE, RIGHT?
NO.
SHOULD I?
THIS IS MORE SERIOUS THAN I THOUGHT, JEZZA.
JACK, WHAT'S THE BEST FOOTBALL SKILLS CHANNEL ON YOUTUBE?
...
HAVE YOU BEEN LIVING UNDER A ROCK?
TIKI TAKA ALL STARS!
THEY'VE GOT SIX MILLION SUBSCRIBERS!
GASP
I DON'T FEEL WELL, JEZZA. I THINK I NEED A LIE DOWN.
EASY, BILL. BREATHE.

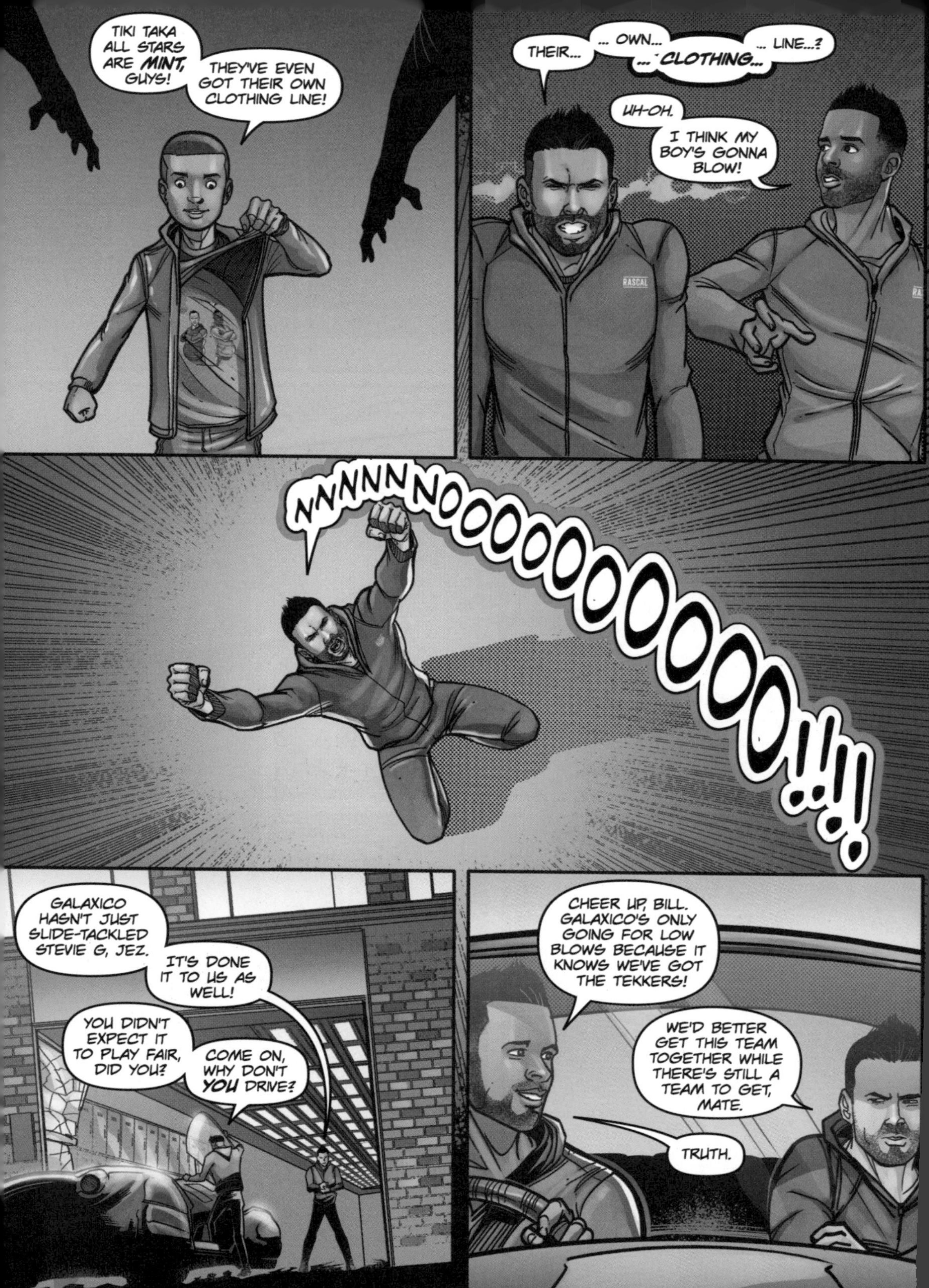
TIKI TAKA ALL STARS ARE **MINT,** GUYS!
THEY'VE EVEN GOT THEIR OWN CLOTHING LINE!
THEIR...
... OWN...
... CLOTHING...
... LINE...?
UH-OH.
I THINK MY BOY'S GONNA BLOW!
RASCAL
NNNNNNOOOOOOOOOO!!!!
GALAXICO HASN'T JUST SLIDE-TACKLED STEVIE G, JEZ.
IT'S DONE IT TO US AS WELL!
YOU DIDN'T EXPECT IT TO PLAY FAIR, DID YOU?
COME ON, WHY DON'T **YOU** DRIVE?
CHEER UP, BILL. GALAXICO'S ONLY GOING FOR LOW BLOWS BECAUSE IT KNOWS WE'VE GOT THE TEKKERS!
WE'D BETTER GET THIS TEAM TOGETHER WHILE THERE'S STILL A TEAM TO GET, MATE.
TRUTH.

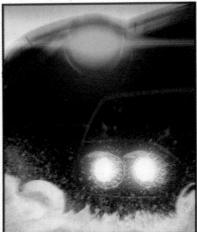

MAGIC FM

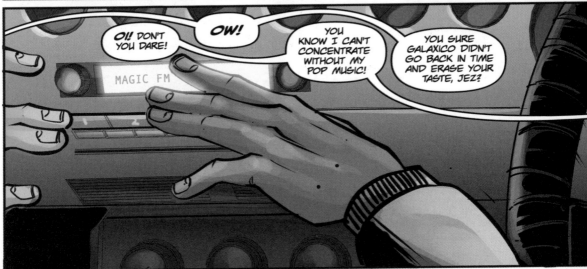

OI! DON'T YOU DARE!

OW!

YOU KNOW I CAN'T CONCENTRATE WITHOUT MY POP MUSIC!

YOU SURE GALAXICO DIDN'T GO BACK IN TIME AND ERASE YOUR TASTE, JEZ?

MAGIC FM

HOLD UP, WHAT HAPPENED TO THAT JAKE KID?

JACK.

HOLD UP, WHAT HAPPENED TO THAT JACK KID?

HE'S PROBABLY CALLING THE COPS ON A COUPLE OF CRAZY FELLAS WHO THINK THEY'RE YOUTUBE STARS.

I WOULD.

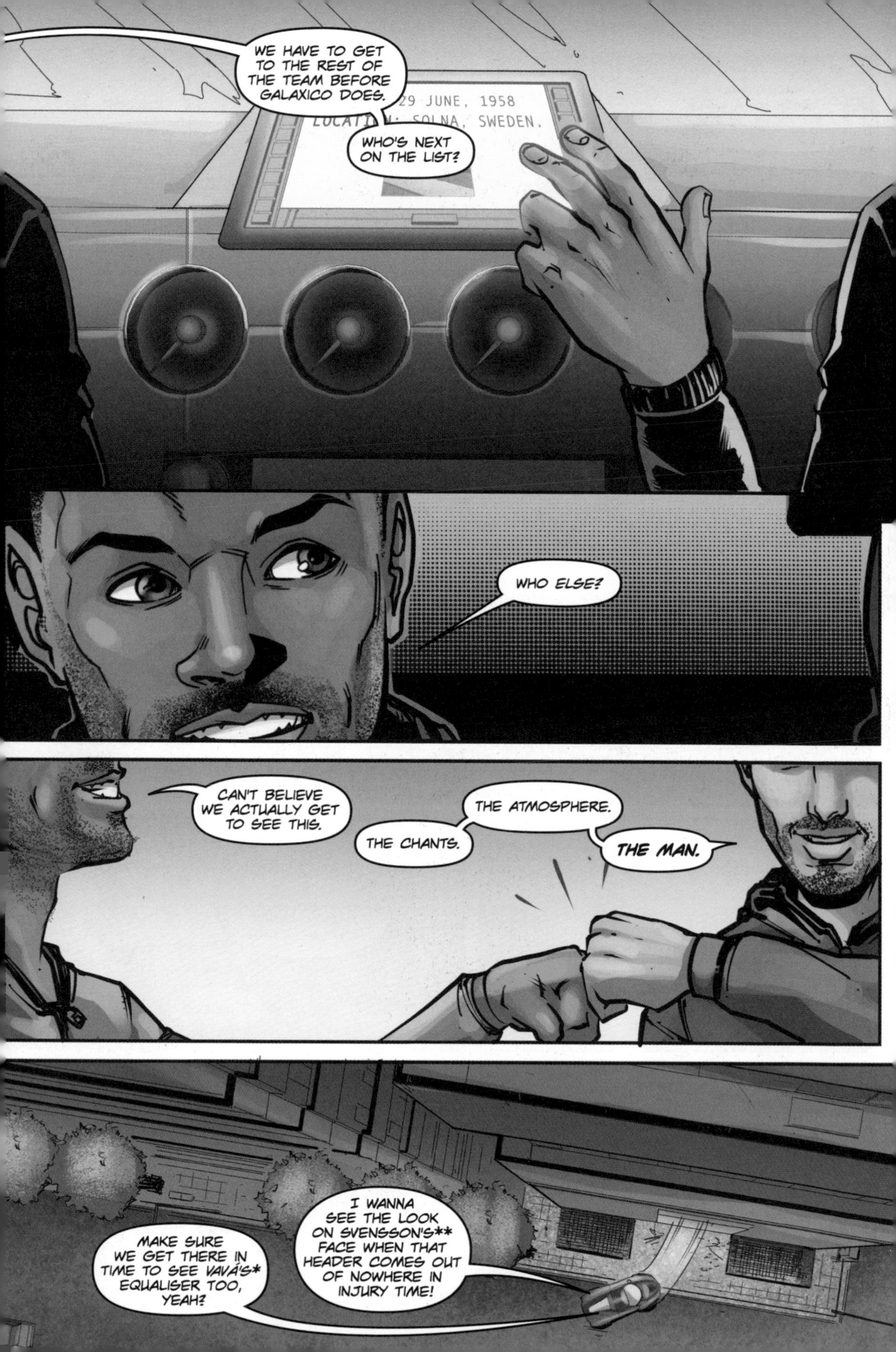
WE HAVE TO GET TO THE REST OF THE TEAM BEFORE GALAXICO DOES.
29 JUNE, 1958
SOLNA, SWEDEN.
WHO'S NEXT ON THE LIST?
WHO ELSE?
CAN'T BELIEVE WE ACTUALLY GET TO SEE THIS.
THE CHANTS.
THE ATMOSPHERE.
THE MAN.
MAKE SURE WE GET THERE IN TIME TO SEE VAVÁ'S* EQUALISER TOO, YEAH?
I WANNA SEE THE LOOK ON SVENSSON'S** FACE WHEN THAT HEADER COMES OUT OF NOWHERE IN INJURY TIME!

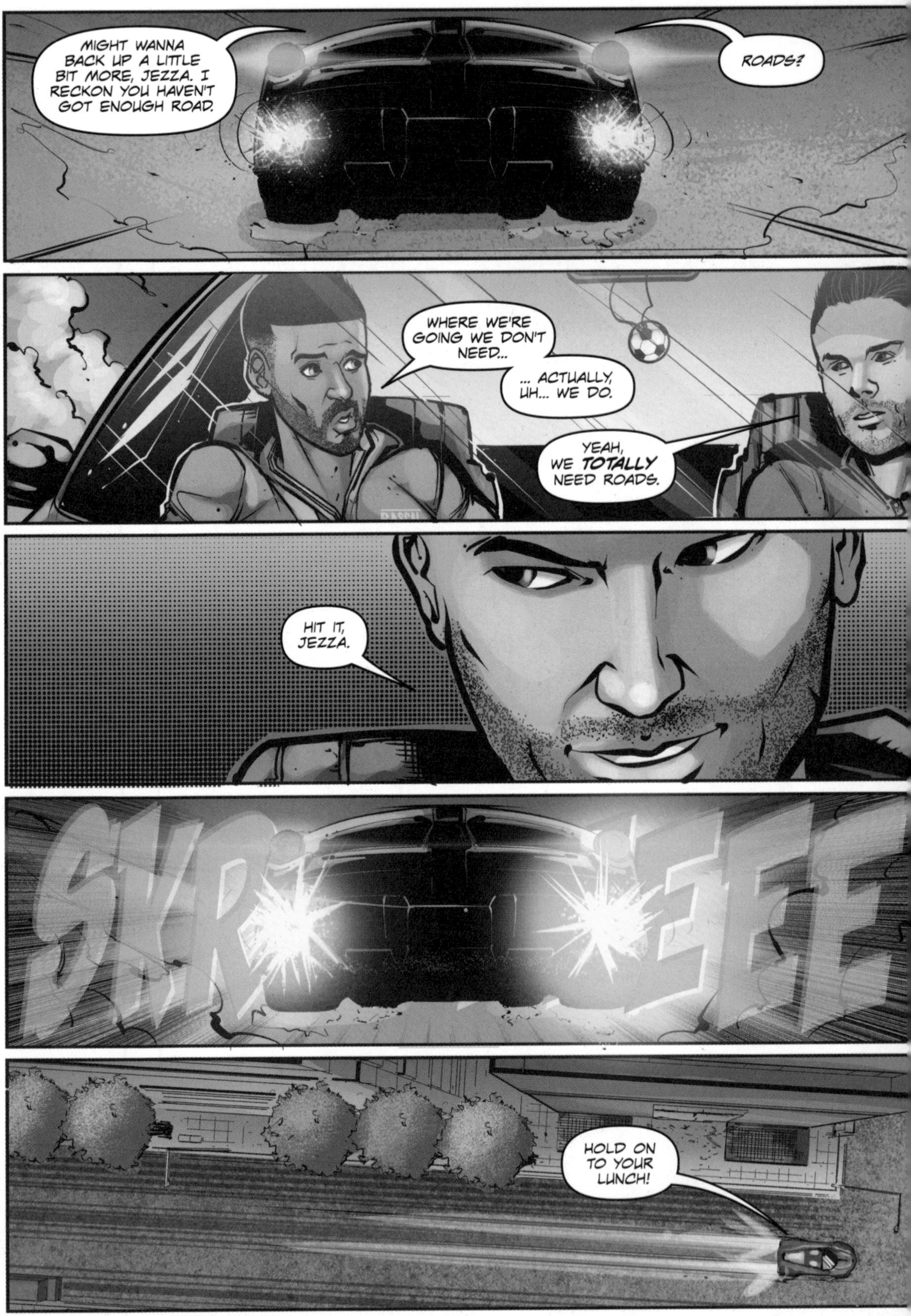
MIGHT WANNA BACK UP A LITTLE BIT MORE, JEZZA. I RECKON YOU HAVEN'T GOT ENOUGH ROAD.
ROADS?
WHERE WE'RE GOING WE DON'T NEED...
... ACTUALLY, UH... WE DO.
YEAH, WE TOTALLY NEED ROADS.
HIT IT, JEZZA.
HOLD ON TO YOUR LUNCH!

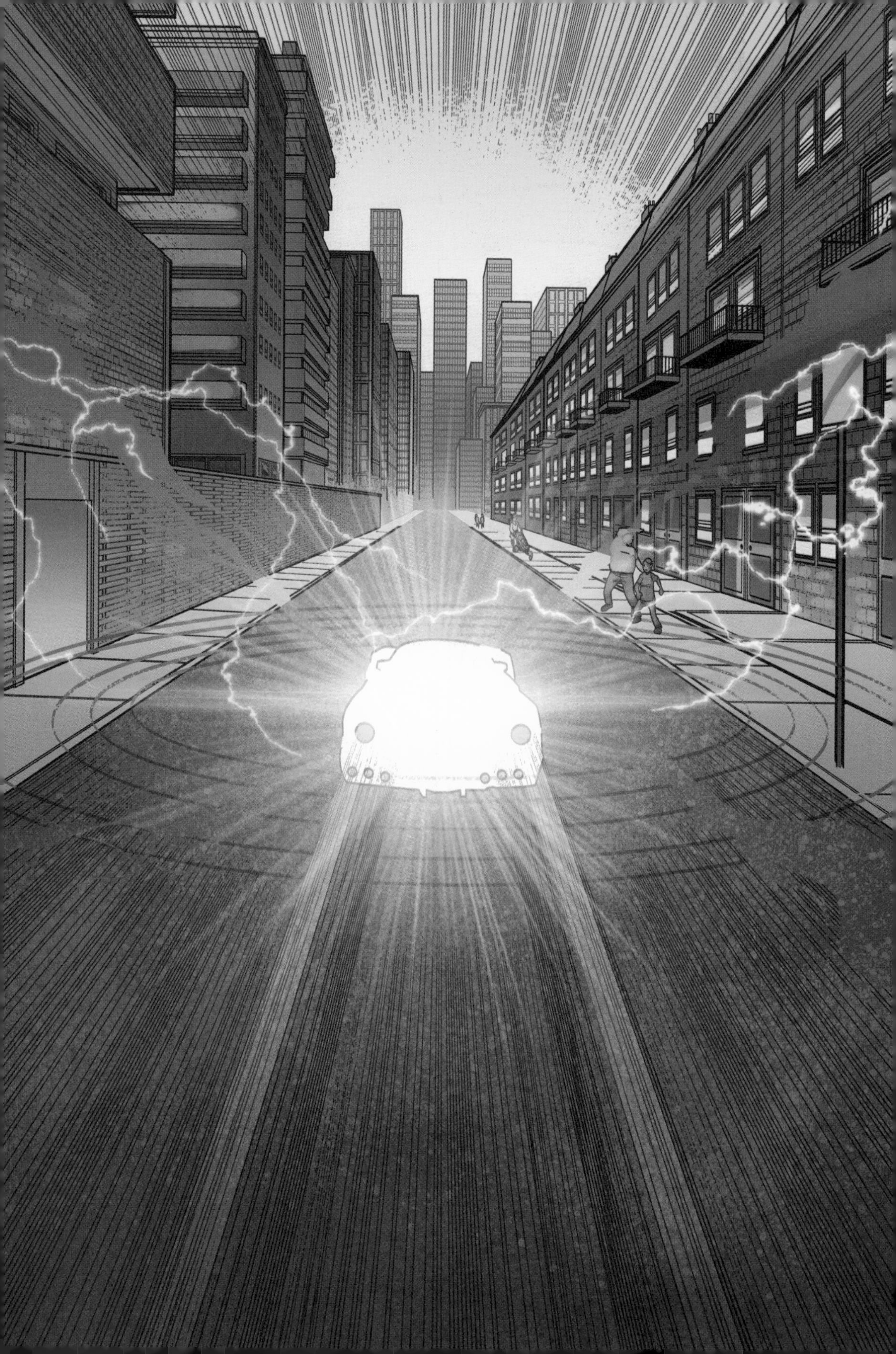

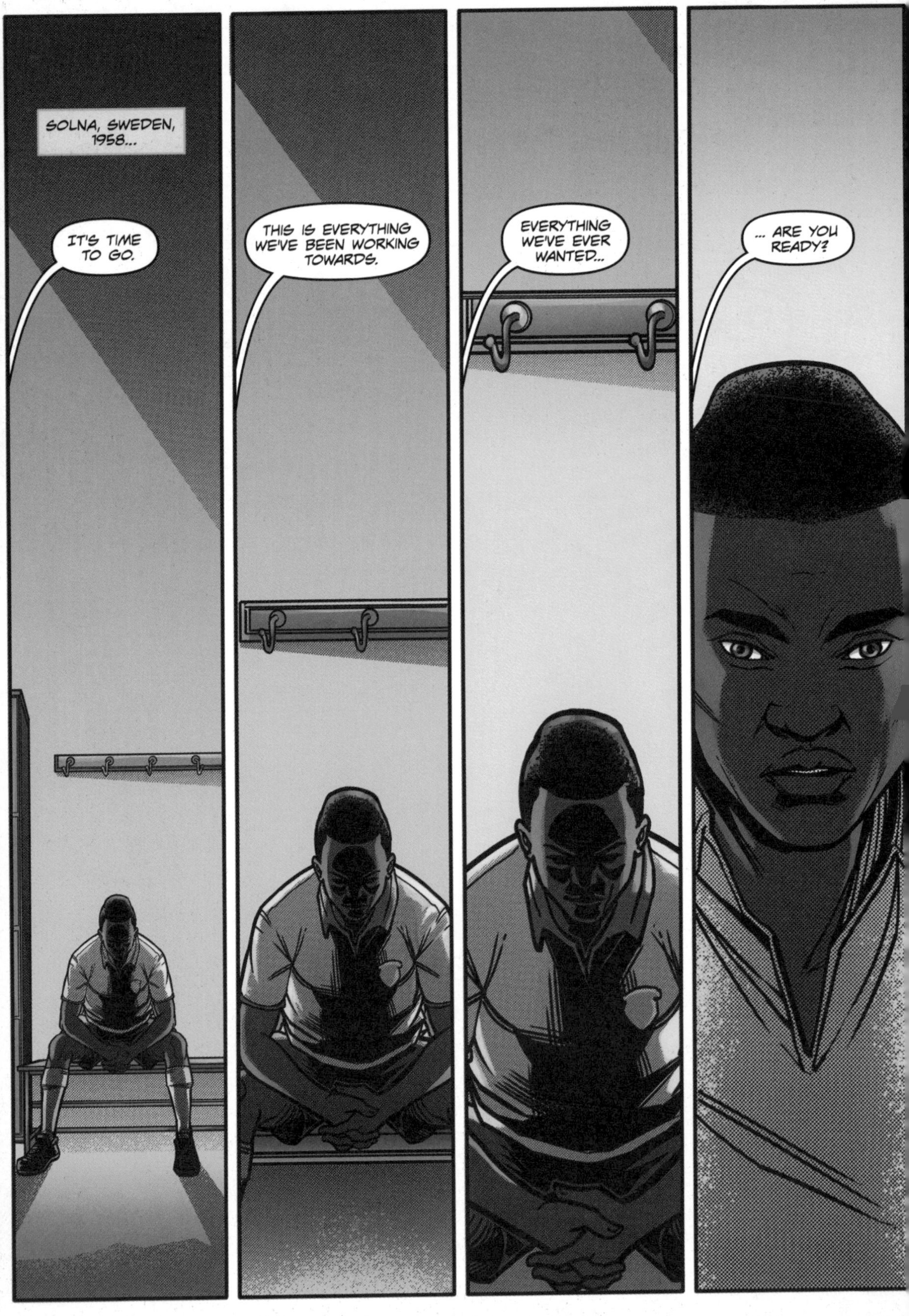
SOLNA, SWEDEN, 1958...
IT'S TIME TO GO.
THIS IS EVERYTHING WE'VE BEEN WORKING TOWARDS.
EVERYTHING WE'VE EVER WANTED...
... ARE YOU READY?

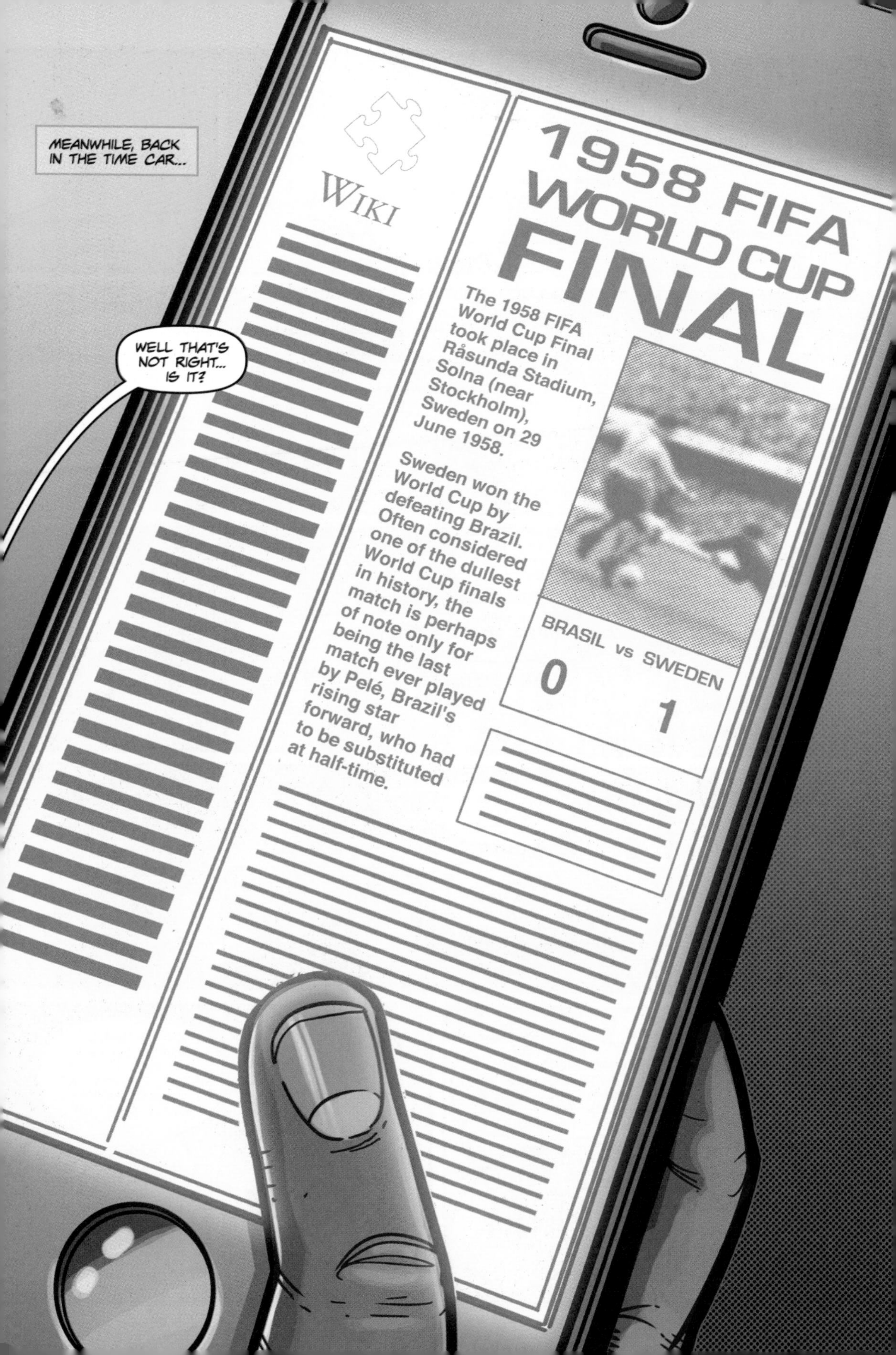

MEANWHILE, BACK IN THE TIME CAR...
WELL THAT'S NOT RIGHT... IS IT?
WIKI
1958 FIFA WORLD CUP FINAL
The 1958 FIFA World Cup Final took place in Råsunda Stadium, Solna (near Stockholm), Sweden on 29 June 1958.
Sweden won the World Cup by defeating Brazil. Often considered one of the dullest World Cup finals in history, the match is perhaps of note only for being the last match ever played by Pelé, Brazil's rising star forward, who had to be substituted at half-time.
BRASIL vs SWEDEN
0 1

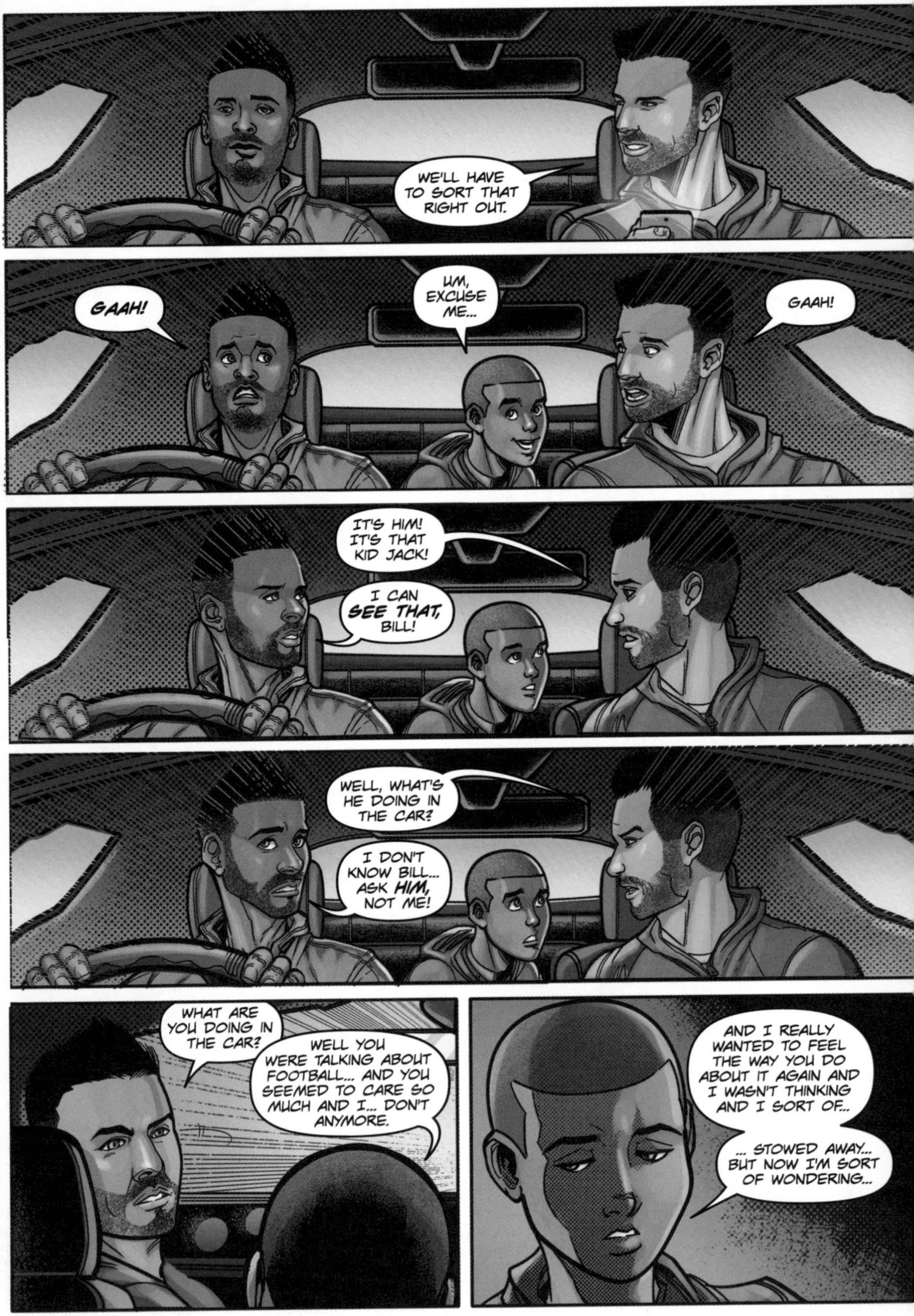
WE'LL HAVE TO SORT THAT RIGHT OUT.
GAAH!
UM, EXCUSE ME...
GAAH!
IT'S HIM! IT'S THAT KID JACK!
I CAN **SEE THAT,** BILL!
WELL, WHAT'S HE DOING IN THE CAR?
I DON'T KNOW BILL... ASK **HIM,** NOT ME!
WHAT ARE YOU DOING IN THE CAR?
WELL YOU WERE TALKING ABOUT FOOTBALL... AND YOU SEEMED TO CARE SO MUCH AND I... DON'T ANYMORE.
AND I REALLY WANTED TO FEEL THE WAY YOU DO ABOUT IT AGAIN AND I WASN'T THINKING AND I SORT OF...
... STOWED AWAY... BUT NOW I'M SORT OF WONDERING...

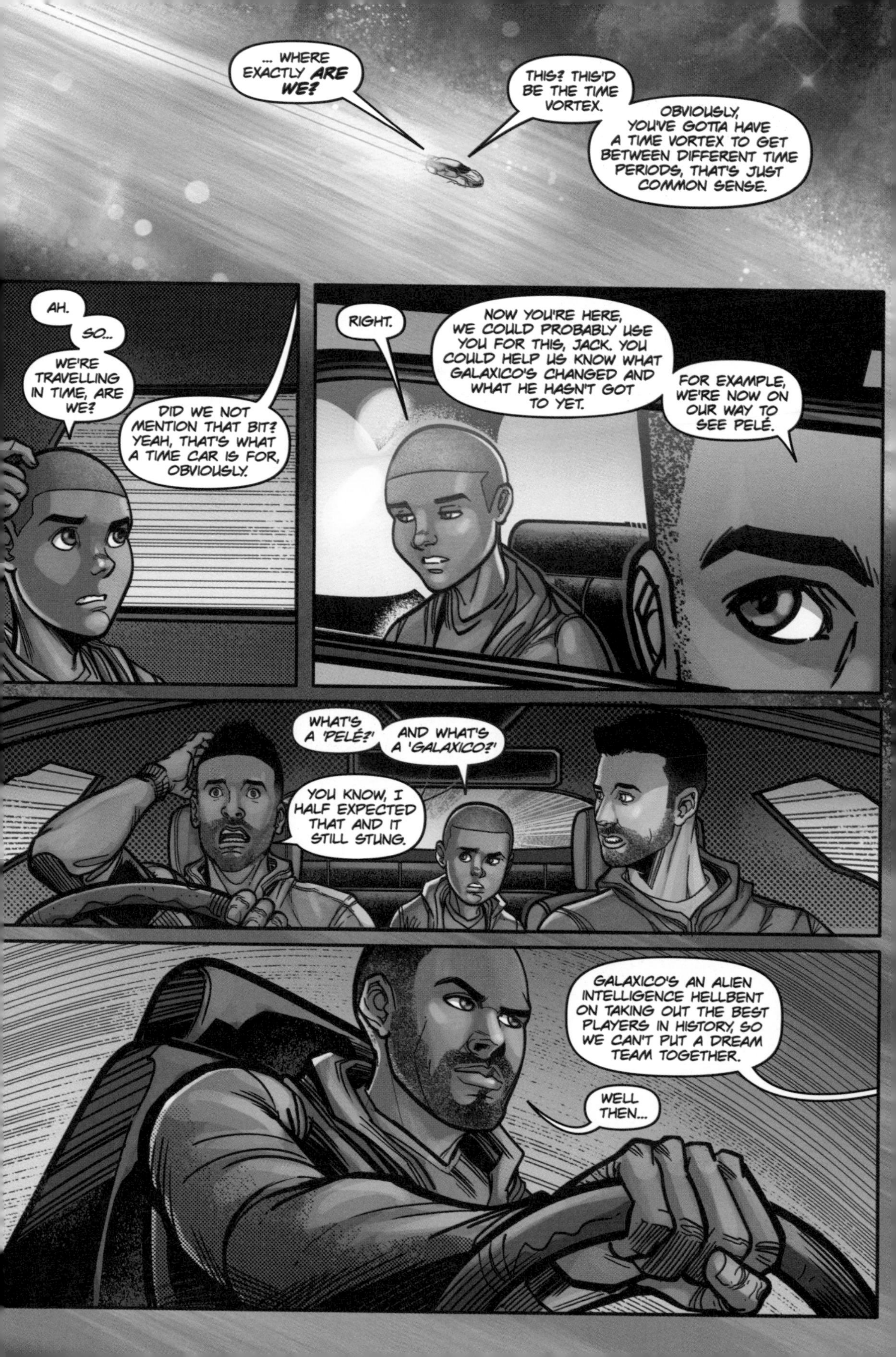
... WHERE EXACTLY ARE WE?
THIS? THIS'D BE THE TIME VORTEX.
OBVIOUSLY, YOU'VE GOTTA HAVE A TIME VORTEX TO GET BETWEEN DIFFERENT TIME PERIODS, THAT'S JUST COMMON SENSE.
AH.
SO...
WE'RE TRAVELLING IN TIME, ARE WE?
DID WE NOT MENTION THAT BIT? YEAH, THAT'S WHAT A TIME CAR IS FOR, OBVIOUSLY.
RIGHT.
NOW YOU'RE HERE, WE COULD PROBABLY USE YOU FOR THIS, JACK. YOU COULD HELP US KNOW WHAT GALAXICO'S CHANGED AND WHAT HE HASN'T GOT TO YET.
FOR EXAMPLE, WE'RE NOW ON OUR WAY TO SEE PELÉ.
WHAT'S A 'PELÉ?'
AND WHAT'S A 'GALAXICO?'
YOU KNOW, I HALF EXPECTED THAT AND IT STILL STUNG.
GALAXICO'S AN ALIEN INTELLIGENCE HELLBENT ON TAKING OUT THE BEST PLAYERS IN HISTORY, SO WE CAN'T PUT A DREAM TEAM TOGETHER.
WELL THEN...

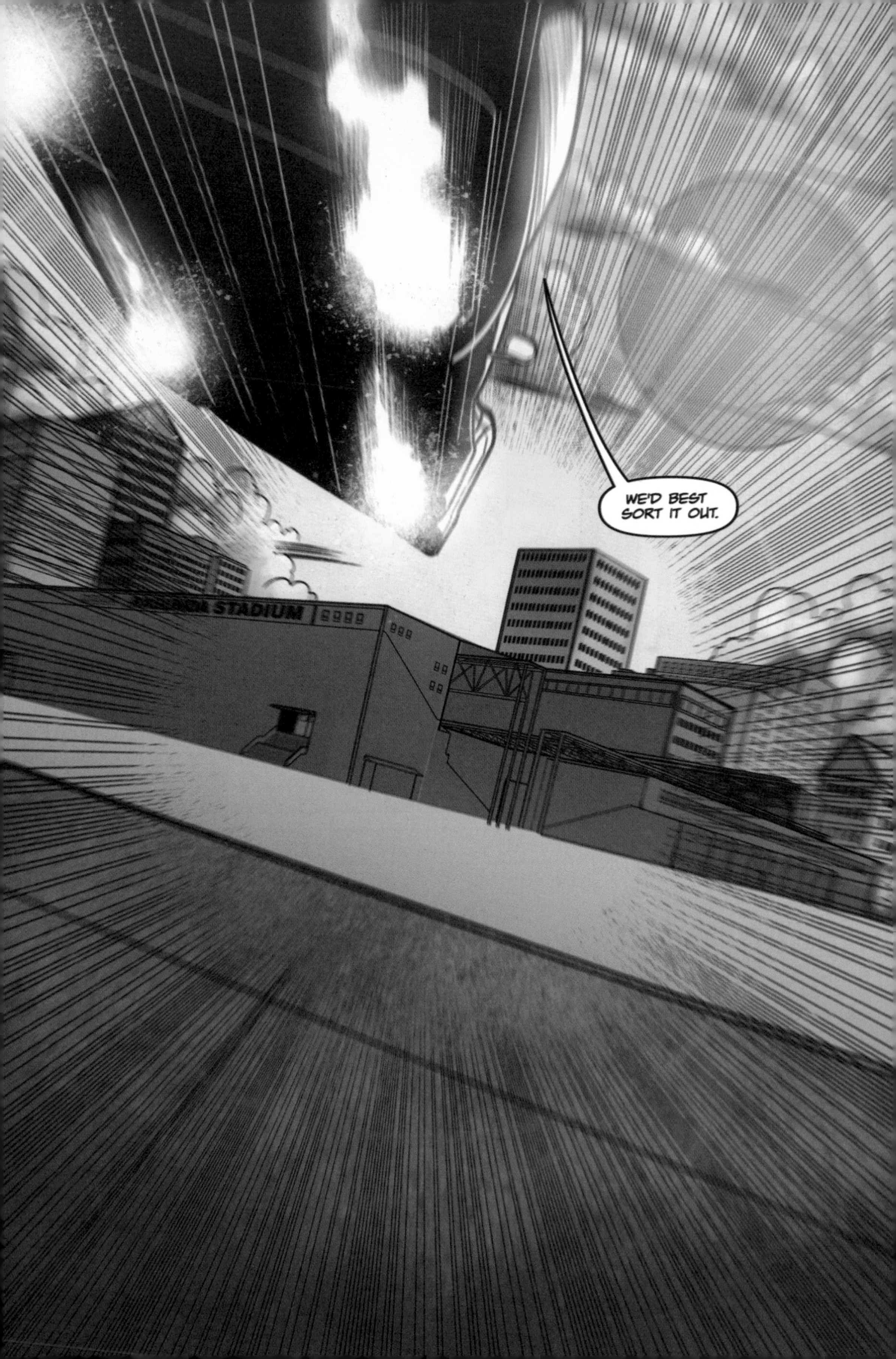
STADIUM
WE'D BEST SORT IT OUT.

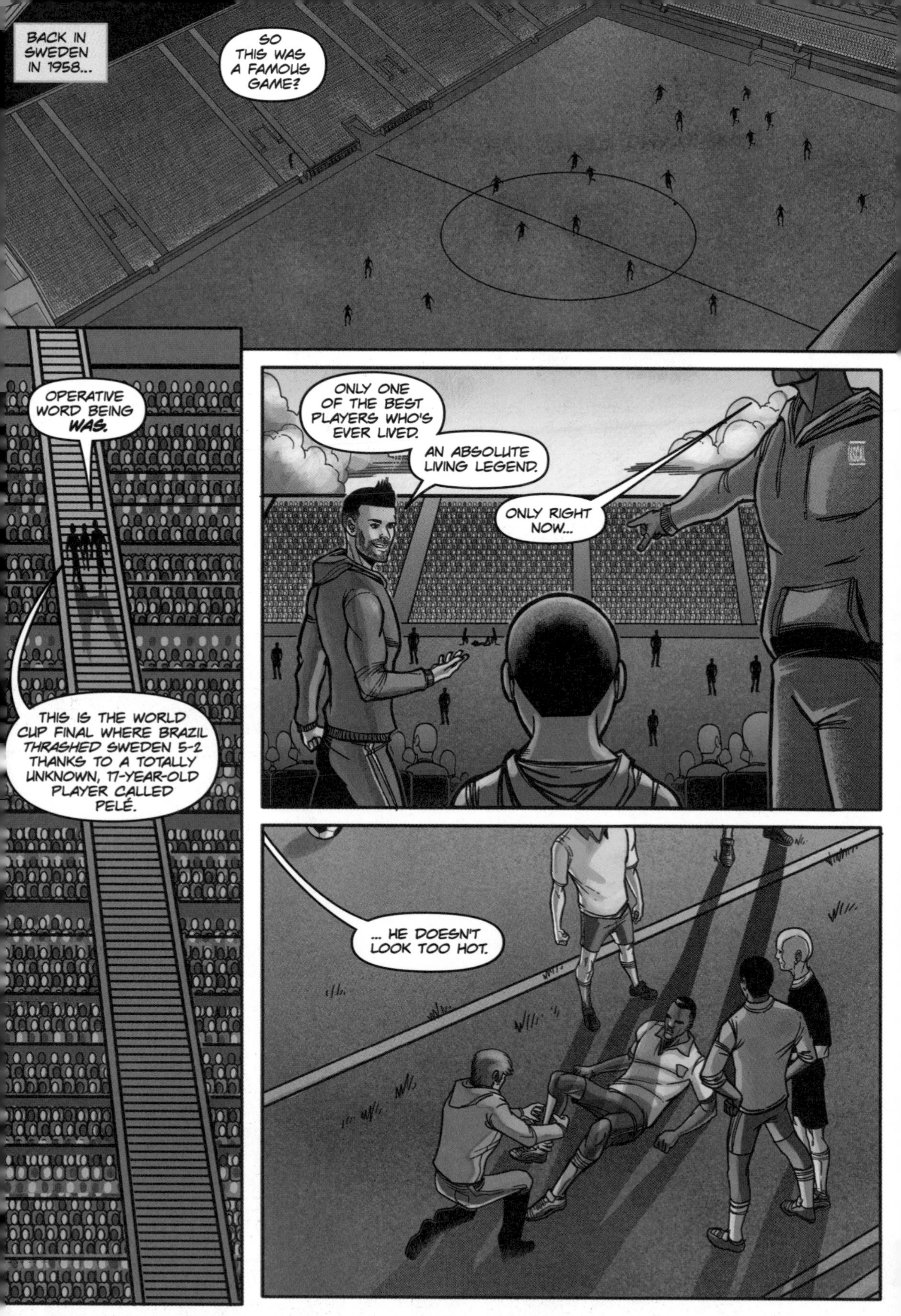
BACK IN SWEDEN IN 1958...
SO THIS WAS A FAMOUS GAME?
OPERATIVE WORD BEING *WAS*.
THIS IS THE WORLD CUP FINAL WHERE BRAZIL *THRASHED* SWEDEN 5-2 THANKS TO A TOTALLY UNKNOWN, 17-YEAR-OLD PLAYER CALLED PELÉ.
ONLY ONE OF THE BEST PLAYERS WHO'S EVER LIVED.
AN ABSOLUTE LIVING LEGEND.
ONLY RIGHT NOW...
... HE DOESN'T LOOK TOO HOT.

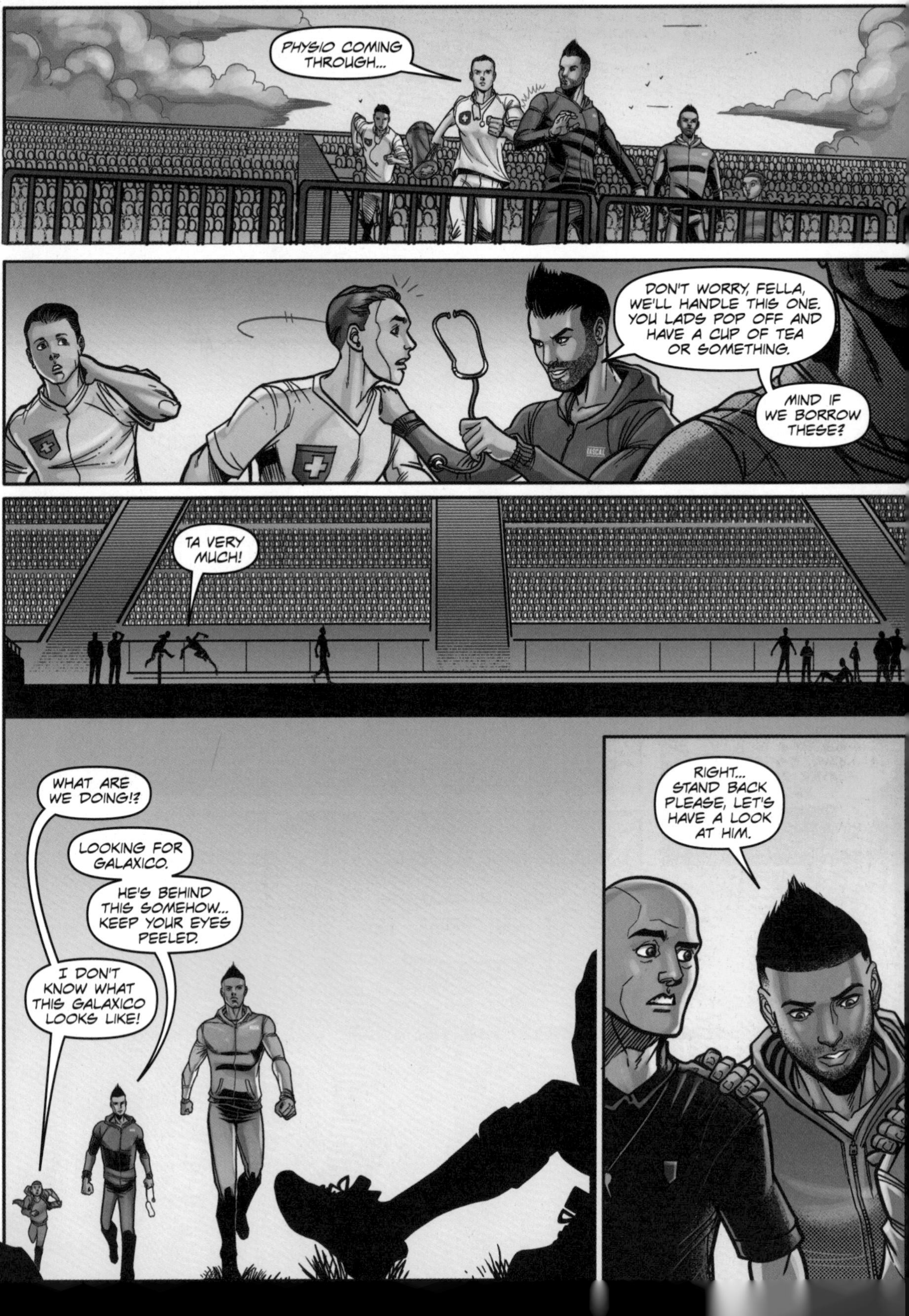
PHYSIO COMING THROUGH...
DON'T WORRY, FELLA, WE'LL HANDLE THIS ONE. YOU LADS POP OFF AND HAVE A CUP OF TEA OR SOMETHING.
MIND IF WE BORROW THESE?
TA VERY MUCH!
WHAT ARE WE DOING!?
LOOKING FOR GALAXICO.
HE'S BEHIND THIS SOMEHOW... KEEP YOUR EYES PEELED.
I DON'T KNOW WHAT THIS GALAXICO LOOKS LIKE!
RIGHT... STAND BACK PLEASE, LET'S HAVE A LOOK AT HIM.

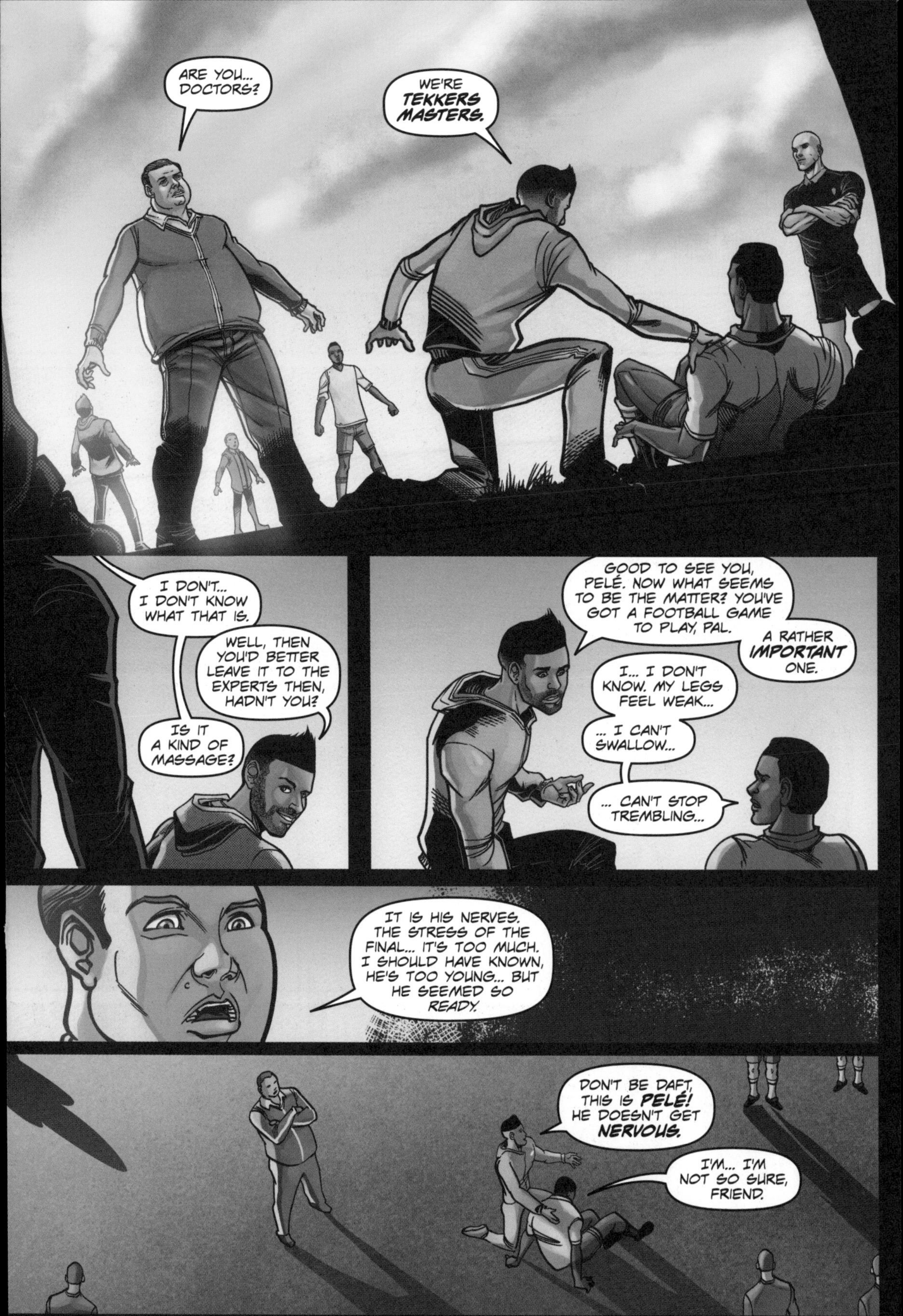
ARE YOU... DOCTORS?
WE'RE ***TEKKERS MASTERS.***
I DON'T... I DON'T KNOW WHAT THAT IS.
WELL, THEN YOU'D BETTER LEAVE IT TO THE EXPERTS THEN, HADN'T YOU?
IS IT A KIND OF MASSAGE?
GOOD TO SEE YOU, PELÉ. NOW WHAT SEEMS TO BE THE MATTER? YOU'VE GOT A FOOTBALL GAME TO PLAY, PAL.
A RATHER ***IMPORTANT*** ONE.
I... I DON'T KNOW. MY LEGS FEEL WEAK...
... I CAN'T SWALLOW...
... CAN'T STOP TREMBLING...
IT IS HIS NERVES. THE STRESS OF THE FINAL... IT'S TOO MUCH. I SHOULD HAVE KNOWN, HE'S TOO YOUNG... BUT HE SEEMED SO *READY.*
DON'T BE DAFT, THIS IS ***PELÉ!*** HE DOESN'T GET ***NERVOUS.***
I'M... I'M NOT SO SURE, FRIEND.

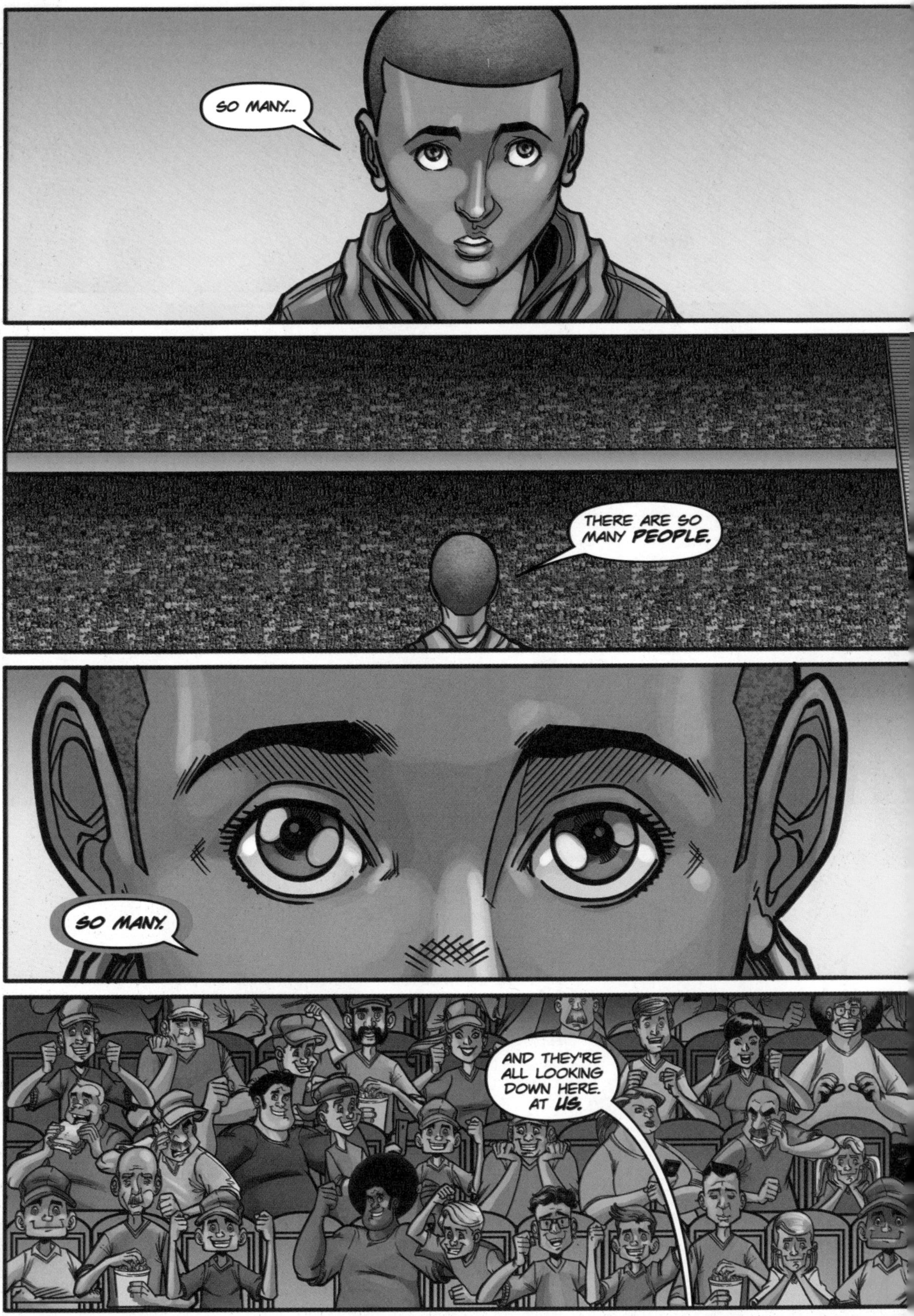
SO MANY...
THERE ARE SO MANY PEOPLE.
SO MANY.
AND THEY'RE ALL LOOKING DOWN HERE. AT US.

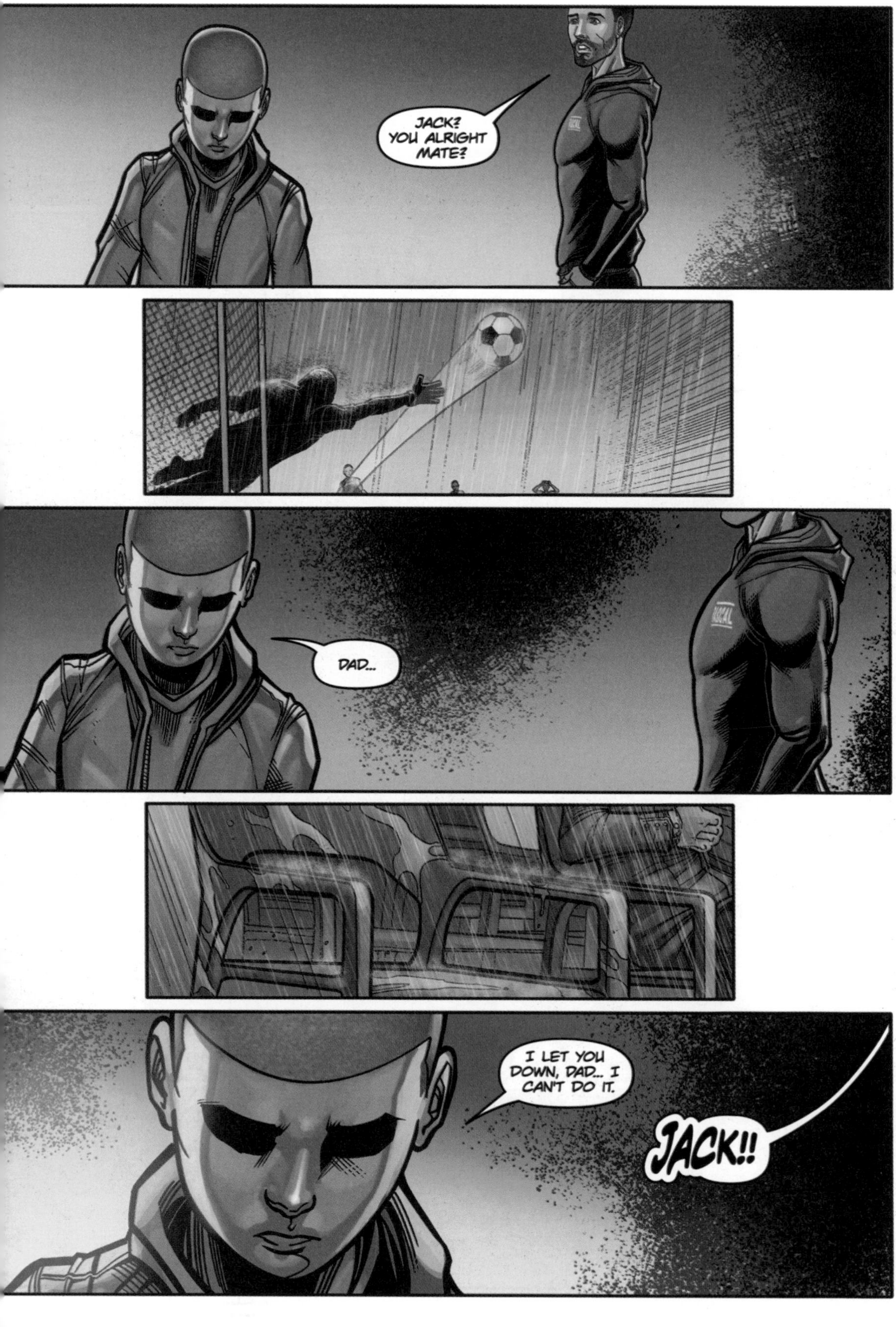
JACK? YOU ALRIGHT MATE?
DAD...
I LET YOU DOWN, DAD... I CAN'T DO IT.
JACK!!

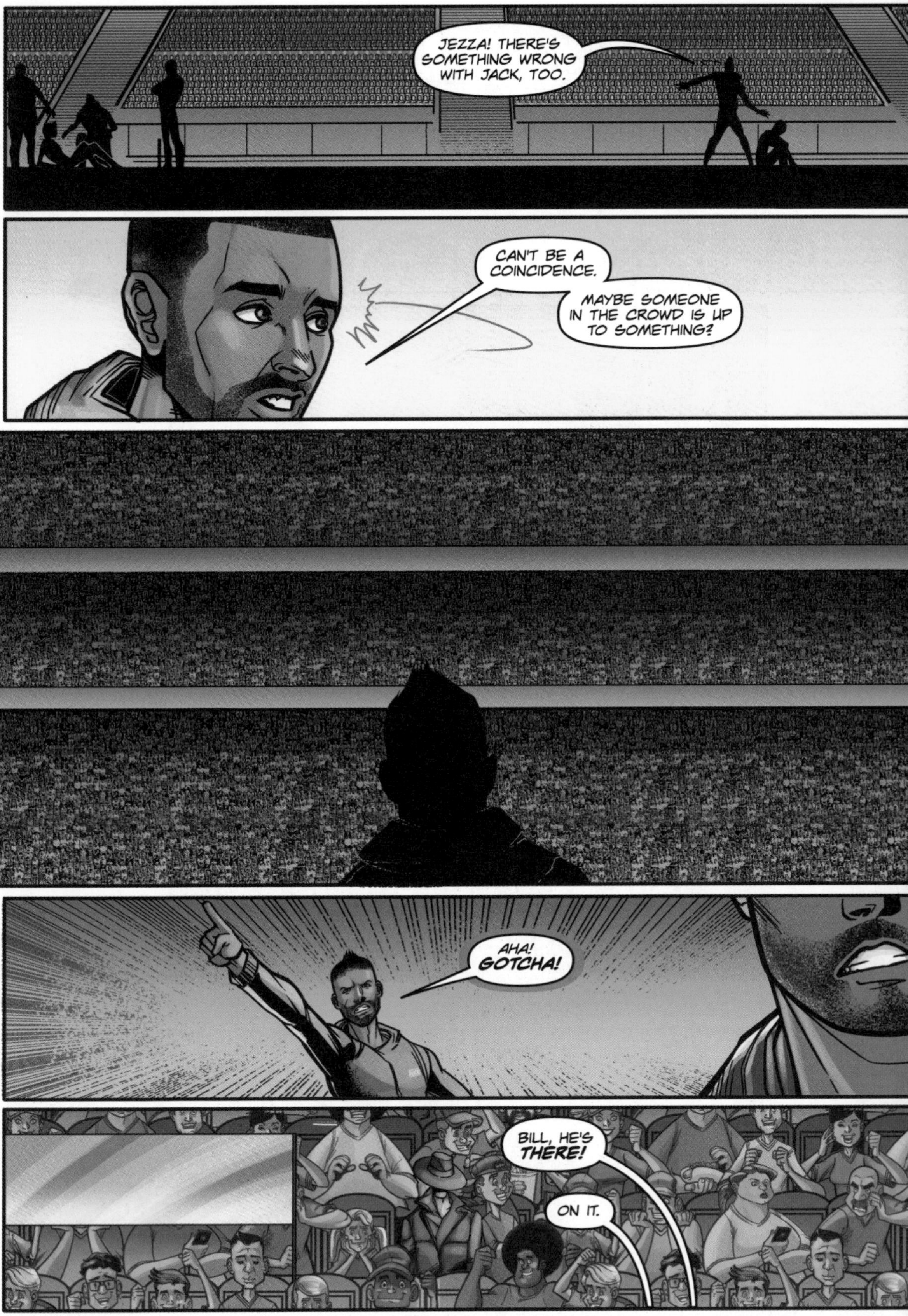
JEZZA! THERE'S SOMETHING WRONG WITH JACK, TOO.
CAN'T BE A COINCIDENCE.
MAYBE SOMEONE IN THE CROWD IS UP TO SOMETHING?
AHA! **GOTCHA!**
BILL, HE'S ***THERE!***
ON IT.

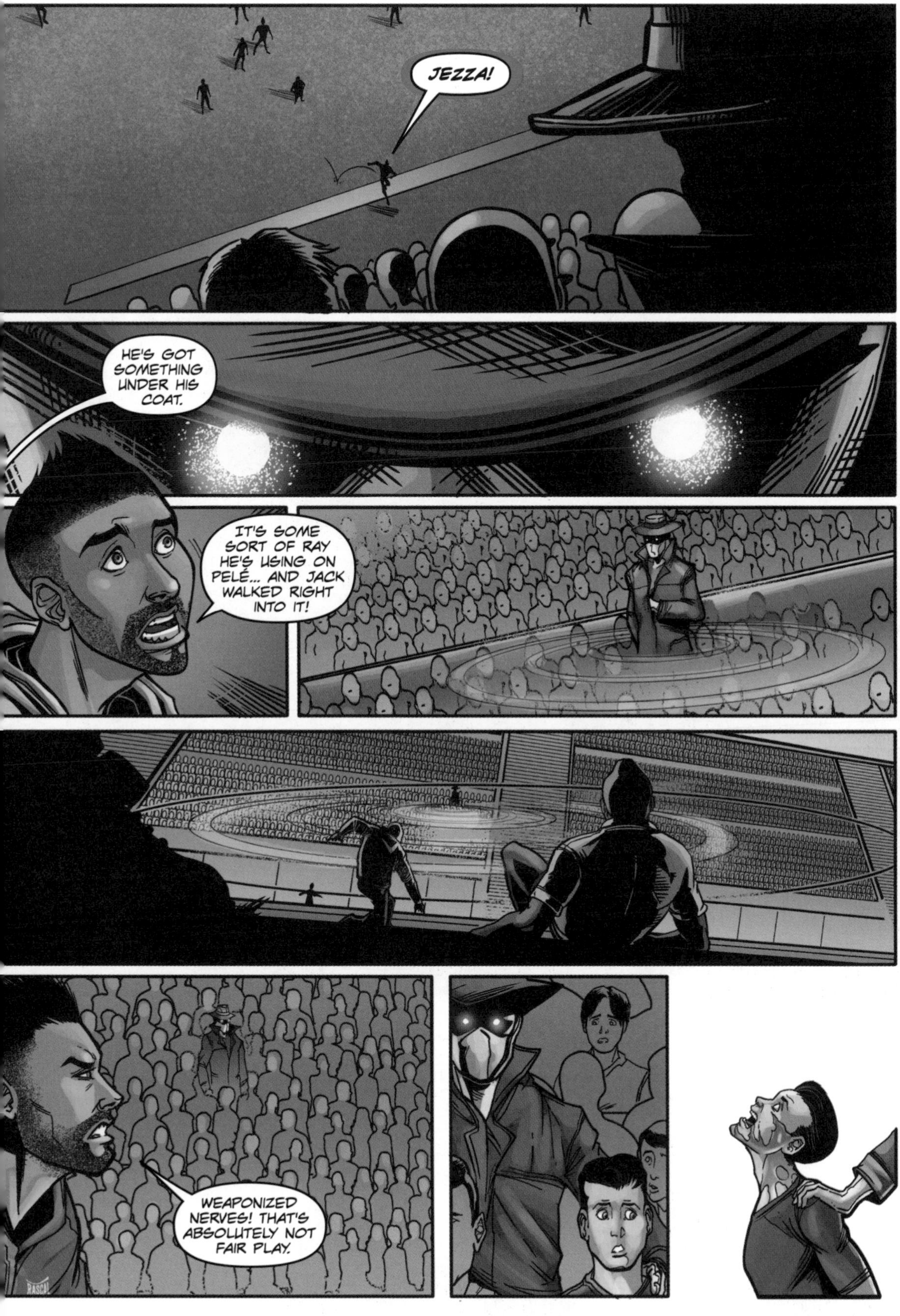
JEZZA!
HE'S GOT SOMETHING UNDER HIS COAT.
IT'S SOME SORT OF RAY HE'S USING ON PELÉ... AND JACK WALKED RIGHT INTO IT!
WEAPONIZED NERVES! THAT'S ABSOLUTELY NOT FAIR PLAY.

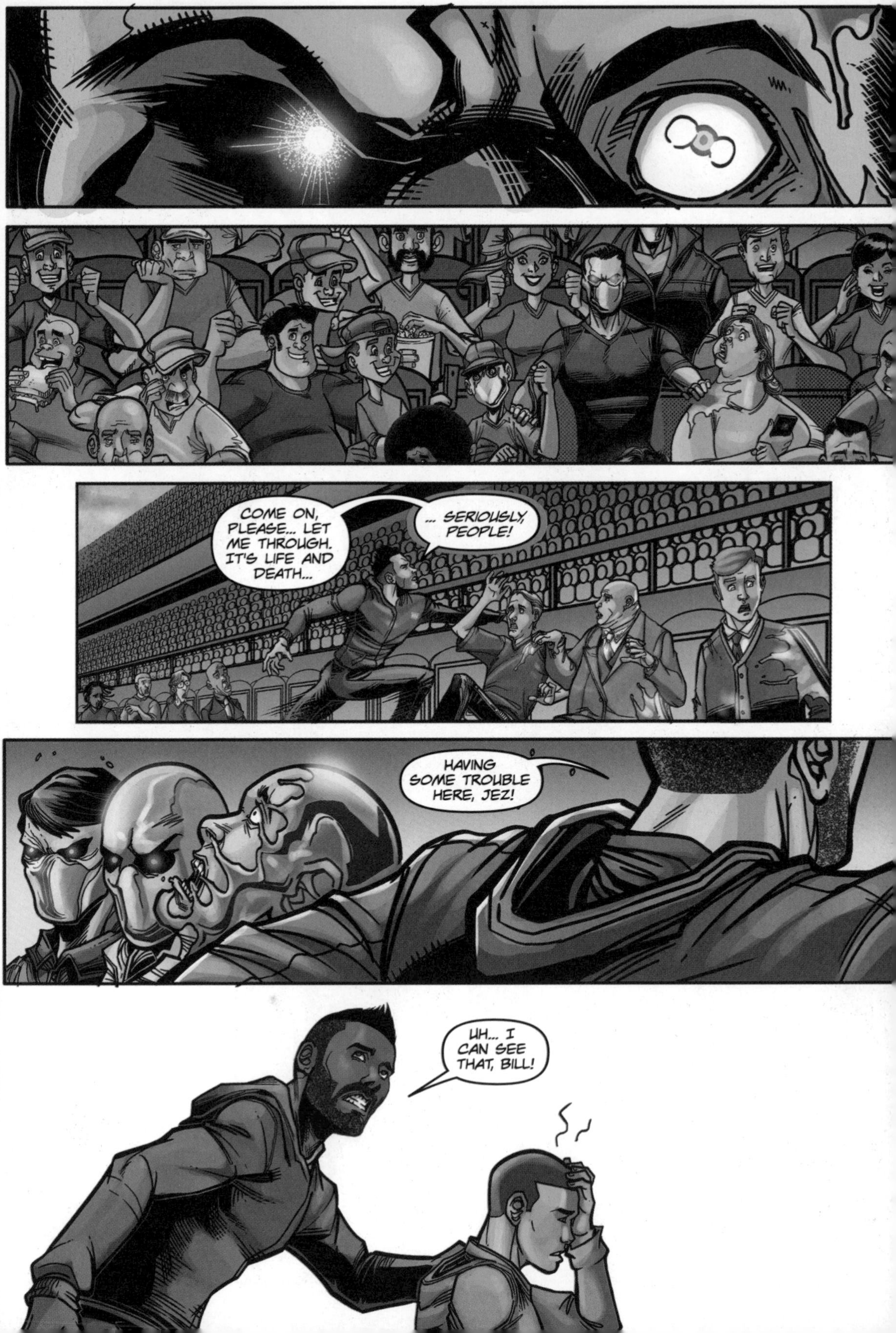
COME ON, PLEASE... LET ME THROUGH. IT'S LIFE AND DEATH...
... SERIOUSLY, PEOPLE!
HAVING SOME TROUBLE HERE, JEZ!
UH... I CAN SEE THAT, BILL!

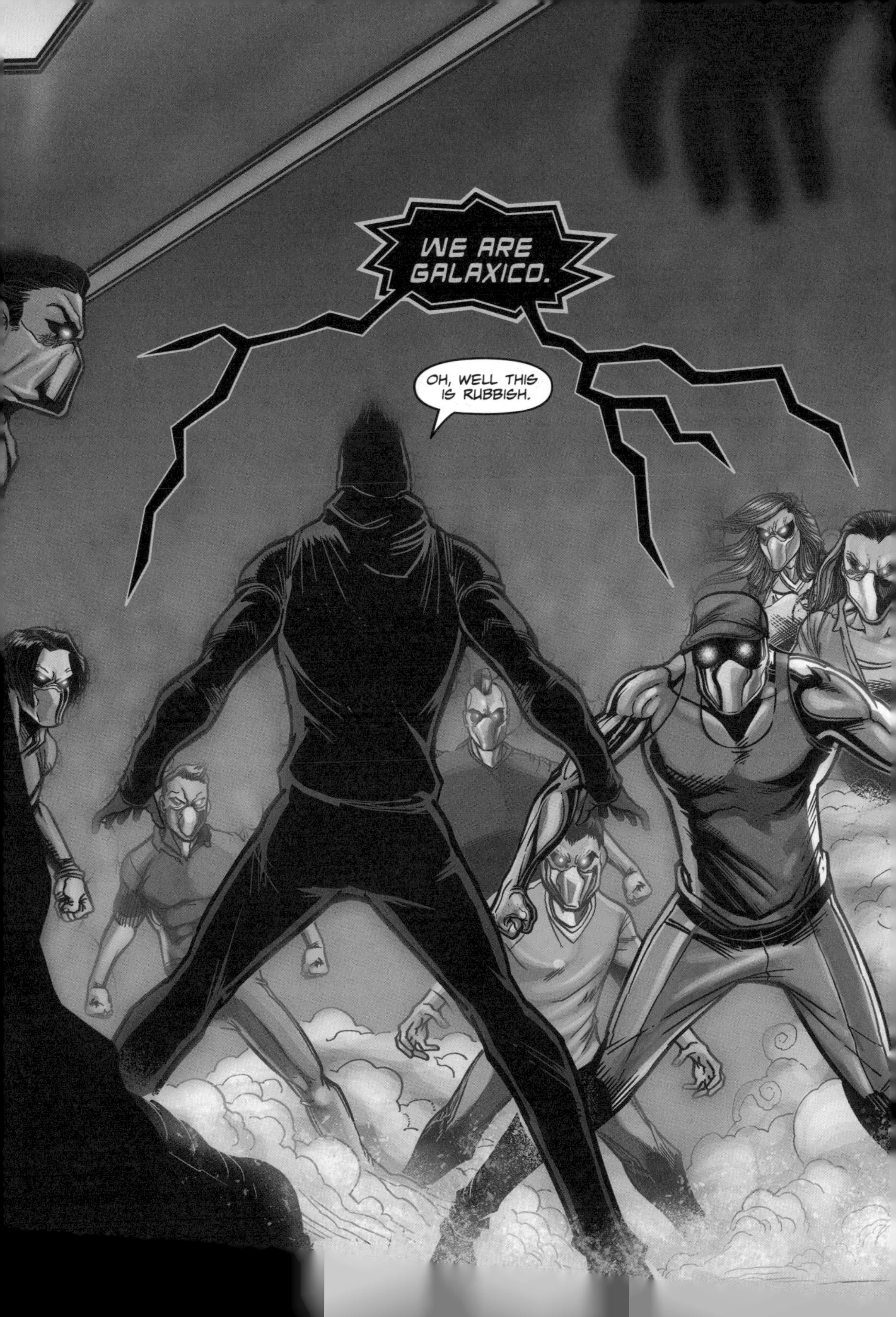
WE ARE GALAXICO.
OH, WELL THIS IS RUBBISH.

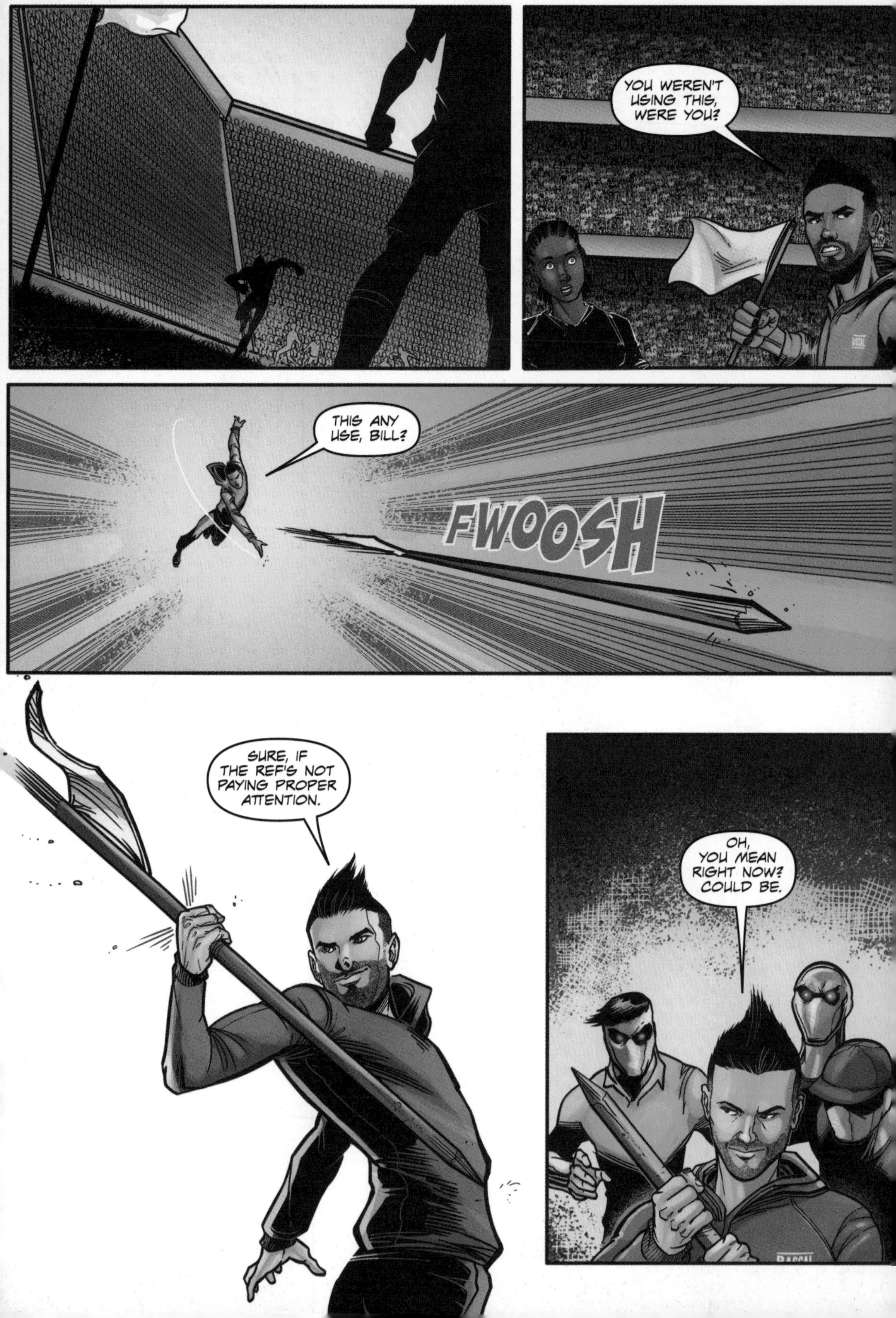
YOU WEREN'T USING THIS, WERE YOU?
THIS ANY USE, BILL?
FWOOSH
SURE, IF THE REF'S NOT PAYING PROPER ATTENTION.
OH, YOU MEAN RIGHT NOW? COULD BE.

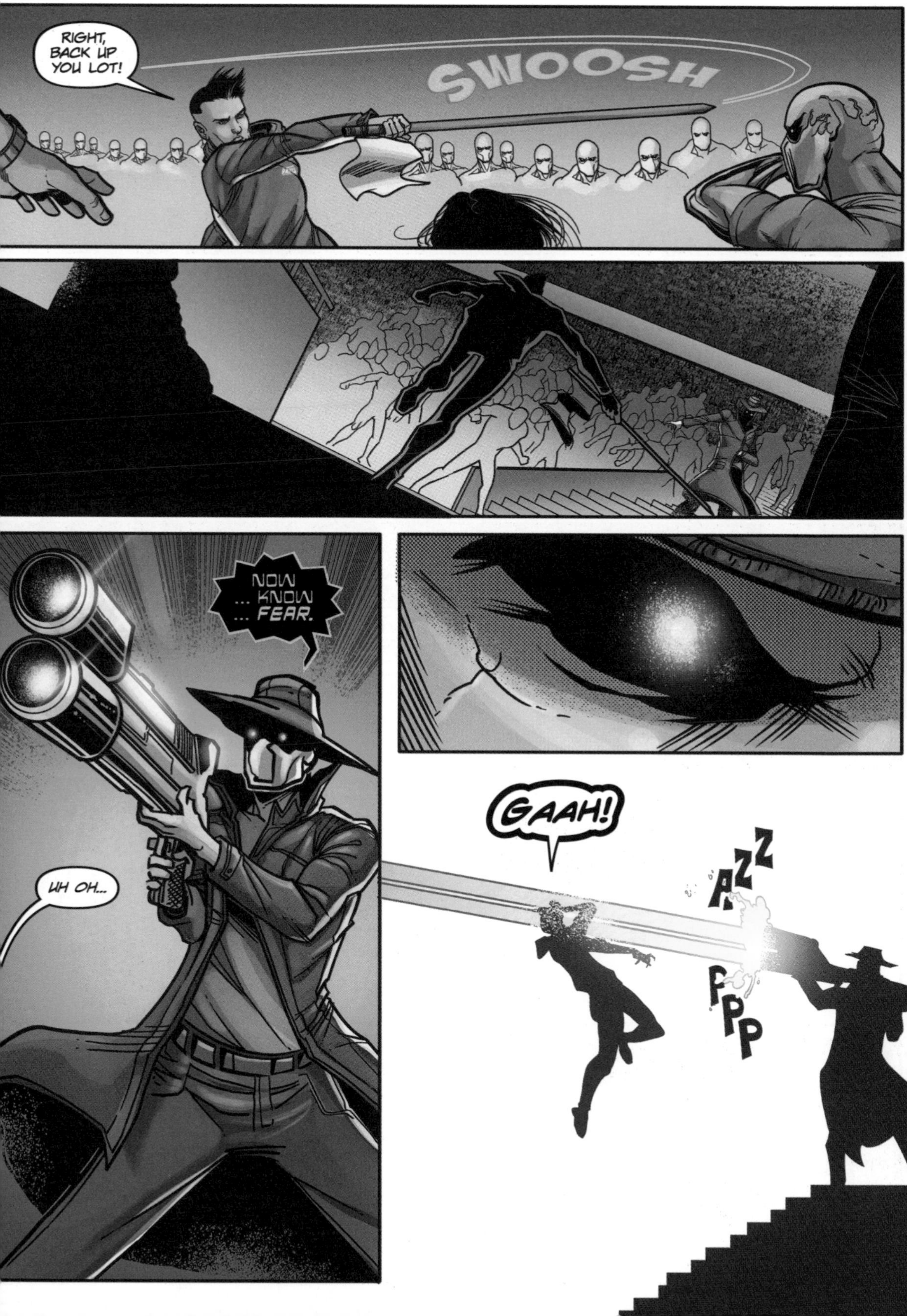
RIGHT, BACK UP YOU LOT!
SWOOSH
NOW ... KNOW ... FEAR.
UH OH...
GAAH!
AZZ
PPPP

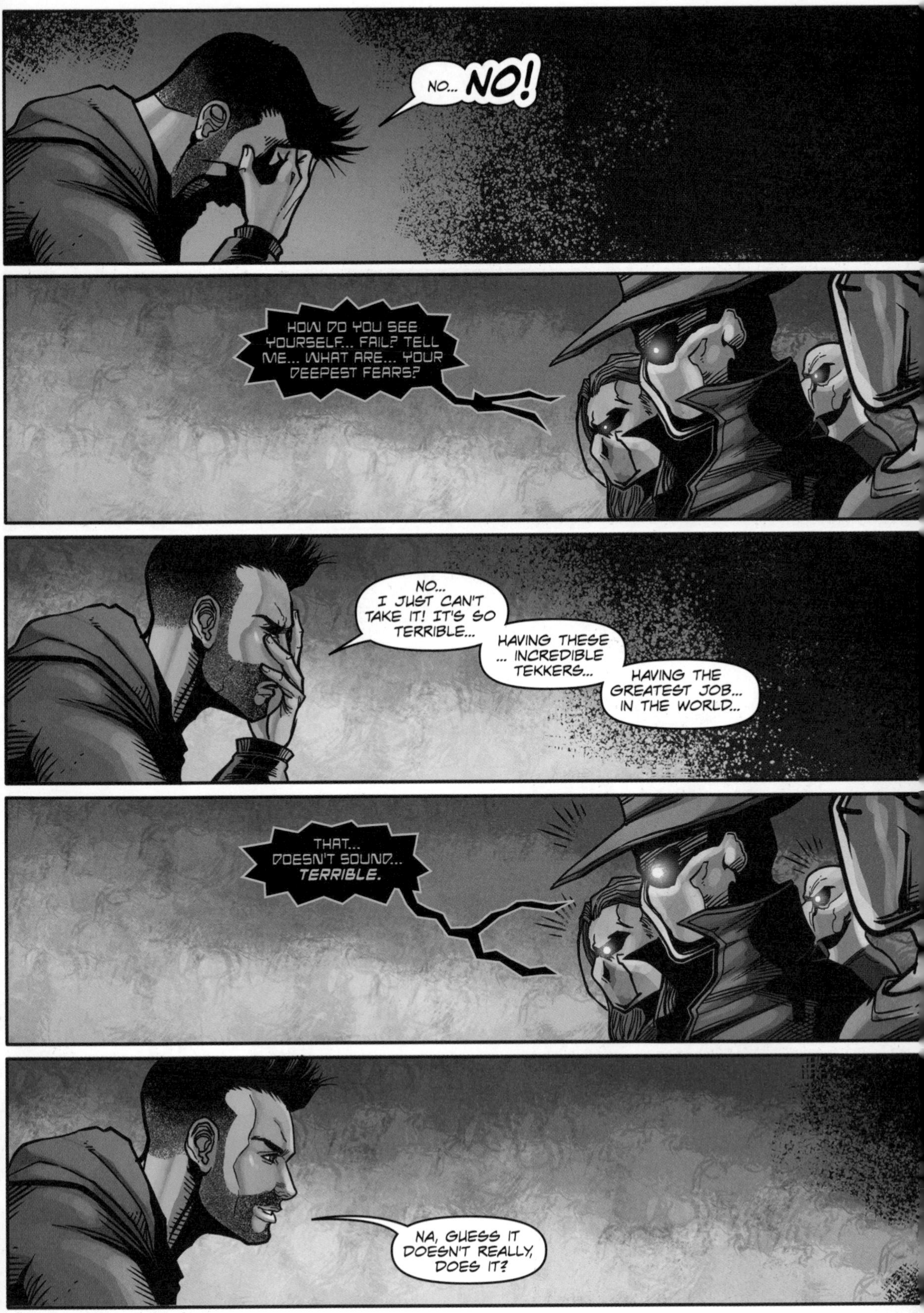
NO... NO!
HOW DO YOU SEE YOURSELF... FAIL? TELL ME... WHAT ARE... YOUR DEEPEST FEARS?
NO... I JUST CAN'T TAKE IT! IT'S SO TERRIBLE...
HAVING THESE ... INCREDIBLE TEKKERS...
HAVING THE GREATEST JOB... IN THE WORLD...
THAT... DOESN'T SOUND... TERRIBLE.
NA, GUESS IT DOESN'T REALLY, DOES IT?

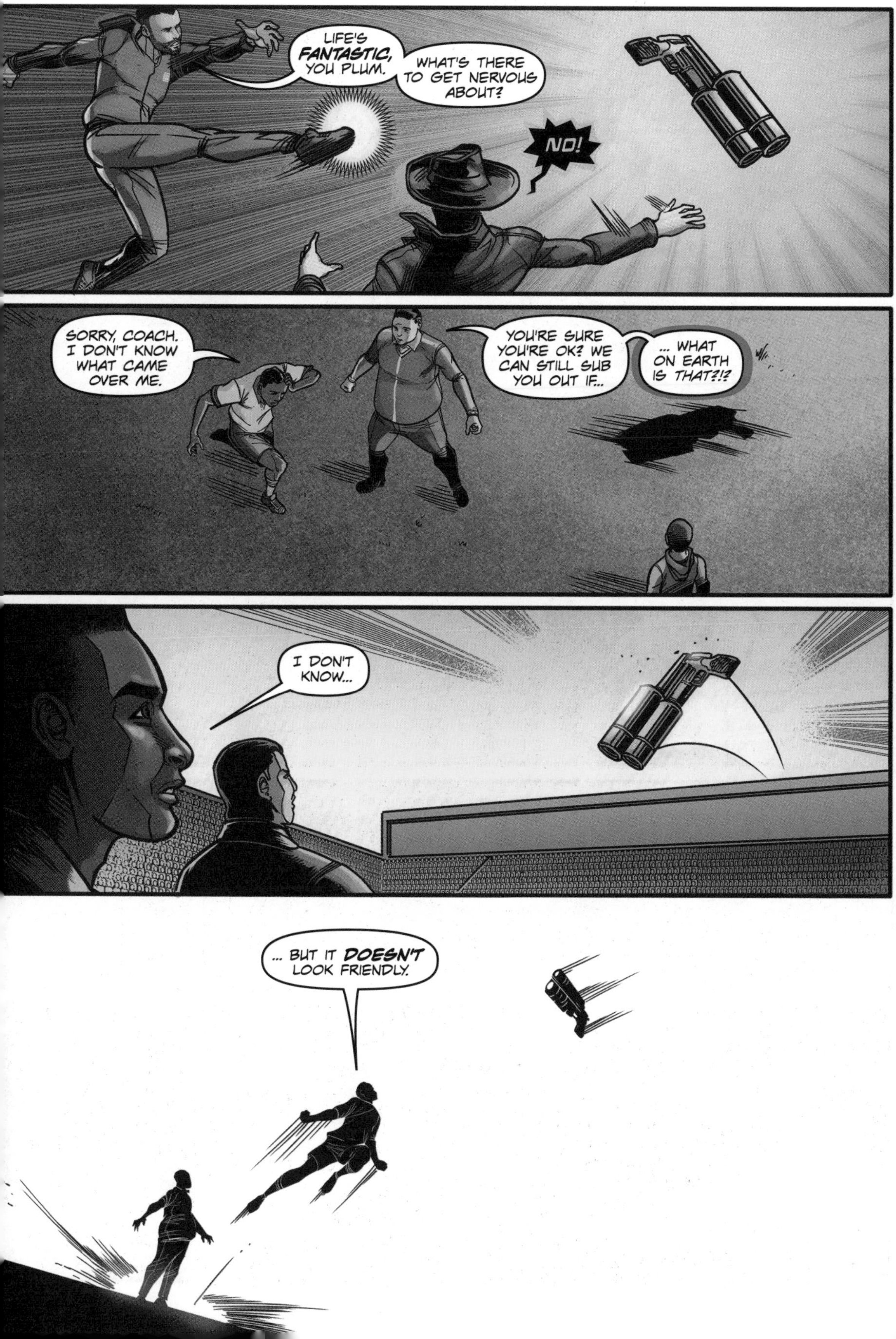
LIFE'S FANTASTIC, YOU PLUM.
WHAT'S THERE TO GET NERVOUS ABOUT?
NO!
SORRY, COACH. I DON'T KNOW WHAT CAME OVER ME.
YOU'RE SURE YOU'RE OK? WE CAN STILL SUB YOU OUT IF...
... WHAT ON EARTH IS THAT?!?
I DON'T KNOW...
... BUT IT DOESN'T LOOK FRIENDLY.

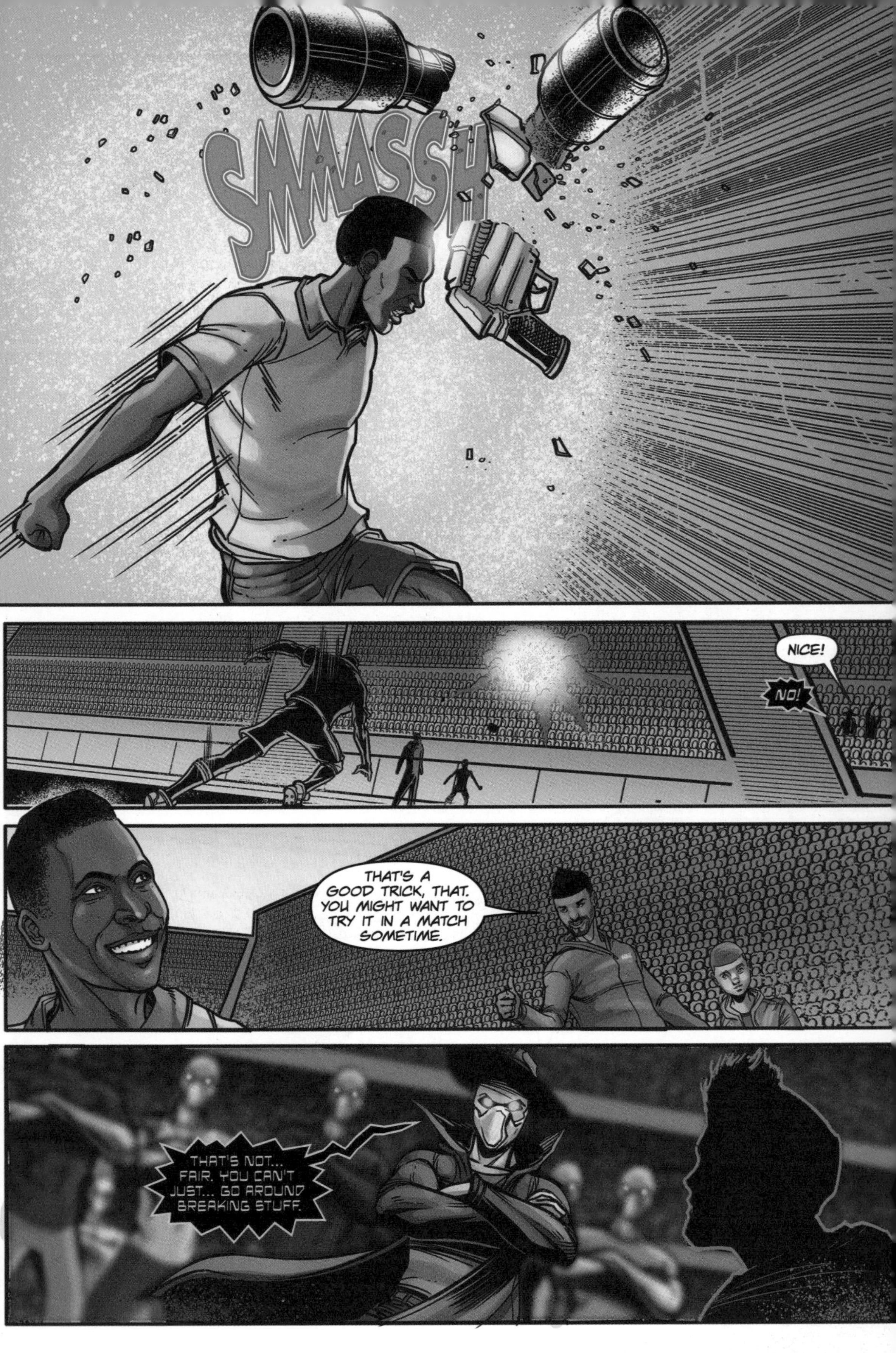
SMMASSH
NICE!
NO!
THAT'S A GOOD TRICK, THAT. YOU MIGHT WANT TO TRY IT IN A MATCH SOMETIME.
THAT'S NOT... FAIR. YOU CAN'T JUST... GO AROUND BREAKING STUFF.

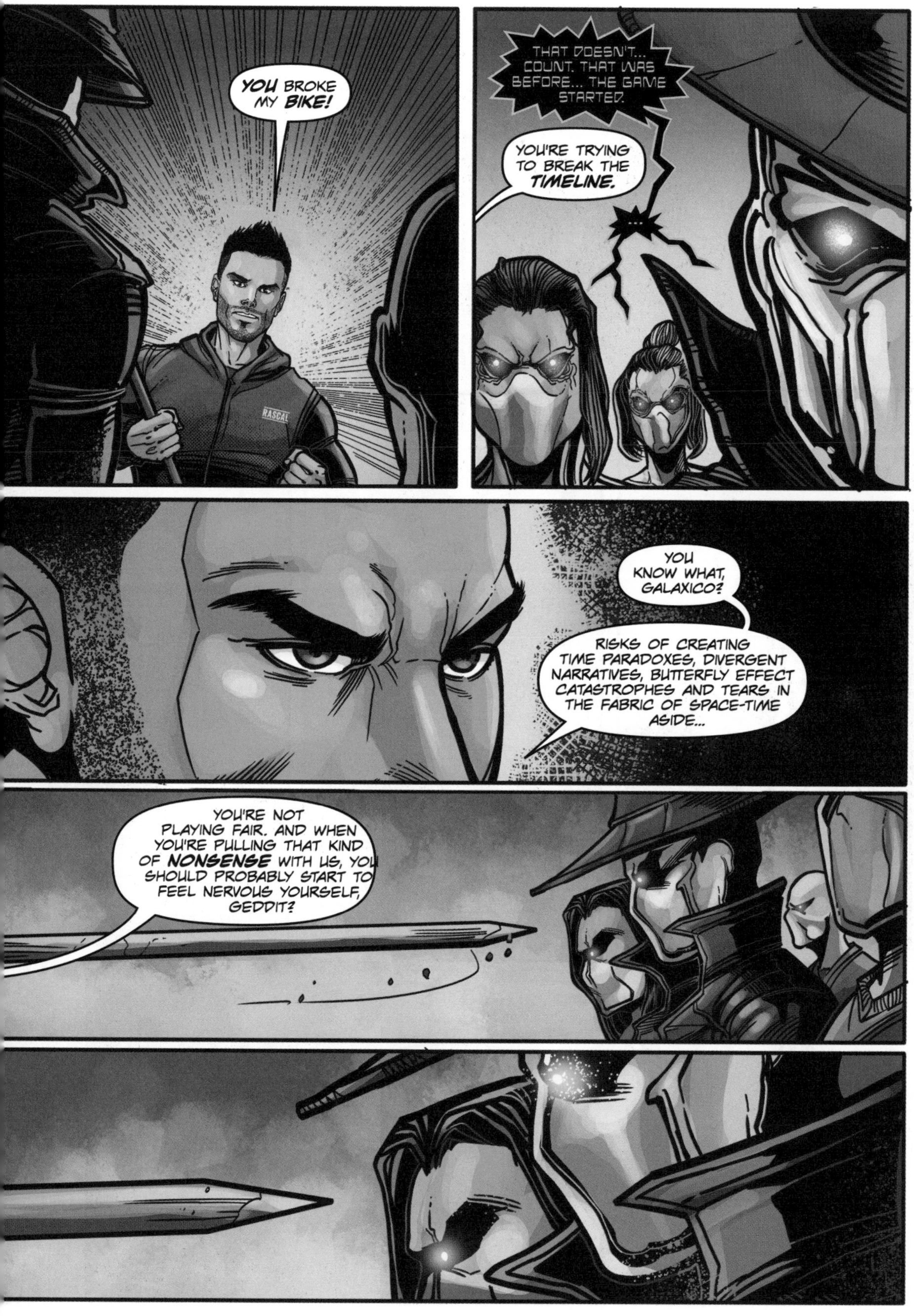
YOU BROKE MY BIKE!
THAT DOESN'T... COUNT. THAT WAS BEFORE... THE GAME STARTED.
YOU'RE TRYING TO BREAK THE TIMELINE.
...
YOU KNOW WHAT, GALAXICO?
RISKS OF CREATING TIME PARADOXES, DIVERGENT NARRATIVES, BUTTERFLY EFFECT CATASTROPHES AND TEARS IN THE FABRIC OF SPACE-TIME ASIDE...
YOU'RE NOT PLAYING FAIR. AND WHEN YOU'RE PULLING THAT KIND OF NONSENSE WITH US, YOU SHOULD PROBABLY START TO FEEL NERVOUS YOURSELF, GEDDIT?

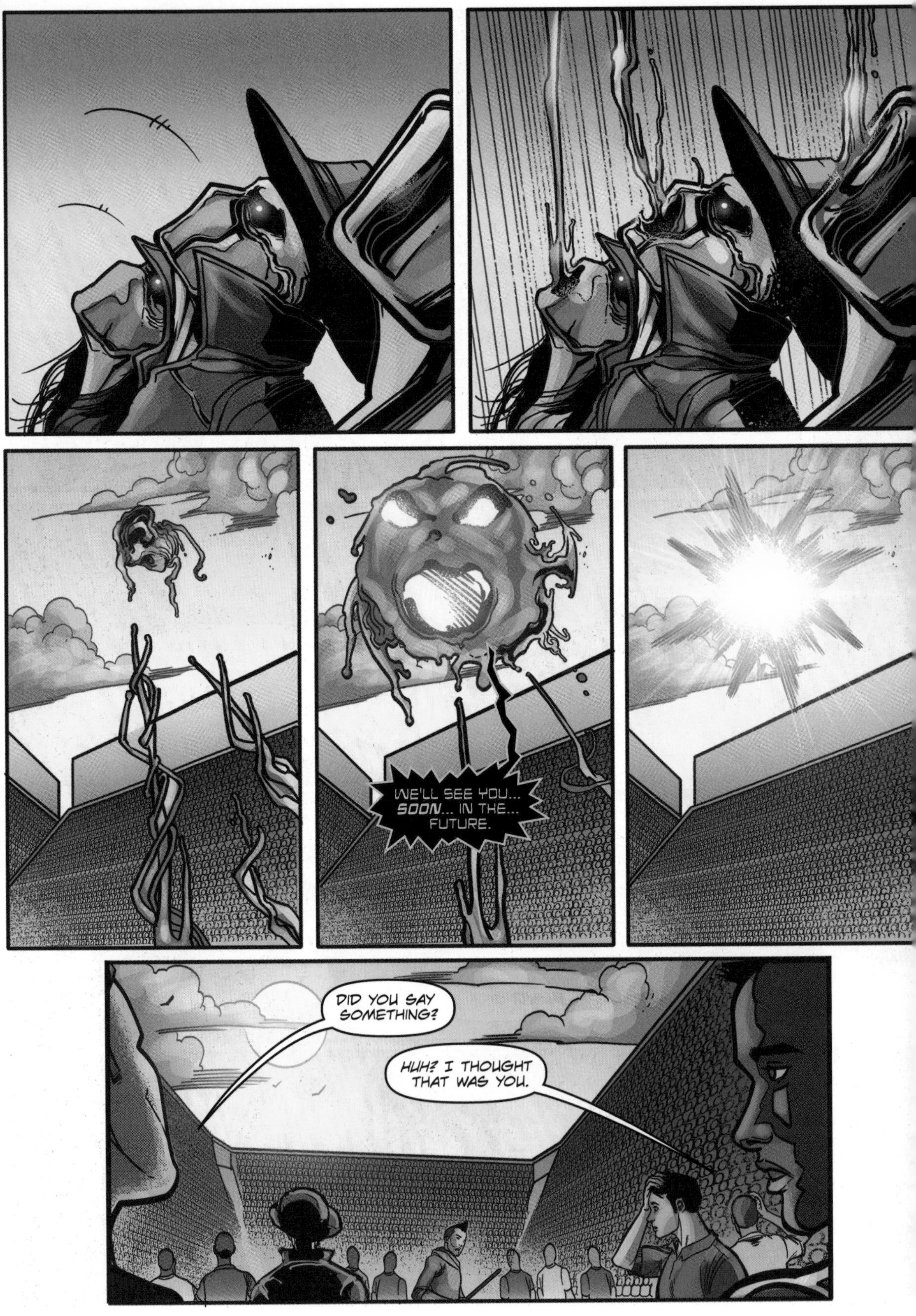
WE'LL SEE YOU... SOON... IN THE... FUTURE.
DID YOU SAY SOMETHING?
HUH? I THOUGHT THAT WAS YOU.

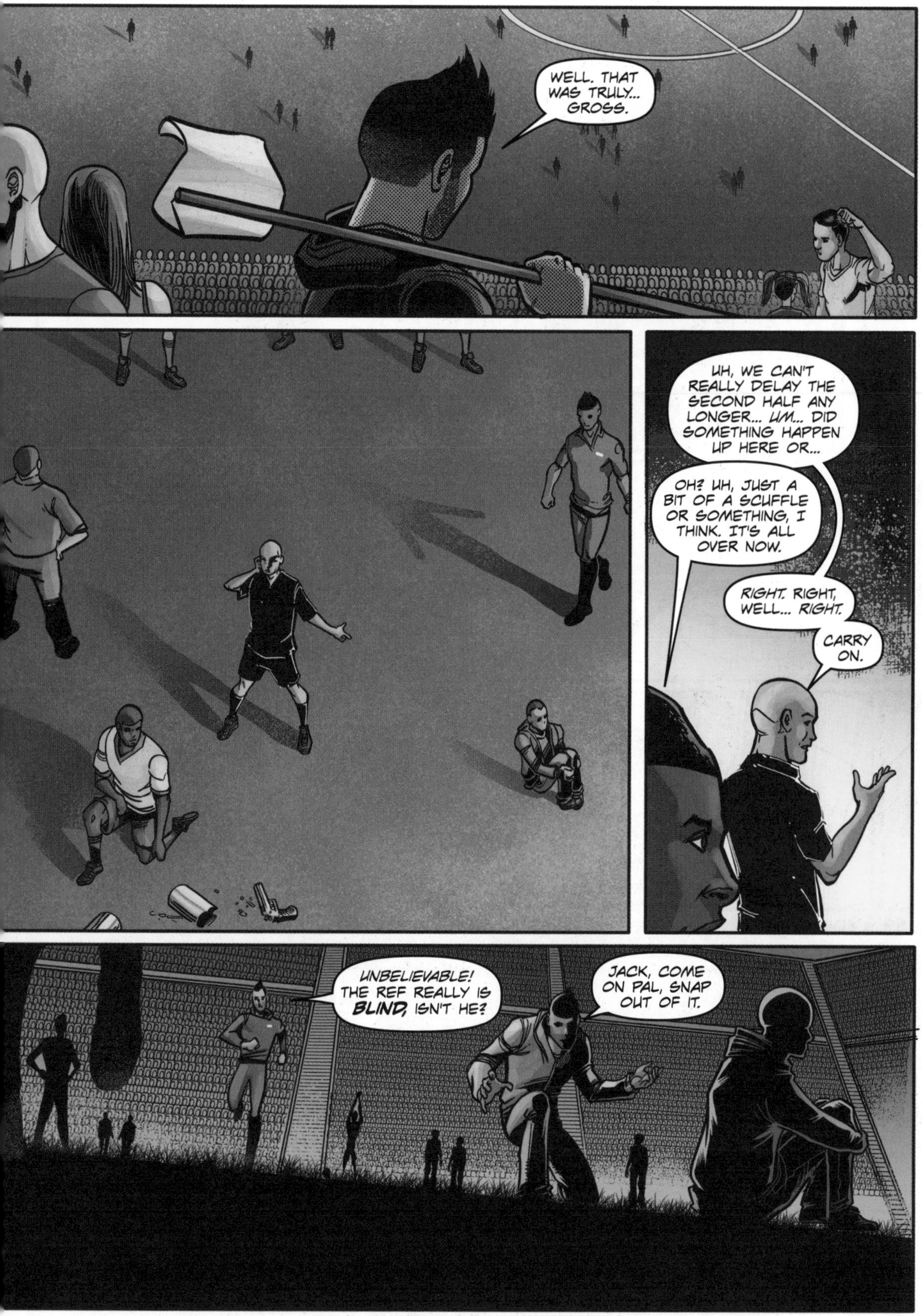
WELL. THAT WAS TRULY... GROSS.
UH, WE CAN'T REALLY DELAY THE SECOND HALF ANY LONGER... UM... DID SOMETHING HAPPEN UP HERE OR...
OH? UH, JUST A BIT OF A SCUFFLE OR SOMETHING, I THINK. IT'S ALL OVER NOW.
RIGHT. RIGHT, WELL... RIGHT.
CARRY ON.
UNBELIEVABLE! THE REF REALLY IS BLIND, ISN'T HE?
JACK, COME ON PAL, SNAP OUT OF IT.

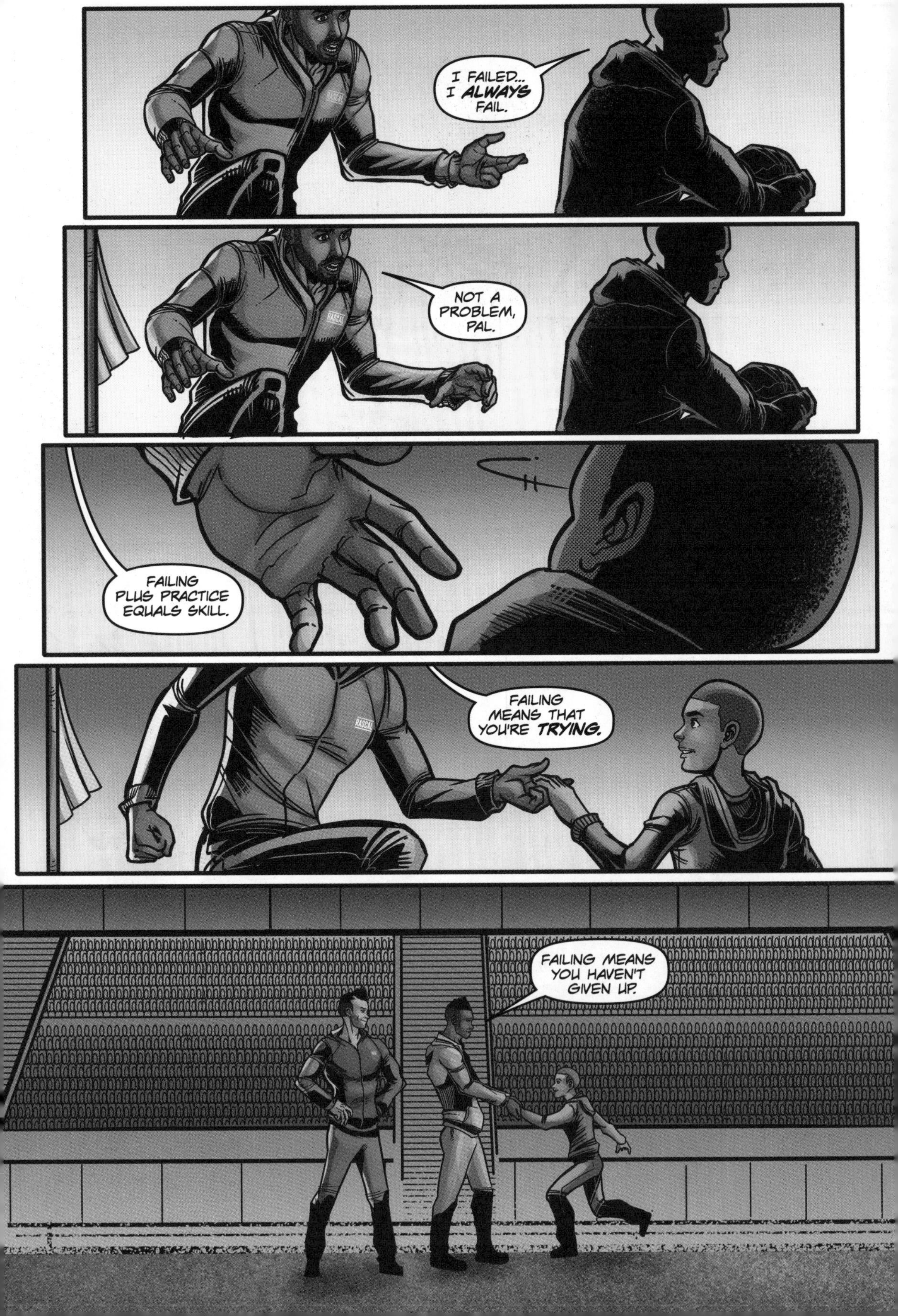
I FAILED... I ALWAYS FAIL.
NOT A PROBLEM, PAL.
FAILING PLUS PRACTICE EQUALS SKILL.
FAILING MEANS THAT YOU'RE TRYING.
FAILING MEANS YOU HAVEN'T GIVEN UP.

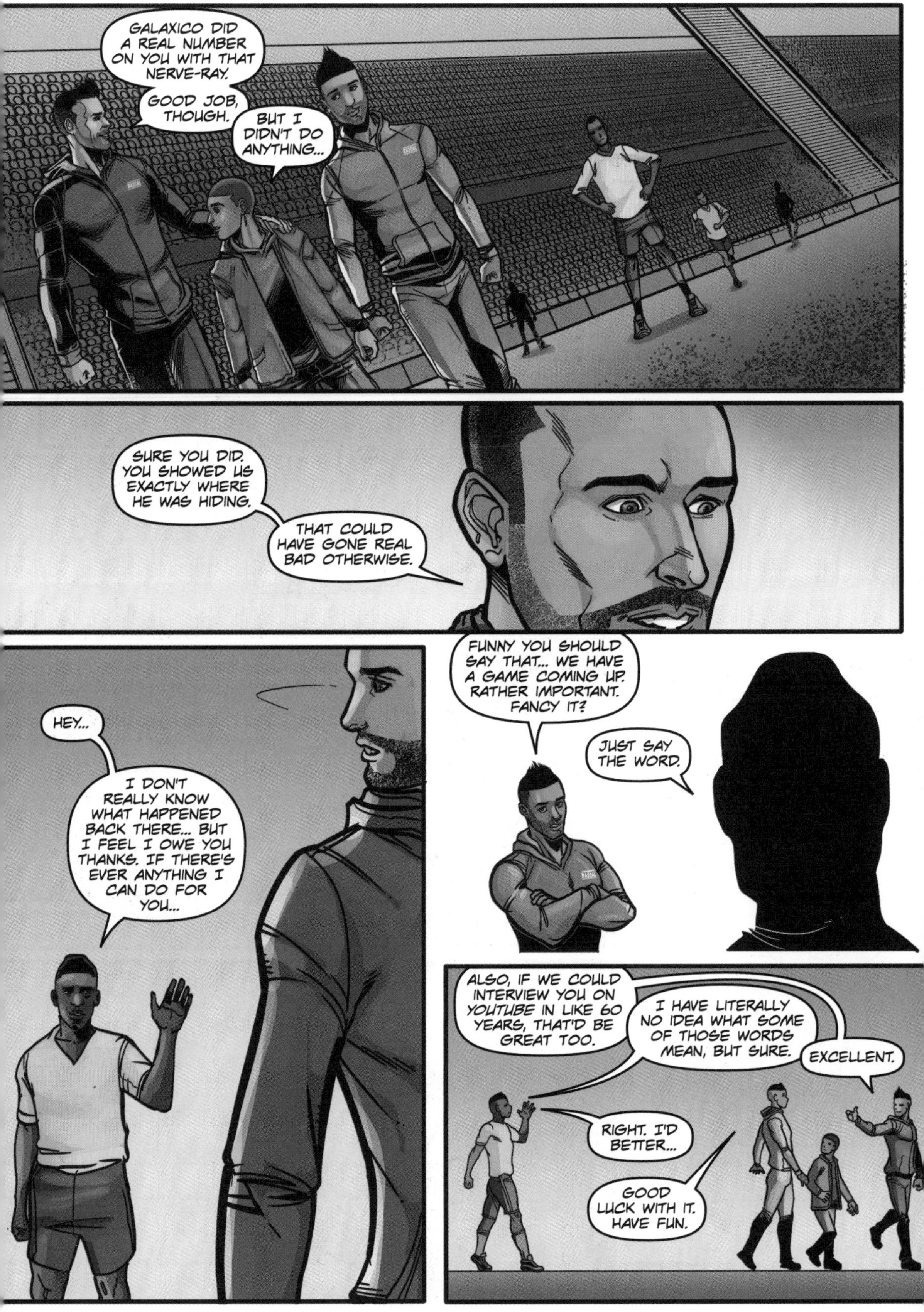
GALAXICO DID A REAL NUMBER ON YOU WITH THAT NERVE-RAY.
GOOD JOB, THOUGH.
BUT I DIDN'T DO ANYTHING...
SURE YOU DID. YOU SHOWED US EXACTLY WHERE HE WAS HIDING.
THAT COULD HAVE GONE REAL BAD OTHERWISE.
HEY...
I DON'T REALLY KNOW WHAT HAPPENED BACK THERE... BUT I FEEL I OWE YOU THANKS. IF THERE'S EVER ANYTHING I CAN DO FOR YOU...
FUNNY YOU SHOULD SAY THAT... WE HAVE A GAME COMING UP. RATHER IMPORTANT. FANCY IT?
JUST SAY THE WORD.
ALSO, IF WE COULD INTERVIEW YOU ON YOUTUBE IN LIKE 60 YEARS, THAT'D BE GREAT TOO.
I HAVE LITERALLY NO IDEA WHAT SOME OF THOSE WORDS MEAN, BUT SURE.
EXCELLENT.
RIGHT. I'D BETTER...
GOOD LUCK WITH IT. HAVE FUN.

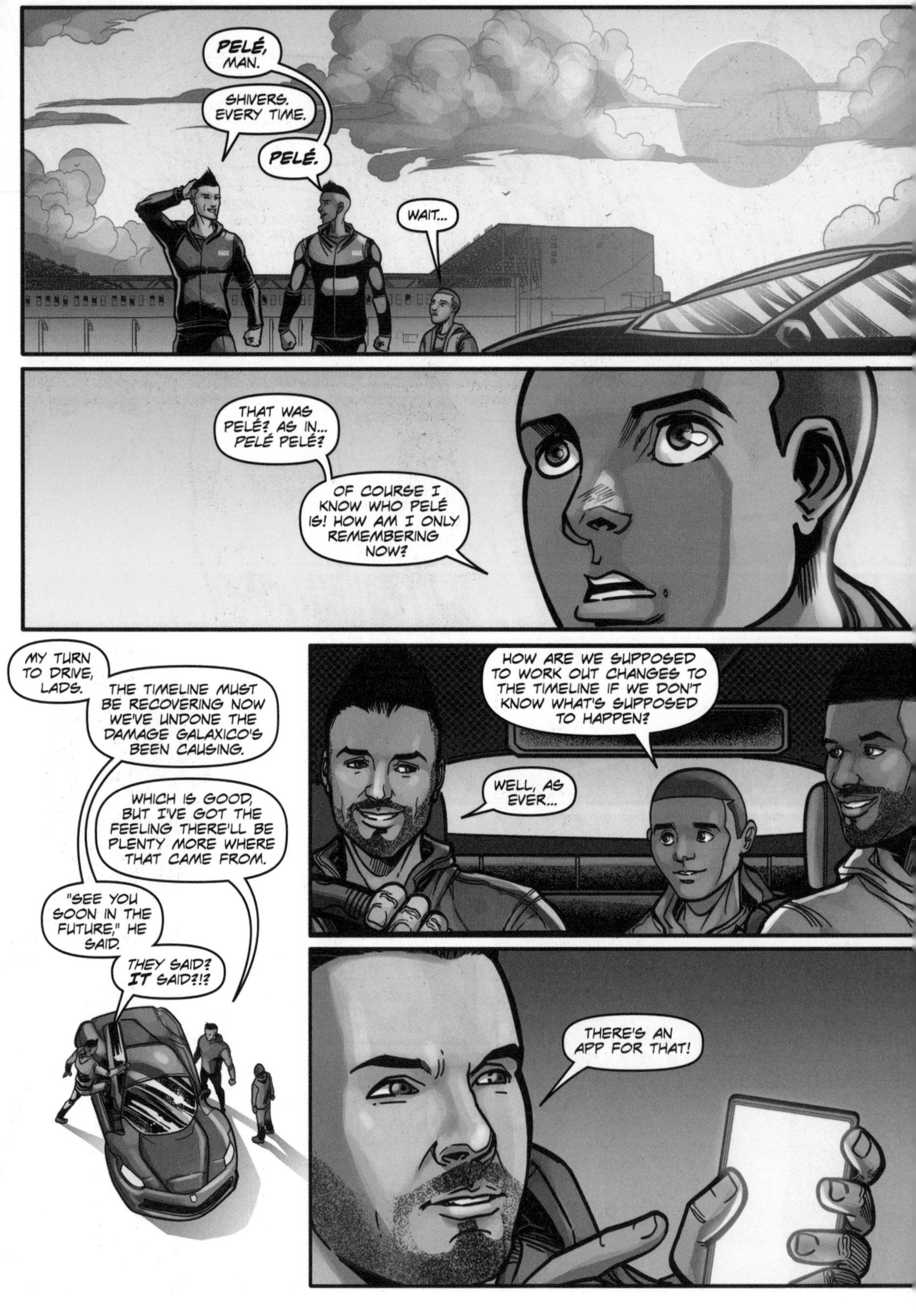
PELÉ, MAN.
SHIVERS. EVERY TIME.
PELÉ.
WAIT...
THAT WAS PELÉ? AS IN... PELÉ PELÉ?
OF COURSE I KNOW WHO PELÉ IS! HOW AM I ONLY REMEMBERING NOW?
MY TURN TO DRIVE, LADS.
THE TIMELINE MUST BE RECOVERING NOW WE'VE UNDONE THE DAMAGE GALAXICO'S BEEN CAUSING.
WHICH IS GOOD, BUT I'VE GOT THE FEELING THERE'LL BE PLENTY MORE WHERE THAT CAME FROM.
"SEE YOU SOON IN THE FUTURE," HE SAID.
THEY SAID? IT SAID?!?
HOW ARE WE SUPPOSED TO WORK OUT CHANGES TO THE TIMELINE IF WE DON'T KNOW WHAT'S SUPPOSED TO HAPPEN?
WELL, AS EVER...
THERE'S AN APP FOR THAT!

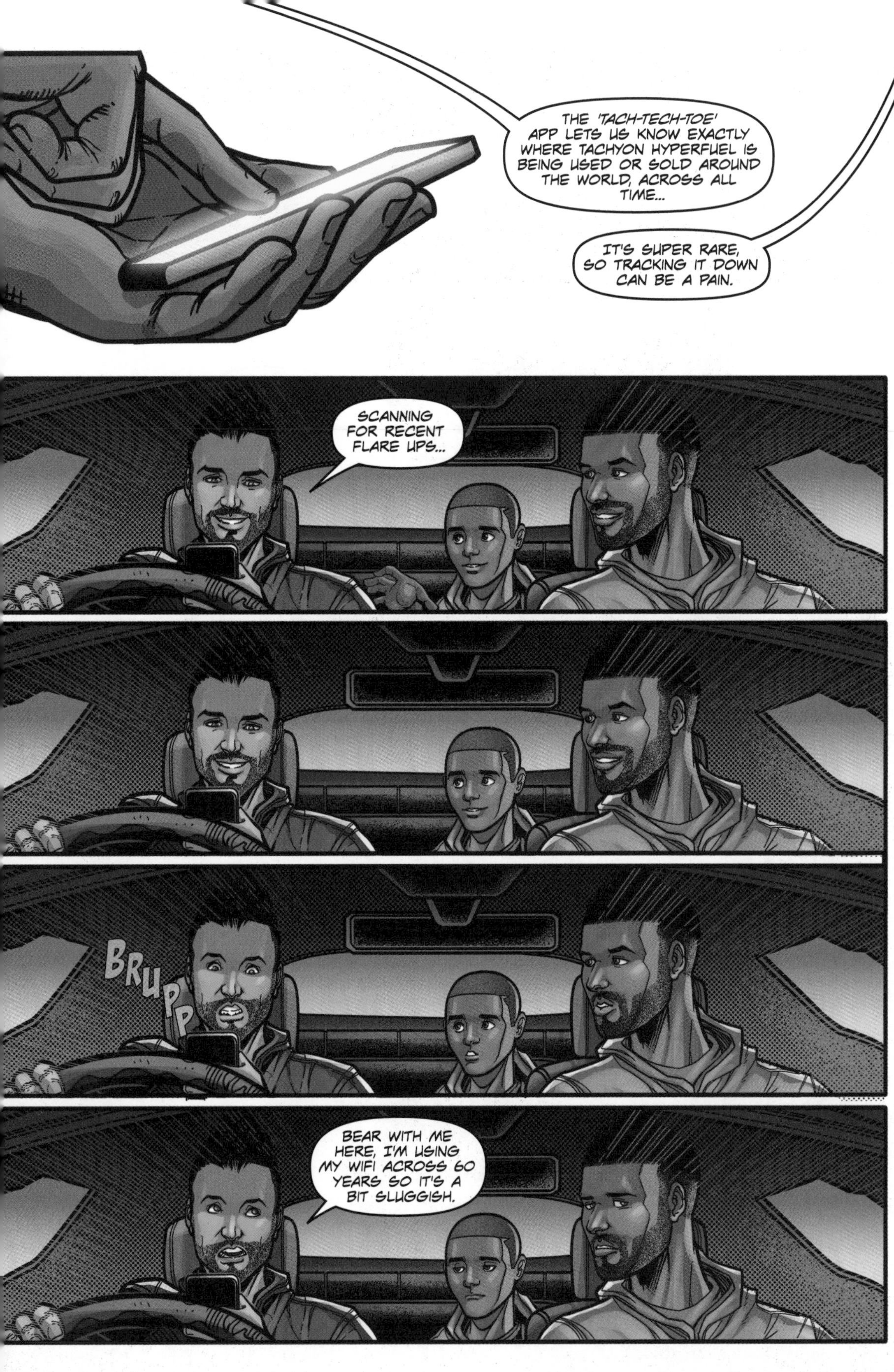
THE 'TACH-TECH-TOE' APP LETS US KNOW EXACTLY WHERE TACHYON HYPERFUEL IS BEING USED OR SOLD AROUND THE WORLD, ACROSS ALL TIME...
IT'S SUPER RARE, SO TRACKING IT DOWN CAN BE A PAIN.
SCANNING FOR RECENT FLARE UPS...
BRUPP
BEAR WITH ME HERE, I'M USING MY WIFI ACROSS 60 YEARS SO IT'S A BIT SLUGGISH.

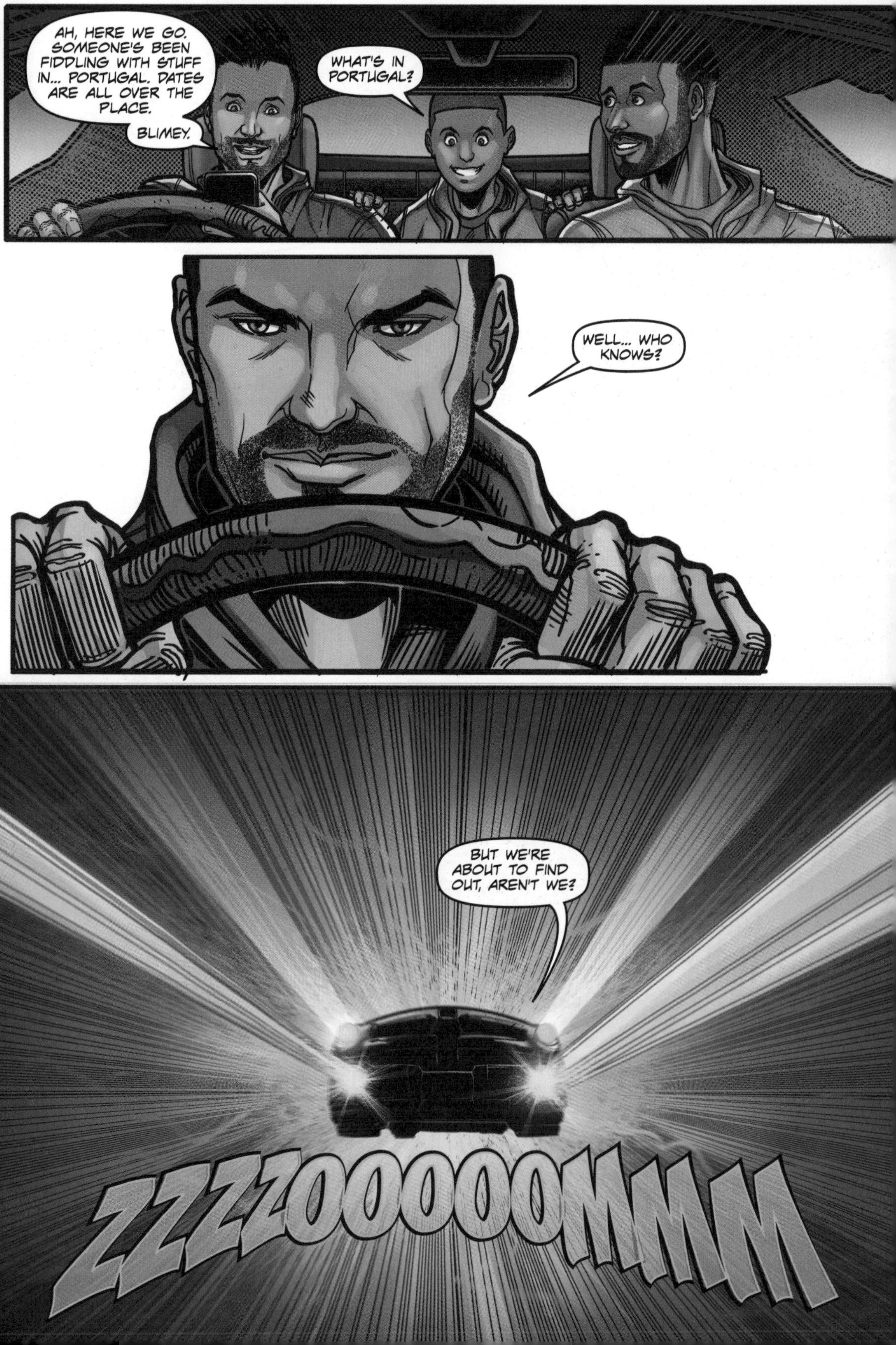
AH, HERE WE GO. SOMEONE'S BEEN FIDDLING WITH STUFF IN... PORTUGAL. DATES ARE ALL OVER THE PLACE.
BLIMEY.
WHAT'S IN PORTUGAL?
WELL... WHO KNOWS?
BUT WE'RE ABOUT TO FIND OUT, AREN'T WE?
ZZZOOOOOMMMM

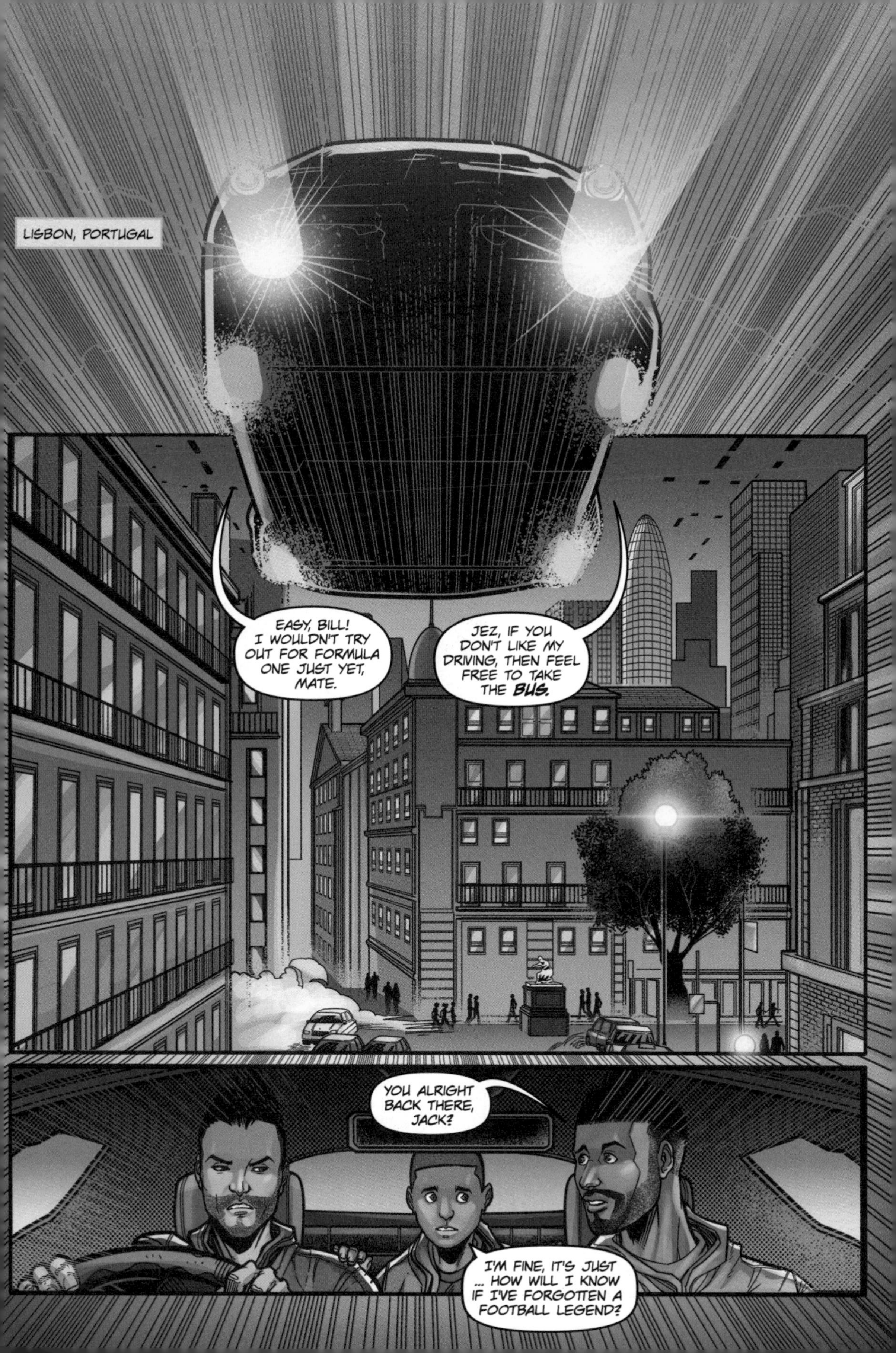
LISBON, PORTUGAL
EASY, BILL! I WOULDN'T TRY OUT FOR FORMULA ONE JUST YET, MATE.
JEZ, IF YOU DON'T LIKE MY DRIVING, THEN FEEL FREE TO TAKE THE BUS.
YOU ALRIGHT BACK THERE, JACK?
I'M FINE, IT'S JUST ... HOW WILL I KNOW IF I'VE FORGOTTEN A FOOTBALL LEGEND?

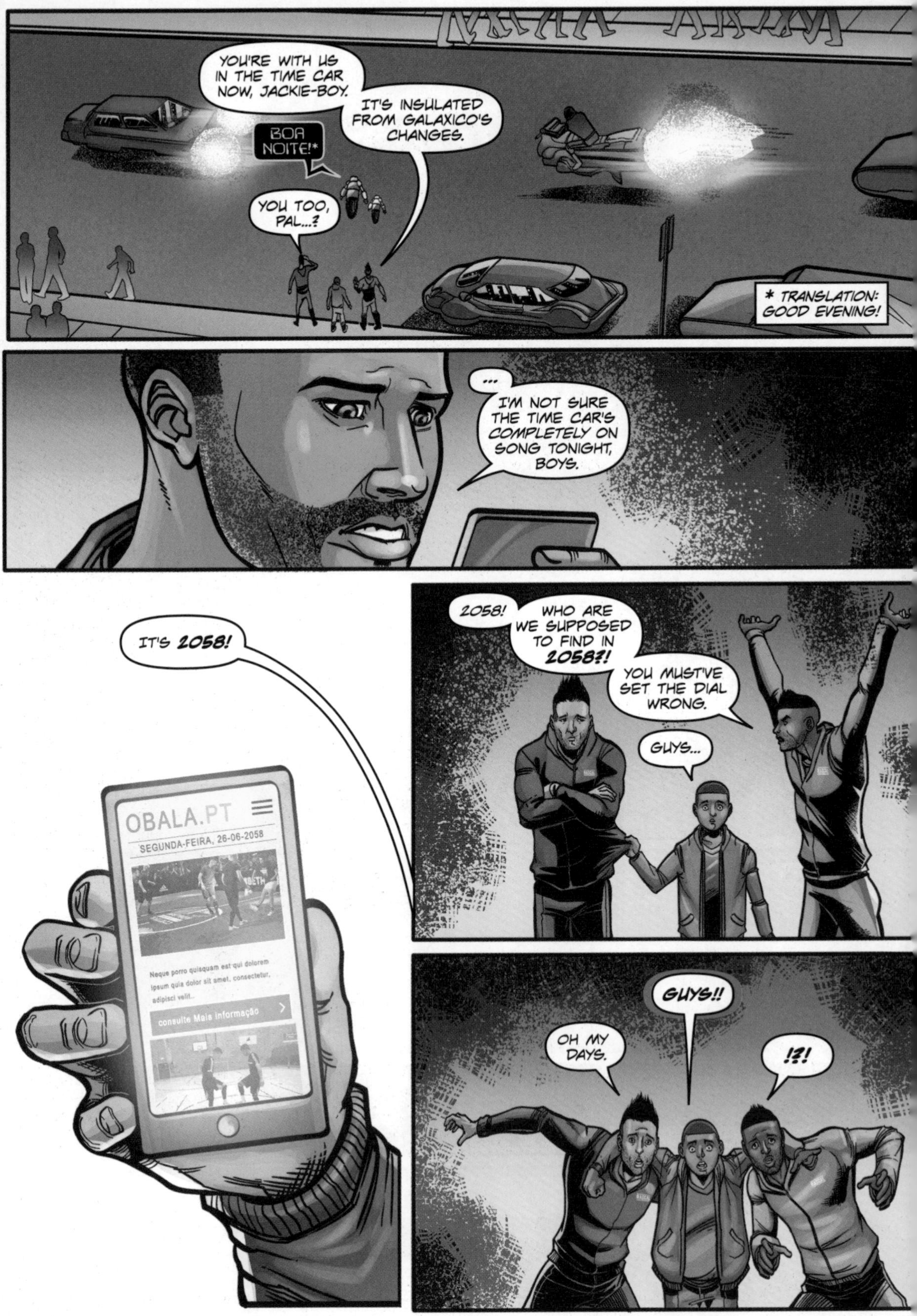
YOU'RE WITH US IN THE TIME CAR NOW, JACKIE-BOY.
BOA NOITE!*
IT'S INSULATED FROM GALAXICO'S CHANGES.
YOU TOO, PAL...?
* TRANSLATION: GOOD EVENING!
...
I'M NOT SURE THE TIME CAR'S COMPLETELY ON SONG TONIGHT, BOYS.
2058!
WHO ARE WE SUPPOSED TO FIND IN 2058?!
YOU MUST'VE SET THE DIAL WRONG.
GUYS...
IT'S 2058!
OBALA.PT
SEGUNDA-FEIRA, 26-06-2058
Neque porro quisquam est qui dolorem ipsum quia dolor sit amet, consectetur, adipisci velit...
consulte Mais informação
GUYS!!
OH MY DAYS.
!?!

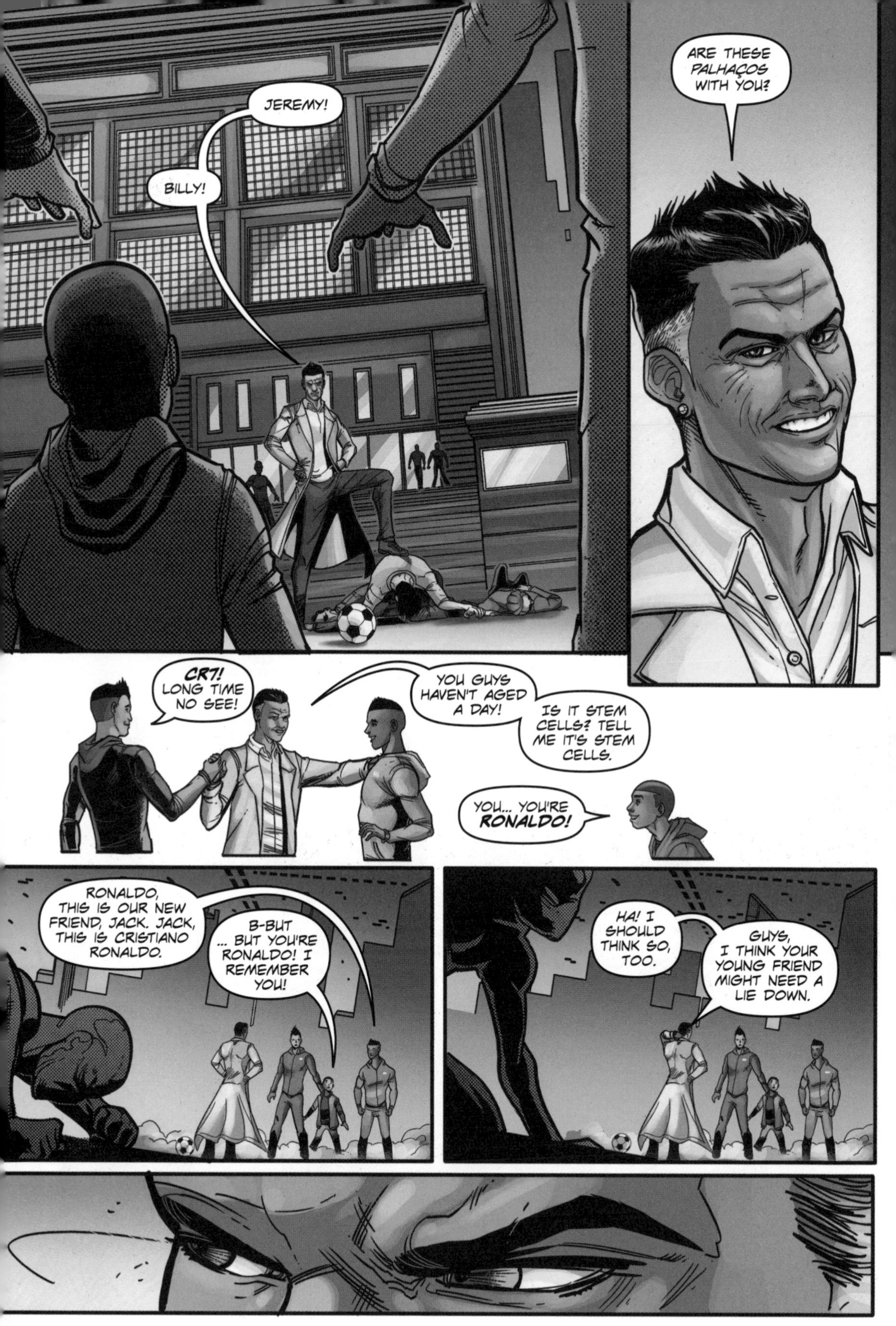
JEREMY!
BILLY!
ARE THESE PALHAÇOS WITH YOU?
CR7! LONG TIME NO SEE!
YOU GUYS HAVEN'T AGED A DAY!
IS IT STEM CELLS? TELL ME IT'S STEM CELLS.
YOU... YOU'RE RONALDO!
RONALDO, THIS IS OUR NEW FRIEND, JACK. JACK, THIS IS CRISTIANO RONALDO.
B-BUT ... BUT YOU'RE RONALDO! I REMEMBER YOU!
HA! I SHOULD THINK SO, TOO.
GUYS, I THINK YOUR YOUNG FRIEND MIGHT NEED A LIE DOWN.

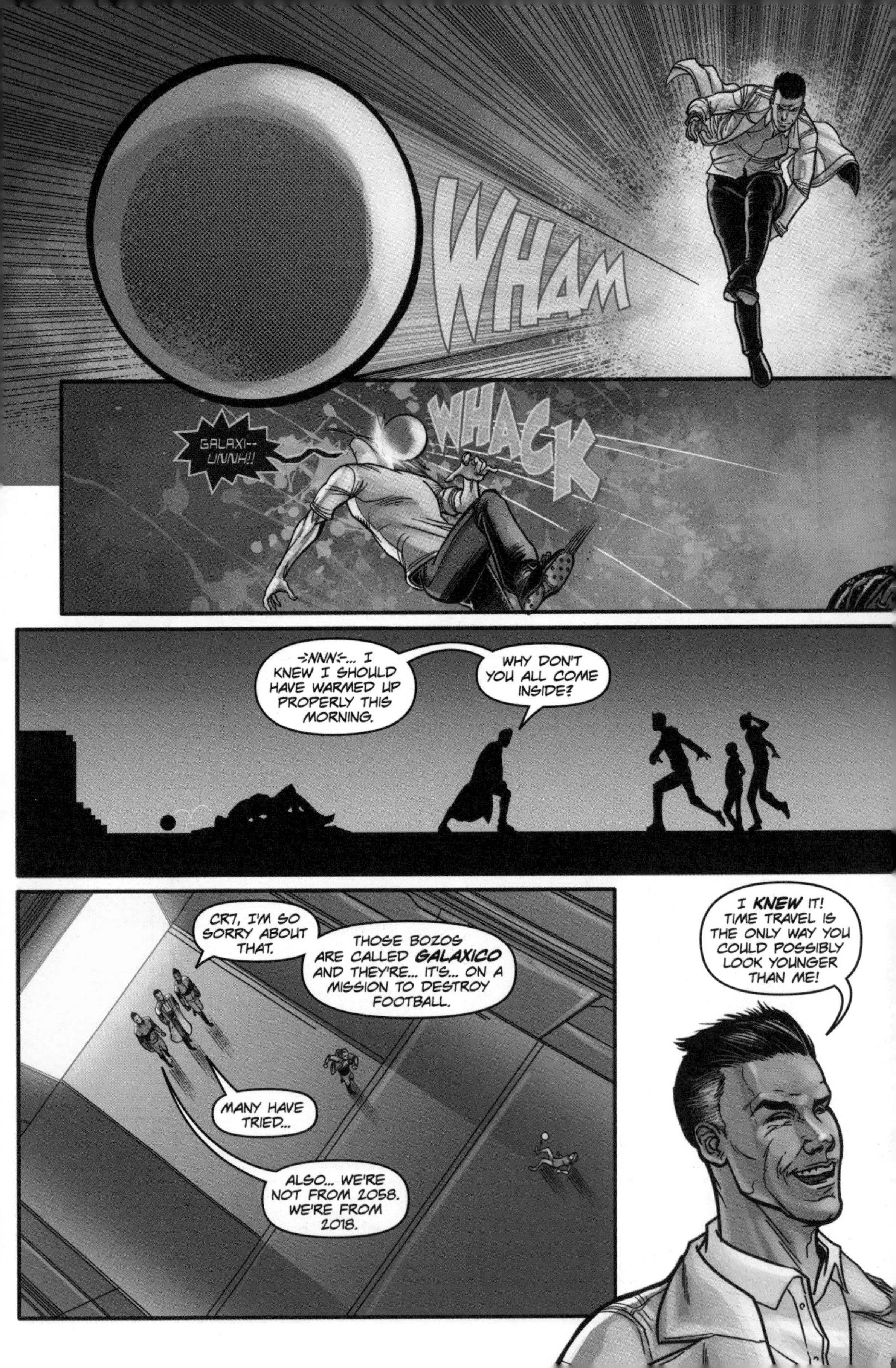
WHAM
GALAXI-- UNNH!!
WHACK
-NNN-... I KNEW I SHOULD HAVE WARMED UP PROPERLY THIS MORNING.
WHY DON'T YOU ALL COME INSIDE?
CR7, I'M SO SORRY ABOUT THAT.
THOSE BOZOS ARE CALLED GALAXICO AND THEY'RE... IT'S... ON A MISSION TO DESTROY FOOTBALL.
MANY HAVE TRIED...
ALSO... WE'RE NOT FROM 2058. WE'RE FROM 2018.
I KNEW IT! TIME TRAVEL IS THE ONLY WAY YOU COULD POSSIBLY LOOK YOUNGER THAN ME!

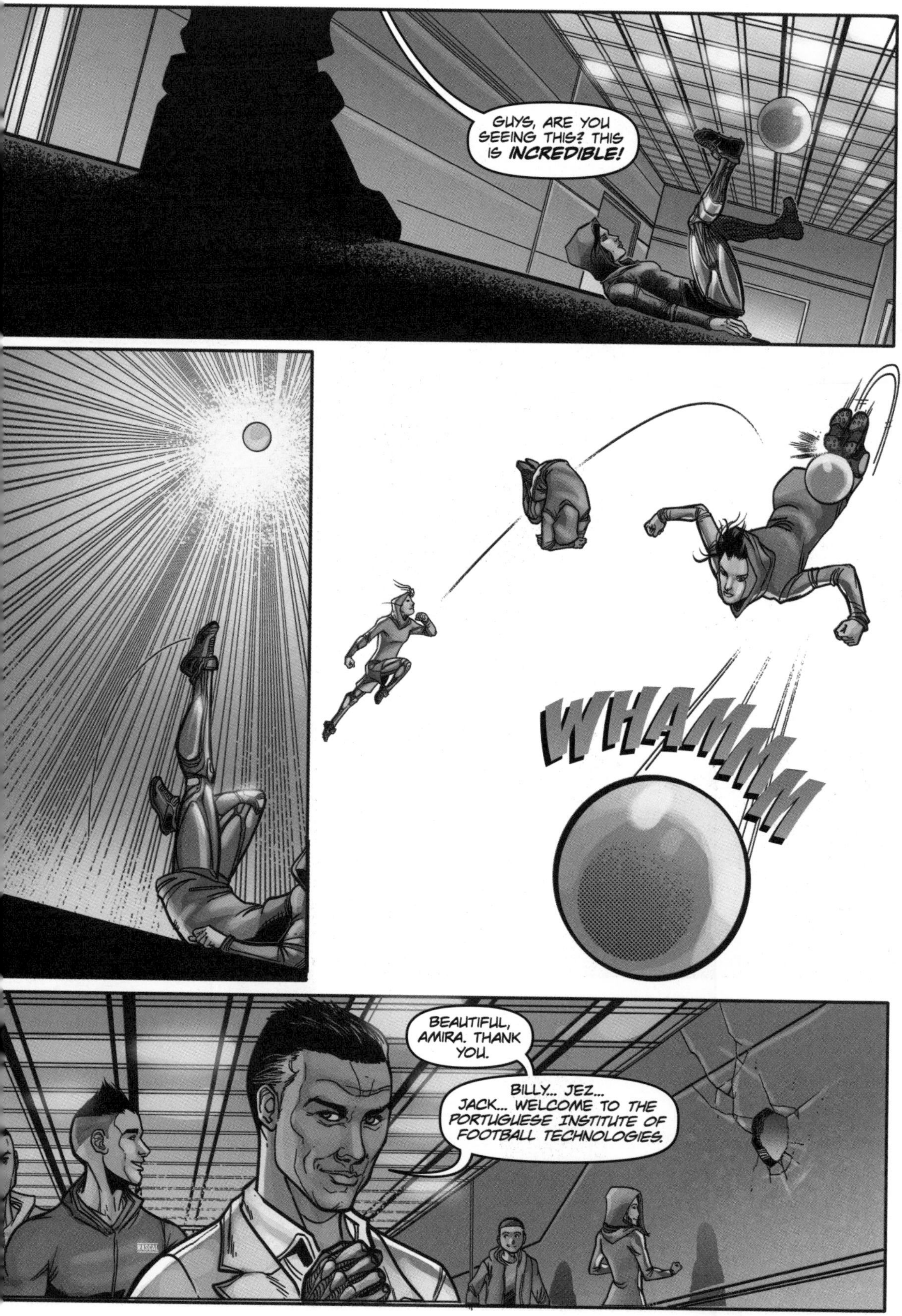
GUYS, ARE YOU SEEING THIS? THIS IS **INCREDIBLE!**
WHAMMM
BEAUTIFUL, AMIRA. THANK YOU.
BILLY... JEZ... JACK... WELCOME TO THE PORTUGUESE INSTITUTE OF FOOTBALL TECHNOLOGIES.
RASCAL

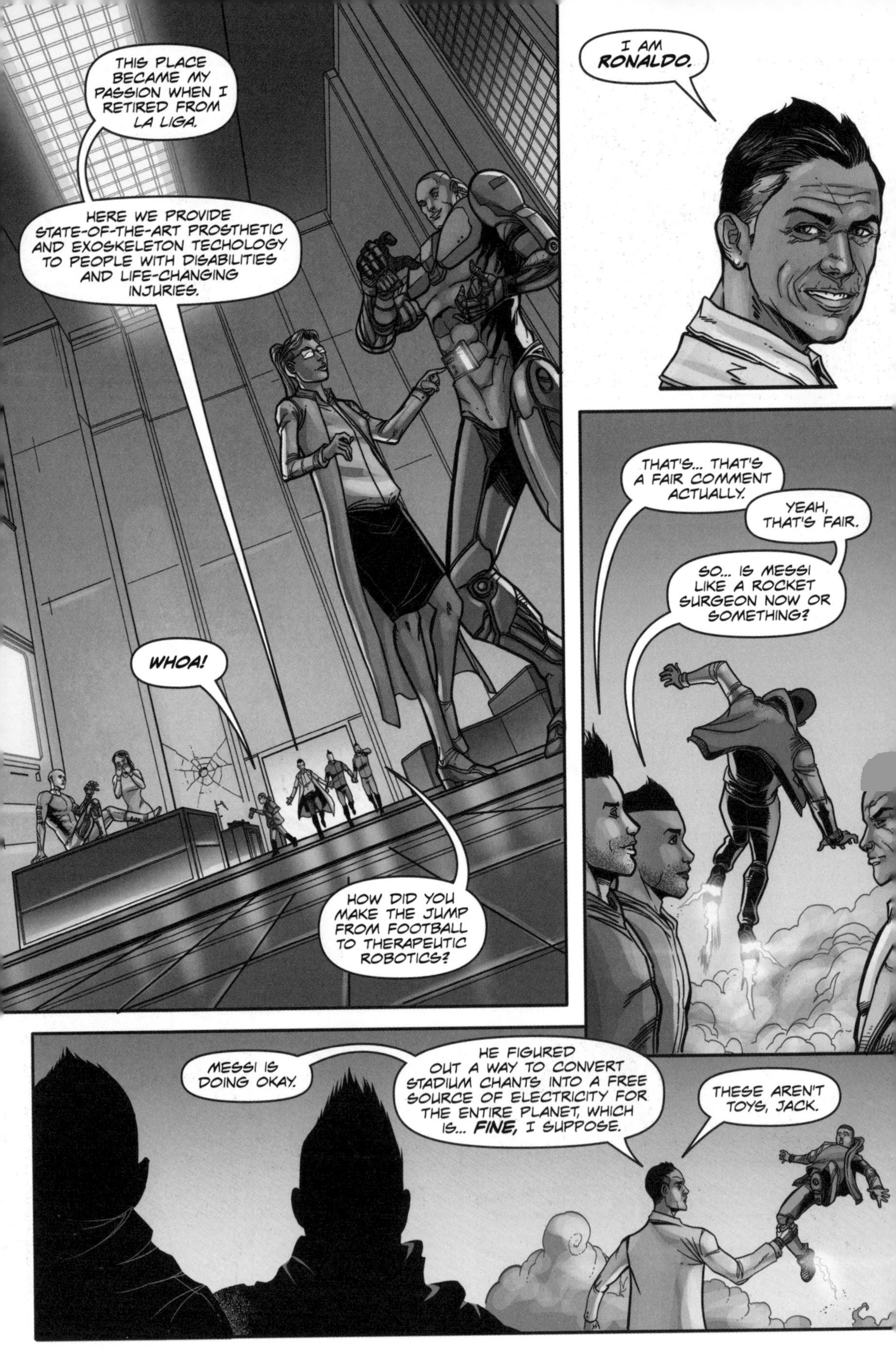
THIS PLACE BECAME MY PASSION WHEN I RETIRED FROM LA LIGA.
HERE WE PROVIDE STATE-OF-THE-ART PROSTHETIC AND EXOSKELETON TECHOLOGY TO PEOPLE WITH DISABILITIES AND LIFE-CHANGING INJURIES.
WHOA!
HOW DID YOU MAKE THE JUMP FROM FOOTBALL TO THERAPEUTIC ROBOTICS?
I AM RONALDO.
THAT'S... THAT'S A FAIR COMMENT ACTUALLY.
YEAH, THAT'S FAIR.
SO... IS MESSI LIKE A ROCKET SURGEON NOW OR SOMETHING?
MESSI IS DOING OKAY.
HE FIGURED OUT A WAY TO CONVERT STADIUM CHANTS INTO A FREE SOURCE OF ELECTRICITY FOR THE ENTIRE PLANET, WHICH IS... FINE, I SUPPOSE.
THESE AREN'T TOYS, JACK.

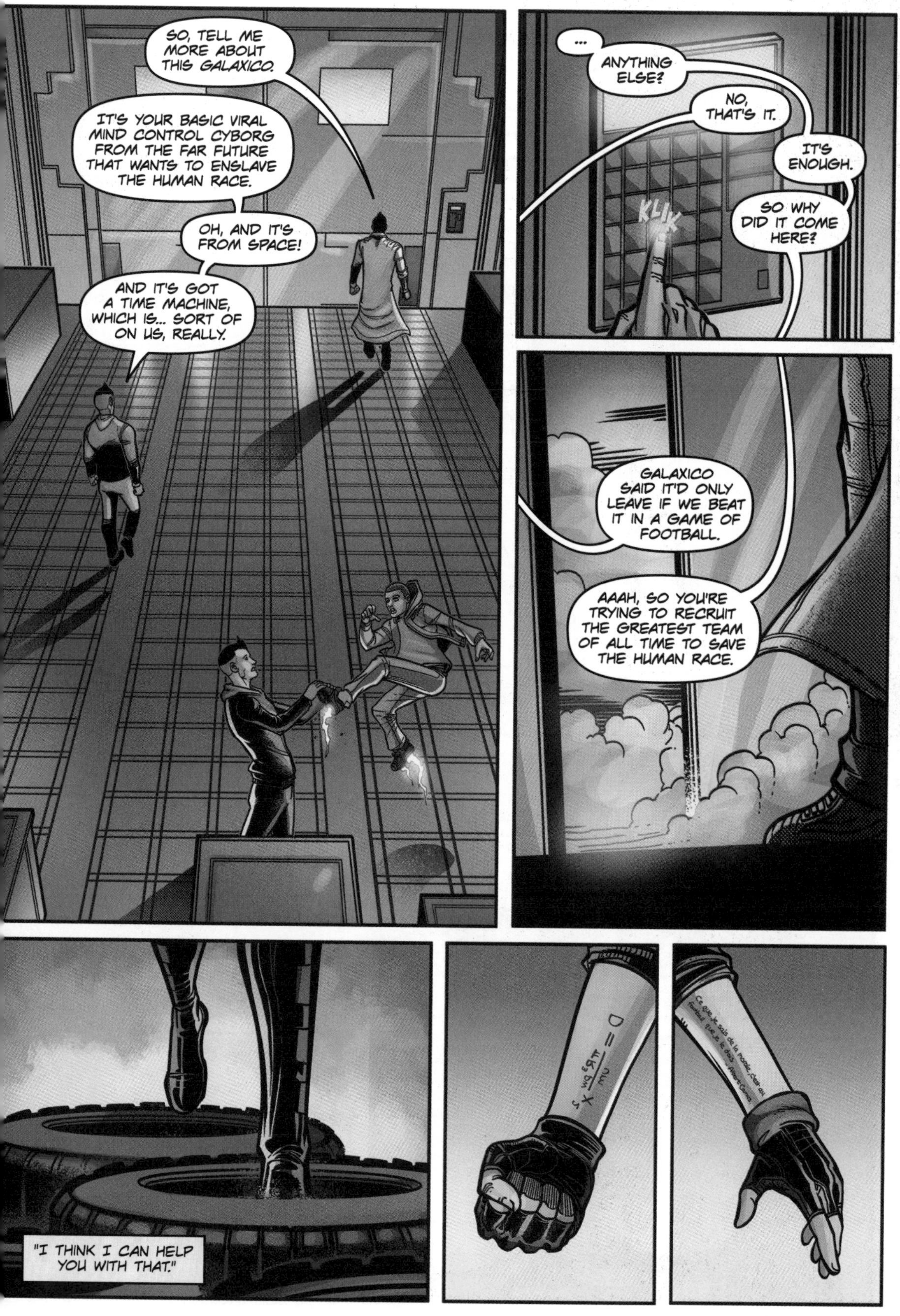
SO, TELL ME MORE ABOUT THIS GALAXICO.
IT'S YOUR BASIC VIRAL MIND CONTROL CYBORG FROM THE FAR FUTURE THAT WANTS TO ENSLAVE THE HUMAN RACE.
OH, AND IT'S FROM SPACE!
AND IT'S GOT A TIME MACHINE, WHICH IS... SORT OF ON US, REALLY.
...
ANYTHING ELSE?
NO, THAT'S IT.
IT'S ENOUGH.
KLIK
SO WHY DID IT COME HERE?
GALAXICO SAID IT'D ONLY LEAVE IF WE BEAT IT IN A GAME OF FOOTBALL.
AAAH, SO YOU'RE TRYING TO RECRUIT THE GREATEST TEAM OF ALL TIME TO SAVE THE HUMAN RACE.
"I THINK I CAN HELP YOU WITH THAT."
Ce que je sais de la morale, c'est au football que je le dois. Albert Camus

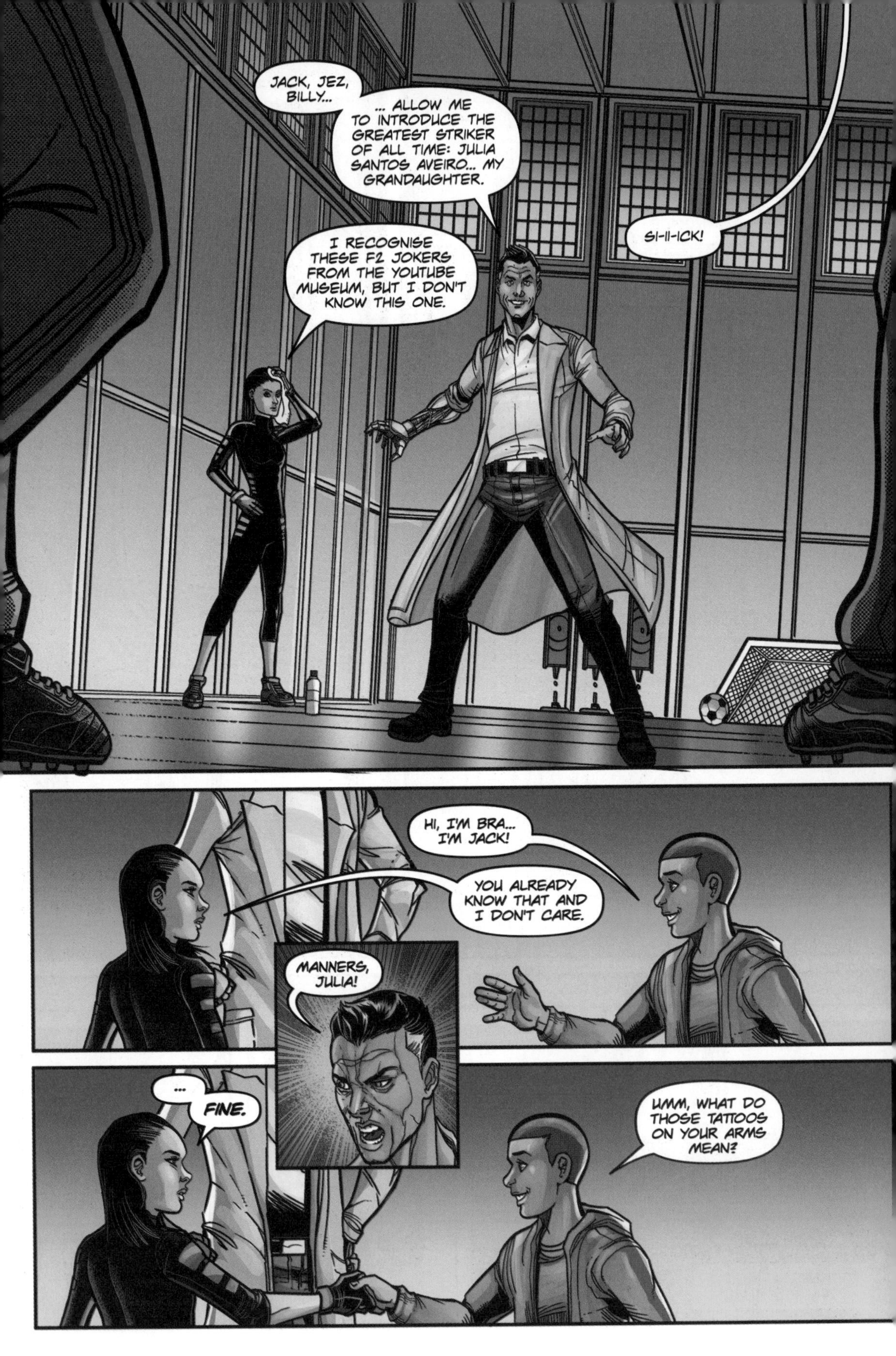
JACK, JEZ, BILLY...
... ALLOW ME TO INTRODUCE THE GREATEST STRIKER OF ALL TIME: JULIA SANTOS AVEIRO... MY GRANDAUGHTER.
SI-II-ICK!
I RECOGNISE THESE F2 JOKERS FROM THE YOUTUBE MUSEUM, BUT I DON'T KNOW THIS ONE.
HI, I'M BRA... I'M JACK!
YOU ALREADY KNOW THAT AND I DON'T CARE.
MANNERS, JULIA!
...
FINE.
UMM, WHAT DO THOSE TATTOOS ON YOUR ARMS MEAN?

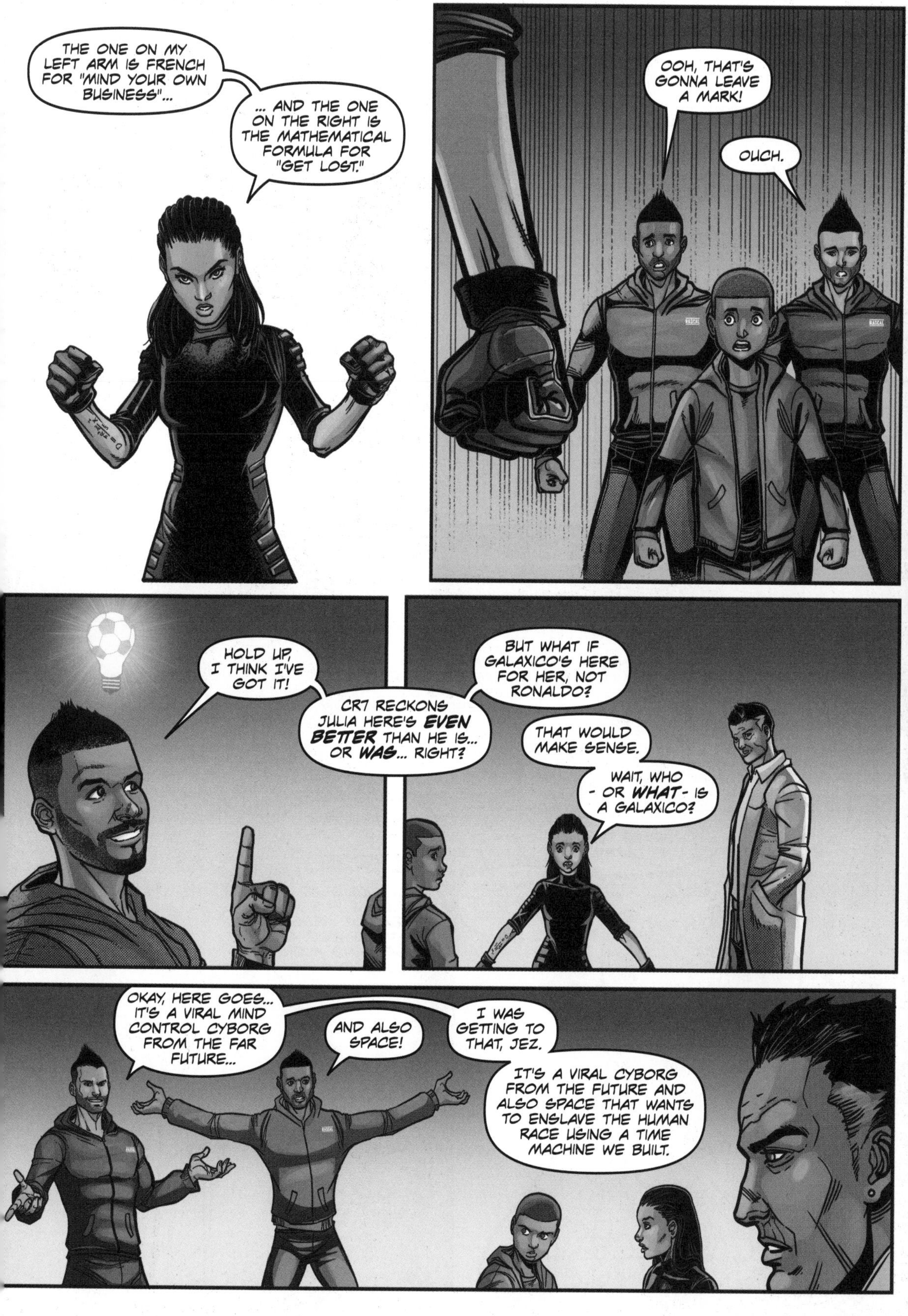
THE ONE ON MY LEFT ARM IS FRENCH FOR "MIND YOUR OWN BUSINESS"...
... AND THE ONE ON THE RIGHT IS THE MATHEMATICAL FORMULA FOR "GET LOST."
OOH, THAT'S GONNA LEAVE A MARK!
OUCH.
HOLD UP, I THINK I'VE GOT IT!
CR7 RECKONS JULIA HERE'S **EVEN BETTER** THAN HE IS... OR **WAS**... RIGHT?
BUT WHAT IF GALAXICO'S HERE FOR HER, NOT RONALDO?
THAT WOULD MAKE SENSE.
WAIT, WHO - OR **WHAT** - IS A GALAXICO?
OKAY, HERE GOES... IT'S A VIRAL MIND CONTROL CYBORG FROM THE FAR FUTURE...
AND ALSO SPACE!
I WAS GETTING TO THAT, JEZ.
IT'S A VIRAL CYBORG FROM THE FUTURE AND ALSO SPACE THAT WANTS TO ENSLAVE THE HUMAN RACE USING A TIME MACHINE WE BUILT.

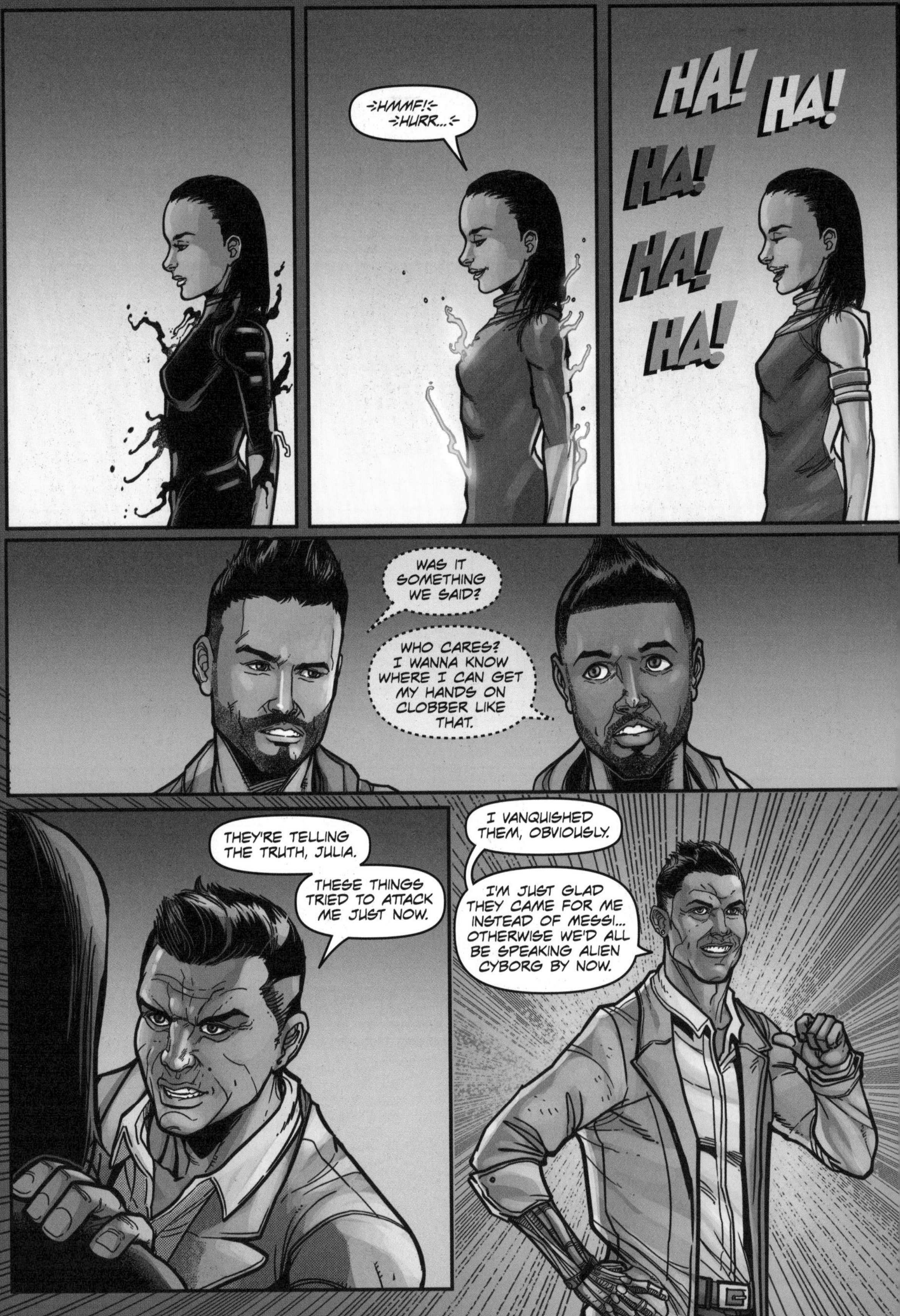

HMMF! HURR...
HA! HA!
HA!
HA!
HA!
WAS IT SOMETHING WE SAID?
WHO CARES? I WANNA KNOW WHERE I CAN GET MY HANDS ON CLOBBER LIKE THAT.
THEY'RE TELLING THE TRUTH, JULIA.
THESE THINGS TRIED TO ATTACK ME JUST NOW.
I VANQUISHED THEM, OBVIOUSLY.
I'M JUST GLAD THEY CAME FOR ME INSTEAD OF MESSI... OTHERWISE WE'D ALL BE SPEAKING ALIEN CYBORG BY NOW.

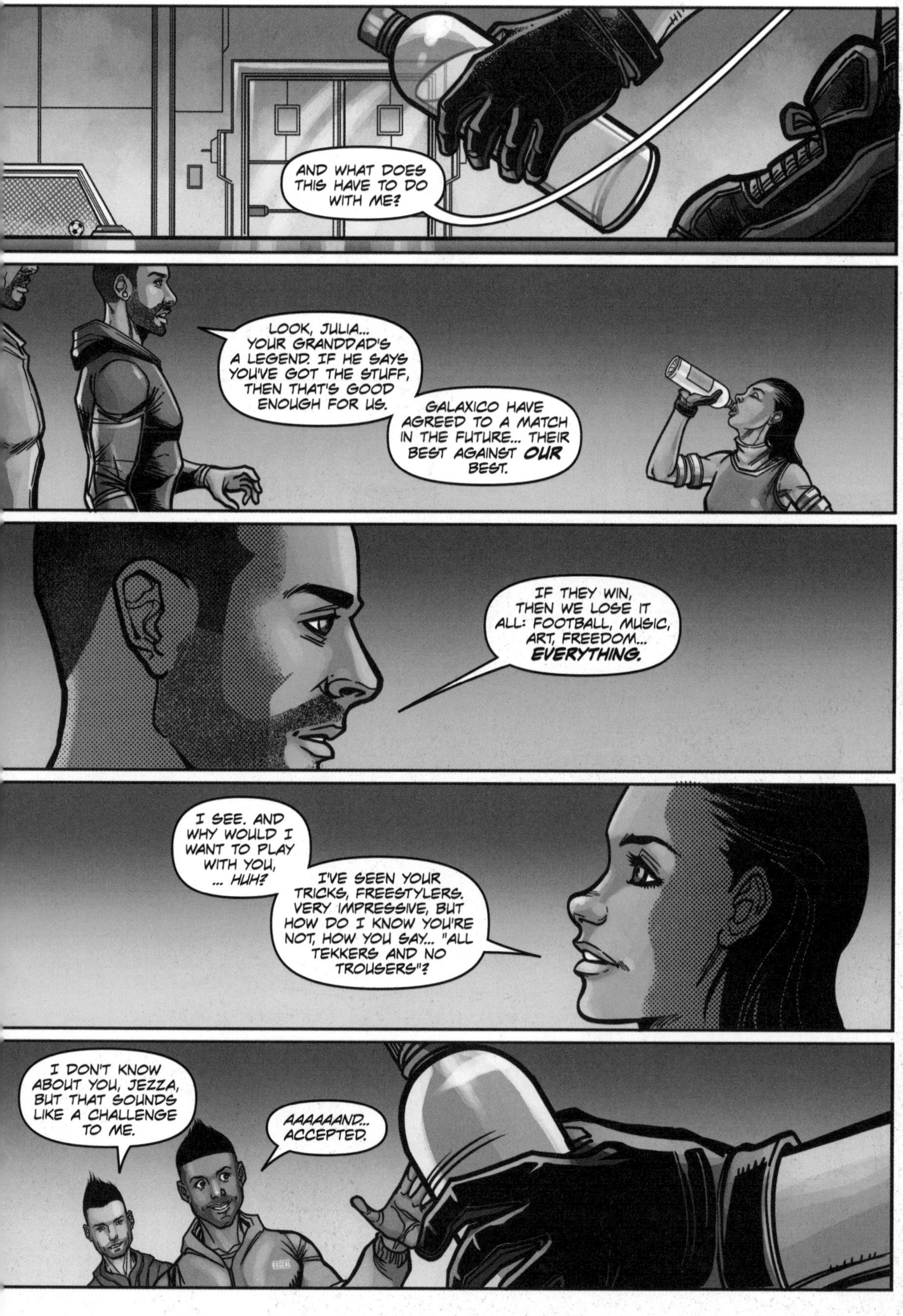
AND WHAT DOES THIS HAVE TO DO WITH ME?
LOOK, JULIA... YOUR GRANDDAD'S A LEGEND. IF HE SAYS YOU'VE GOT THE STUFF, THEN THAT'S GOOD ENOUGH FOR US.
GALAXICO HAVE AGREED TO A MATCH IN THE FUTURE... THEIR BEST AGAINST **OUR** BEST.
IF THEY WIN, THEN WE LOSE IT ALL: FOOTBALL, MUSIC, ART, FREEDOM... ***EVERYTHING.***
I SEE. AND WHY WOULD I WANT TO PLAY WITH YOU, ... *HUH?*
I'VE SEEN YOUR TRICKS, FREESTYLERS. VERY IMPRESSIVE, BUT HOW DO I KNOW YOU'RE NOT, HOW YOU SAY... "ALL TEKKERS AND NO TROUSERS"?
I DON'T KNOW ABOUT YOU, JEZZA, BUT THAT SOUNDS LIKE A CHALLENGE TO ME.
AAAAAAND... ACCEPTED.

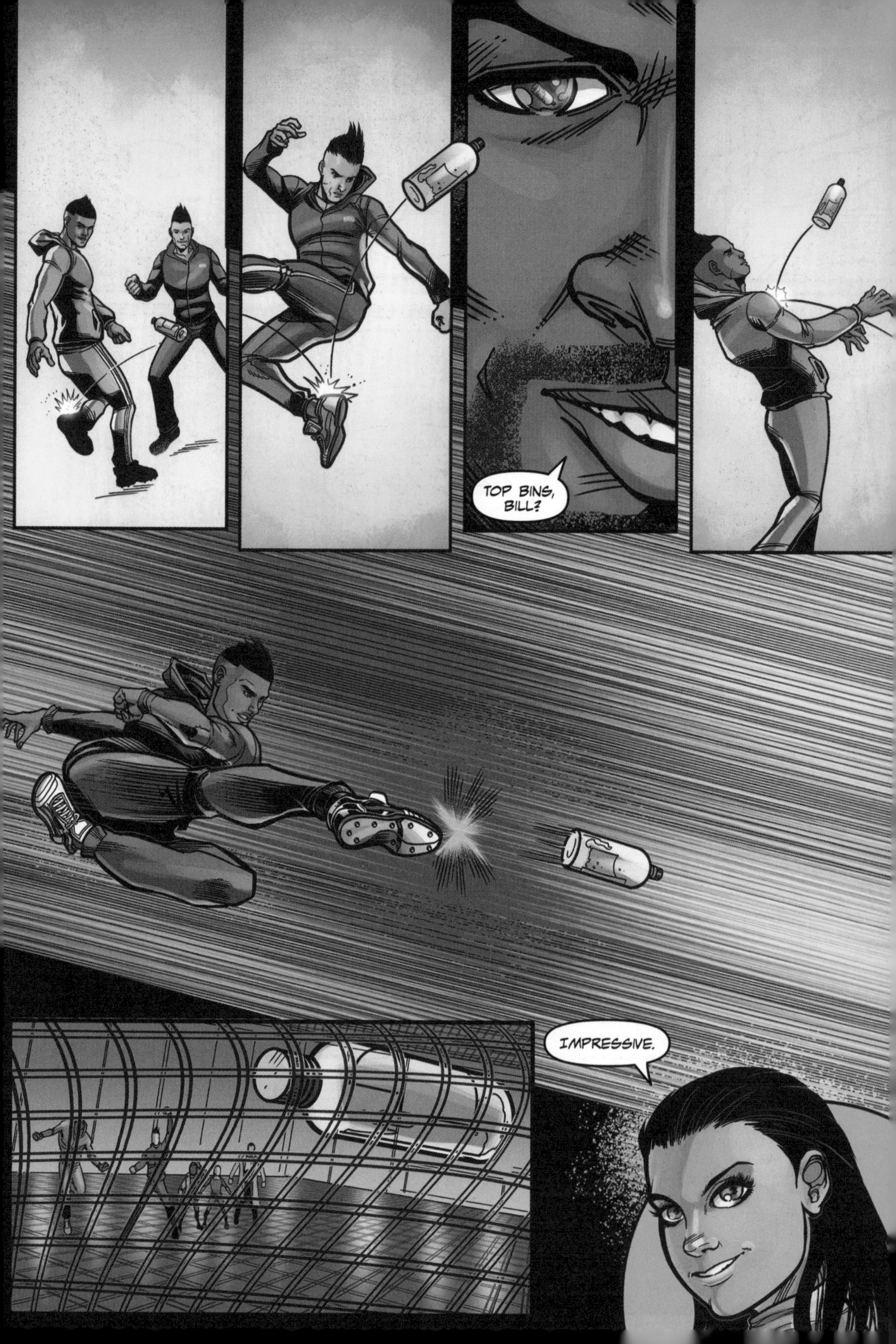
TOP BINS, BILL?
IMPRESSIVE.

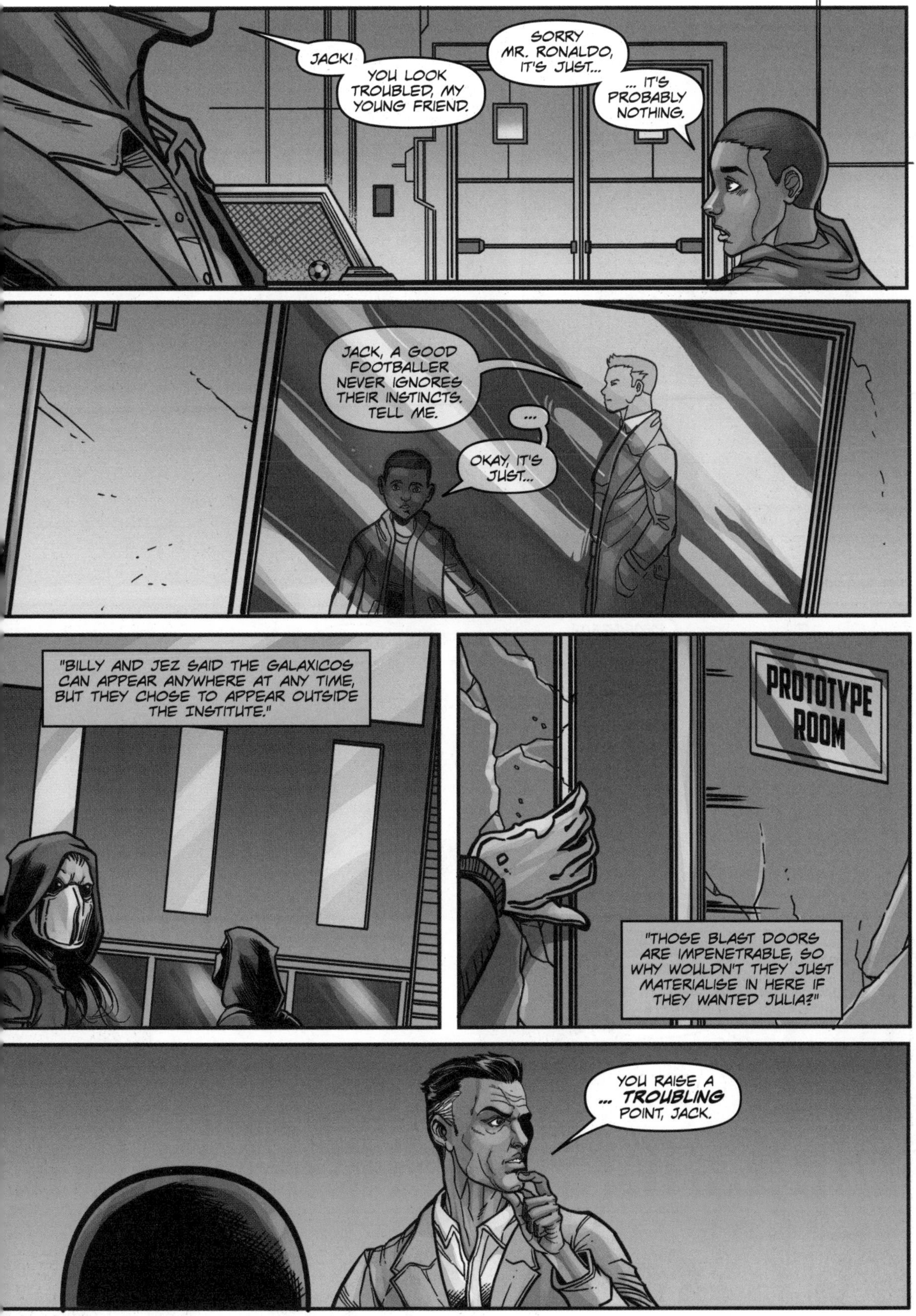
JACK!
YOU LOOK TROUBLED, MY YOUNG FRIEND.
SORRY MR. RONALDO, IT'S JUST...
... IT'S PROBABLY NOTHING.
JACK, A GOOD FOOTBALLER NEVER IGNORES THEIR INSTINCTS. TELL ME.
...
OKAY, IT'S JUST...
"BILLY AND JEZ SAID THE GALAXICOS CAN APPEAR ANYWHERE AT ANY TIME, BUT THEY CHOSE TO APPEAR OUTSIDE THE INSTITUTE."
PROTOTYPE ROOM
"THOSE BLAST DOORS ARE IMPENETRABLE, SO WHY WOULDN'T THEY JUST MATERIALISE IN HERE IF THEY WANTED JULIA?"
YOU RAISE A ... TROUBLING POINT, JACK.

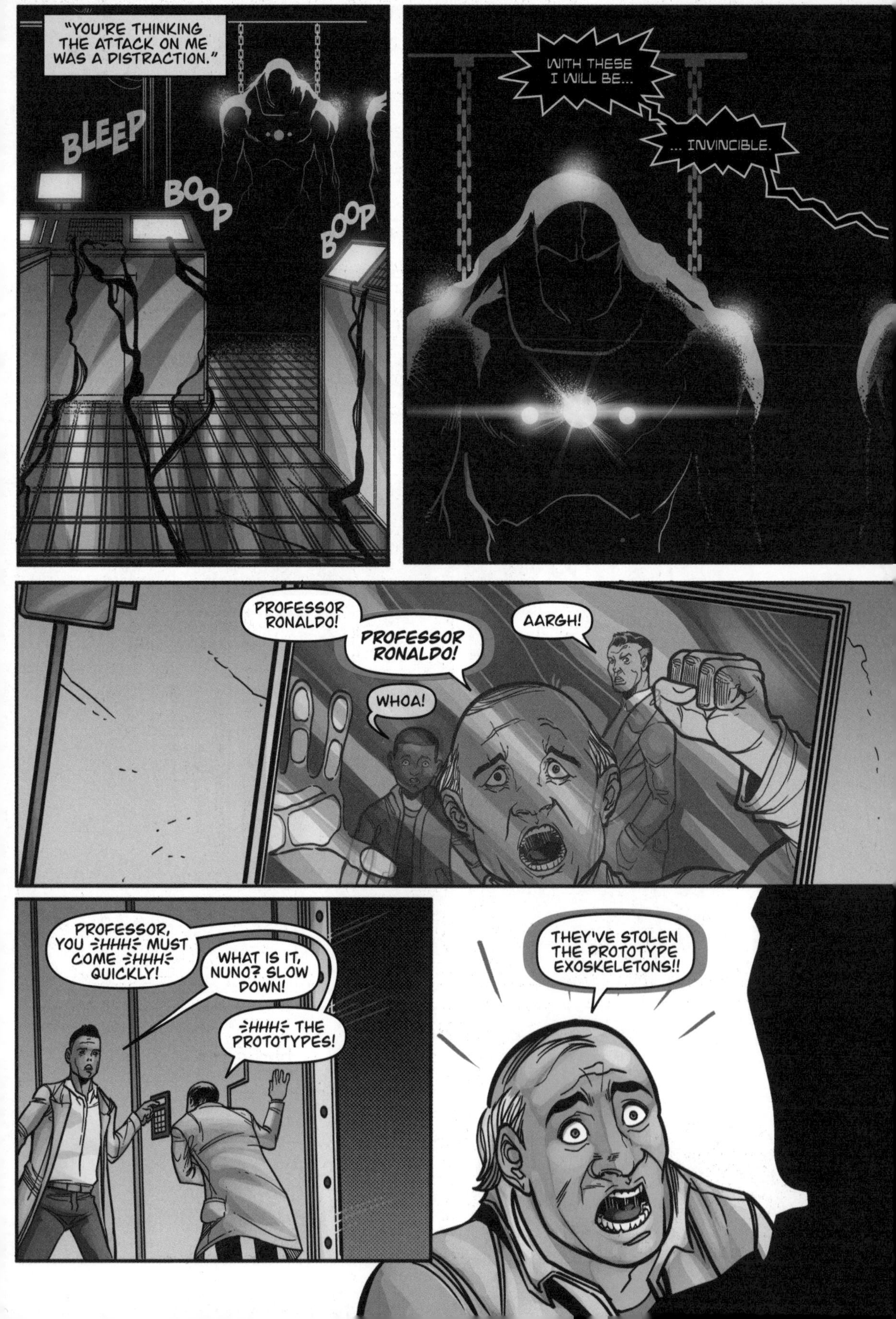
"YOU'RE THINKING THE ATTACK ON ME WAS A DISTRACTION."
BLEEP
BOOP
BOOP
WITH THESE I WILL BE...
... INVINCIBLE.
PROFESSOR RONALDO!
PROFESSOR RONALDO!
AARGH!
WHOA!
PROFESSOR, YOU =HHH= MUST COME =HHH= QUICKLY!
WHAT IS IT, NUNO? SLOW DOWN!
=HHH= THE PROTOTYPES!
THEY'VE STOLEN THE PROTOTYPE EXOSKELETONS!!

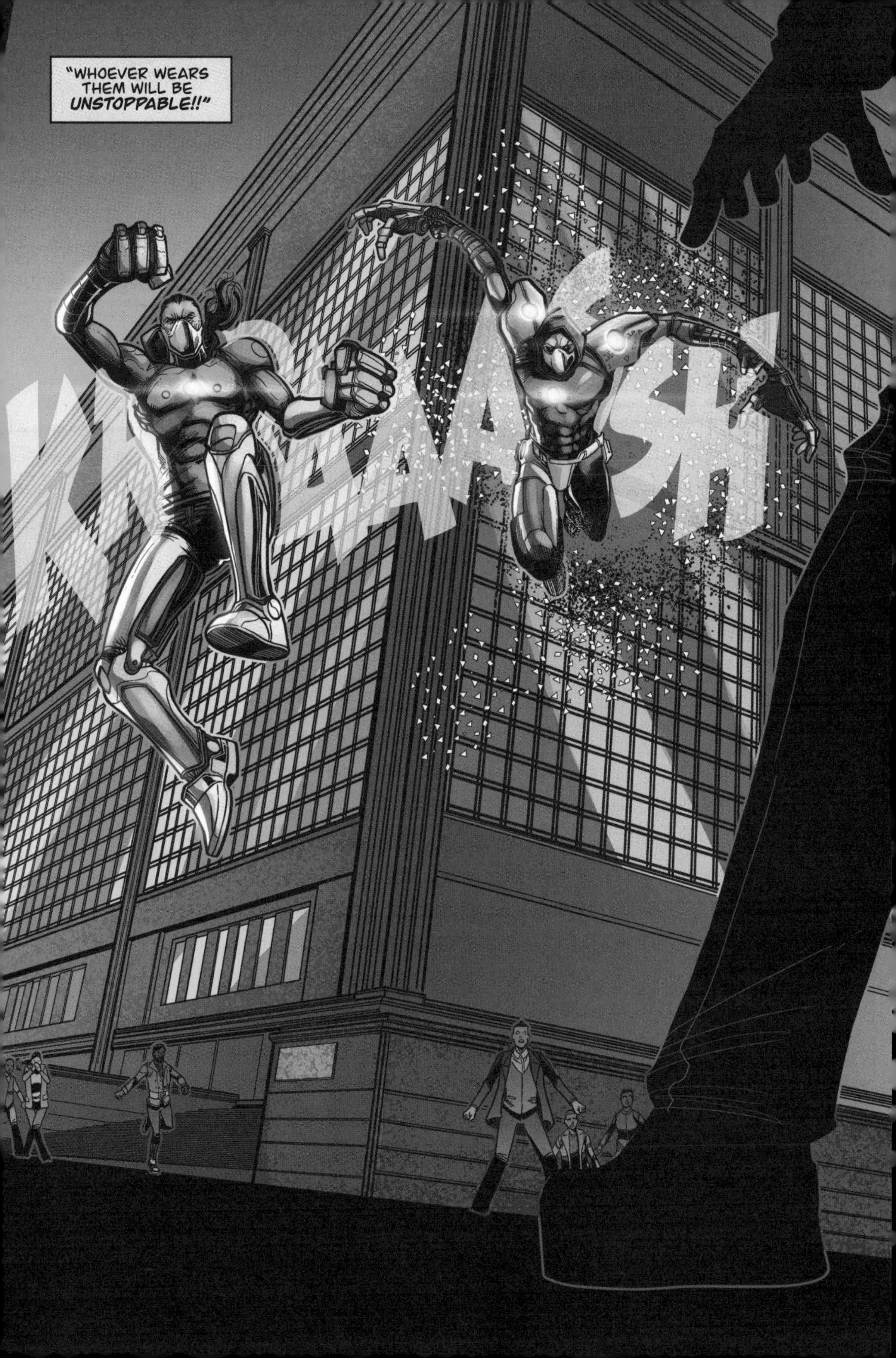
"WHOEVER WEARS THEM WILL BE *UNSTOPPABLE!!*"

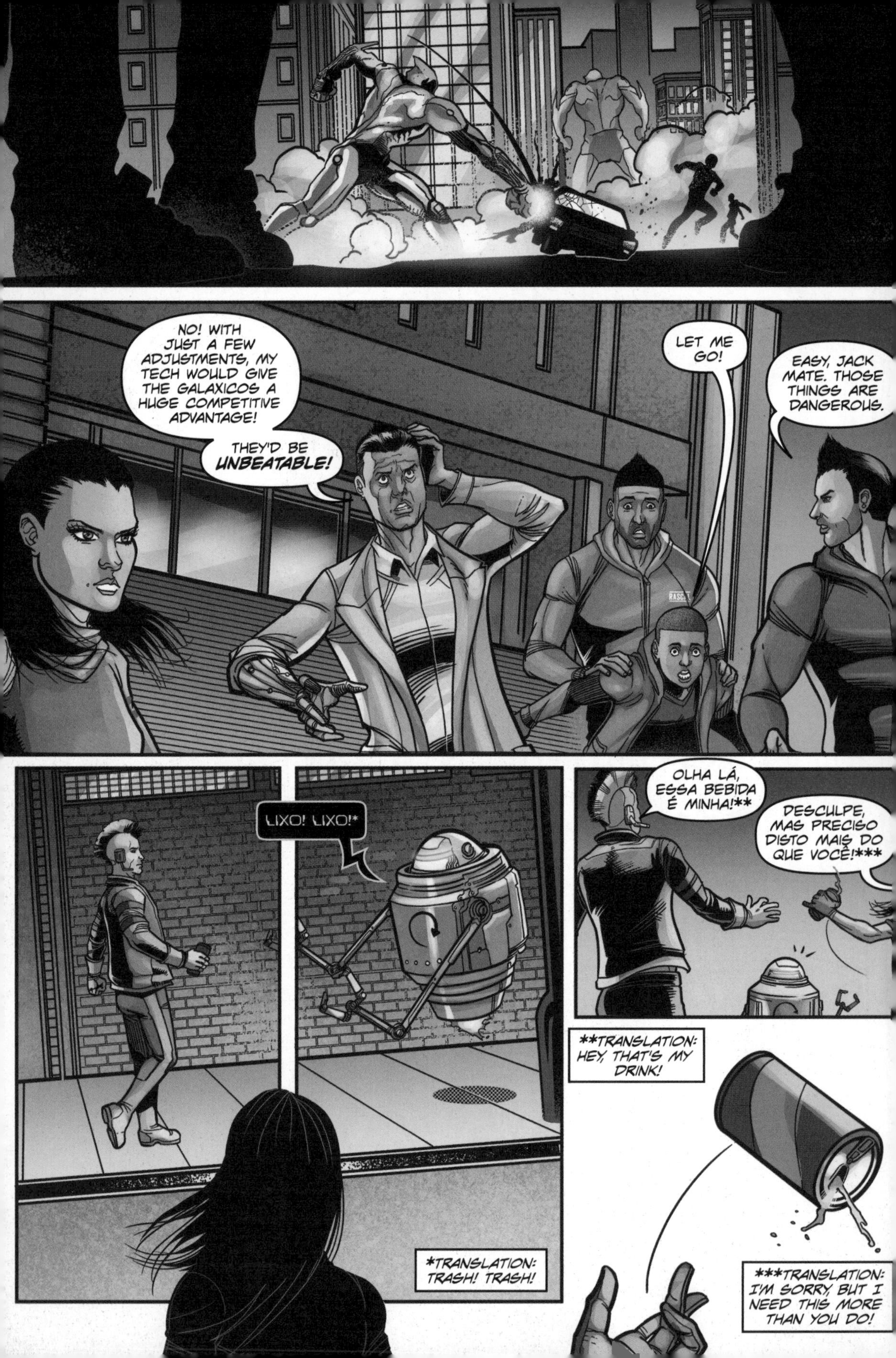
NO! WITH JUST A FEW ADJUSTMENTS, MY TECH WOULD GIVE THE GALAXICOS A HUGE COMPETITIVE ADVANTAGE!
THEY'D BE UNBEATABLE!
LET ME GO!
EASY, JACK MATE. THOSE THINGS ARE DANGEROUS.
LIXO! LIXO!*
*TRANSLATION: TRASH! TRASH!
OLHA LÁ, ESSA BEBIDA É MINHA!**
DESCULPE, MAS PRECISO DISTO MAIS DO QUE VOCÊ!***
**TRANSLATION: HEY, THAT'S MY DRINK!
***TRANSLATION: I'M SORRY, BUT I NEED THIS MORE THAN YOU DO!

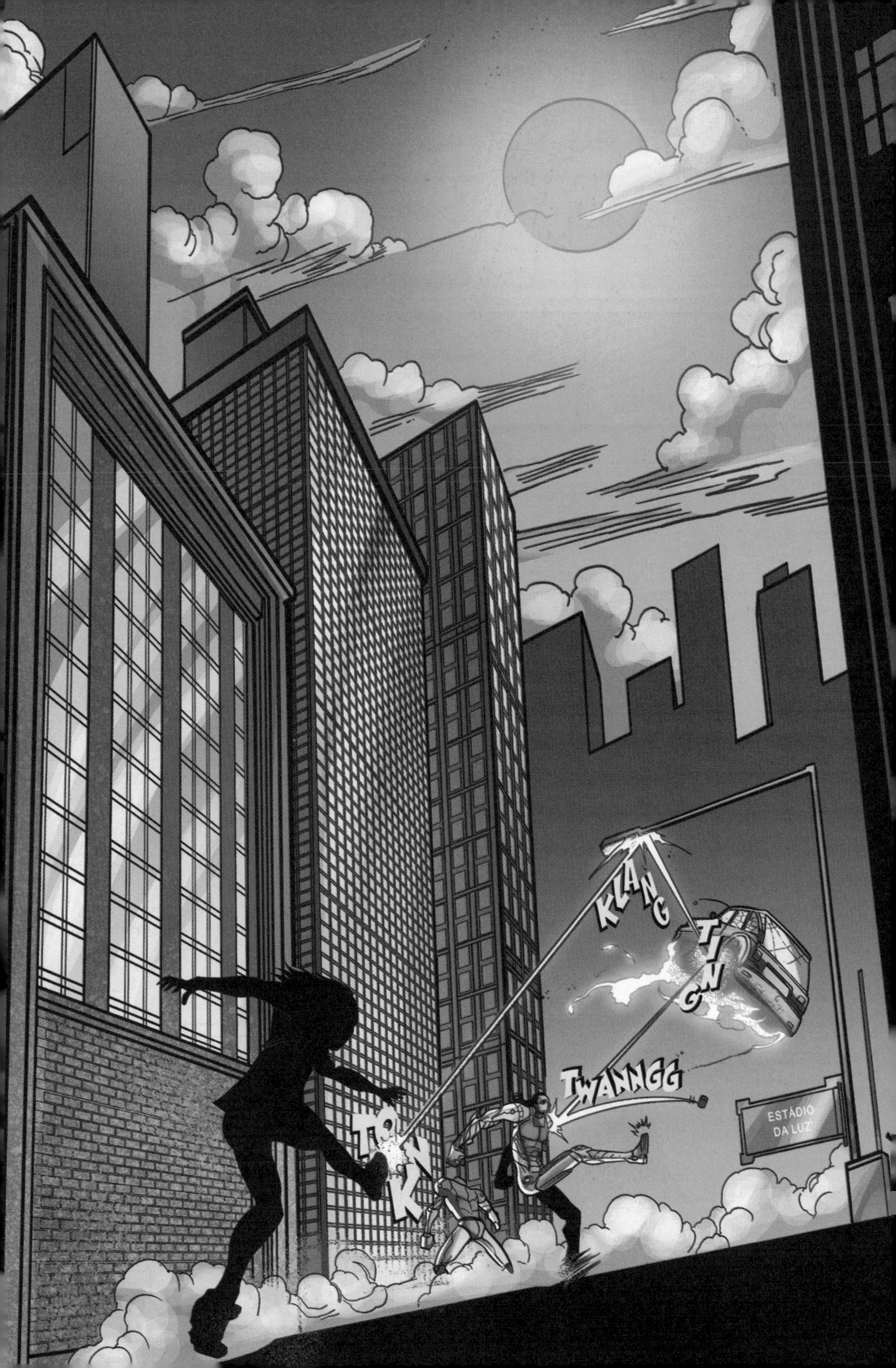
TONK
KLANG
TING
TWANNGG
ESTÁDIO
DA LUZ

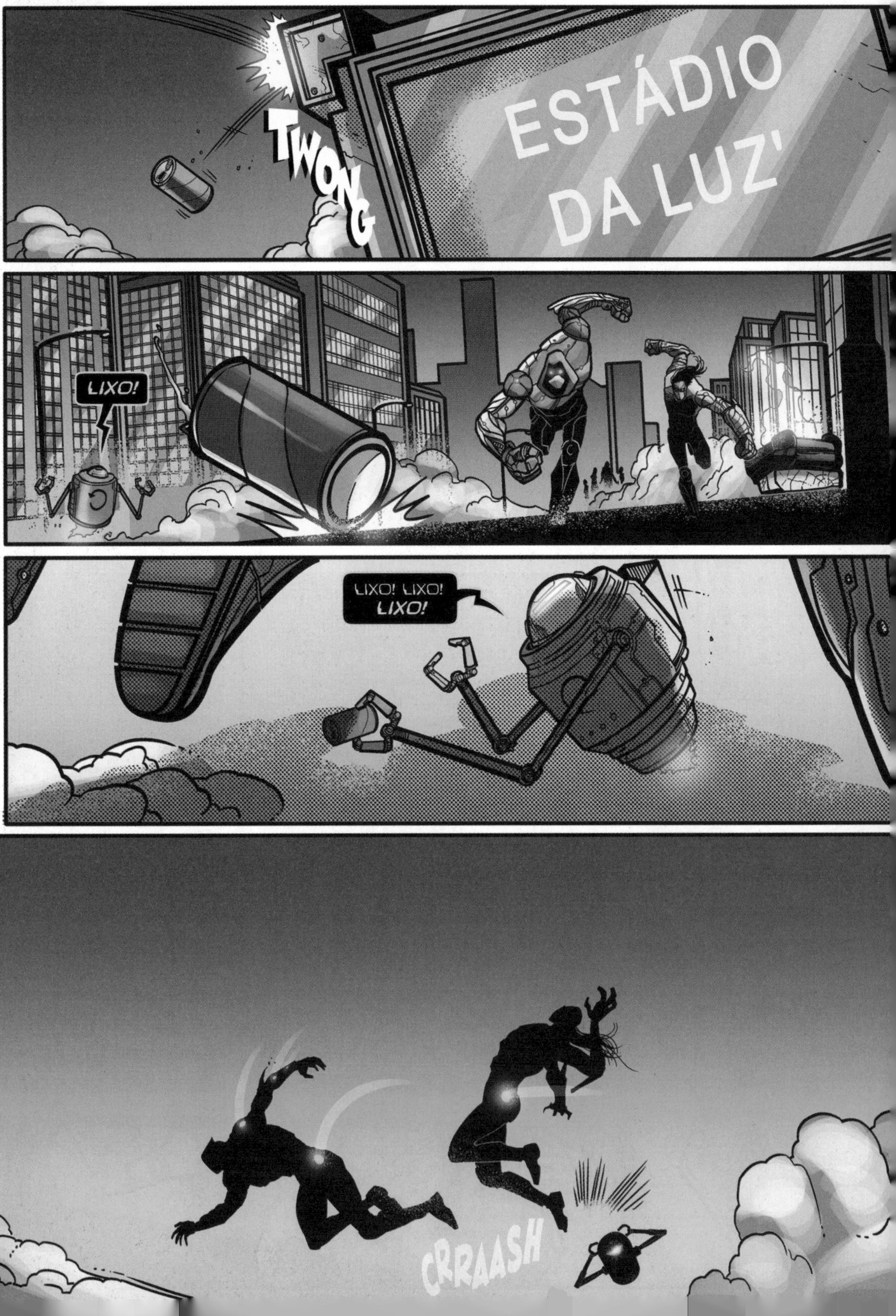
TWONG
ESTÁDIO DA LUZ'
LIXO!
LIXO! LIXO! LIXO!
CRRAASH

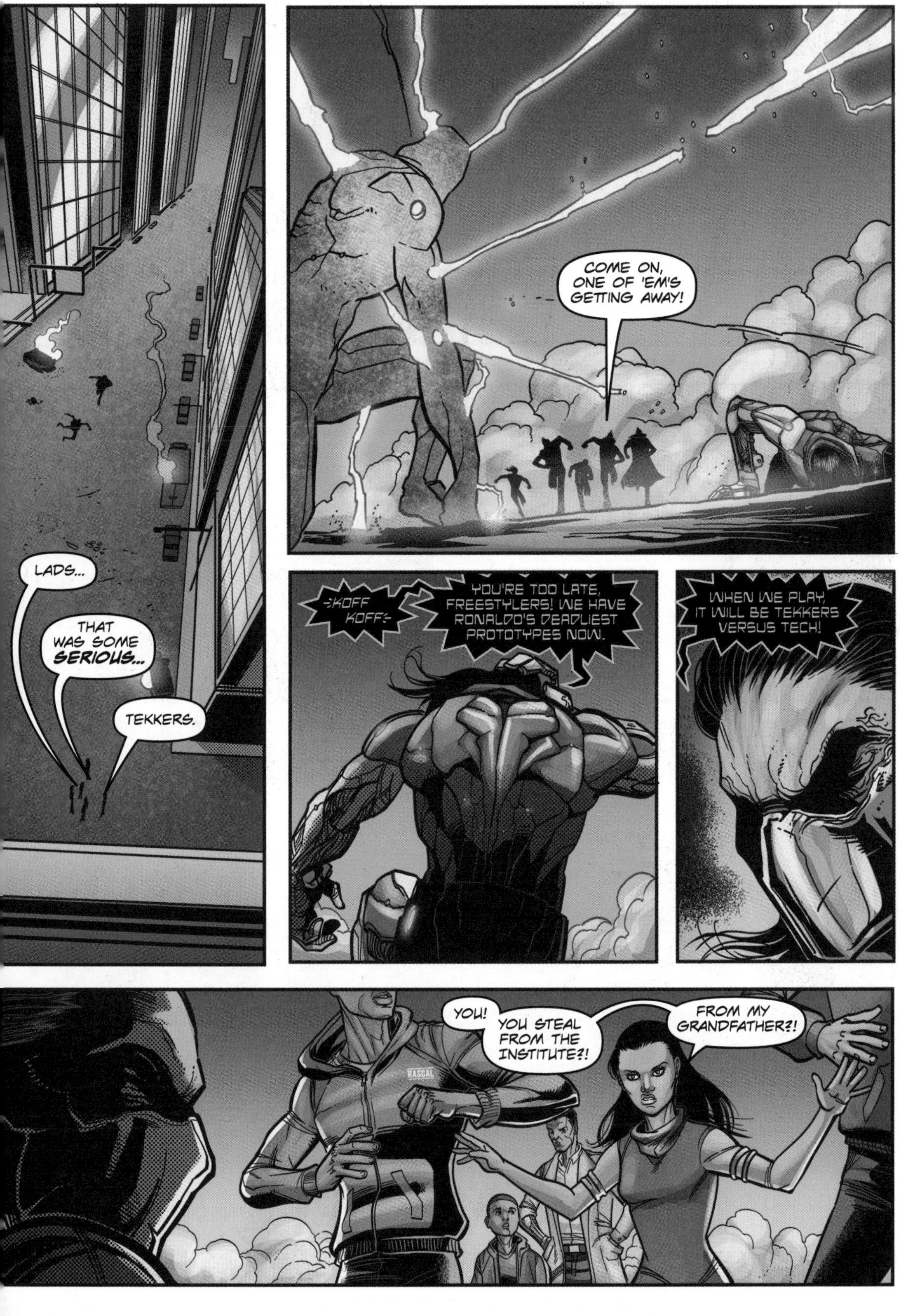
LADS...
THAT WAS SOME SERIOUS...
TEKKERS.
COME ON, ONE OF 'EM'S GETTING AWAY!
-KOFF KOFF-
YOU'RE TOO LATE, FREESTYLERS! WE HAVE RONALDO'S DEADLIEST PROTOTYPES NOW.
WHEN WE PLAY, IT WILL BE TEKKERS VERSUS TECH!
YOU!
YOU STEAL FROM THE INSTITUTE?!
FROM MY GRANDFATHER?!
RASCAL

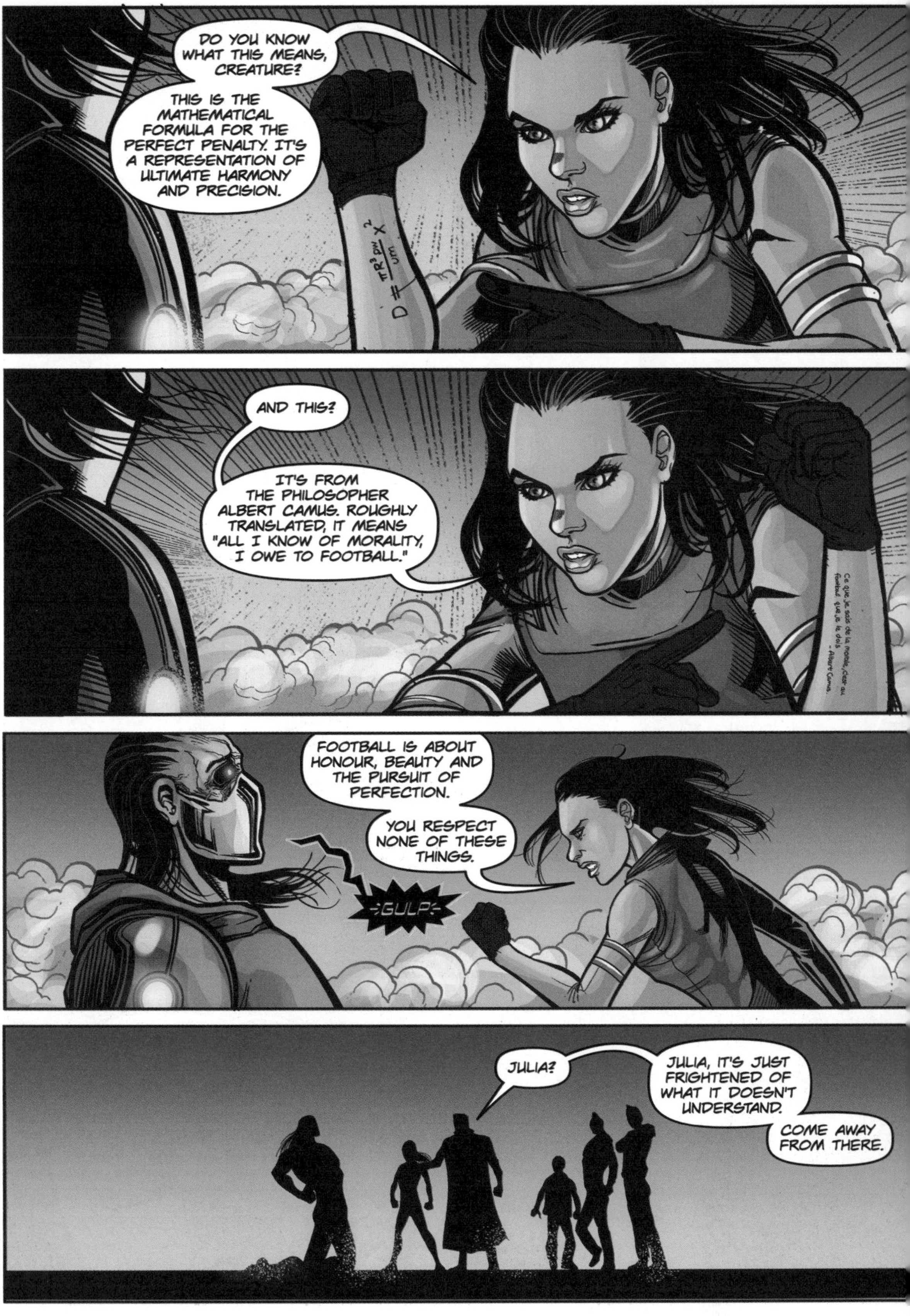
DO YOU KNOW WHAT THIS MEANS, CREATURE?
THIS IS THE MATHEMATICAL FORMULA FOR THE PERFECT PENALTY. IT'S A REPRESENTATION OF ULTIMATE HARMONY AND PRECISION.
AND THIS?
IT'S FROM THE PHILOSOPHER ALBERT CAMUS. ROUGHLY TRANSLATED, IT MEANS "ALL I KNOW OF MORALITY, I OWE TO FOOTBALL."
Ce que je sais de la morale, c'est au football que je le dois
- Albert Camus.
FOOTBALL IS ABOUT HONOUR, BEAUTY AND THE PURSUIT OF PERFECTION.
YOU RESPECT NONE OF THESE THINGS.
GULP
JULIA?
JULIA, IT'S JUST FRIGHTENED OF WHAT IT DOESN'T UNDERSTAND.
COME AWAY FROM THERE.

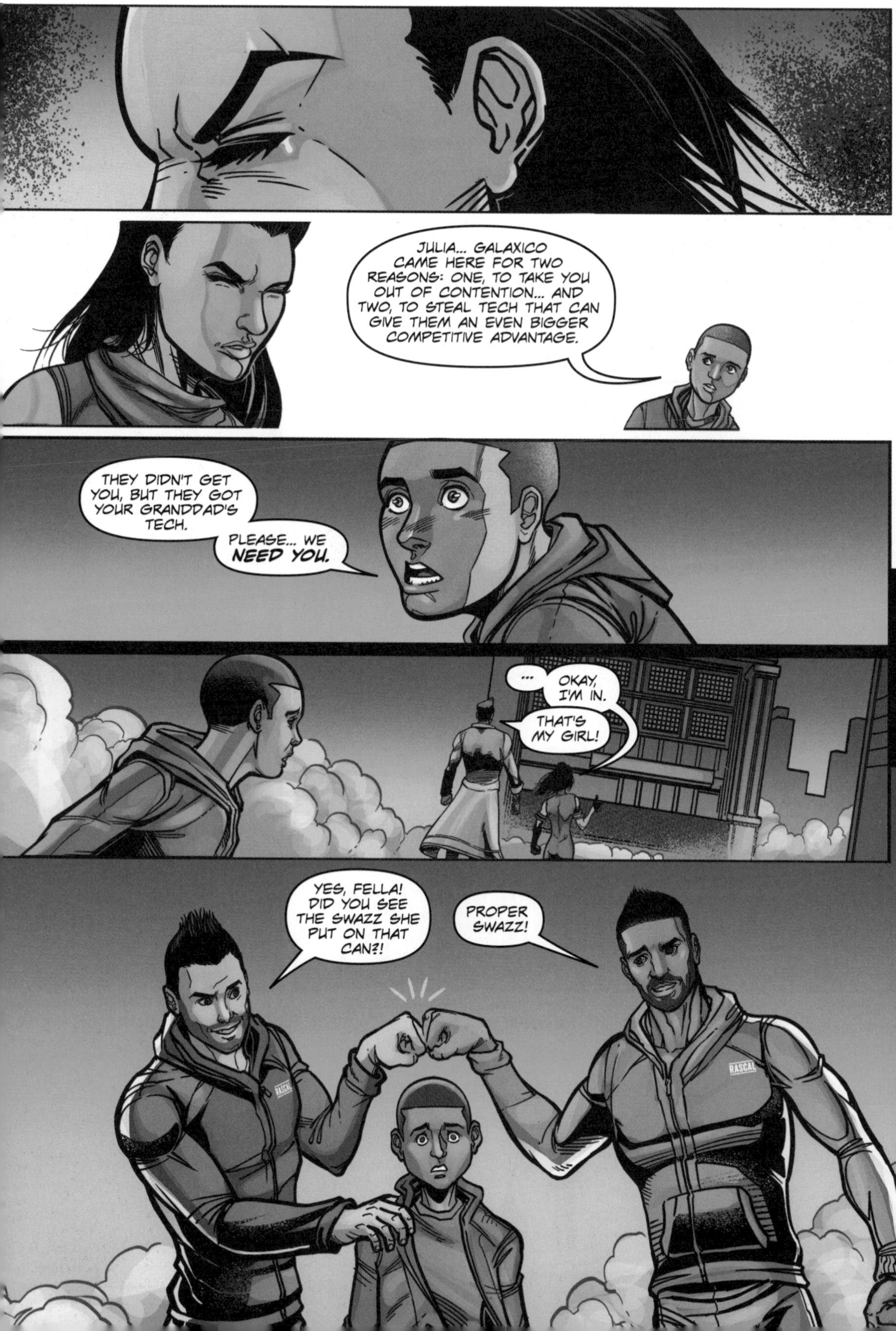
JULIA... GALAXICO CAME HERE FOR TWO REASONS: ONE, TO TAKE YOU OUT OF CONTENTION... AND TWO, TO STEAL TECH THAT CAN GIVE THEM AN EVEN BIGGER COMPETITIVE ADVANTAGE.
THEY DIDN'T GET YOU, BUT THEY GOT YOUR GRANDDAD'S TECH.
PLEASE... WE NEED YOU.
...
OKAY, I'M IN.
THAT'S MY GIRL!
YES, FELLA! DID YOU SEE THE SWAZZ SHE PUT ON THAT CAN?!
PROPER SWAZZ!
RASCAL
RASCAL

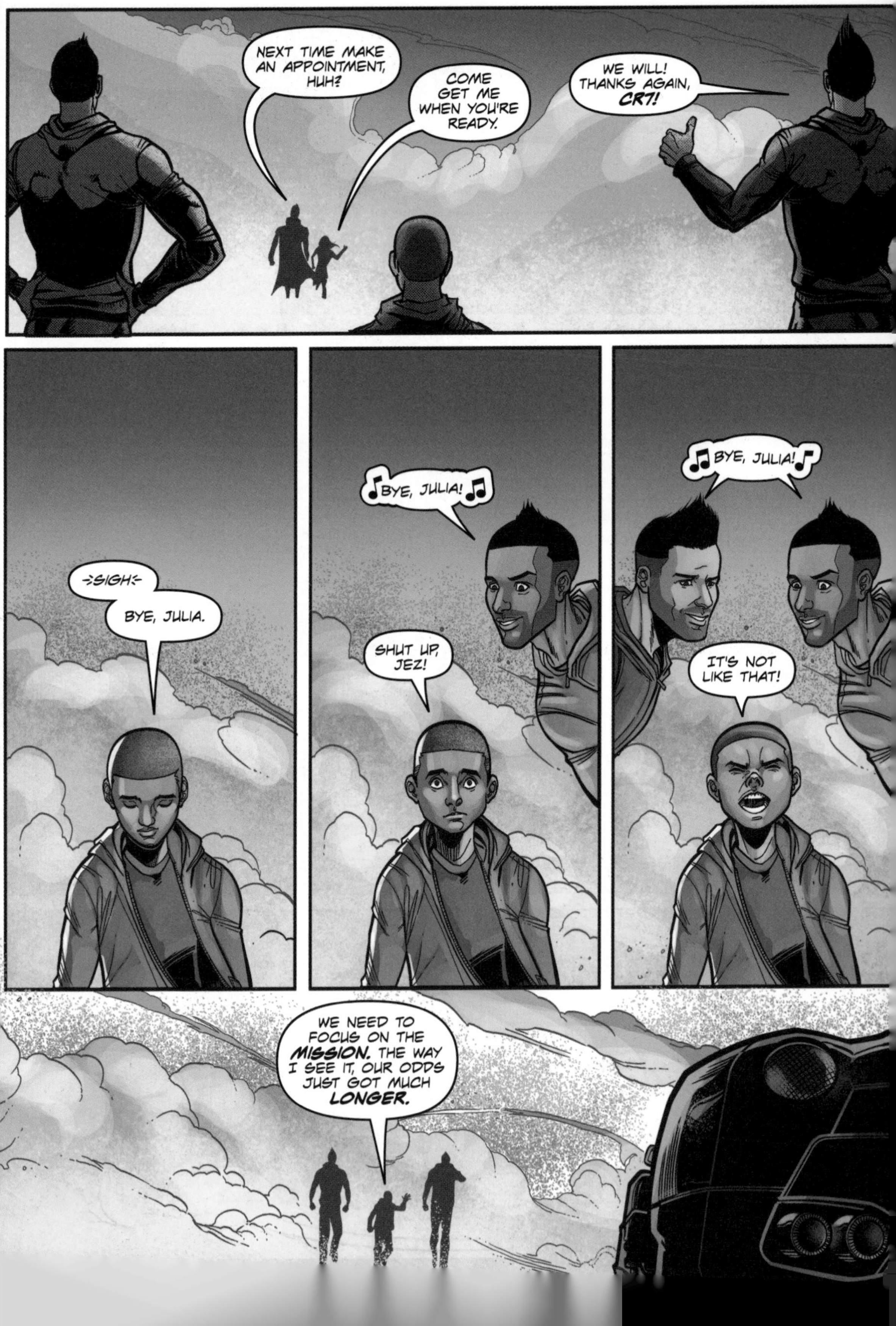
NEXT TIME MAKE AN APPOINTMENT, HUH?
COME GET ME WHEN YOU'RE READY.
WE WILL! THANKS AGAIN, CR7!
-SIGH-
BYE, JULIA.
BYE, JULIA!
SHUT UP, JEZ!
BYE, JULIA!
IT'S NOT LIKE THAT!
WE NEED TO FOCUS ON THE MISSION. THE WAY I SEE IT, OUR ODDS JUST GOT MUCH LONGER.

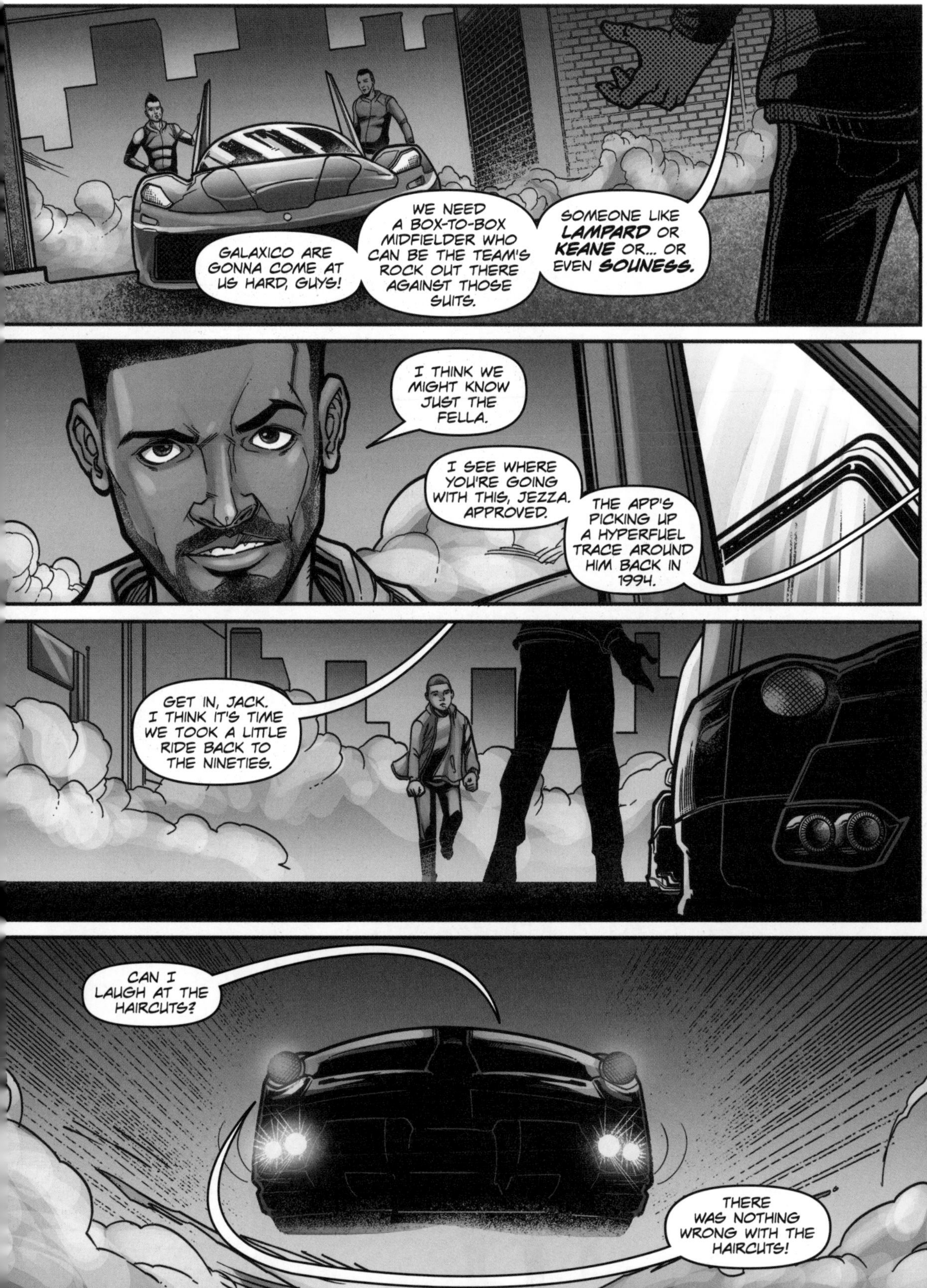
GALAXICO ARE GONNA COME AT US HARD, GUYS!
WE NEED A BOX-TO-BOX MIDFIELDER WHO CAN BE THE TEAM'S ROCK OUT THERE AGAINST THOSE SUITS.
SOMEONE LIKE LAMPARD OR KEANE OR... OR EVEN SOUNESS.
I THINK WE MIGHT KNOW JUST THE FELLA.
I SEE WHERE YOU'RE GOING WITH THIS, JEZZA. APPROVED.
THE APP'S PICKING UP A HYPERFUEL TRACE AROUND HIM BACK IN 1994.
GET IN, JACK. I THINK IT'S TIME WE TOOK A LITTLE RIDE BACK TO THE NINETIES.
CAN I LAUGH AT THE HAIRCUTS?
THERE WAS NOTHING WRONG WITH THE HAIRCUTS!

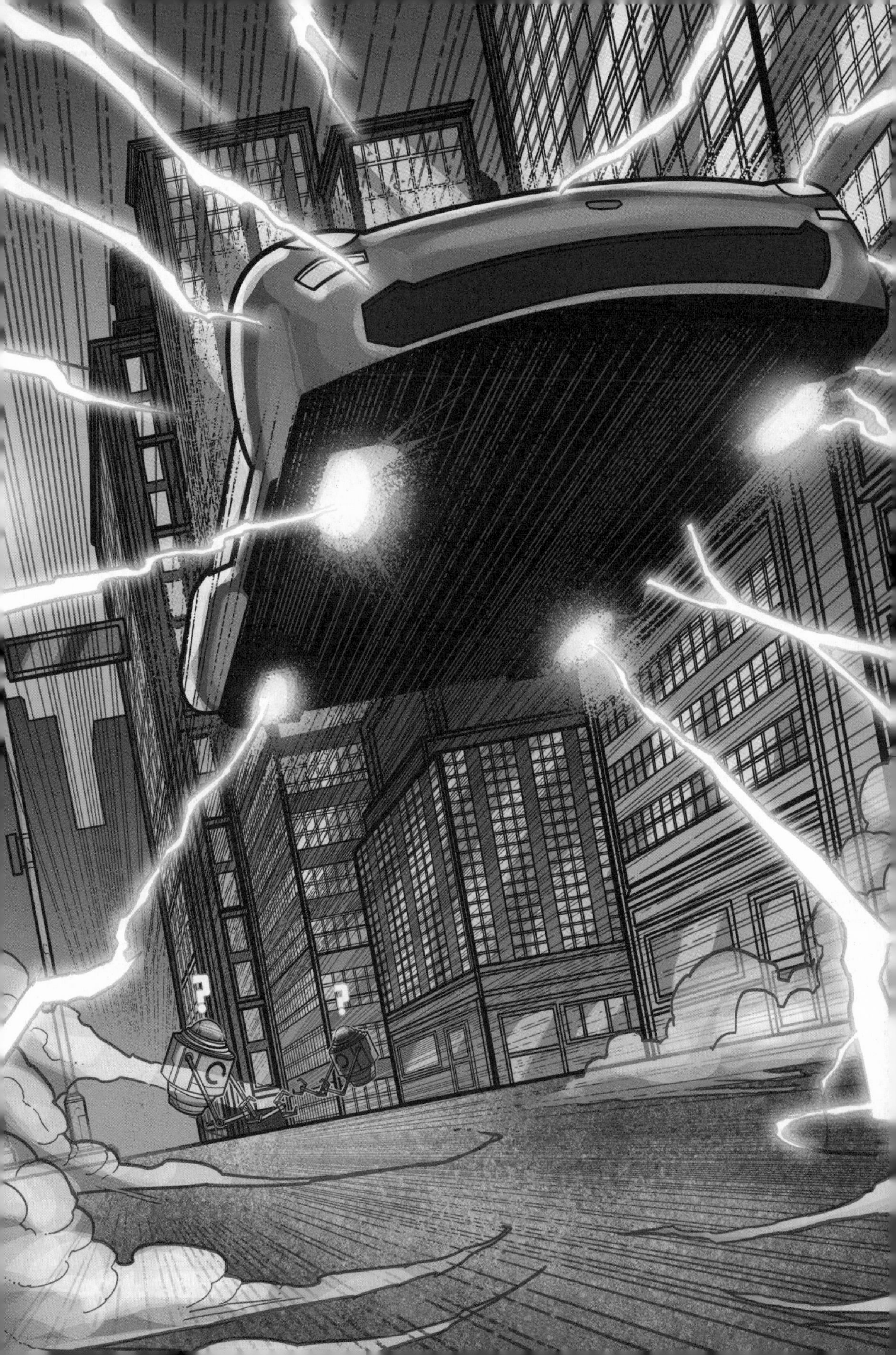
?
?

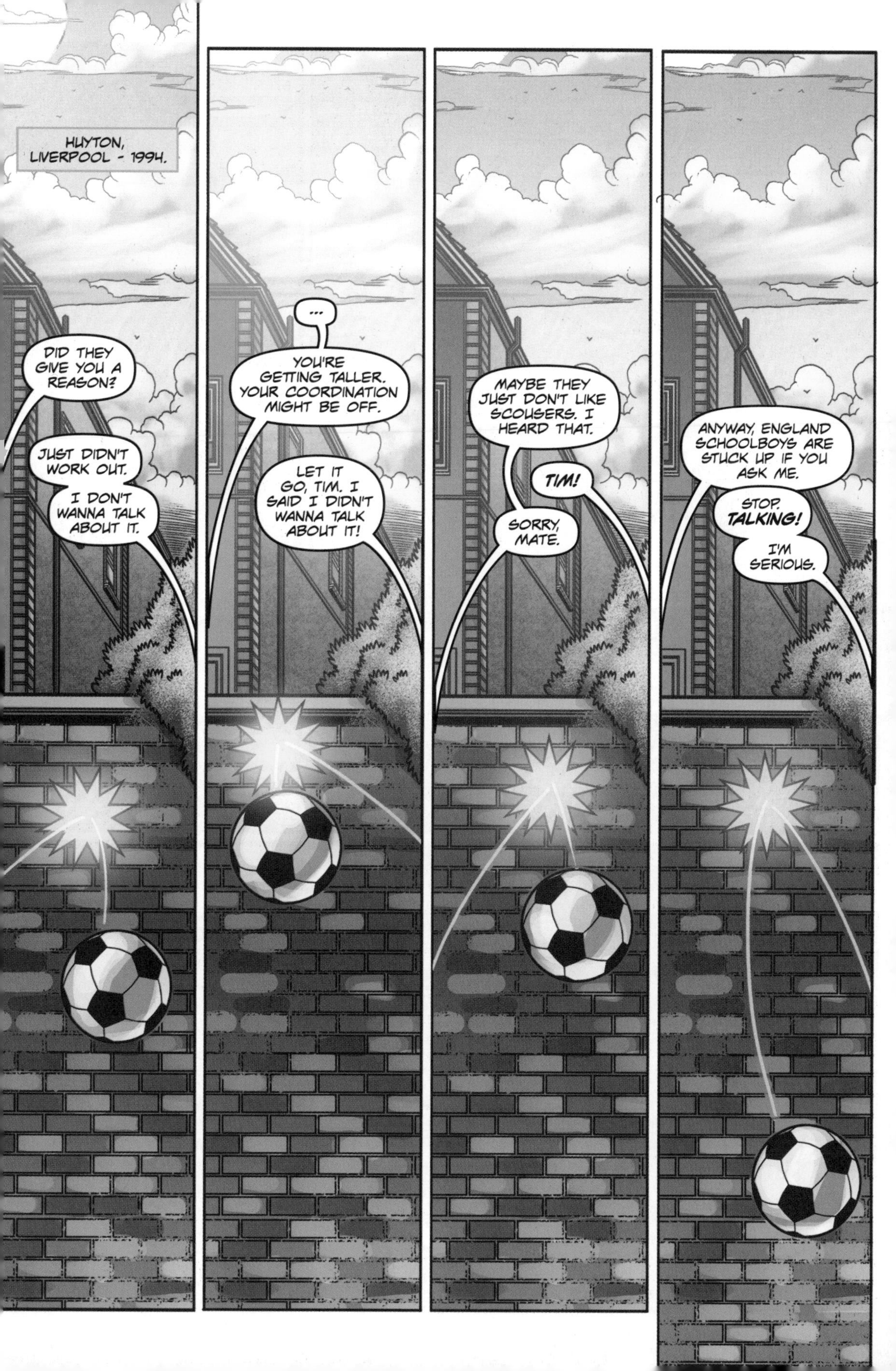
HUYTON, LIVERPOOL - 1994.
DID THEY GIVE YOU A REASON?
JUST DIDN'T WORK OUT.
I DON'T WANNA TALK ABOUT IT.
...
YOU'RE GETTING TALLER. YOUR COORDINATION MIGHT BE OFF.
LET IT GO, TIM. I SAID I DIDN'T WANNA TALK ABOUT IT!
MAYBE THEY JUST DON'T LIKE SCOUSERS. I HEARD THAT.
TIM!
SORRY, MATE.
ANYWAY, ENGLAND SCHOOLBOYS ARE STUCK UP IF YOU ASK ME.
STOP. TALKING!
I'M SERIOUS.

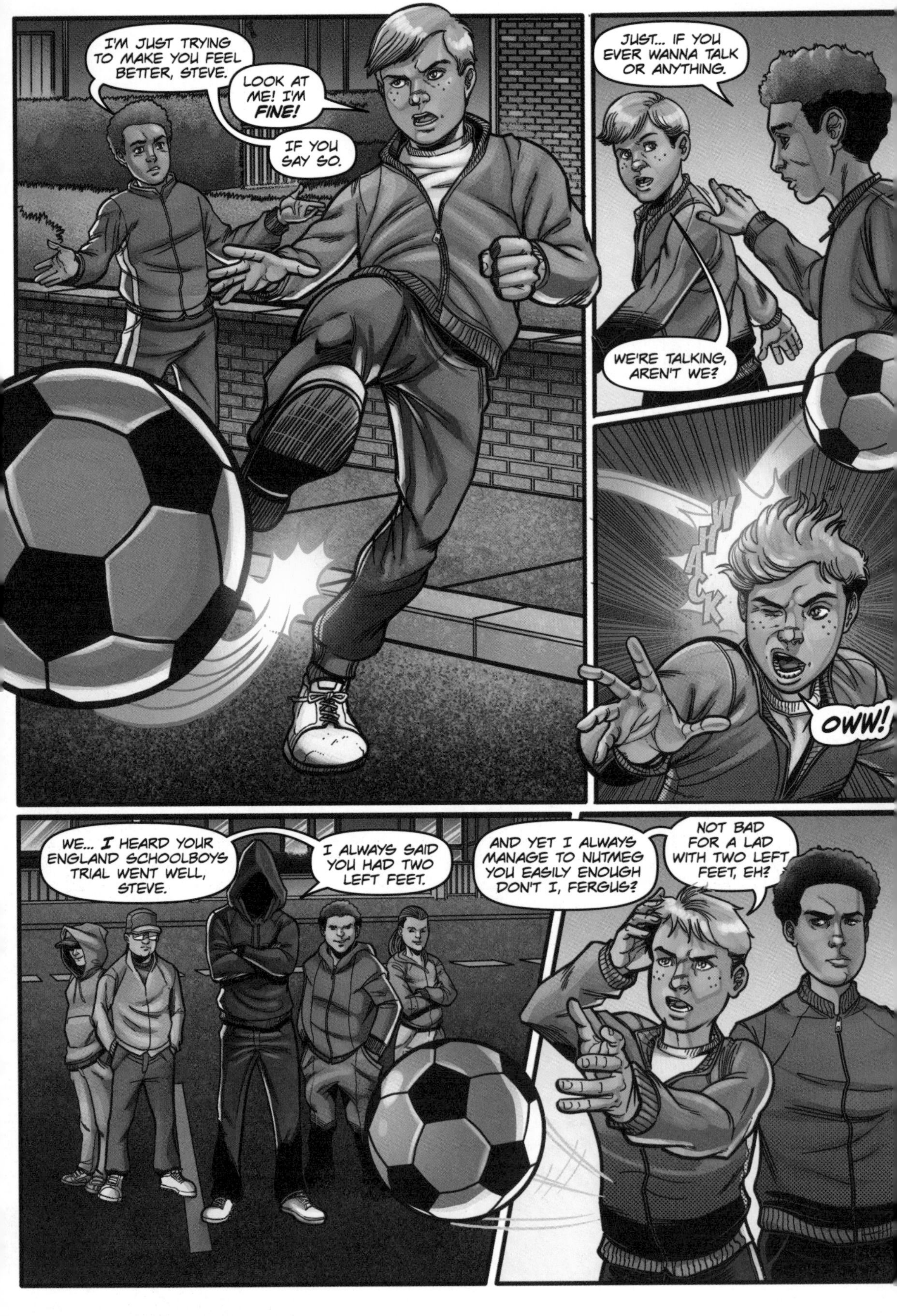
I'M JUST TRYING TO MAKE YOU FEEL BETTER, STEVE.
LOOK AT ME! I'M FINE!
IF YOU SAY SO.
JUST... IF YOU EVER WANNA TALK OR ANYTHING.
WE'RE TALKING, AREN'T WE?
WHHACK
OWW!
WE... I HEARD YOUR ENGLAND SCHOOLBOYS TRIAL WENT WELL, STEVE.
I ALWAYS SAID YOU HAD TWO LEFT FEET.
AND YET I ALWAYS MANAGE TO NUTMEG YOU EASILY ENOUGH DON'T I, FERGUS?
NOT BAD FOR A LAD WITH TWO LEFT FEET, EH?

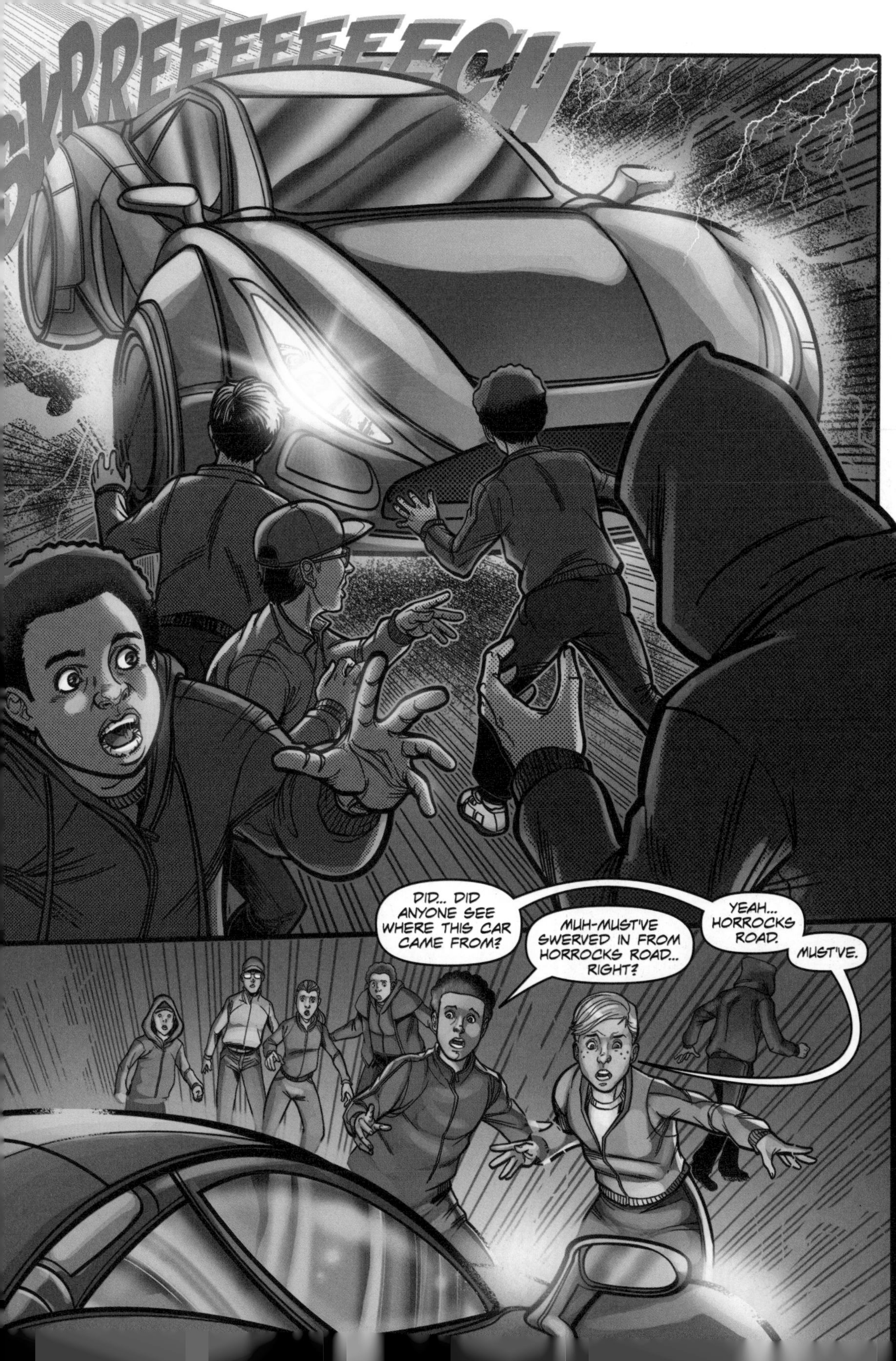
SKRREEEEEEEECH
DID... DID ANYONE SEE WHERE THIS CAR CAME FROM?
MUH-MUST'VE SWERVED IN FROM HORROCKS ROAD... RIGHT?
YEAH... HORROCKS ROAD.
MUST'VE.

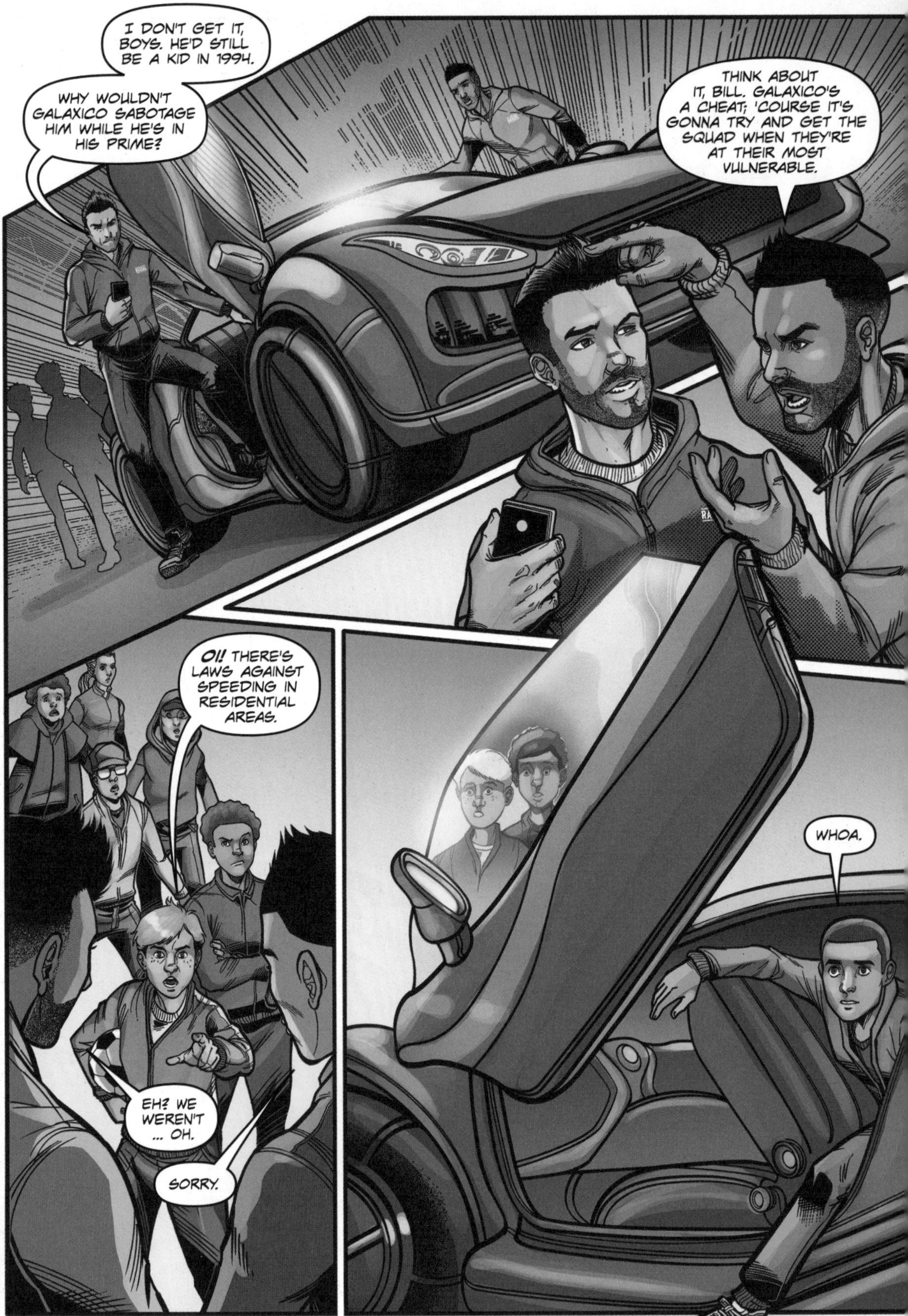
I DON'T GET IT, BOYS. HE'D STILL BE A KID IN 1994.
WHY WOULDN'T GALAXICO SABOTAGE HIM WHILE HE'S IN HIS PRIME?
THINK ABOUT IT, BILL. GALAXICO'S A CHEAT; 'COURSE IT'S GONNA TRY AND GET THE SQUAD WHEN THEY'RE AT THEIR MOST VULNERABLE.
OI! THERE'S LAWS AGAINST SPEEDING IN RESIDENTIAL AREAS.
EH? WE WEREN'T ... OH.
SORRY.
WHOA.

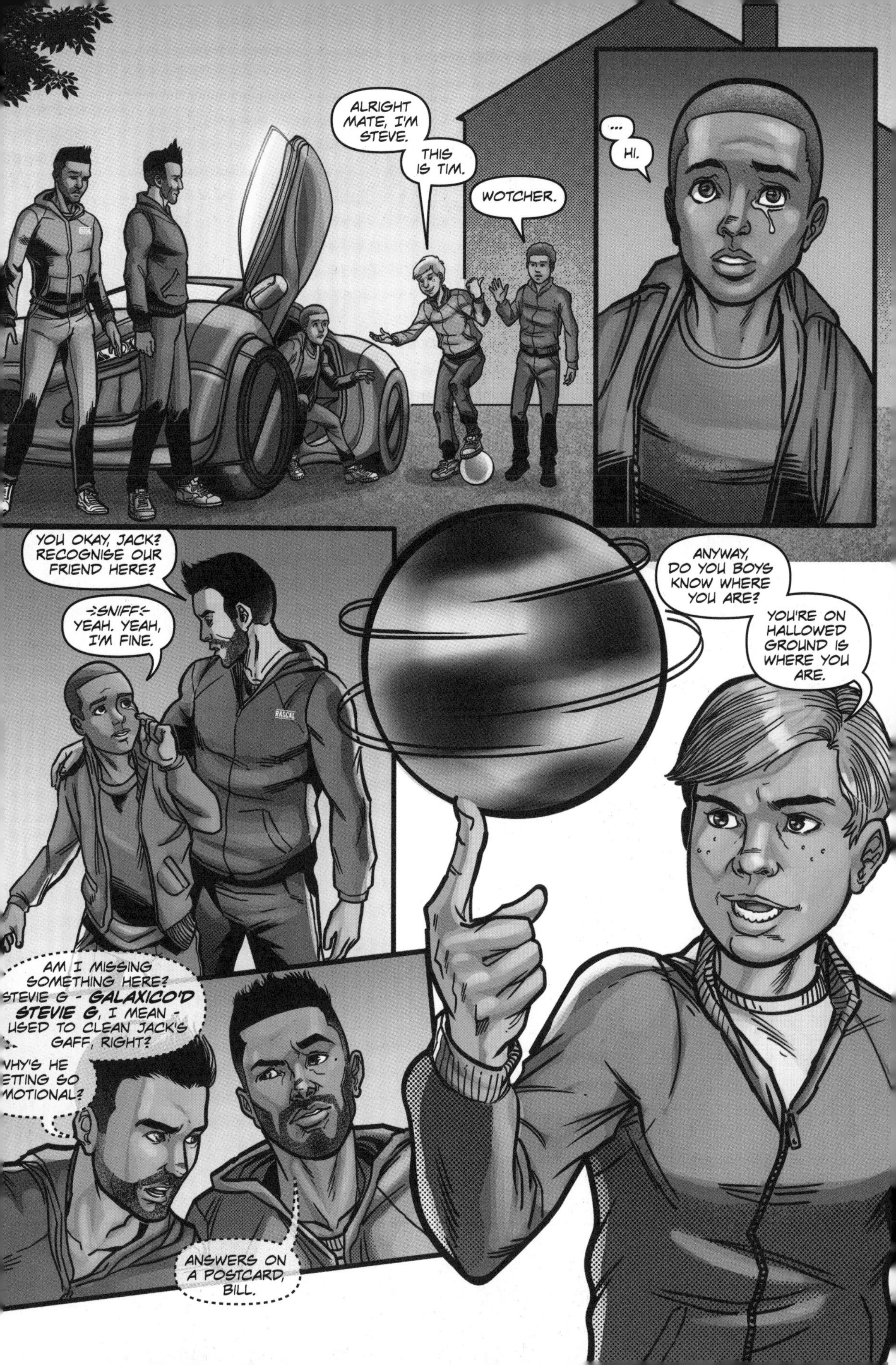
ALRIGHT MATE, I'M STEVE.
THIS IS TIM.
WOTCHER.
...
HI.
YOU OKAY, JACK? RECOGNISE OUR FRIEND HERE?
SNIFF
YEAH. YEAH, I'M FINE.
ANYWAY, DO YOU BOYS KNOW WHERE YOU ARE?
YOU'RE ON HALLOWED GROUND IS WHERE YOU ARE.
AM I MISSING SOMETHING HERE? STEVIE G - GALAXICO'D STEVIE G, I MEAN - USED TO CLEAN JACK'S GAFF, RIGHT?
WHY'S HE GETTING SO EMOTIONAL?
ANSWERS ON A POSTCARD, BILL.

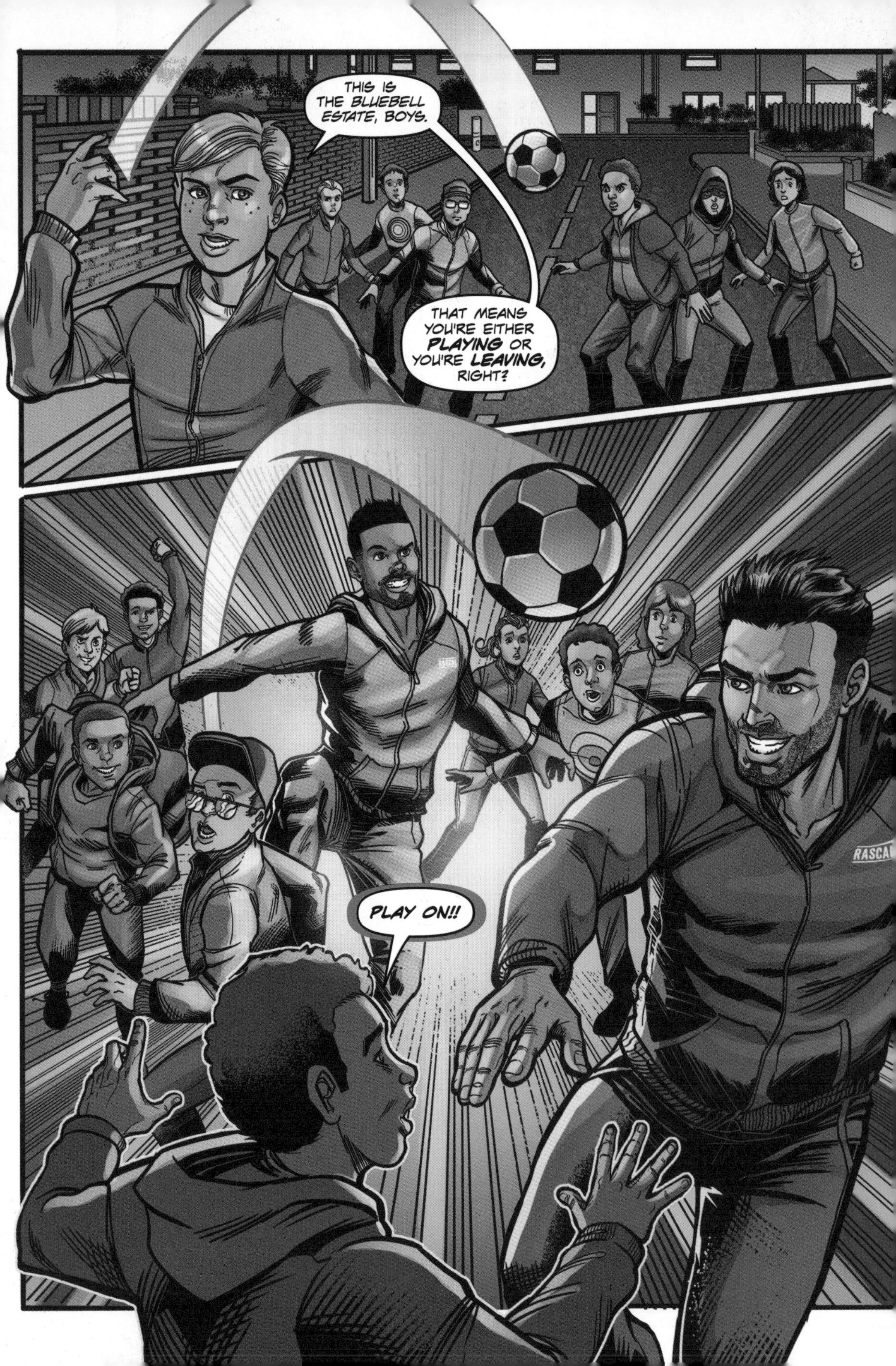
THIS IS THE BLUEBELL ESTATE, BOYS.
THAT MEANS YOU'RE EITHER PLAYING OR YOU'RE LEAVING, RIGHT?
RASCAL
PLAY ON!!

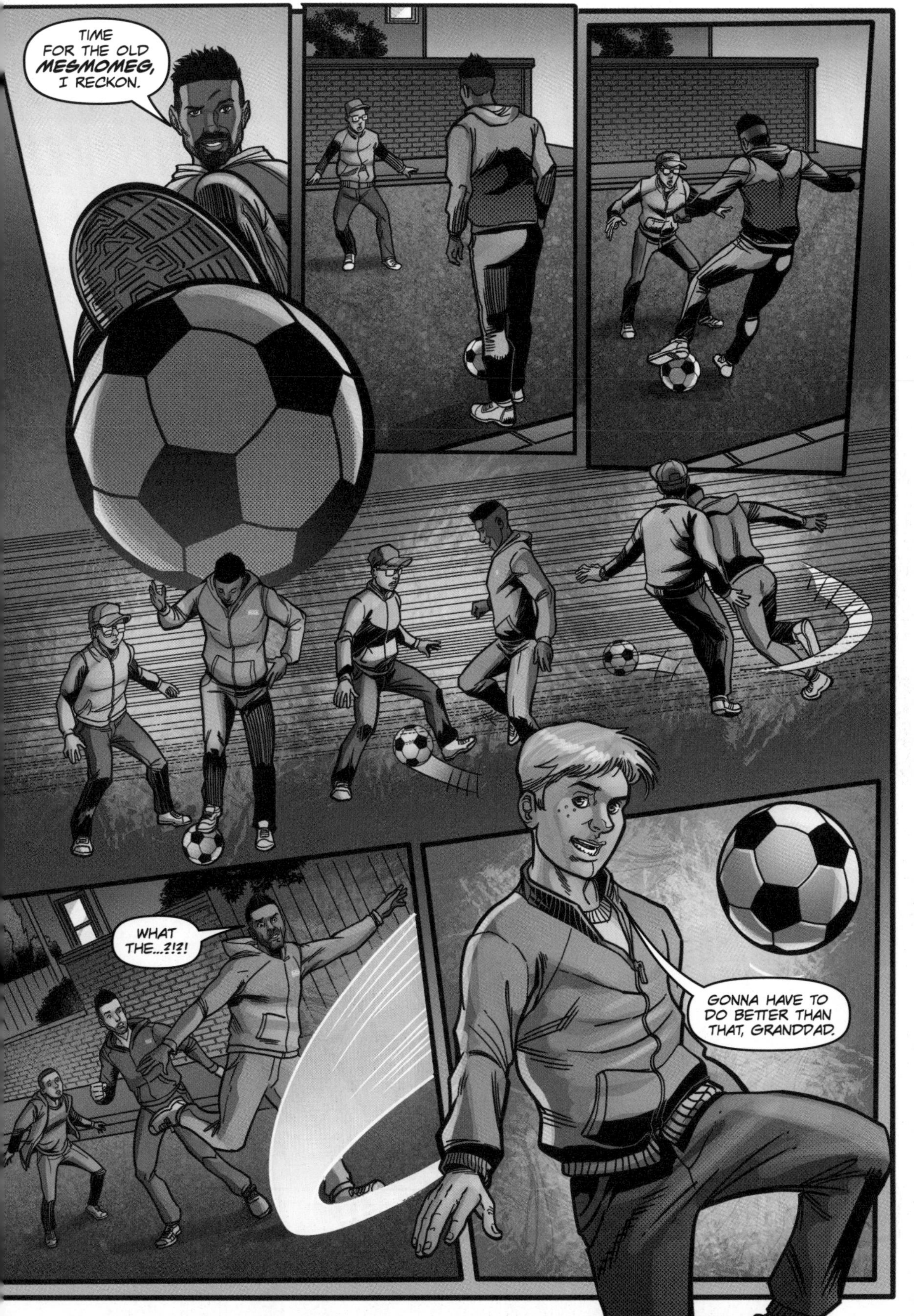
TIME FOR THE OLD MESMOMEG, I RECKON.
WHAT THE...?!?!
GONNA HAVE TO DO BETTER THAN THAT, GRANDDAD.

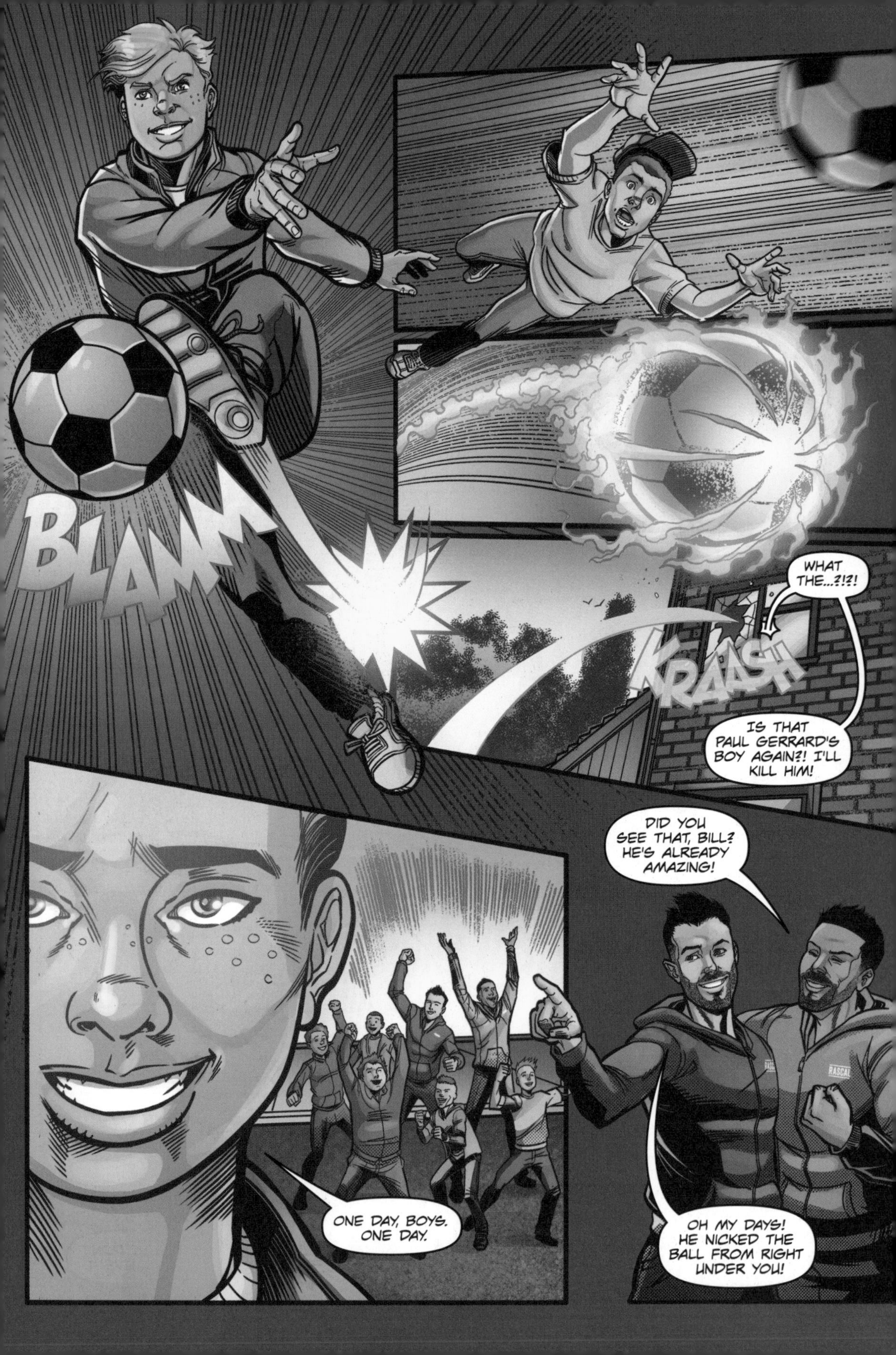
BLAM
KRAASH
WHAT THE...?!?!
IS THAT PAUL GERRARD'S BOY AGAIN?! I'LL KILL HIM!
DID YOU SEE THAT, BILL? HE'S ALREADY AMAZING!
RASCAL
ONE DAY, BOYS. ONE DAY.
OH MY DAYS! HE NICKED THE BALL FROM RIGHT UNDER YOU!

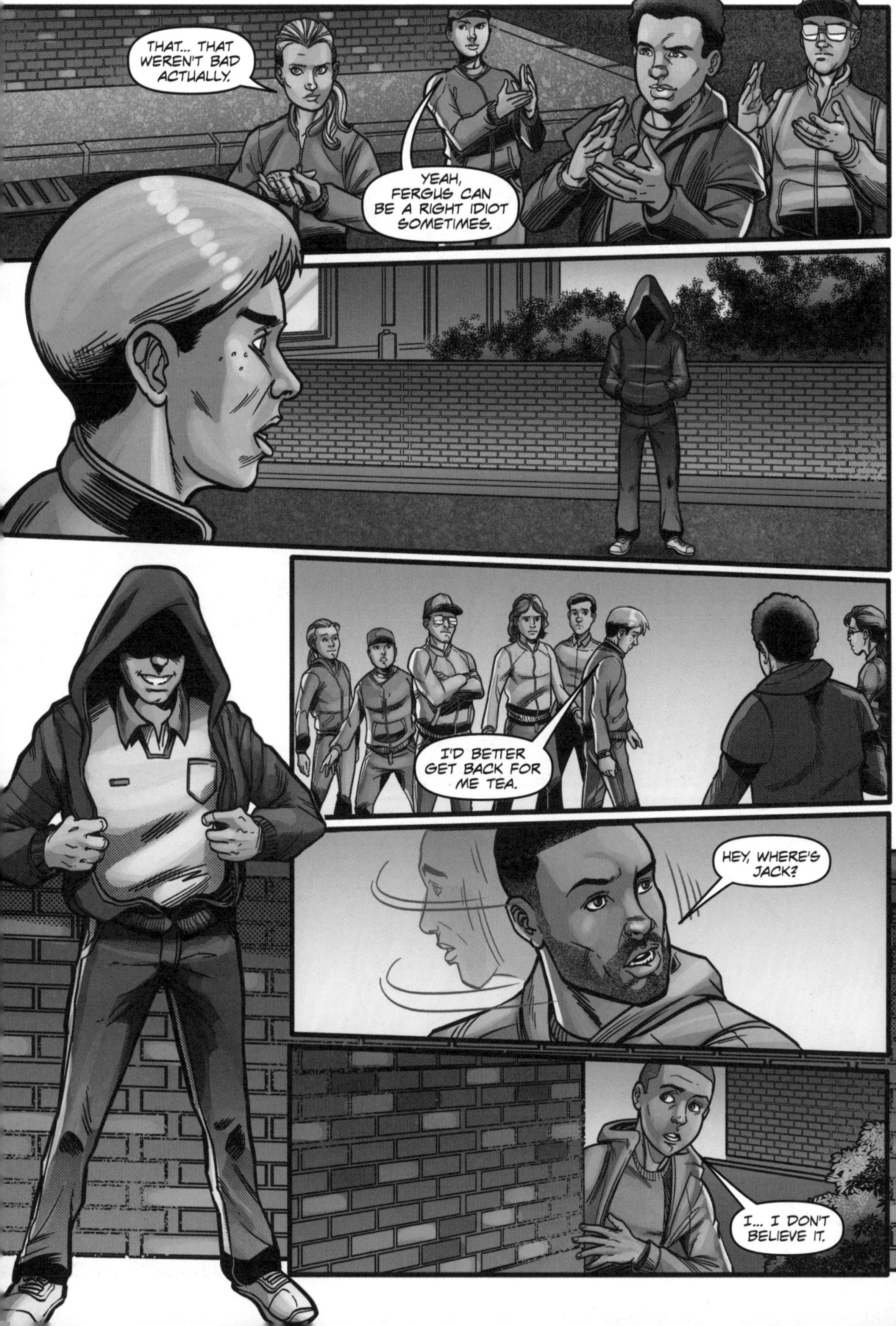
THAT... THAT WEREN'T BAD ACTUALLY.
YEAH, FERGUS CAN BE A RIGHT IDIOT SOMETIMES.
I'D BETTER GET BACK FOR ME TEA.
HEY, WHERE'S JACK?
I... I DON'T BELIEVE IT.

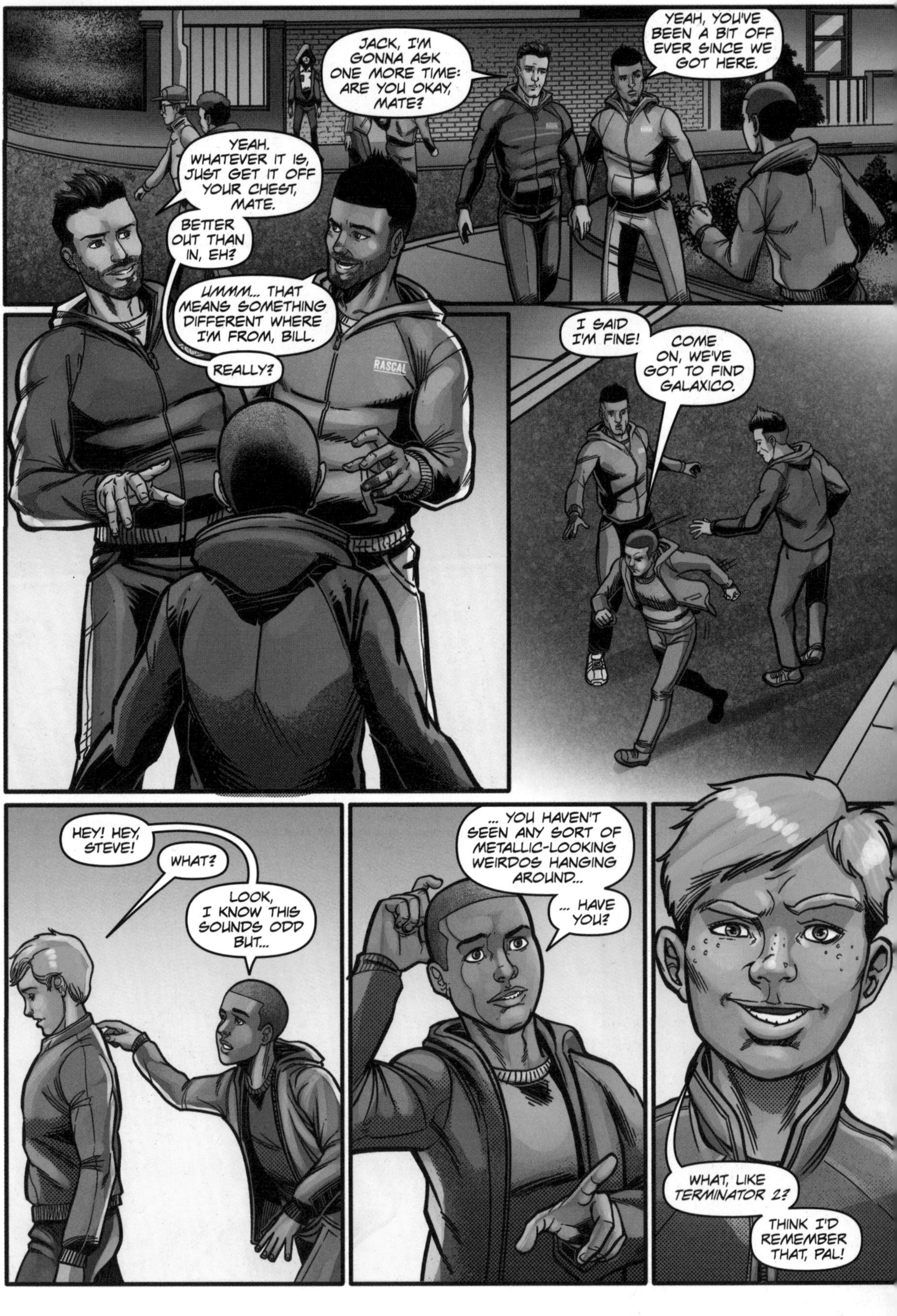
JACK, I'M GONNA ASK ONE MORE TIME: ARE YOU OKAY, MATE?
YEAH, YOU'VE BEEN A BIT OFF EVER SINCE WE GOT HERE.
YEAH. WHATEVER IT IS, JUST GET IT OFF YOUR CHEST, MATE.
BETTER OUT THAN IN, EH?
UMMM... THAT MEANS SOMETHING DIFFERENT WHERE I'M FROM, BILL.
REALLY?
RASCAL
I SAID I'M FINE!
COME ON, WE'VE GOT TO FIND GALAXICO.
HEY! HEY, STEVE!
WHAT?
LOOK, I KNOW THIS SOUNDS ODD BUT...
... YOU HAVEN'T SEEN ANY SORT OF METALLIC-LOOKING WEIRDOS HANGING AROUND...
... HAVE YOU?
WHAT, LIKE *TERMINATOR 2*?
THINK I'D REMEMBER THAT, PAL!

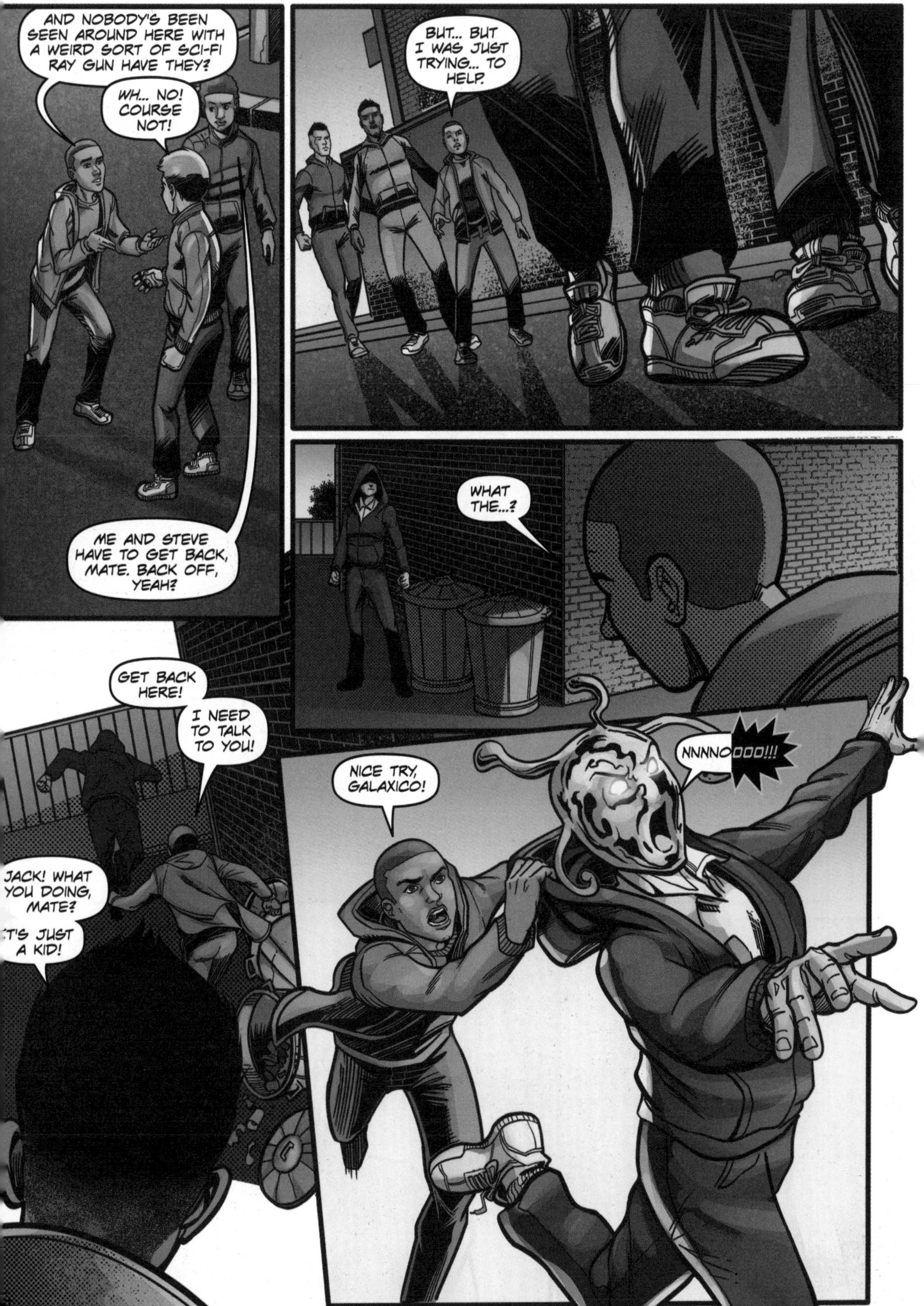
AND NOBODY'S BEEN SEEN AROUND HERE WITH A WEIRD SORT OF SCI-FI RAY GUN HAVE THEY?
WH... NO! COURSE NOT!
ME AND STEVE HAVE TO GET BACK, MATE. BACK OFF, YEAH?
BUT... BUT I WAS JUST TRYING... TO HELP.
WHAT THE...?
GET BACK HERE!
I NEED TO TALK TO YOU!
JACK! WHAT YOU DOING, MATE?
T'S JUST A KID!
NICE TRY, GALAXICO!
NNNNOOOO!!!

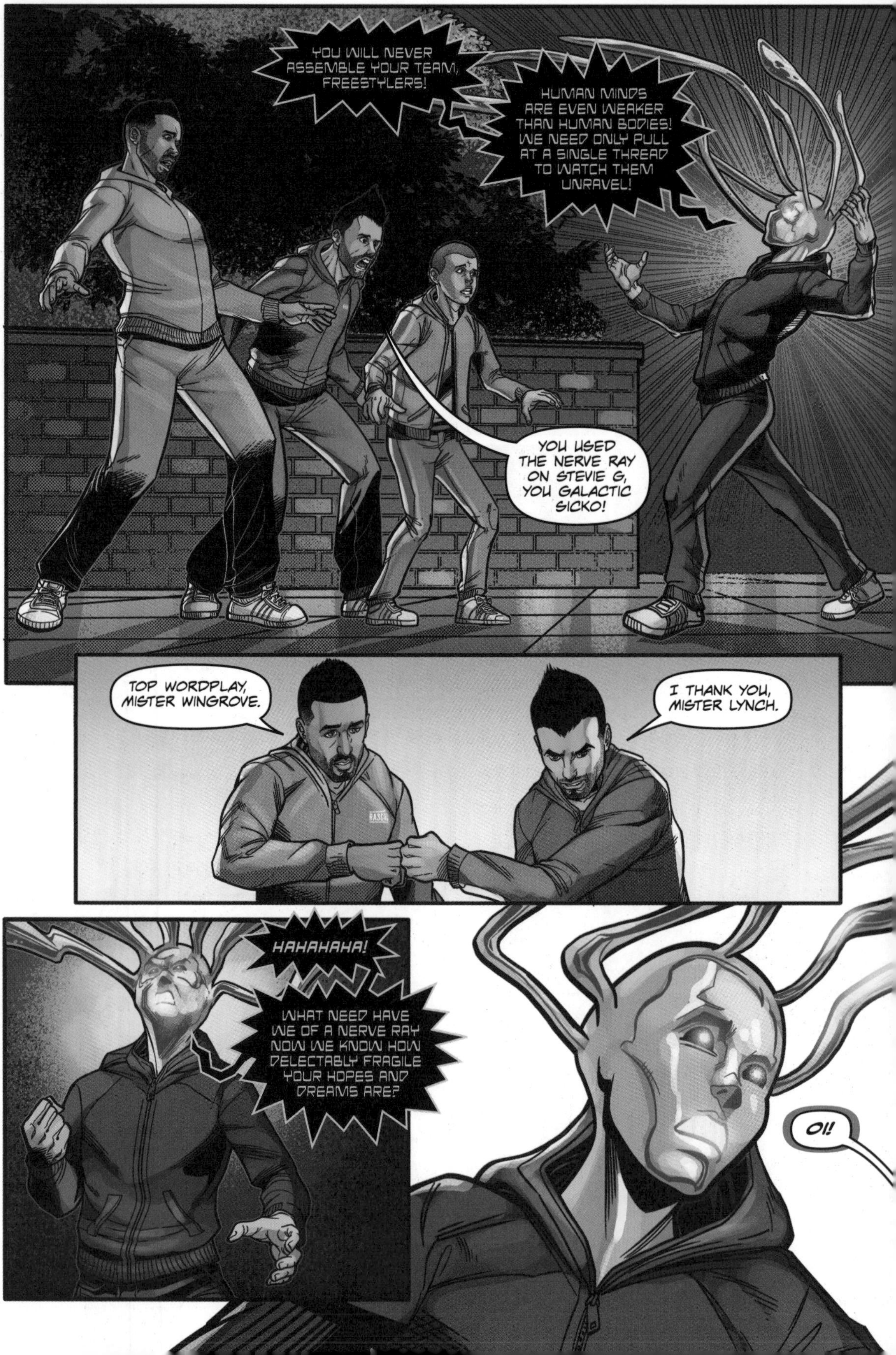
YOU WILL NEVER ASSEMBLE YOUR TEAM, FREESTYLERS!
HUMAN MINDS ARE EVEN WEAKER THAN HUMAN BODIES! WE NEED ONLY PULL AT A SINGLE THREAD TO WATCH THEM UNRAVEL!
YOU USED THE NERVE RAY ON STEVIE G, YOU GALACTIC SICKO!
TOP WORDPLAY, MISTER WINGROVE.
I THANK YOU, MISTER LYNCH.
HAHAHAHA!
WHAT NEED HAVE WE OF A NERVE RAY NOW WE KNOW HOW DELECTABLY FRAGILE YOUR HOPES AND DREAMS ARE?
OI!

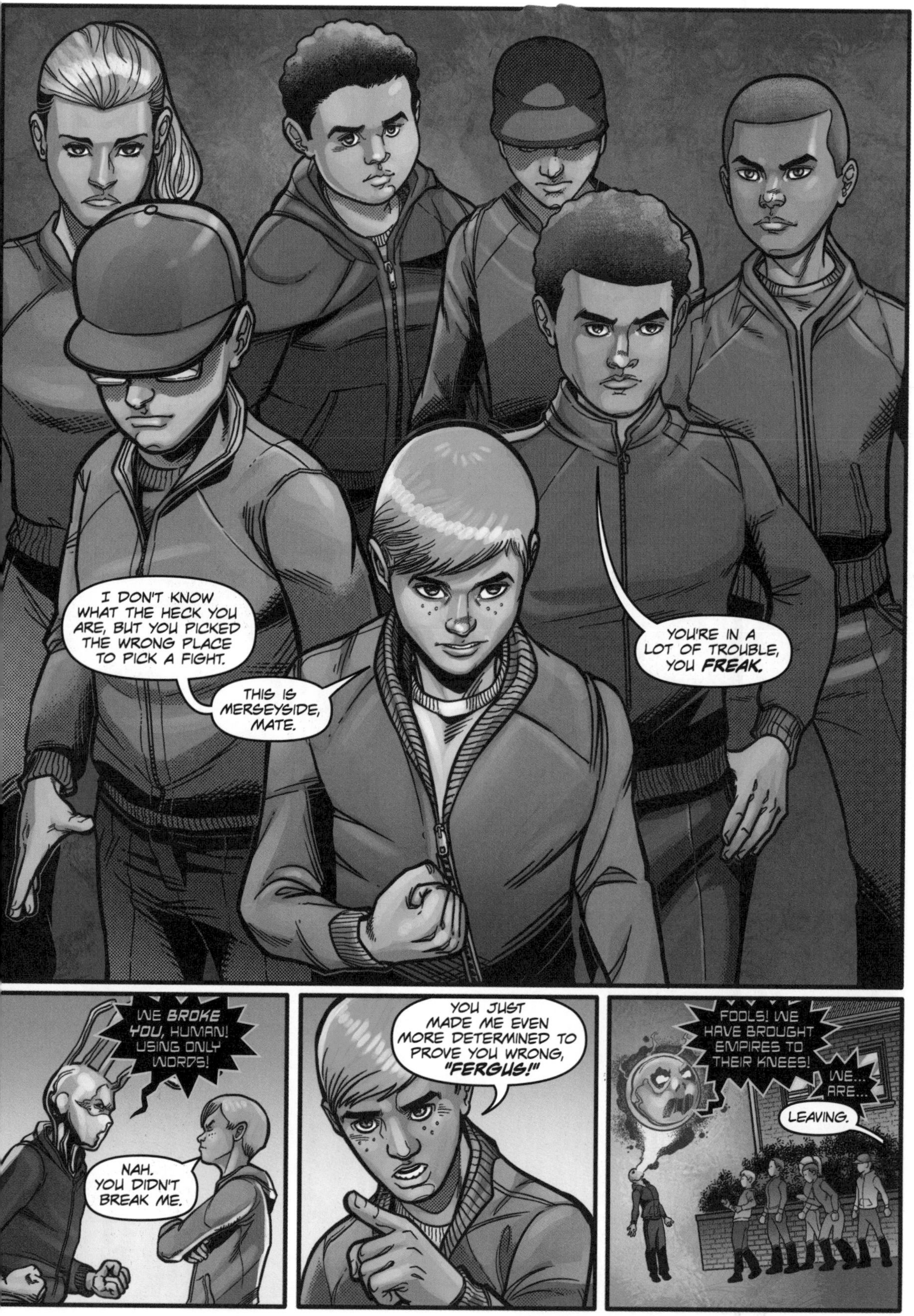
I DON'T KNOW WHAT THE HECK YOU ARE, BUT YOU PICKED THE WRONG PLACE TO PICK A FIGHT.
THIS IS MERSEYSIDE, MATE.
YOU'RE IN A LOT OF TROUBLE, YOU FREAK.
WE BROKE YOU, HUMAN! USING ONLY WORDS!
NAH. YOU DIDN'T BREAK ME.
YOU JUST MADE ME EVEN MORE DETERMINED TO PROVE YOU WRONG, "FERGUS!"
FOOLS! WE HAVE BROUGHT EMPIRES TO THEIR KNEES!
WE... ARE...
LEAVING.

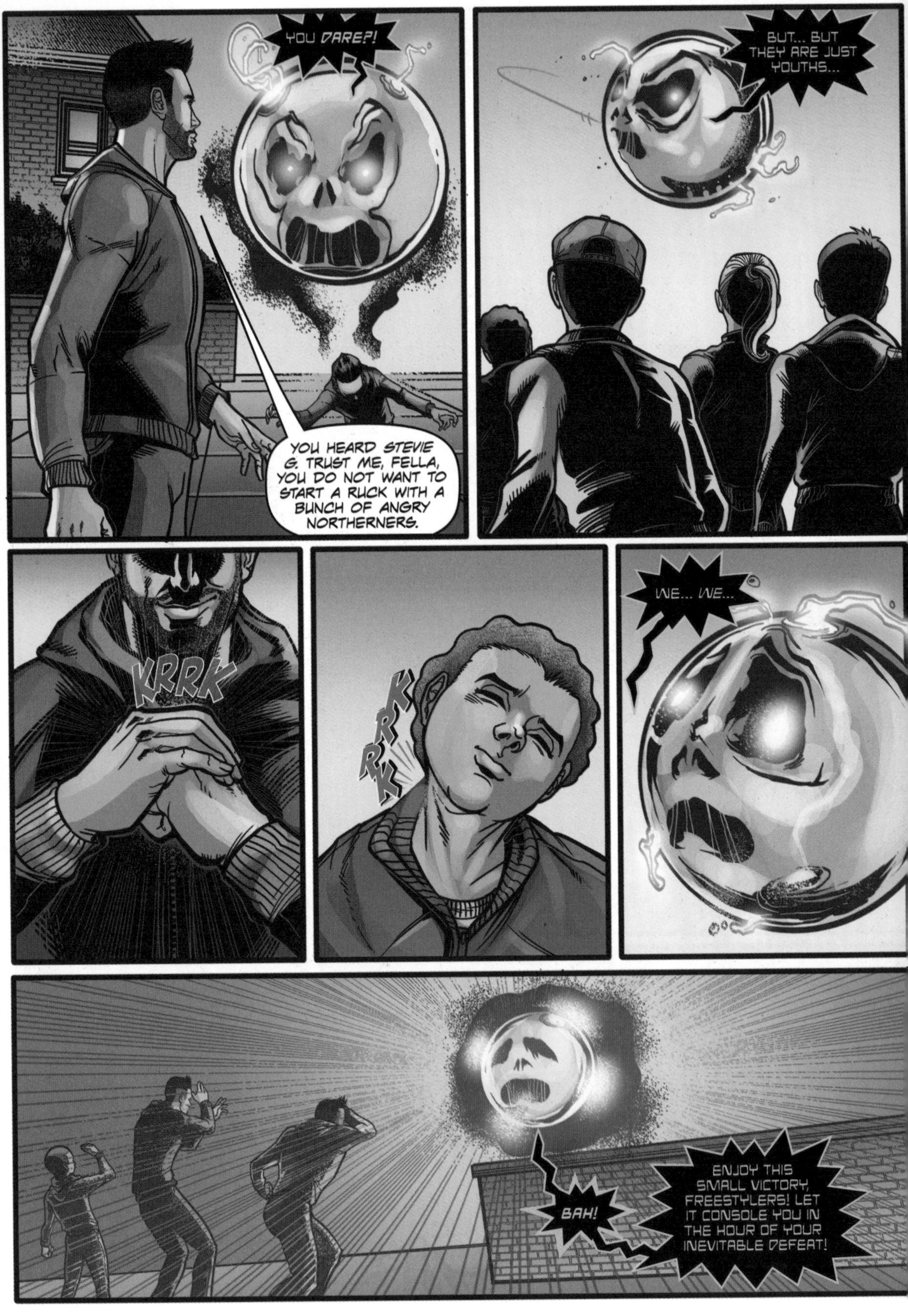
YOU DARE?!
YOU HEARD STEVIE G. TRUST ME, FELLA, YOU DO NOT WANT TO START A RUCK WITH A BUNCH OF ANGRY NORTHERNERS.
BUT... BUT THEY ARE JUST YOUTHS...
KRRK
KRRK
WE... WE...
BAH!
ENJOY THIS SMALL VICTORY, FREESTYLERS! LET IT CONSOLE YOU IN THE HOUR OF YOUR INEVITABLE DEFEAT!

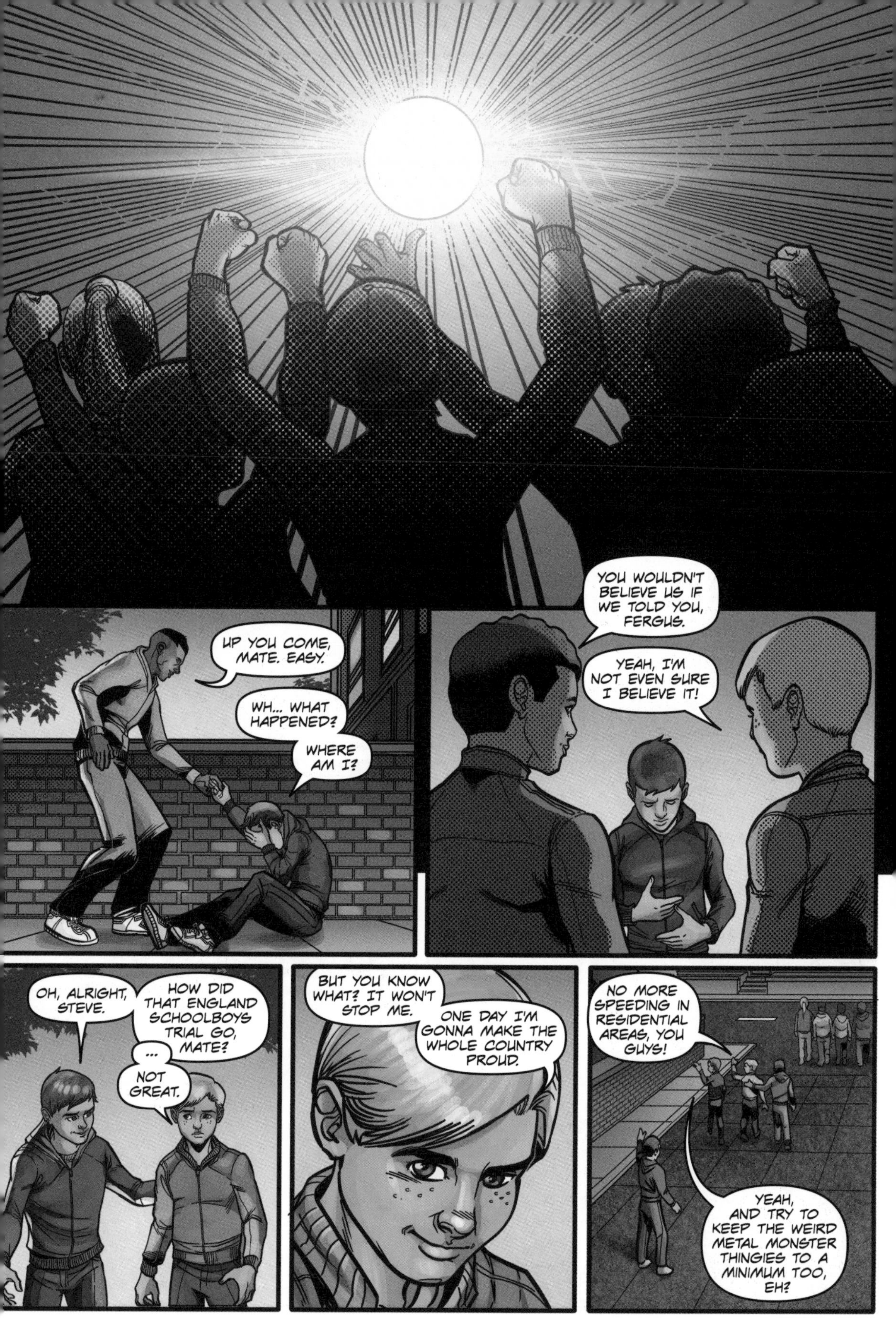
YOU WOULDN'T BELIEVE US IF WE TOLD YOU, FERGUS.
UP YOU COME, MATE. EASY.
WH... WHAT HAPPENED?
WHERE AM I?
YEAH, I'M NOT EVEN SURE I BELIEVE IT!
OH, ALRIGHT, STEVE.
HOW DID THAT ENGLAND SCHOOLBOYS TRIAL GO, MATE?
...
NOT GREAT.
BUT YOU KNOW WHAT? IT WON'T STOP ME.
ONE DAY I'M GONNA MAKE THE WHOLE COUNTRY PROUD.
NO MORE SPEEDING IN RESIDENTIAL AREAS, YOU GUYS!
YEAH, AND TRY TO KEEP THE WEIRD METAL MONSTER THINGIES TO A MINIMUM TOO, EH?

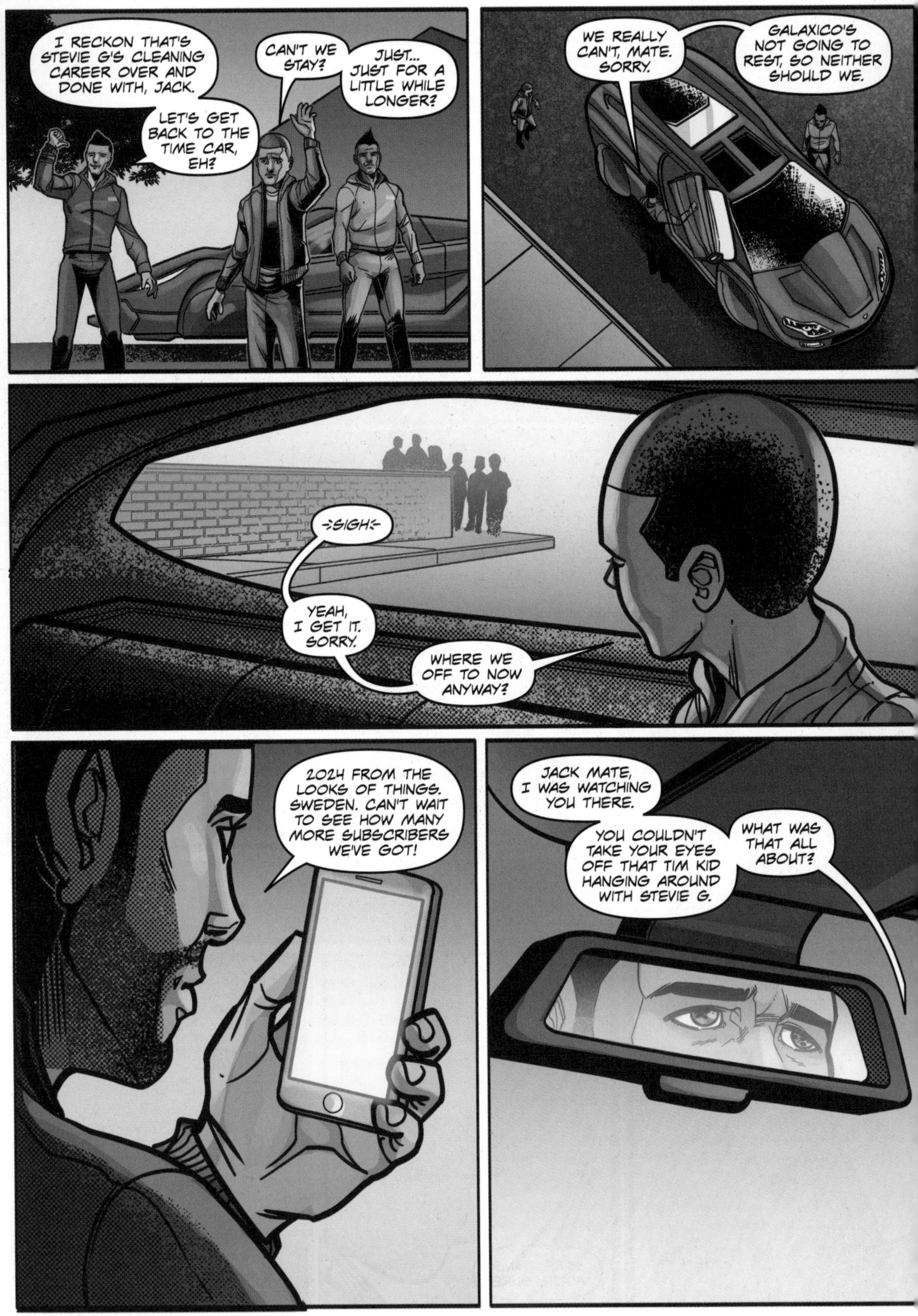
I RECKON THAT'S STEVIE G'S CLEANING CAREER OVER AND DONE WITH, JACK.
LET'S GET BACK TO THE TIME CAR, EH?
CAN'T WE STAY?
JUST... JUST FOR A LITTLE WHILE LONGER?
WE REALLY CAN'T, MATE. SORRY.
GALAXICO'S NOT GOING TO REST, SO NEITHER SHOULD WE.
SIGH
YEAH, I GET IT. SORRY.
WHERE WE OFF TO NOW ANYWAY?
2024 FROM THE LOOKS OF THINGS. SWEDEN. CAN'T WAIT TO SEE HOW MANY MORE SUBSCRIBERS WE'VE GOT!
JACK MATE, I WAS WATCHING YOU THERE.
YOU COULDN'T TAKE YOUR EYES OFF THAT TIM KID HANGING AROUND WITH STEVIE G.
WHAT WAS THAT ALL ABOUT?

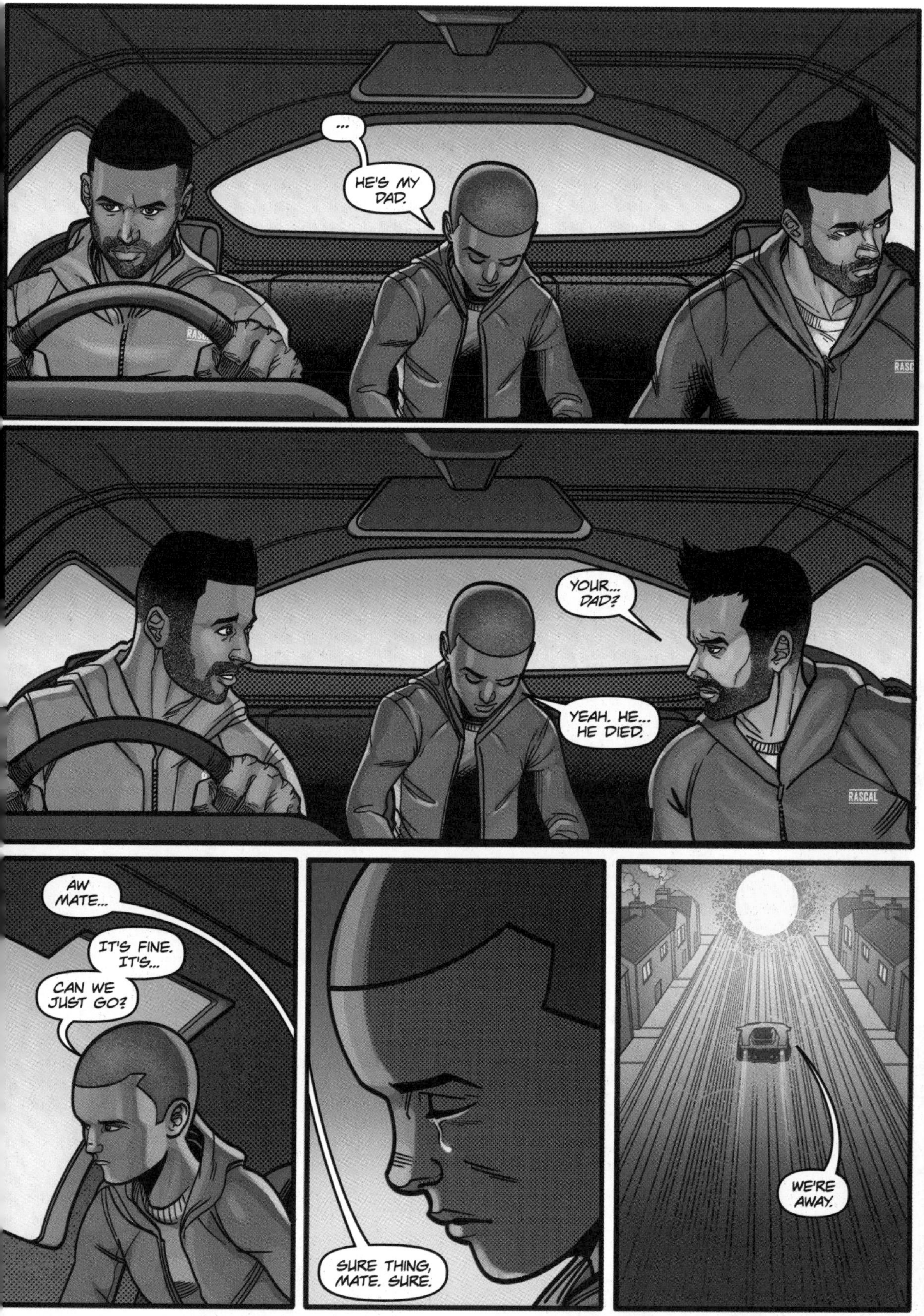
...
HE'S MY DAD.
YOUR... DAD?
YEAH. HE... HE DIED.
AW MATE...
IT'S FINE. IT'S...
CAN WE JUST GO?
SURE THING, MATE. SURE.
WE'RE AWAY.

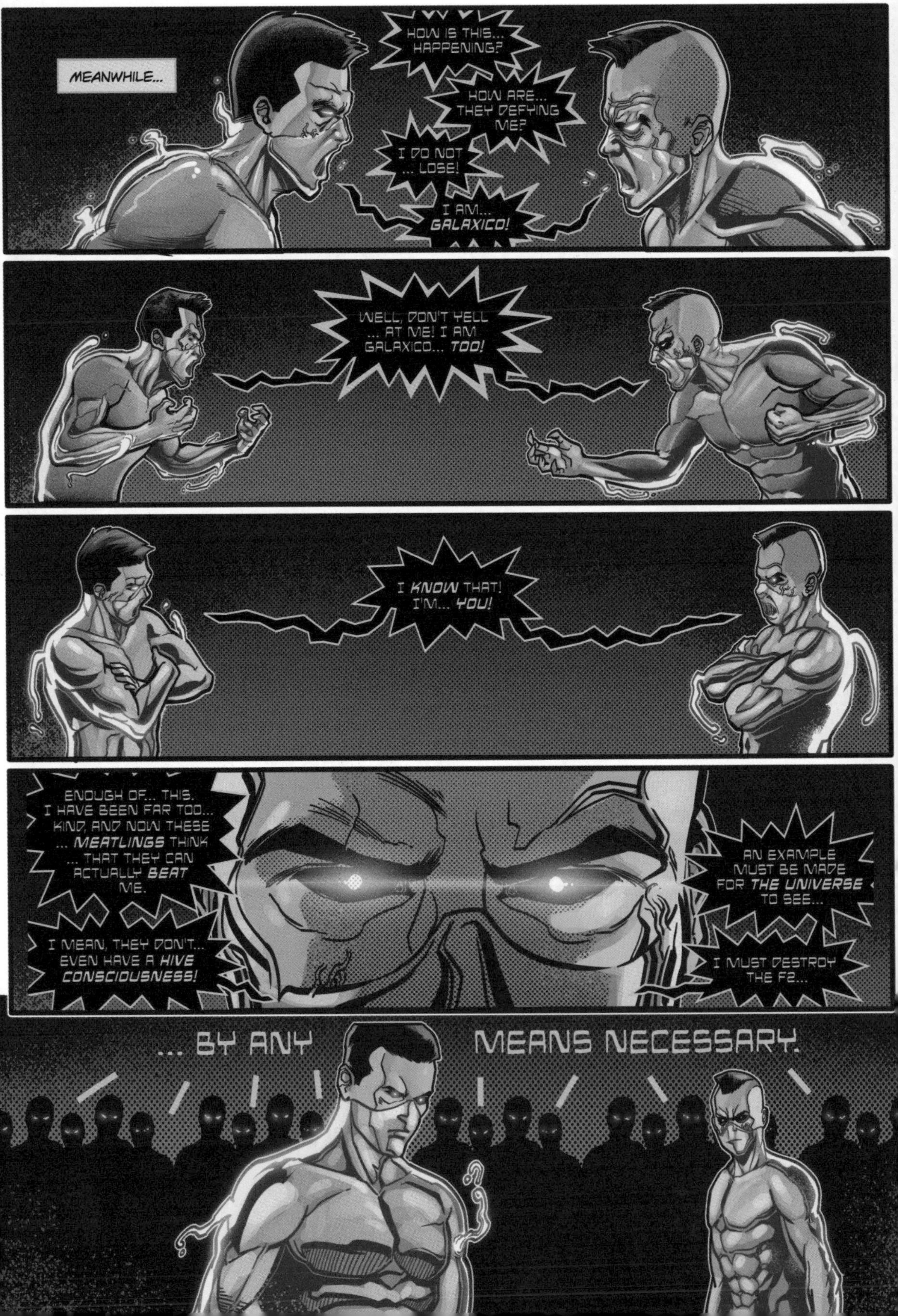
MEANWHILE...
HOW IS THIS... HAPPENING?
HOW ARE... THEY DEFYING ME?
I DO NOT ... LOSE!
I AM... GALAXICO!
WELL, DON'T YELL ... AT ME! I AM GALAXICO... TOO!
I KNOW THAT! I'M... YOU!
ENOUGH OF... THIS. I HAVE BEEN FAR TOO... KIND, AND NOW THESE ... MEATLINGS THINK ... THAT THEY CAN ACTUALLY BEAT ME.
I MEAN, THEY DON'T... EVEN HAVE A HIVE CONSCIOUSNESS!
AN EXAMPLE MUST BE MADE FOR THE UNIVERSE TO SEE...
I MUST DESTROY THE F2...
... BY ANY MEANS NECESSARY.

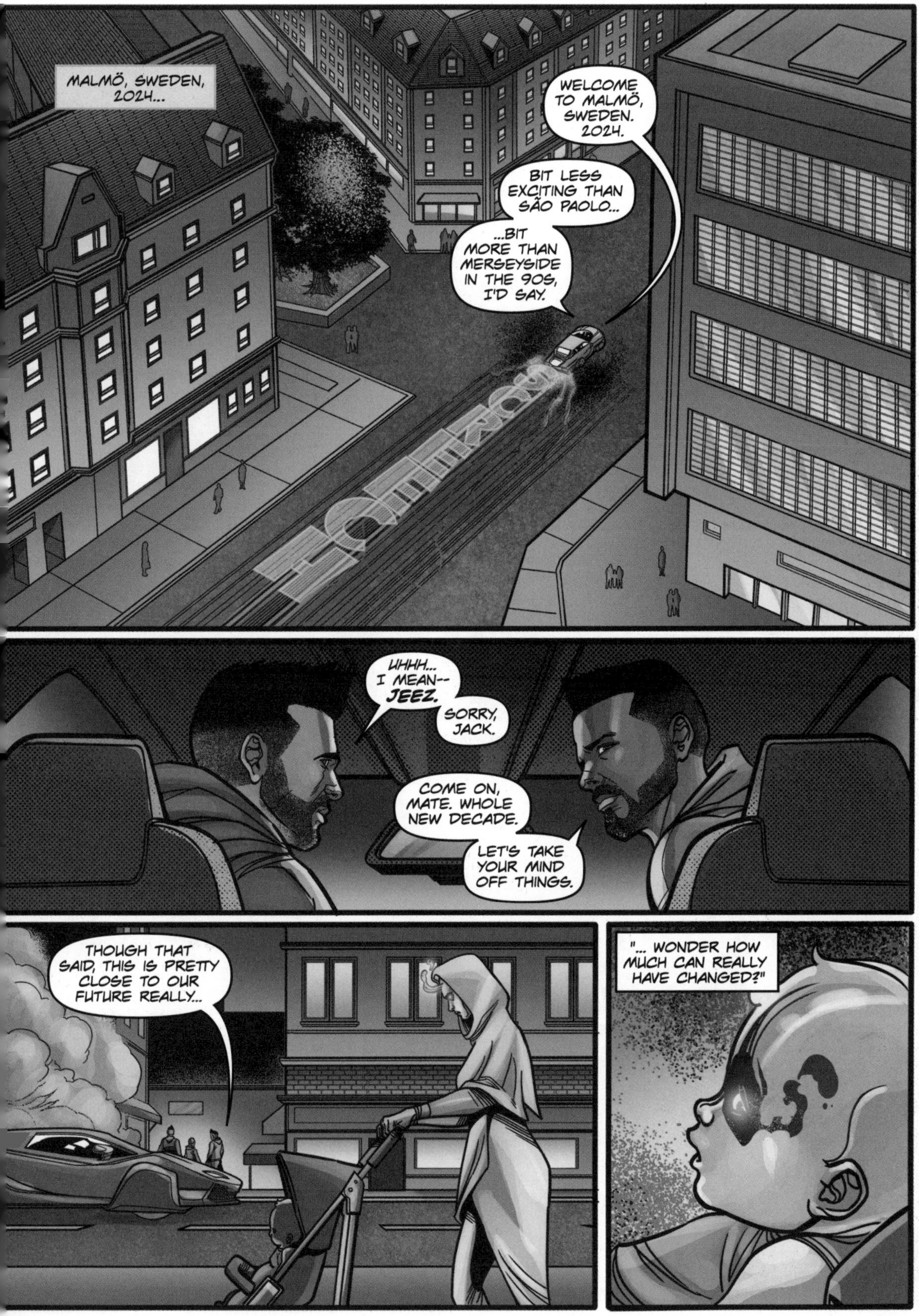

MALMÖ, SWEDEN, 2024...
WELCOME TO MALMÖ, SWEDEN. 2024.
BIT LESS EXCITING THAN SÃO PAOLO...
...BIT MORE THAN MERSEYSIDE IN THE 90S, I'D SAY.
UHHH... I MEAN-- JEEZ.
SORRY, JACK.
COME ON, MATE. WHOLE NEW DECADE.
LET'S TAKE YOUR MIND OFF THINGS.
THOUGH THAT SAID, THIS IS PRETTY CLOSE TO OUR FUTURE REALLY...
"... WONDER HOW MUCH CAN REALLY HAVE CHANGED?"

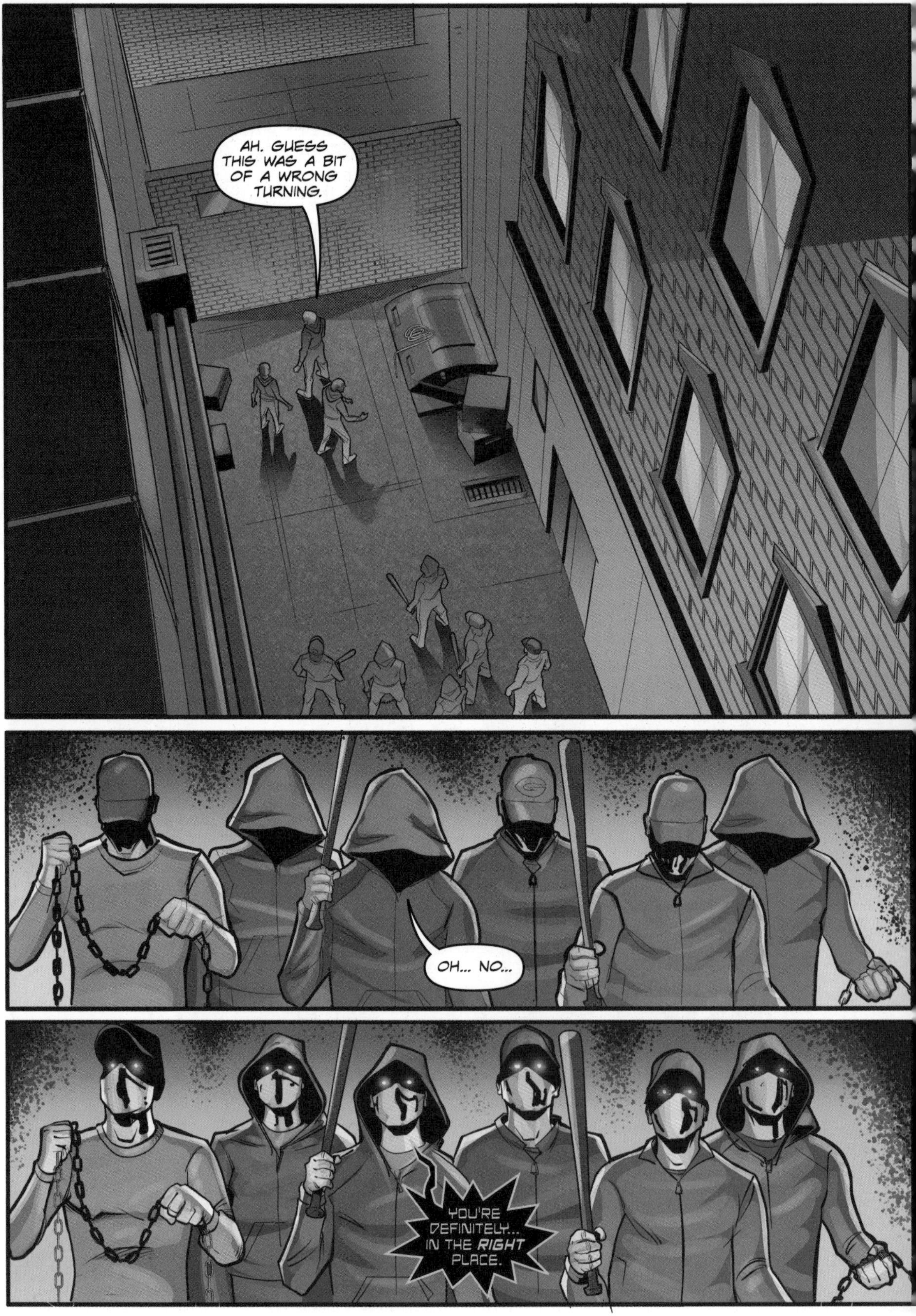
AH. GUESS THIS WAS A BIT OF A WRONG TURNING.
OH... NO...
YOU'RE DEFINITELY... IN THE *RIGHT* PLACE.

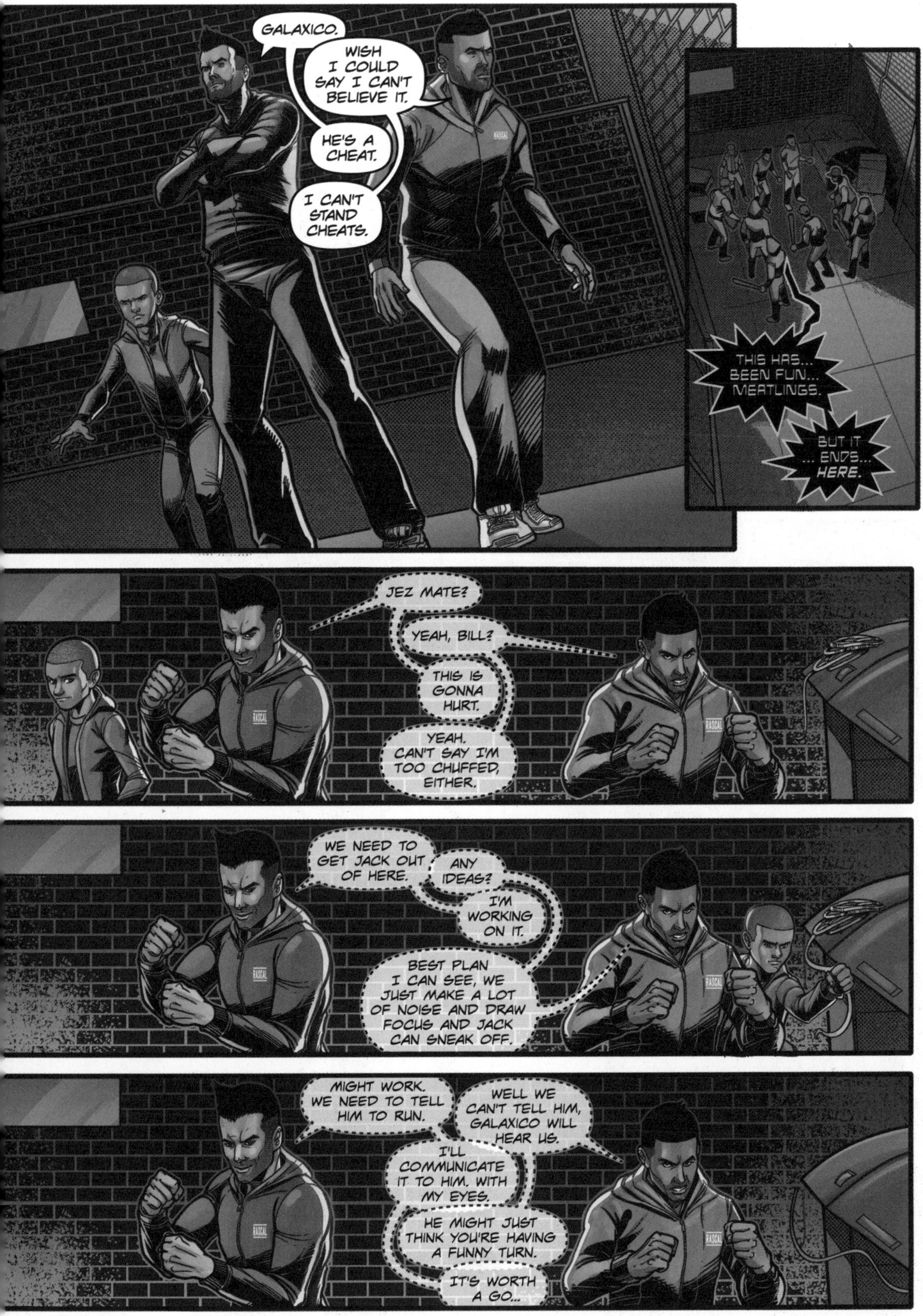
GALAXICO.
WISH I COULD SAY I CAN'T BELIEVE IT.
HE'S A CHEAT.
I CAN'T STAND CHEATS.
THIS HAS... BEEN FUN... MEATLINGS.
BUT IT ... ENDS... HERE.
JEZ MATE?
YEAH, BILL?
THIS IS GONNA HURT.
YEAH. CAN'T SAY I'M TOO CHUFFED, EITHER.
WE NEED TO GET JACK OUT OF HERE.
ANY IDEAS?
I'M WORKING ON IT.
BEST PLAN I CAN SEE, WE JUST MAKE A LOT OF NOISE AND DRAW FOCUS AND JACK CAN SNEAK OFF.
MIGHT WORK. WE NEED TO TELL HIM TO RUN.
WELL WE CAN'T TELL HIM, GALAXICO WILL HEAR US.
I'LL COMMUNICATE IT TO HIM. WITH MY EYES.
HE MIGHT JUST THINK YOU'RE HAVING A FUNNY TURN.
IT'S WORTH A GO...

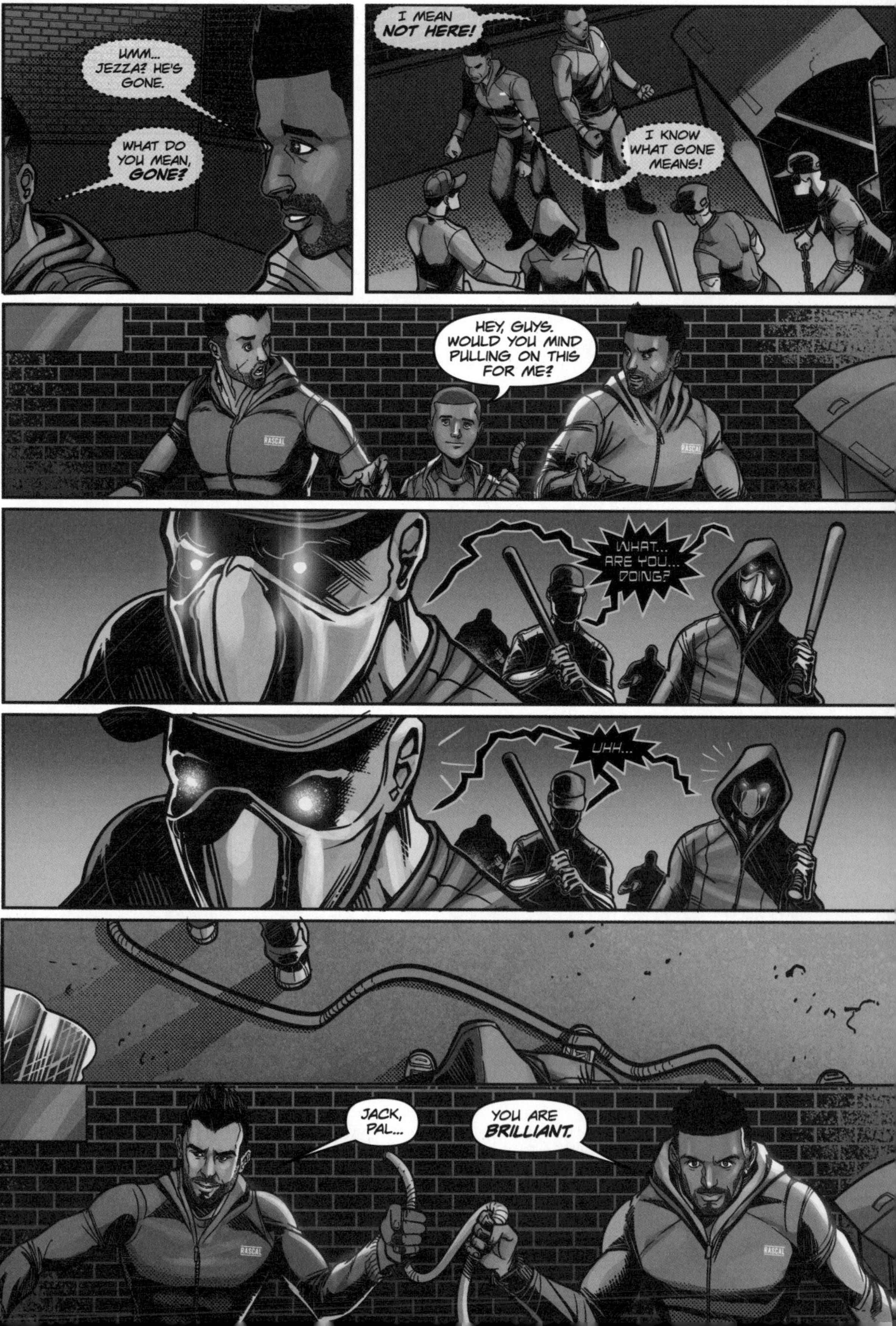
UMM... JEZZA? HE'S GONE.
WHAT DO YOU MEAN, GONE?
I MEAN NOT HERE!
I KNOW WHAT GONE MEANS!
HEY, GUYS. WOULD YOU MIND PULLING ON THIS FOR ME?
RASCAL
RASCAL
WHAT... ARE YOU... DOING?
UHH...
JACK, PAL...
YOU ARE BRILLIANT.
RASCAL
RASCAL

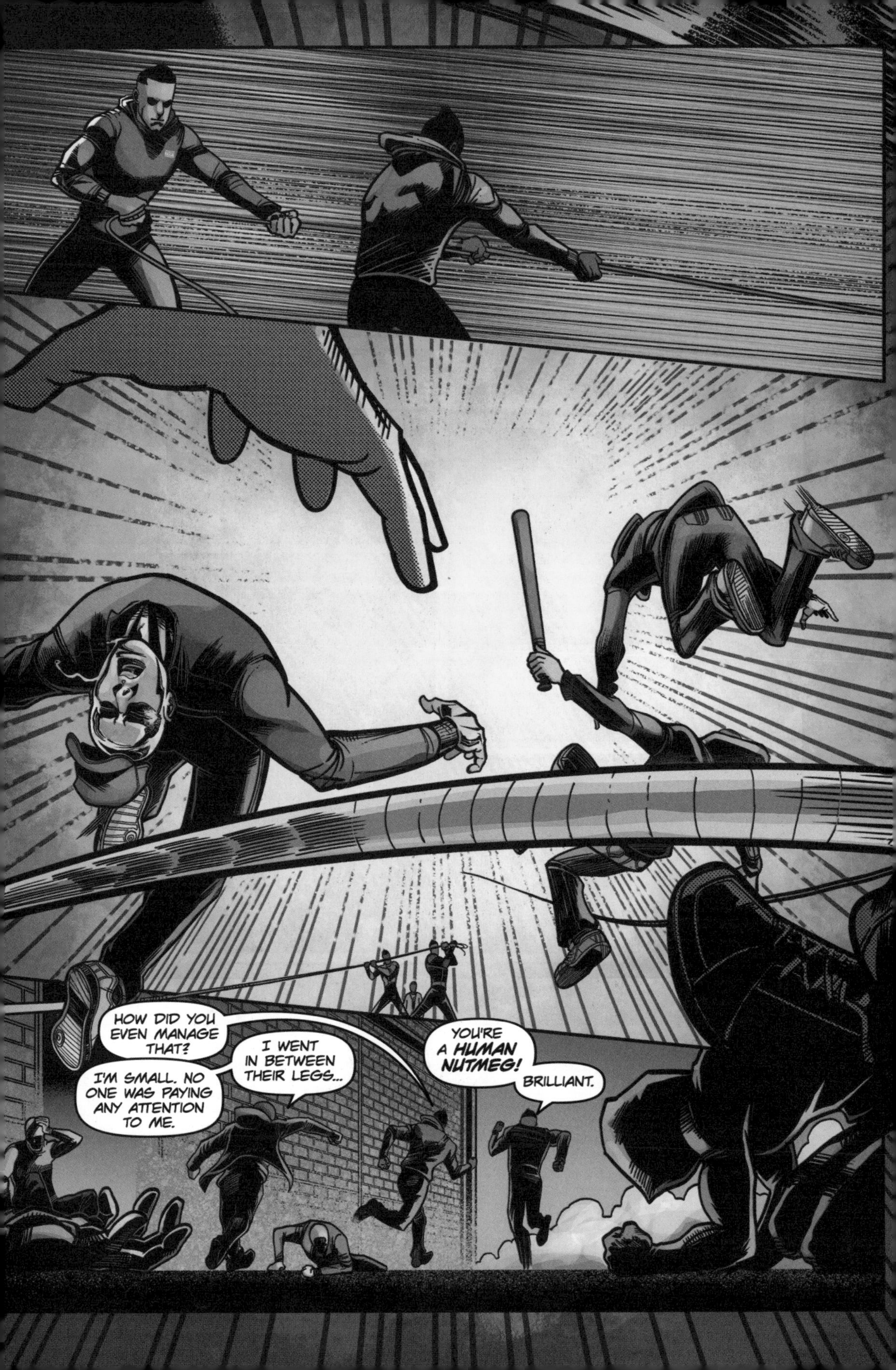
HOW DID YOU EVEN MANAGE THAT?
I'M SMALL. NO ONE WAS PAYING ANY ATTENTION TO ME.
I WENT IN BETWEEN THEIR LEGS...
YOU'RE A **HUMAN NUTMEG!**
BRILLIANT.

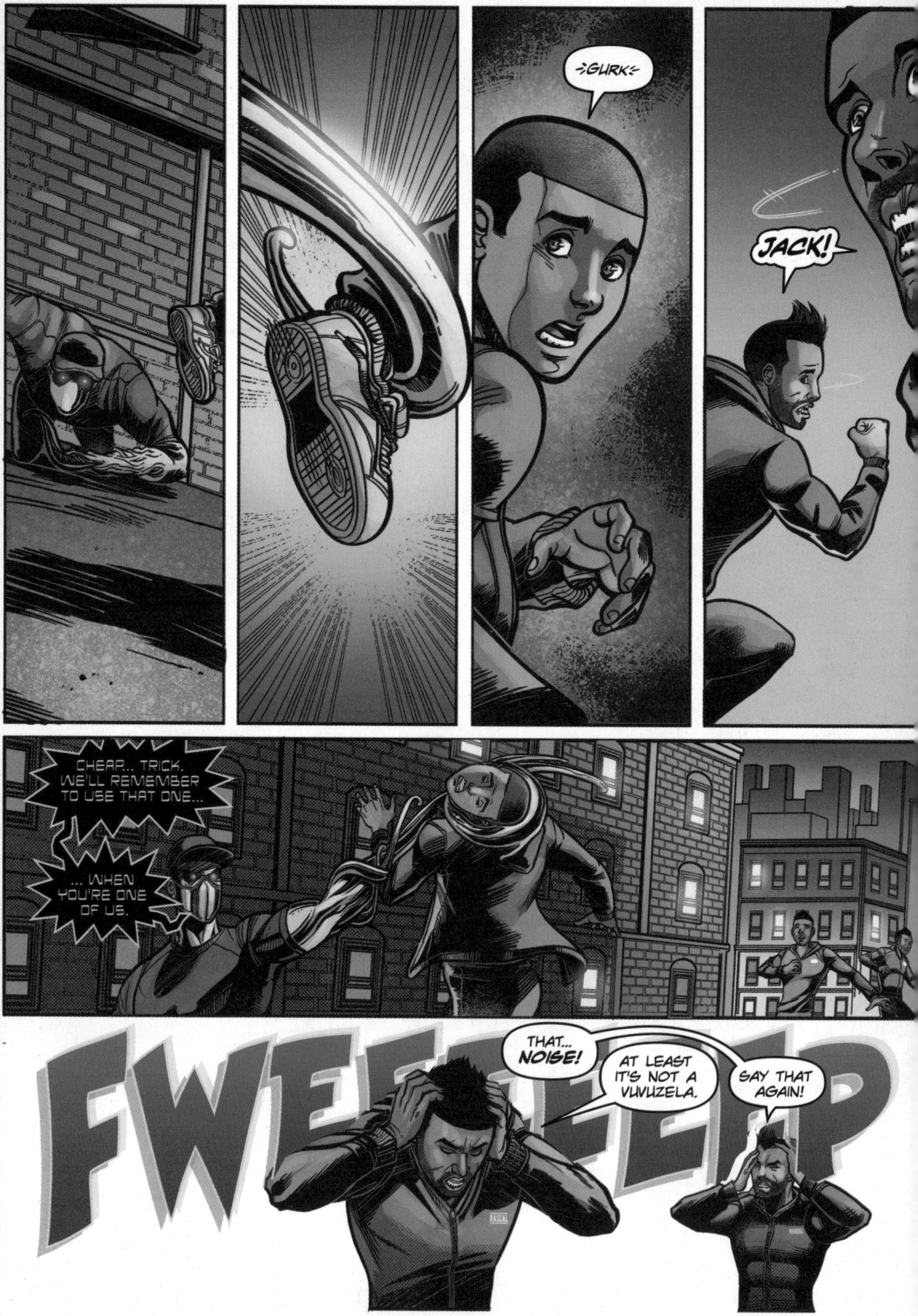
GURK
JACK!
CHEAP... TRICK. WE'LL REMEMBER TO USE THAT ONE...
... WHEN YOU'RE ONE OF US.
THAT... NOISE!
AT LEAST IT'S NOT A VUVUZELA.
SAY THAT AGAIN!

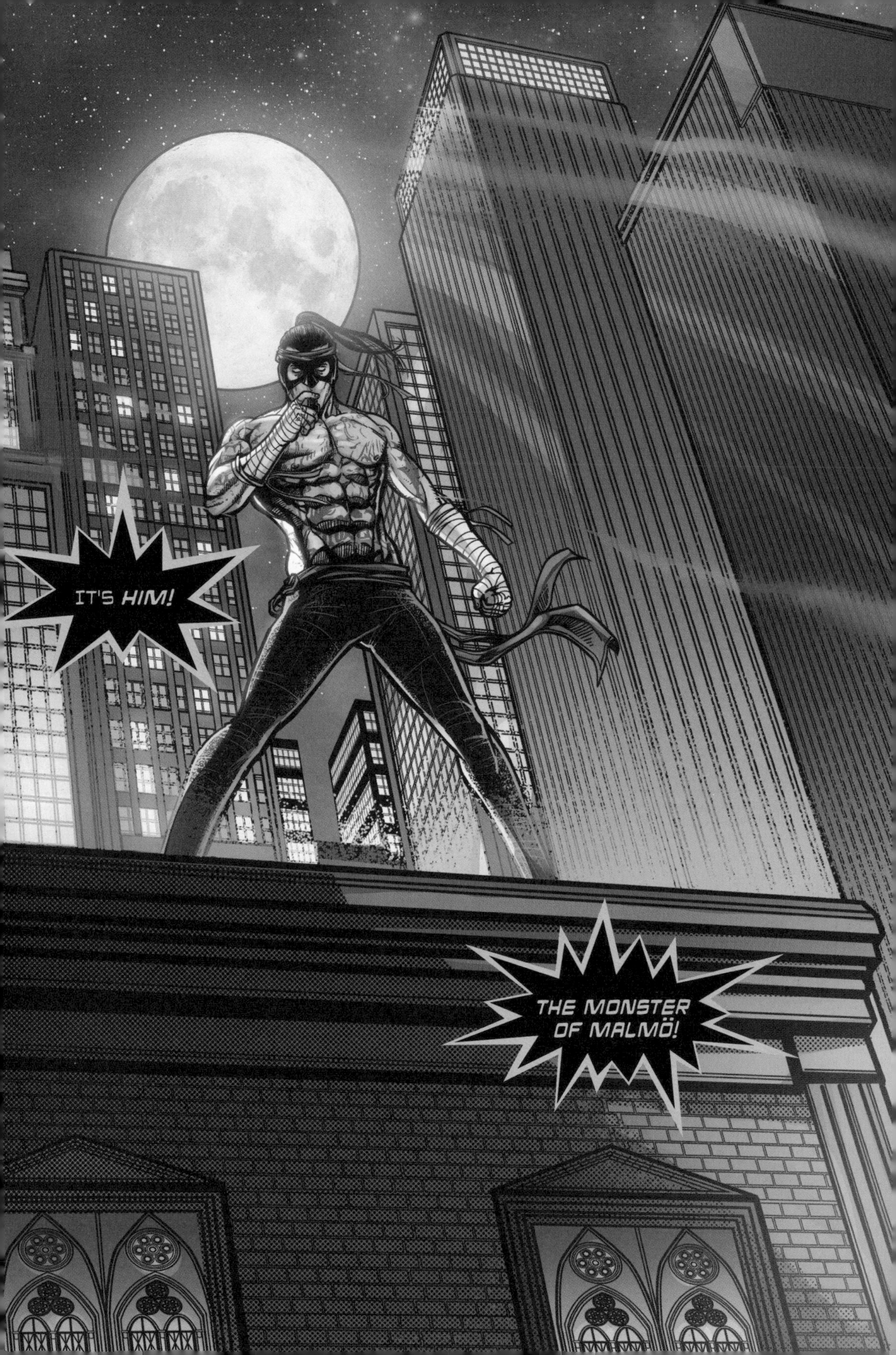
IT'S *HIM!*
THE MONSTER OF MALMÖ!

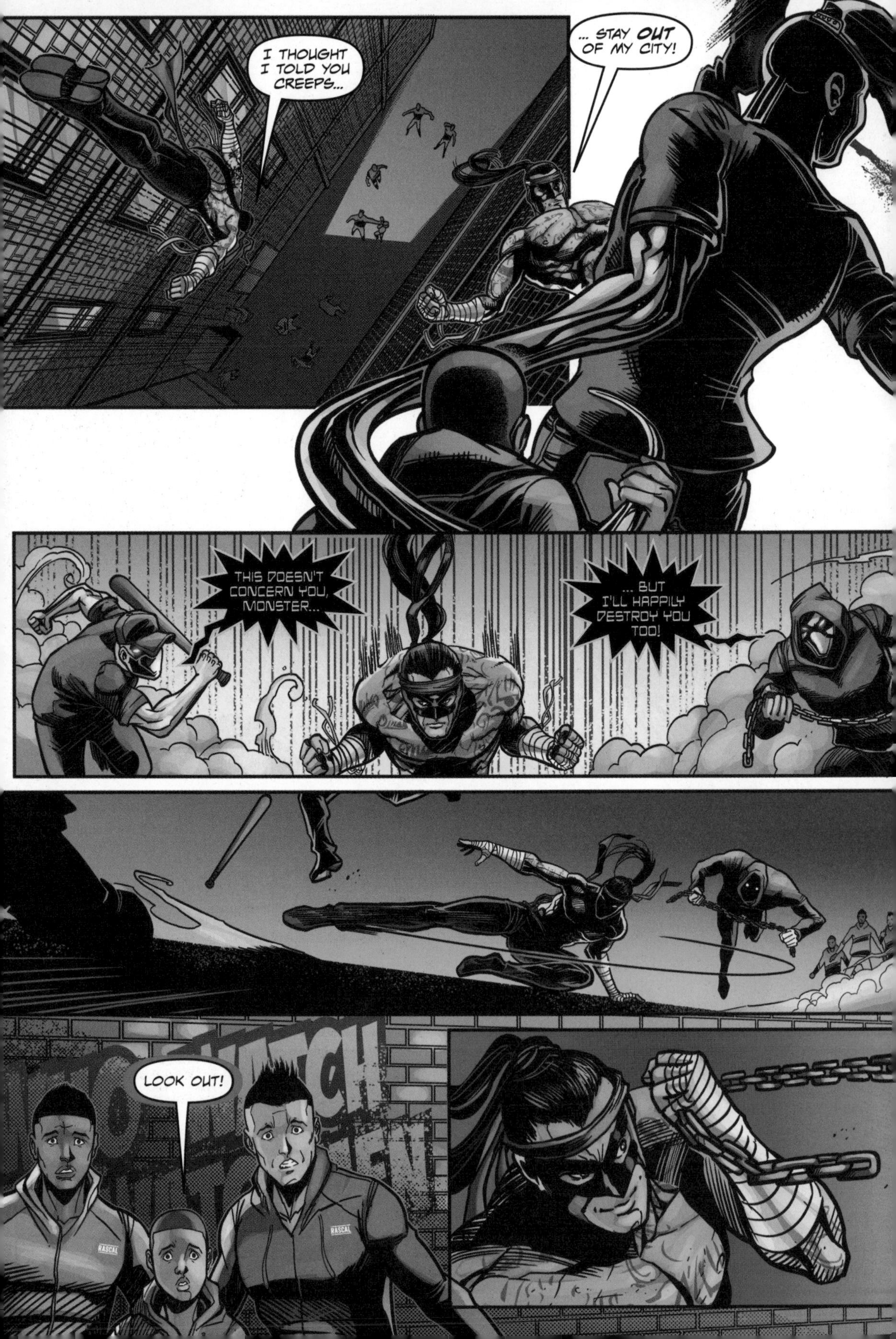
I THOUGHT I TOLD YOU CREEPS...
... STAY OUT OF MY CITY!
THIS DOESN'T CONCERN YOU, MONSTER...
... BUT I'LL HAPPILY DESTROY YOU TOO!
LOOK OUT!
RASCAL
RASCAL

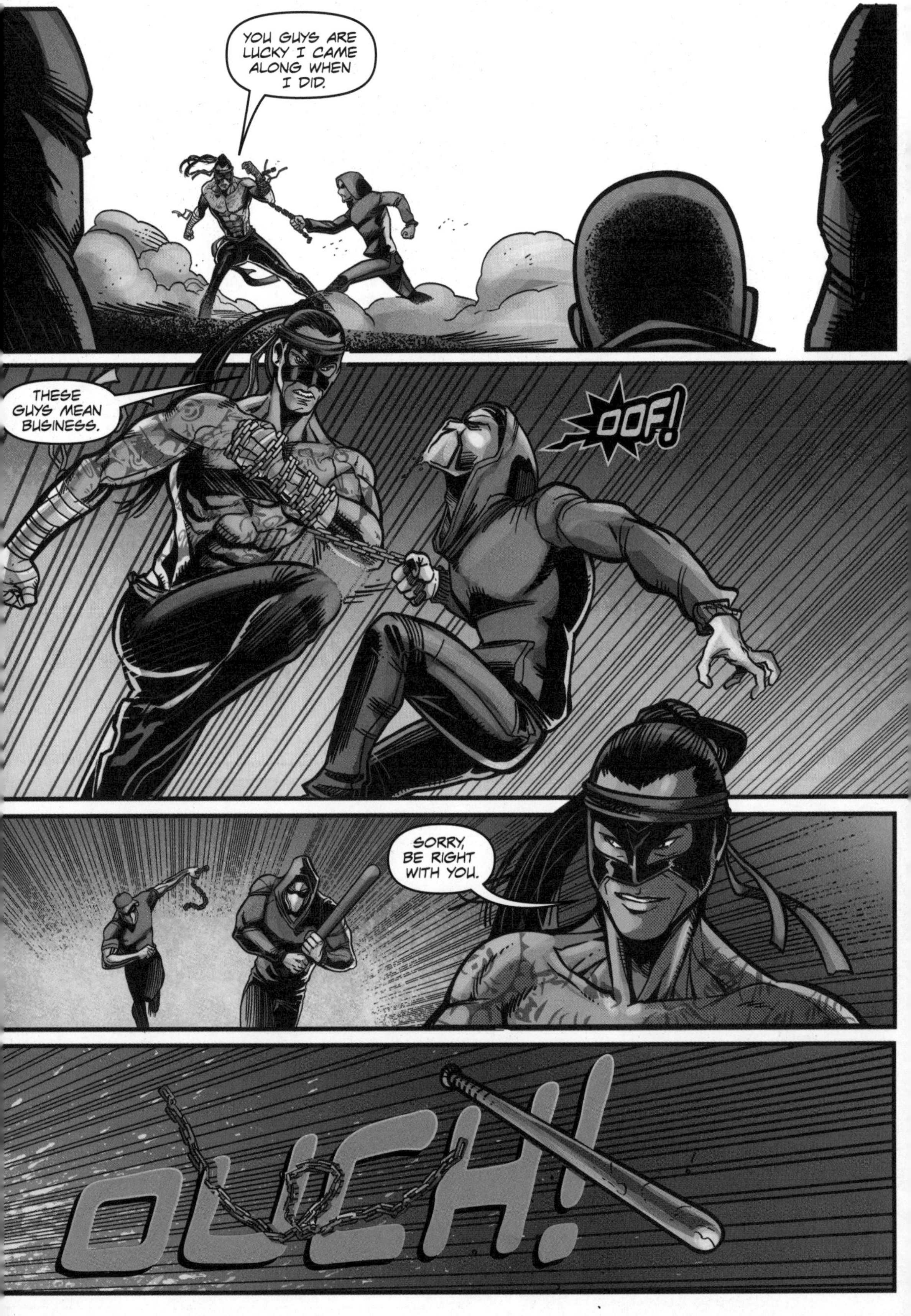
YOU GUYS ARE LUCKY I CAME ALONG WHEN I DID.
THESE GUYS MEAN BUSINESS.
OOF!
SORRY, BE RIGHT WITH YOU.
OUCH!

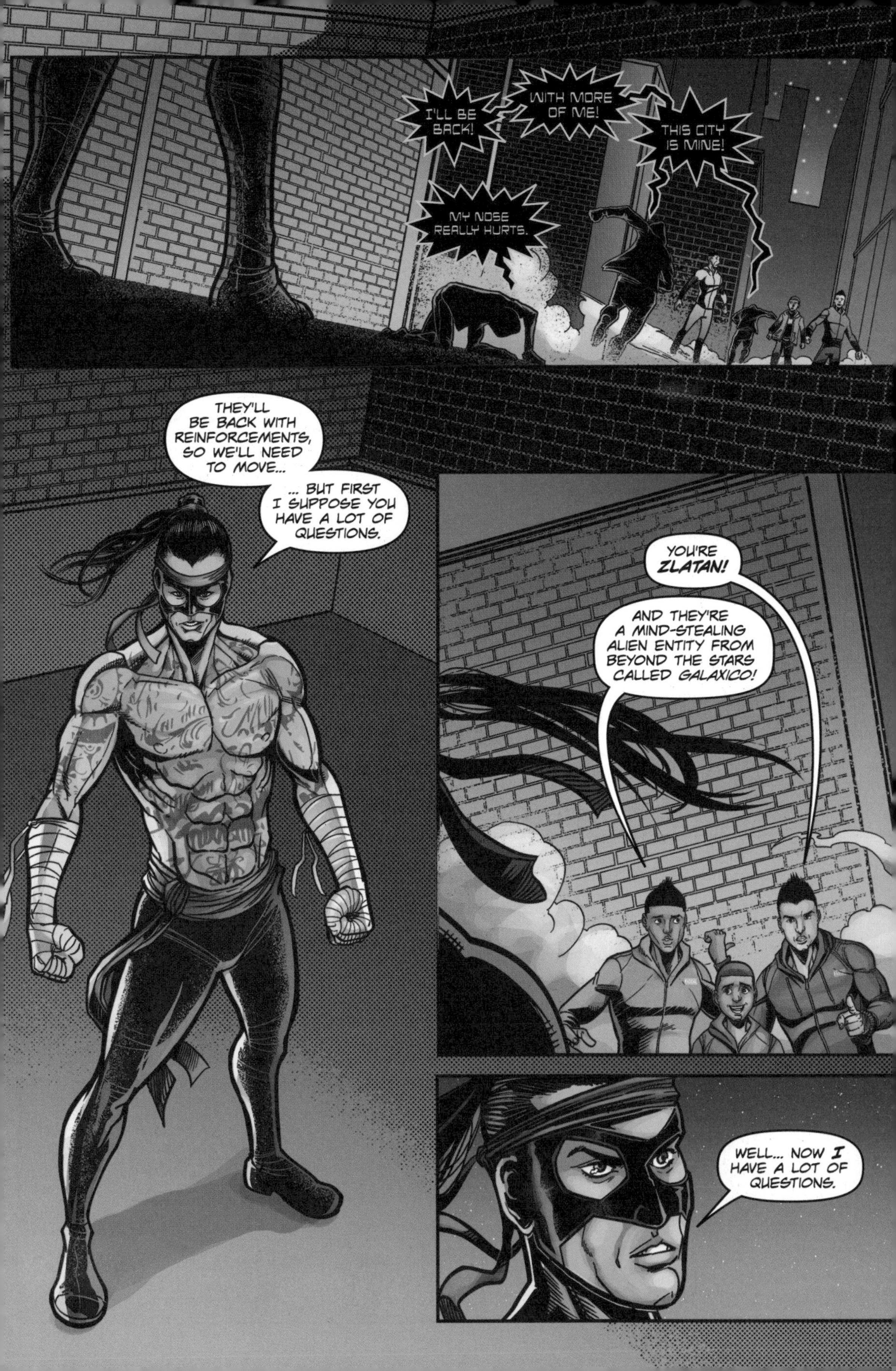
I'LL BE BACK!
WITH MORE OF ME!
THIS CITY IS MINE!
MY NOSE REALLY HURTS.
THEY'LL BE BACK WITH REINFORCEMENTS, SO WE'LL NEED TO MOVE...
... BUT FIRST I SUPPOSE YOU HAVE A LOT OF QUESTIONS.
YOU'RE ZLATAN!
AND THEY'RE A MIND-STEALING ALIEN ENTITY FROM BEYOND THE STARS CALLED GALAXICO!
WELL... NOW I HAVE A LOT OF QUESTIONS.

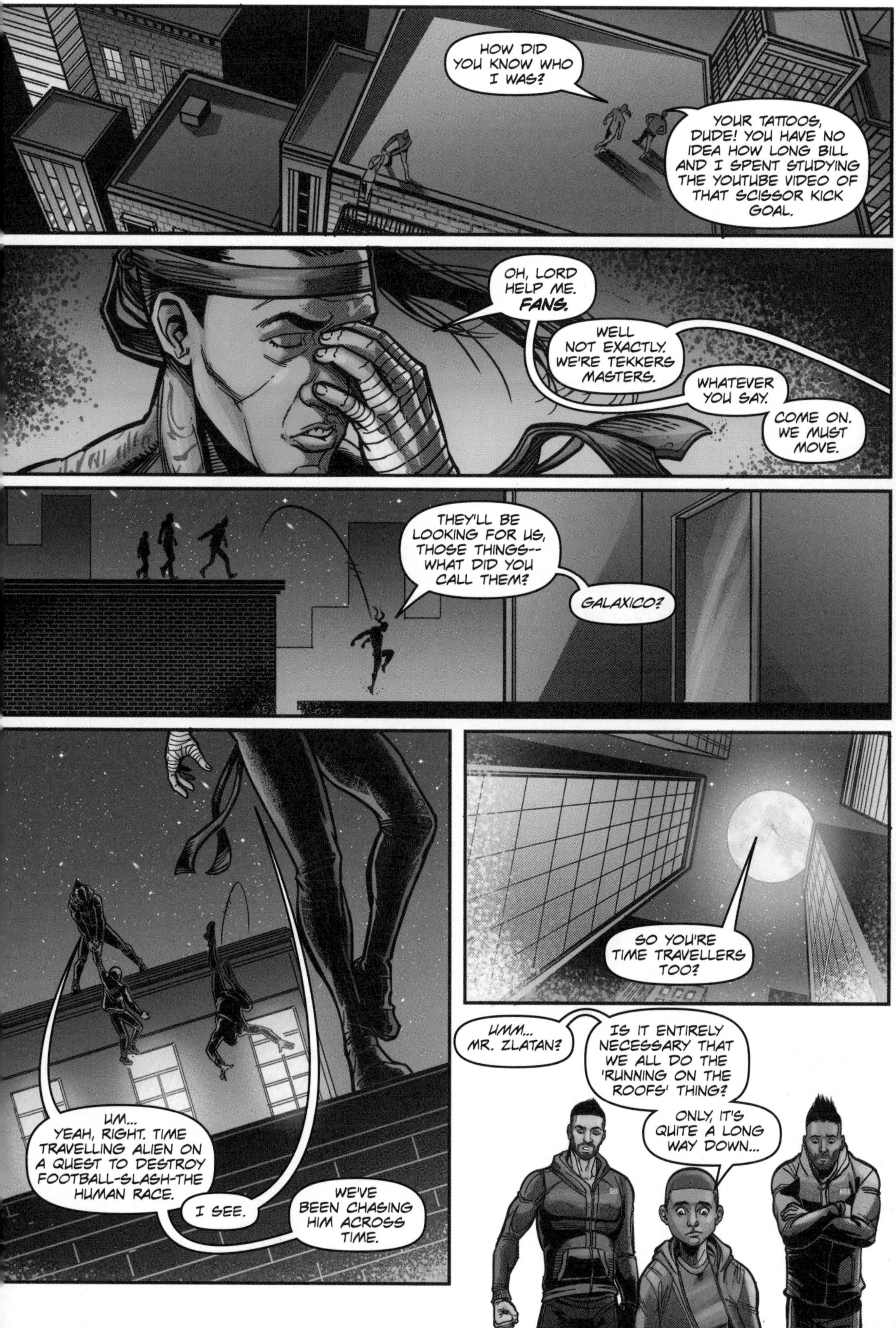
HOW DID YOU KNOW WHO I WAS?
YOUR TATTOOS, DUDE! YOU HAVE NO IDEA HOW LONG BILL AND I SPENT STUDYING THE YOUTUBE VIDEO OF THAT SCISSOR KICK GOAL.
OH, LORD HELP ME. FANS.
WELL NOT EXACTLY. WE'RE TEKKERS MASTERS.
WHATEVER YOU SAY.
COME ON. WE MUST MOVE.
THEY'LL BE LOOKING FOR US, THOSE THINGS-- WHAT DID YOU CALL THEM?
GALAXICO?
UM... YEAH, RIGHT. TIME TRAVELLING ALIEN ON A QUEST TO DESTROY FOOTBALL-SLASH-THE HUMAN RACE.
I SEE.
WE'VE BEEN CHASING HIM ACROSS TIME.
SO YOU'RE TIME TRAVELLERS TOO?
UMM... MR. ZLATAN?
IS IT ENTIRELY NECESSARY THAT WE ALL DO THE 'RUNNING ON THE ROOFS' THING?
ONLY, IT'S QUITE A LONG WAY DOWN...

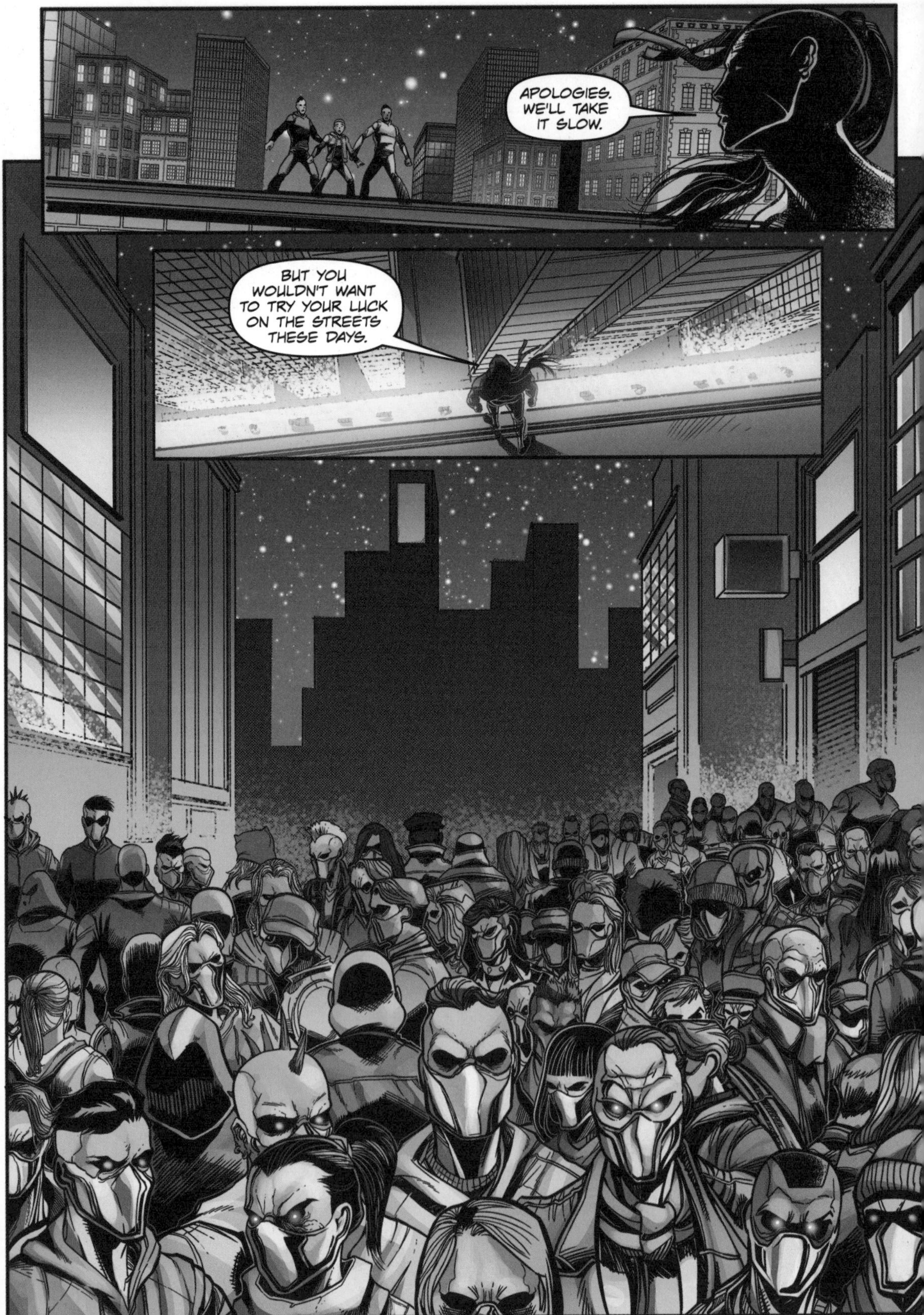
APOLOGIES. WE'LL TAKE IT SLOW.
BUT YOU WOULDN'T WANT TO TRY YOUR LUCK ON THE STREETS THESE DAYS.

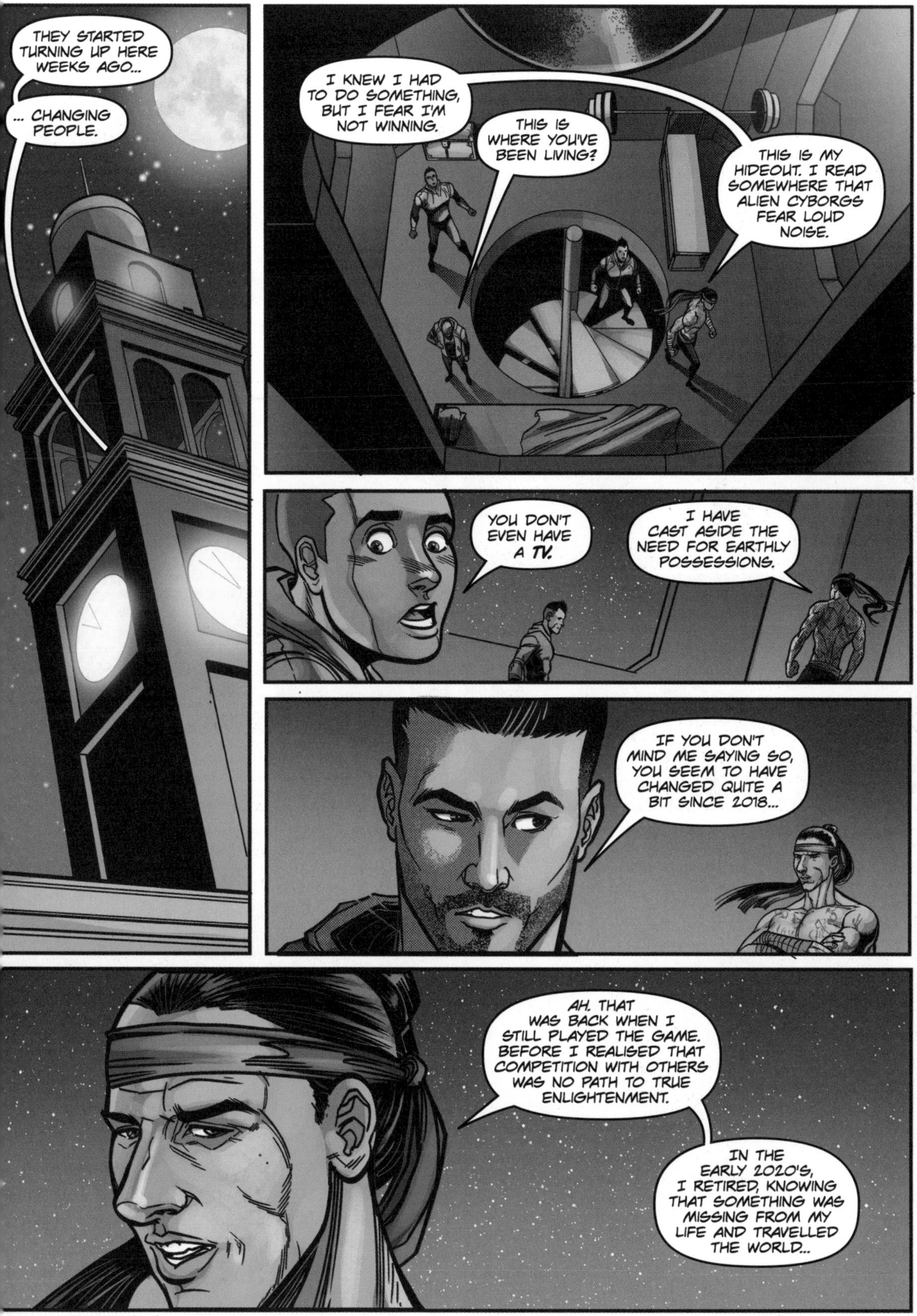
THEY STARTED TURNING UP HERE WEEKS AGO...
... CHANGING PEOPLE.
I KNEW I HAD TO DO SOMETHING, BUT I FEAR I'M NOT WINNING.
THIS IS WHERE YOU'VE BEEN LIVING?
THIS IS MY HIDEOUT. I READ SOMEWHERE THAT ALIEN CYBORGS FEAR LOUD NOISE.
YOU DON'T EVEN HAVE A TV.
I HAVE CAST ASIDE THE NEED FOR EARTHLY POSSESSIONS.
IF YOU DON'T MIND ME SAYING SO, YOU SEEM TO HAVE CHANGED QUITE A BIT SINCE 2018...
AH. THAT WAS BACK WHEN I STILL PLAYED THE GAME. BEFORE I REALISED THAT COMPETITION WITH OTHERS WAS NO PATH TO TRUE ENLIGHTENMENT.
IN THE EARLY 2020'S, I RETIRED, KNOWING THAT SOMETHING WAS MISSING FROM MY LIFE AND TRAVELLED THE WORLD...

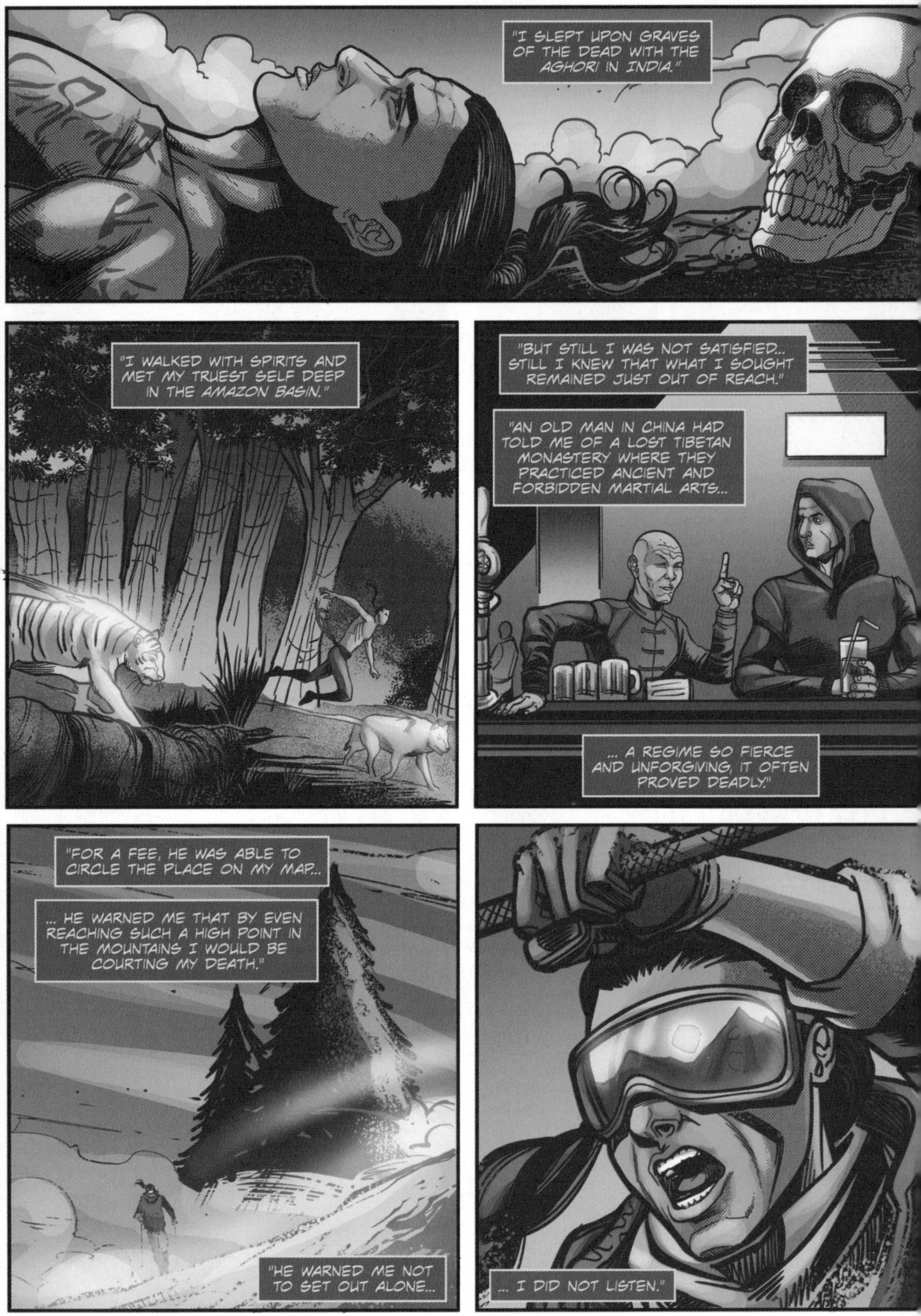
"I SLEPT UPON GRAVES OF THE DEAD WITH THE AGHORI IN INDIA."
"I WALKED WITH SPIRITS AND MET MY TRUEST SELF DEEP IN THE AMAZON BASIN."
"BUT STILL I WAS NOT SATISFIED... STILL I KNEW THAT WHAT I SOUGHT REMAINED JUST OUT OF REACH."
"AN OLD MAN IN CHINA HAD TOLD ME OF A LOST TIBETAN MONASTERY WHERE THEY PRACTICED ANCIENT AND FORBIDDEN MARTIAL ARTS...
... A REGIME SO FIERCE AND UNFORGIVING, IT OFTEN PROVED DEADLY."
"FOR A FEE, HE WAS ABLE TO CIRCLE THE PLACE ON MY MAP...
... HE WARNED ME THAT BY EVEN REACHING SUCH A HIGH POINT IN THE MOUNTAINS I WOULD BE COURTING MY DEATH."
"HE WARNED ME NOT TO SET OUT ALONE...
... I DID NOT LISTEN."

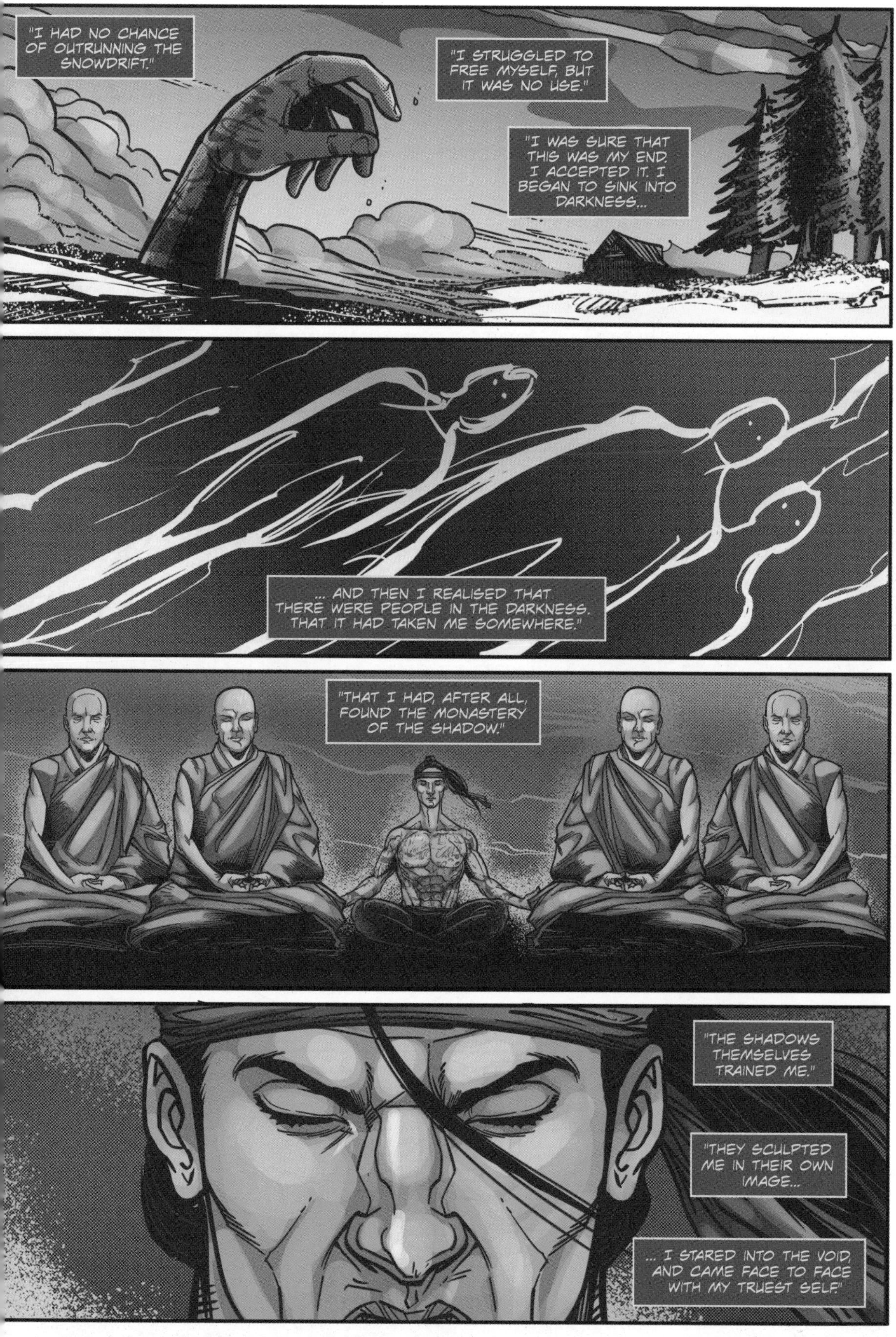
"I HAD NO CHANCE OF OUTRUNNING THE SNOWDRIFT."
"I STRUGGLED TO FREE MYSELF, BUT IT WAS NO USE."
"I WAS SURE THAT THIS WAS MY END. I ACCEPTED IT. I BEGAN TO SINK INTO DARKNESS...
... AND THEN I REALISED THAT THERE WERE PEOPLE IN THE DARKNESS. THAT IT HAD TAKEN ME SOMEWHERE."
"THAT I HAD, AFTER ALL, FOUND THE MONASTERY OF THE SHADOW."
"THE SHADOWS THEMSELVES TRAINED ME."
"THEY SCULPTED ME IN THEIR OWN IMAGE...
... I STARED INTO THE VOID, AND CAME FACE TO FACE WITH MY TRUEST SELF."

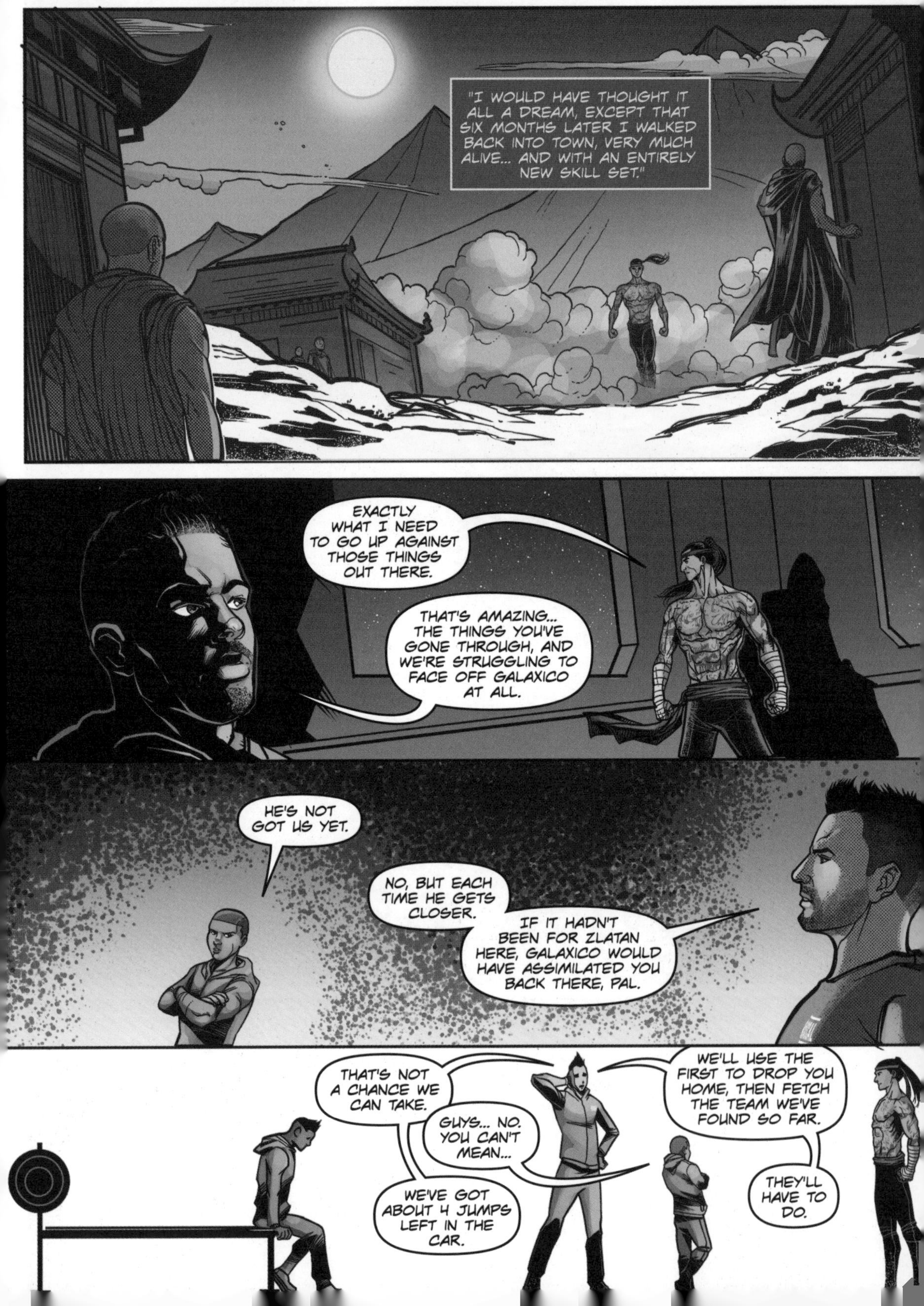
"I WOULD HAVE THOUGHT IT ALL A DREAM, EXCEPT THAT SIX MONTHS LATER I WALKED BACK INTO TOWN, VERY MUCH ALIVE... AND WITH AN ENTIRELY NEW SKILL SET."
EXACTLY WHAT I NEED TO GO UP AGAINST THOSE THINGS OUT THERE.
THAT'S AMAZING... THE THINGS YOU'VE GONE THROUGH, AND WE'RE STRUGGLING TO FACE OFF GALAXICO AT ALL.
HE'S NOT GOT US YET.
NO, BUT EACH TIME HE GETS CLOSER.
IF IT HADN'T BEEN FOR ZLATAN HERE, GALAXICO WOULD HAVE ASSIMILATED YOU BACK THERE, PAL.
THAT'S NOT A CHANCE WE CAN TAKE.
WE'VE GOT ABOUT 4 JUMPS LEFT IN THE CAR.
GUYS... NO. YOU CAN'T MEAN...
WE'LL USE THE FIRST TO DROP YOU HOME, THEN FETCH THE TEAM WE'VE FOUND SO FAR.
THEY'LL HAVE TO DO.

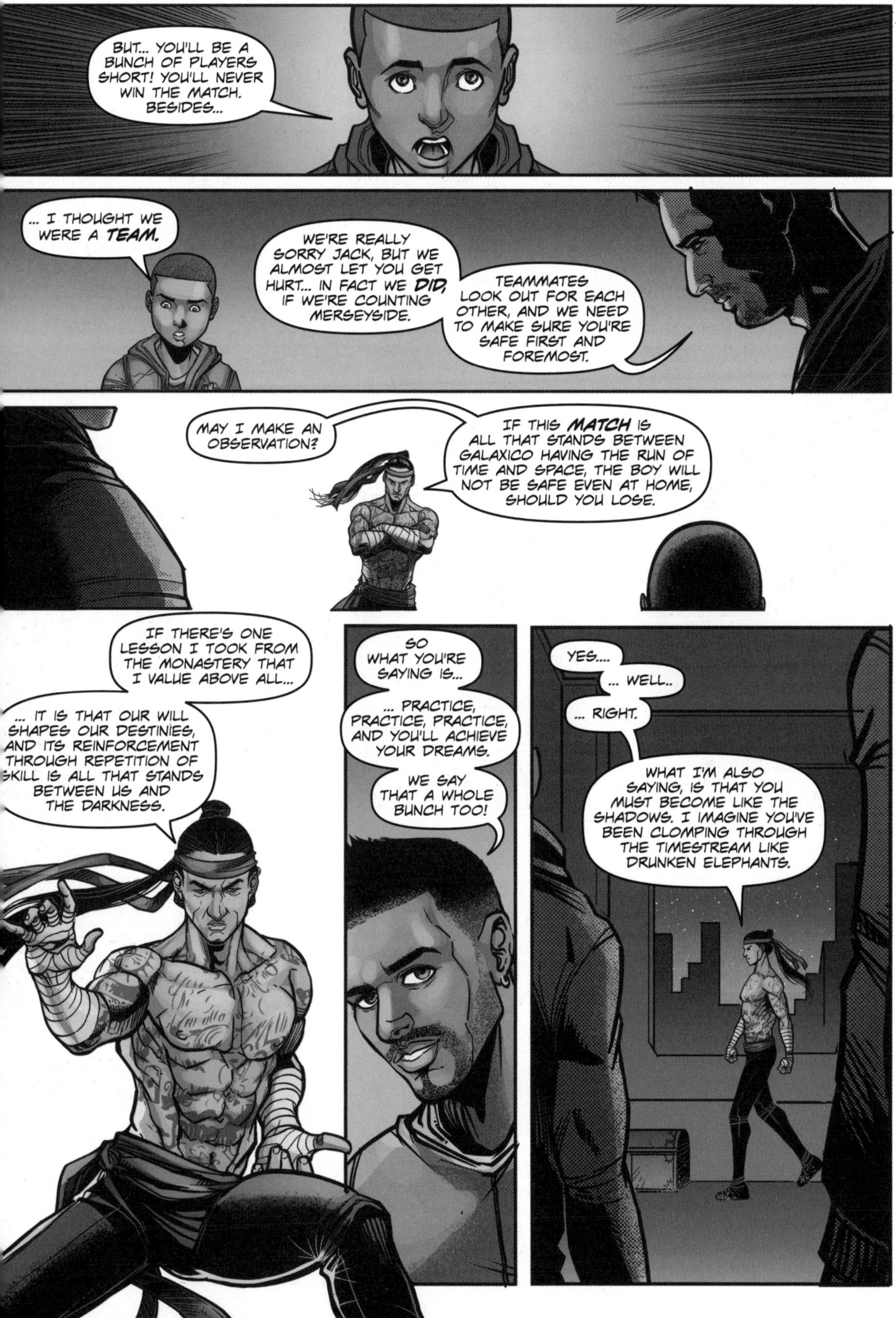
BUT... YOU'LL BE A BUNCH OF PLAYERS SHORT! YOU'LL NEVER WIN THE MATCH. BESIDES...
... I THOUGHT WE WERE A TEAM.
WE'RE REALLY SORRY JACK, BUT WE ALMOST LET YOU GET HURT... IN FACT WE DID, IF WE'RE COUNTING MERSEYSIDE.
TEAMMATES LOOK OUT FOR EACH OTHER, AND WE NEED TO MAKE SURE YOU'RE SAFE FIRST AND FOREMOST.
MAY I MAKE AN OBSERVATION?
IF THIS MATCH IS ALL THAT STANDS BETWEEN GALAXICO HAVING THE RUN OF TIME AND SPACE, THE BOY WILL NOT BE SAFE EVEN AT HOME, SHOULD YOU LOSE.
IF THERE'S ONE LESSON I TOOK FROM THE MONASTERY THAT I VALUE ABOVE ALL...
... IT IS THAT OUR WILL SHAPES OUR DESTINIES, AND ITS REINFORCEMENT THROUGH REPETITION OF SKILL IS ALL THAT STANDS BETWEEN US AND THE DARKNESS.
SO WHAT YOU'RE SAYING IS...
... PRACTICE, PRACTICE, PRACTICE, AND YOU'LL ACHIEVE YOUR DREAMS.
WE SAY THAT A WHOLE BUNCH TOO!
YES....
... WELL..
... RIGHT.
WHAT I'M ALSO SAYING, IS THAT YOU MUST BECOME LIKE THE SHADOWS. I IMAGINE YOU'VE BEEN CLOMPING THROUGH THE TIMESTREAM LIKE DRUNKEN ELEPHANTS.

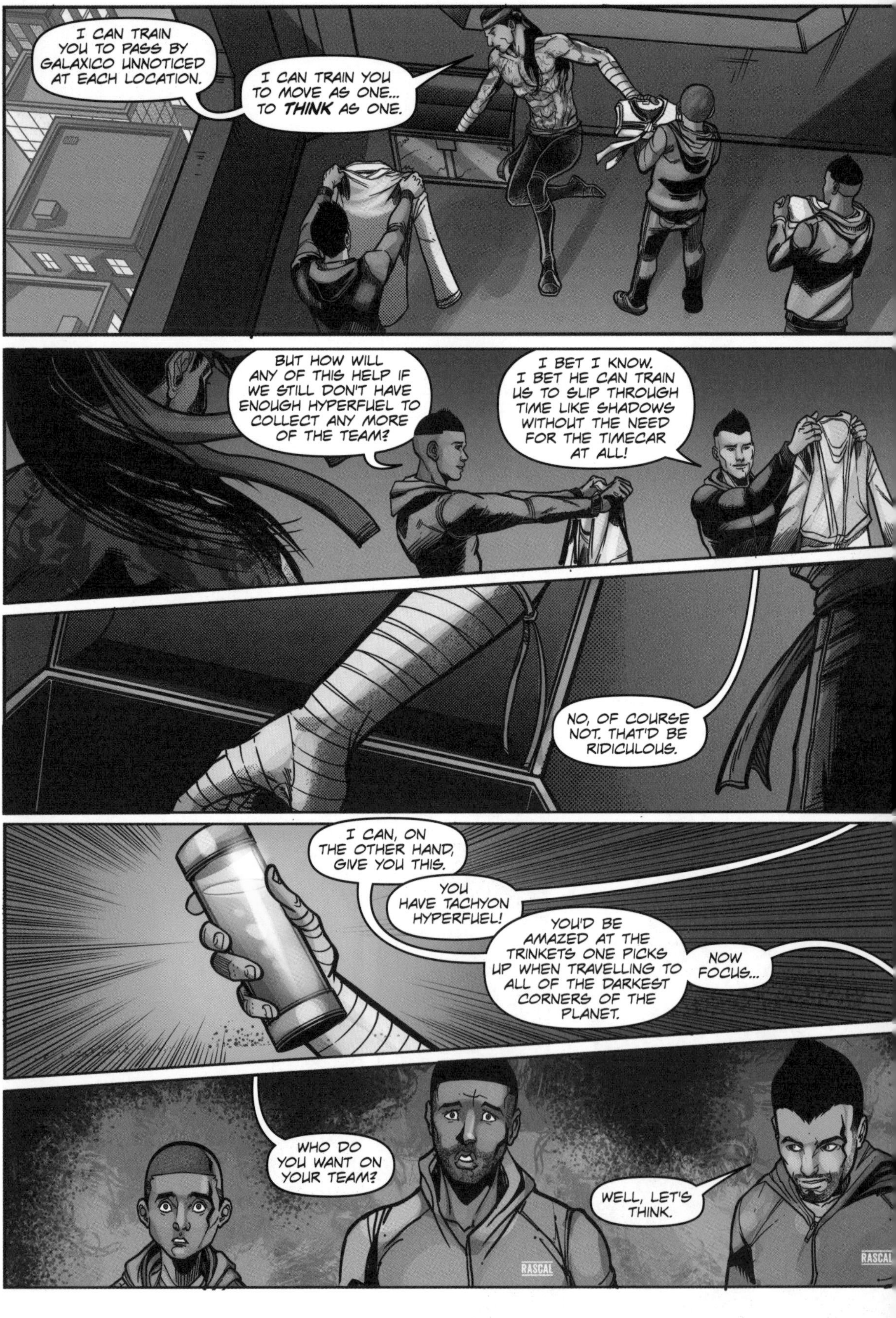
I CAN TRAIN YOU TO PASS BY GALAXICO UNNOTICED AT EACH LOCATION.
I CAN TRAIN YOU TO MOVE AS ONE... TO *THINK* AS ONE.
BUT HOW WILL ANY OF THIS HELP IF WE STILL DON'T HAVE ENOUGH HYPERFUEL TO COLLECT ANY MORE OF THE TEAM?
I BET I KNOW. I BET HE CAN TRAIN US TO SLIP THROUGH TIME LIKE SHADOWS WITHOUT THE NEED FOR THE TIMECAR AT ALL!
NO, OF COURSE NOT. THAT'D BE RIDICULOUS.
I CAN, ON THE OTHER HAND, GIVE YOU THIS.
YOU HAVE TACHYON HYPERFUEL!
YOU'D BE AMAZED AT THE TRINKETS ONE PICKS UP WHEN TRAVELLING TO ALL OF THE DARKEST CORNERS OF THE PLANET.
NOW FOCUS...
WHO DO YOU WANT ON YOUR TEAM?
WELL, LET'S THINK.
RASCAL
RASCAL

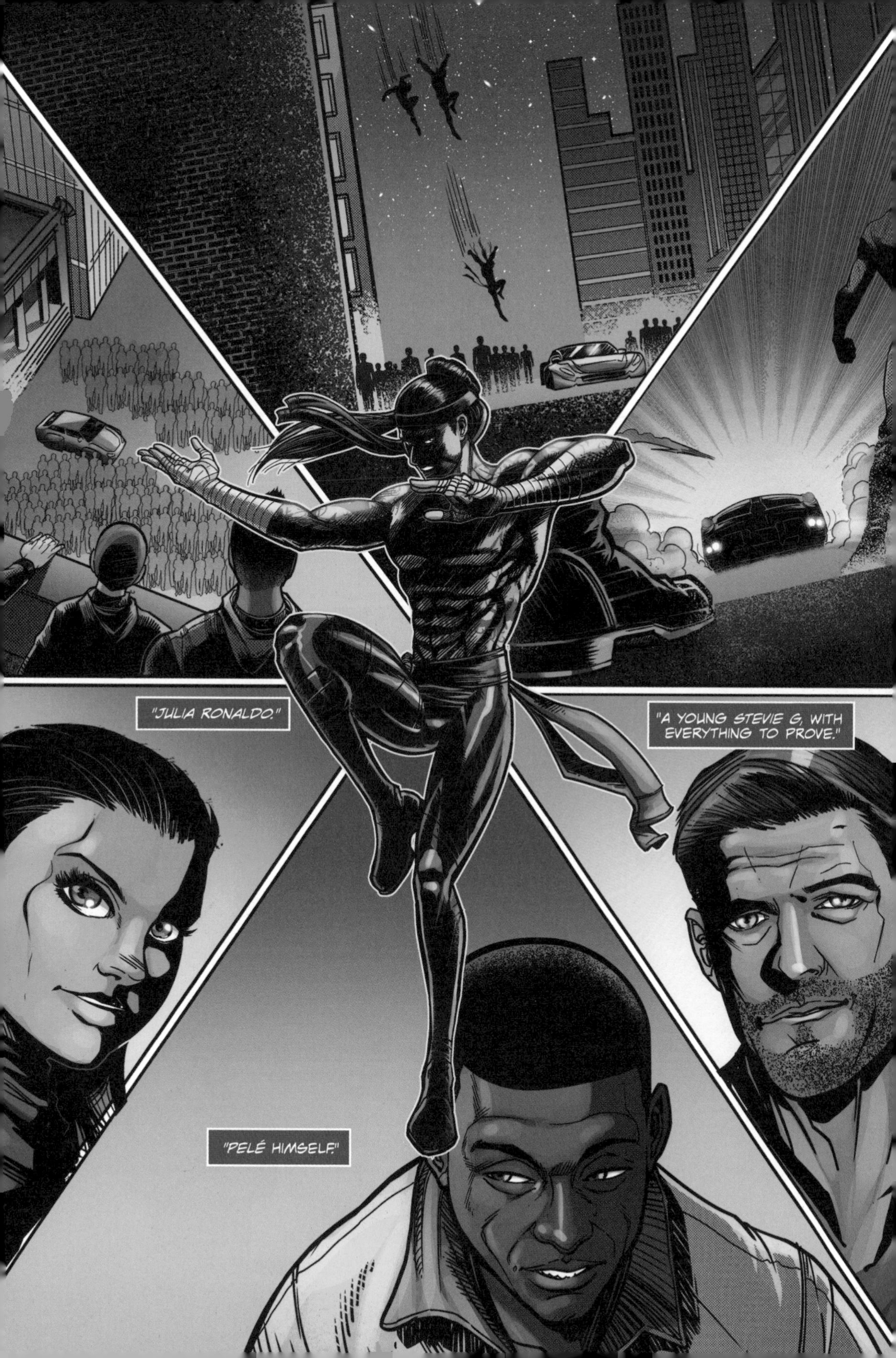
"JULIA RONALDO."
"A YOUNG STEVIE G, WITH EVERYTHING TO PROVE."
"PELÉ HIMSELF."

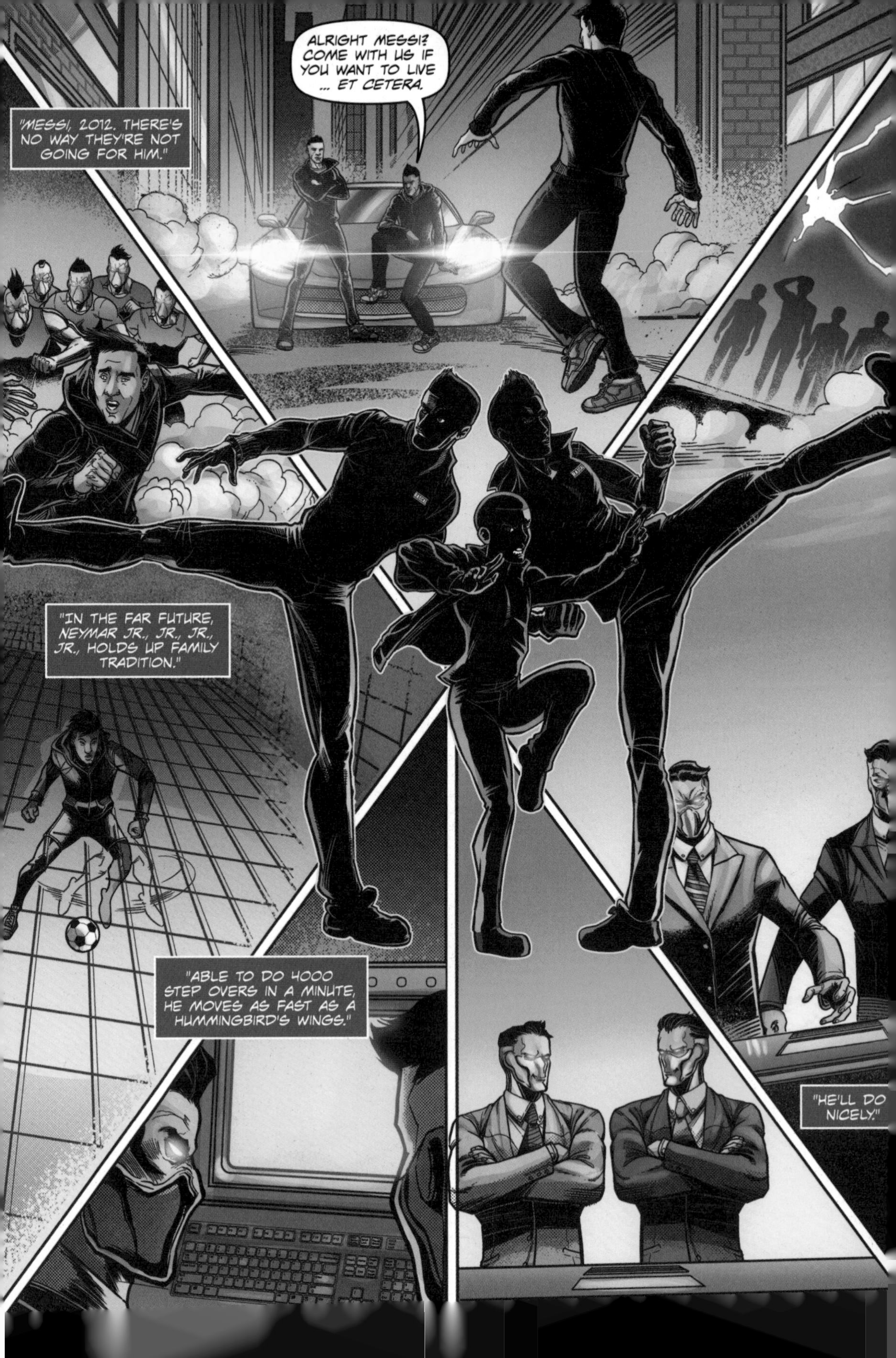
"MESSI, 2012. THERE'S NO WAY THEY'RE NOT GOING FOR HIM."
ALRIGHT MESSI? COME WITH US IF YOU WANT TO LIVE ... ET CETERA.
"IN THE FAR FUTURE, NEYMAR JR., JR., JR., JR., HOLDS UP FAMILY TRADITION."
"ABLE TO DO 4000 STEP OVERS IN A MINUTE, HE MOVES AS FAST AS A HUMMINGBIRD'S WINGS."
"HE'LL DO NICELY."

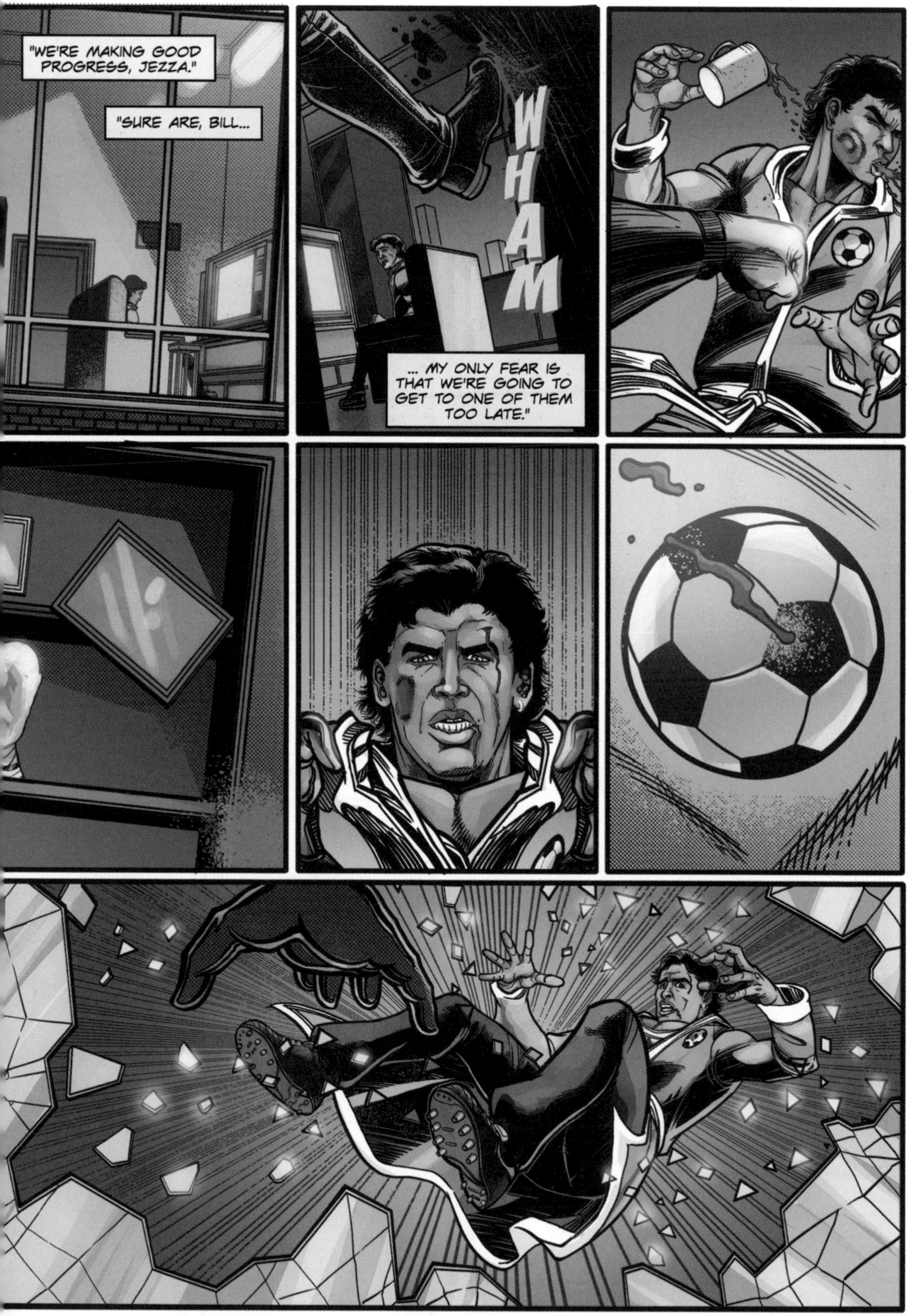
"WE'RE MAKING GOOD PROGRESS, JEZZA."
"SURE ARE, BILL...
WHAM
... MY ONLY FEAR IS THAT WE'RE GOING TO GET TO ONE OF THEM TOO LATE."

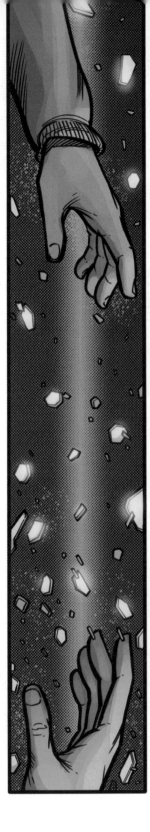

ONCE AGAIN, SAVED BY THE HAND OF GOD!

FANCY A KICKAROUND?

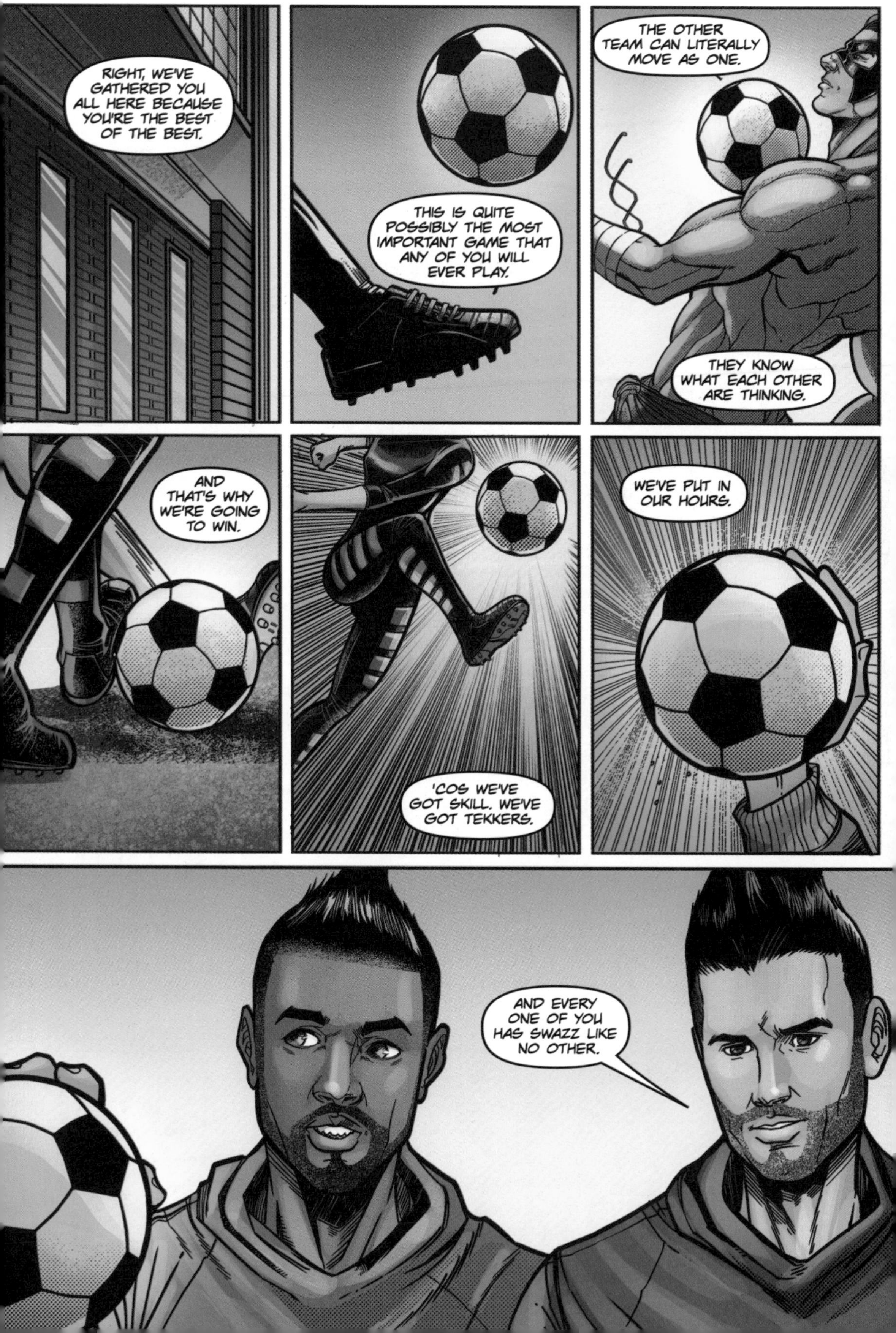
RIGHT, WE'VE GATHERED YOU ALL HERE BECAUSE YOU'RE THE BEST OF THE BEST.
THIS IS QUITE POSSIBLY THE MOST IMPORTANT GAME THAT ANY OF YOU WILL EVER PLAY.
THE OTHER TEAM CAN LITERALLY MOVE AS ONE.
THEY KNOW WHAT EACH OTHER ARE THINKING.
AND THAT'S WHY WE'RE GOING TO WIN.
'COS WE'VE GOT SKILL. WE'VE GOT TEKKERS.
WE'VE PUT IN OUR HOURS.
AND EVERY ONE OF YOU HAS SWAZZ LIKE NO OTHER.

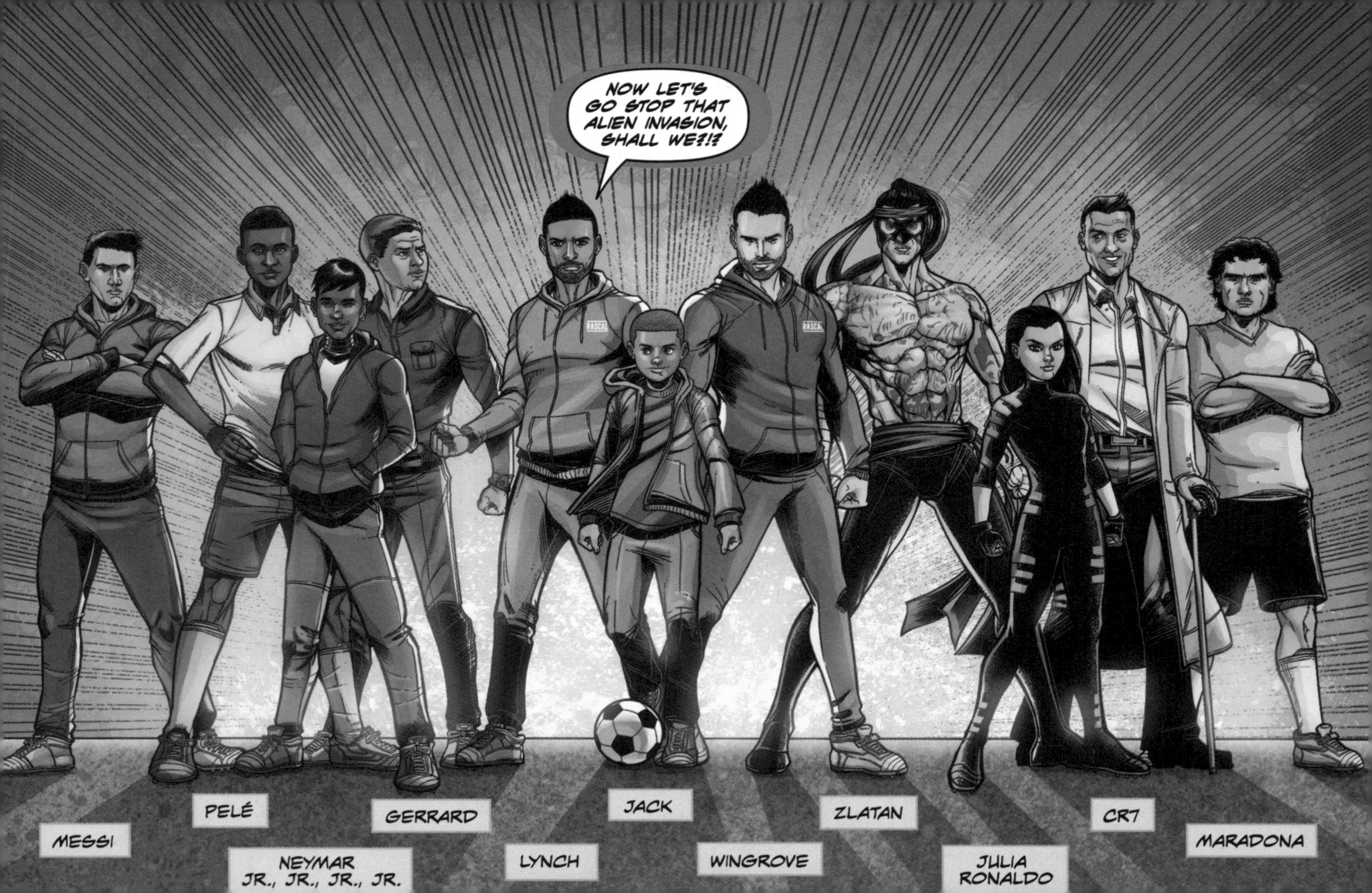
NOW LET'S GO STOP THAT ALIEN INVASION, SHALL WE?!?
MESSI
PELÉ
NEYMAR JR., JR., JR., JR.
GERRARD
LYNCH
JACK
WINGROVE
ZLATAN
JULIA RONALDO
CR7
MARADONA

THAT'S EVERYONE... BUT HANG ON...

... RONALDO'S NOT PLAYING... AND EVEN IF HE WAS, YOU'RE A PLAYER SHORT!

I MAY HAVE HUNG UP MY FOOTBALL BOOTS... BUT I DO HAVE SOMEONE ELSE TO OFFER.

MEET THE G-O2-1B...

... PROTOTYPE TRAINER.

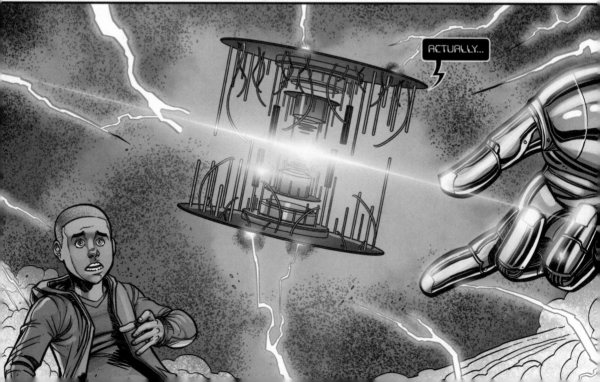

ACTUALLY...

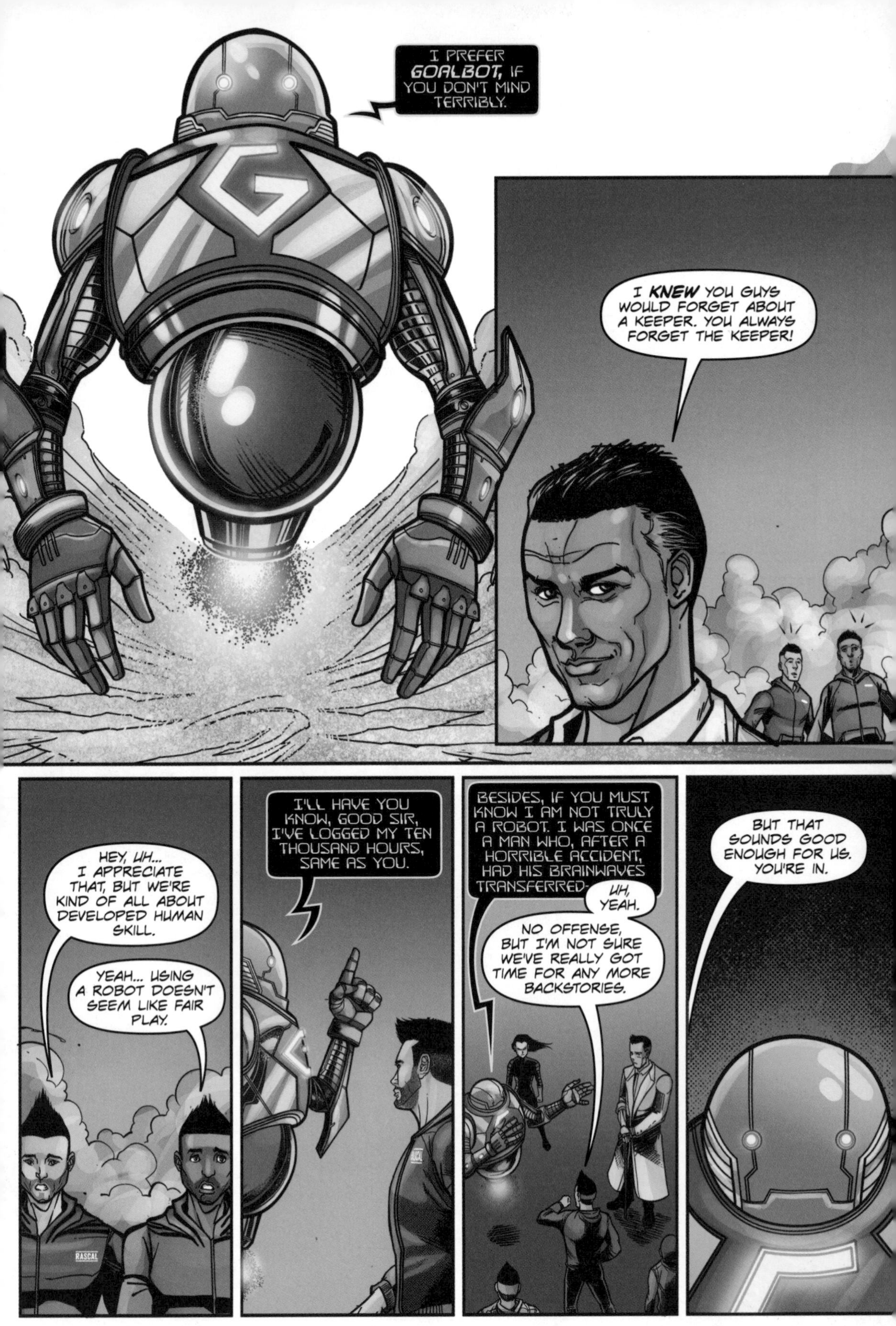
I PREFER GOALBOT, IF YOU DON'T MIND TERRIBLY.
I KNEW YOU GUYS WOULD FORGET ABOUT A KEEPER. YOU ALWAYS FORGET THE KEEPER!
HEY, UH... I APPRECIATE THAT, BUT WE'RE KIND OF ALL ABOUT DEVELOPED HUMAN SKILL.
YEAH... USING A ROBOT DOESN'T SEEM LIKE FAIR PLAY.
RASCAL
I'LL HAVE YOU KNOW, GOOD SIR, I'VE LOGGED MY TEN THOUSAND HOURS, SAME AS YOU.
RASCAL
BESIDES, IF YOU MUST KNOW I AM NOT TRULY A ROBOT. I WAS ONCE A MAN WHO, AFTER A HORRIBLE ACCIDENT, HAD HIS BRAINWAVES TRANSFERRED-
UH, YEAH.
NO OFFENSE, BUT I'M NOT SURE WE'VE REALLY GOT TIME FOR ANY MORE BACKSTORIES.
BUT THAT SOUNDS GOOD ENOUGH FOR US. YOU'RE IN.

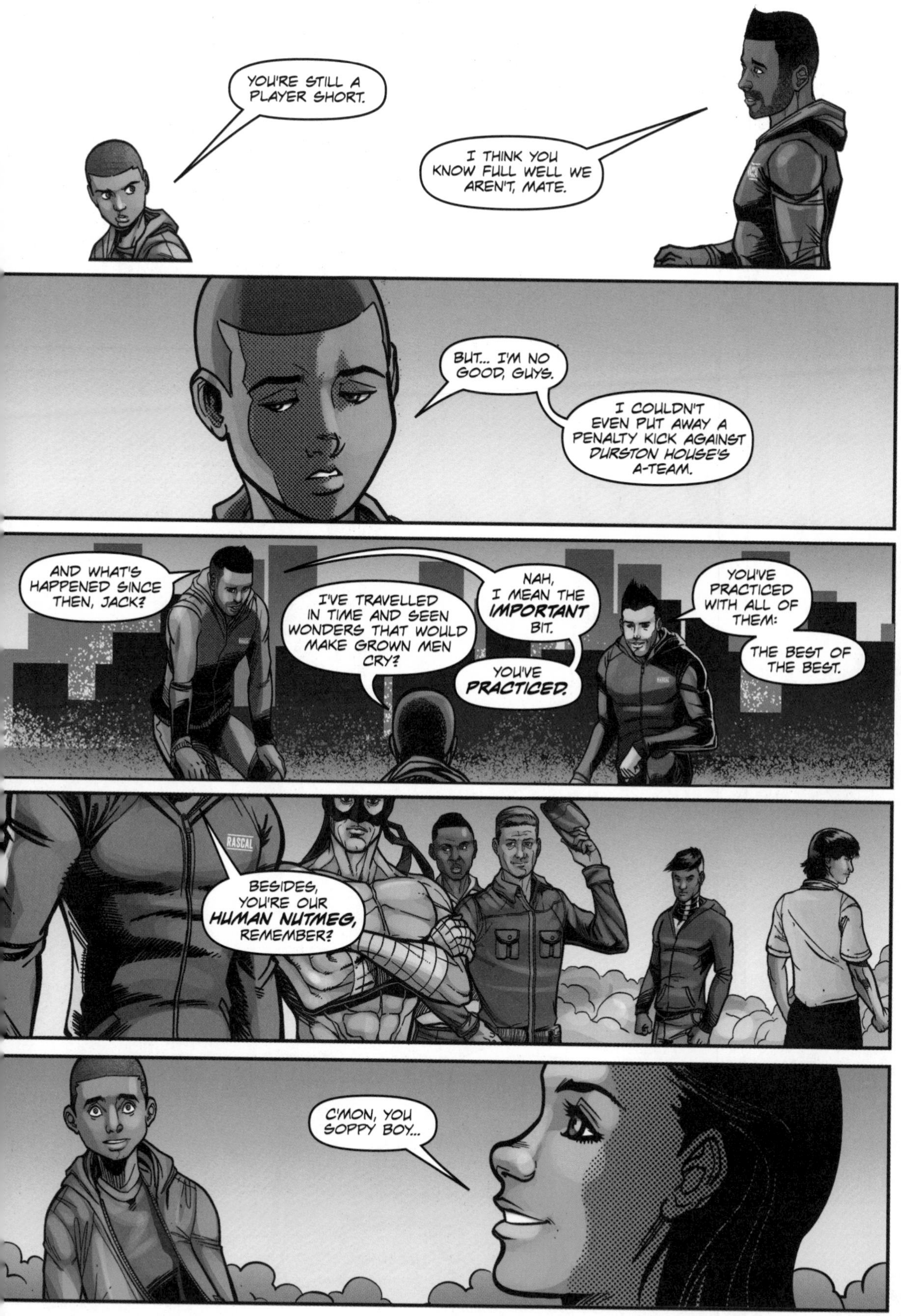
YOU'RE STILL A PLAYER SHORT.
I THINK YOU KNOW FULL WELL WE AREN'T, MATE.
BUT... I'M NO GOOD, GUYS.
I COULDN'T EVEN PUT AWAY A PENALTY KICK AGAINST DURSTON HOUSE'S A-TEAM.
AND WHAT'S HAPPENED SINCE THEN, JACK?
I'VE TRAVELLED IN TIME AND SEEN WONDERS THAT WOULD MAKE GROWN MEN CRY?
NAH, I MEAN THE IMPORTANT BIT.
YOU'VE PRACTICED.
YOU'VE PRACTICED WITH ALL OF THEM:
THE BEST OF THE BEST.
RASCAL
BESIDES, YOU'RE OUR HUMAN NUTMEG, REMEMBER?
C'MON, YOU SOPPY BOY...

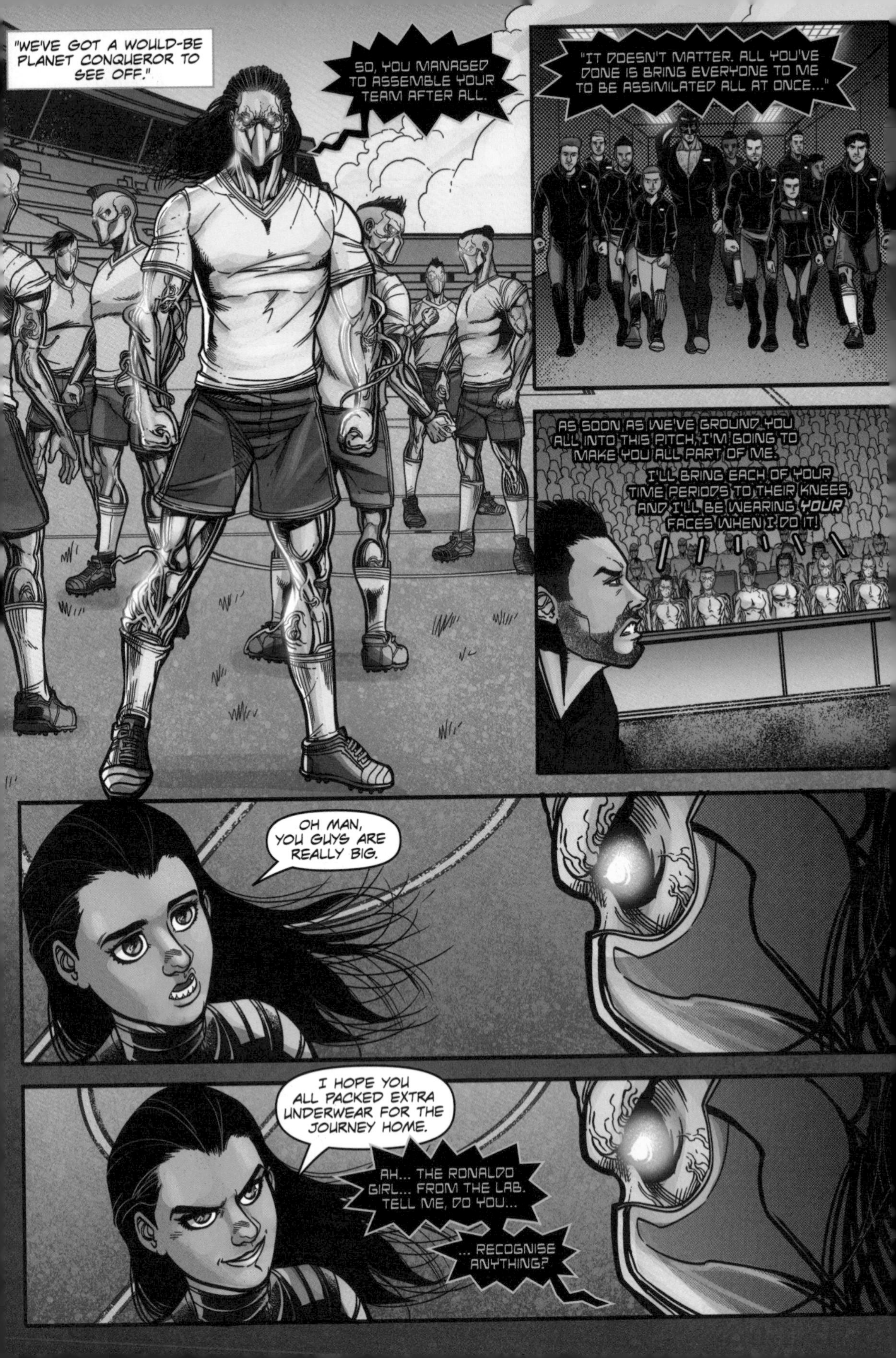
"WE'VE GOT A WOULD-BE PLANET CONQUEROR TO SEE OFF."
SO, YOU MANAGED TO ASSEMBLE YOUR TEAM AFTER ALL.
"IT DOESN'T MATTER. ALL YOU'VE DONE IS BRING EVERYONE TO ME TO BE ASSIMILATED ALL AT ONCE..."
AS SOON AS WE'VE GROUND YOU ALL INTO THIS PITCH, I'M GOING TO MAKE YOU ALL PART OF ME.
I'LL BRING EACH OF YOUR TIME PERIODS TO THEIR KNEES, AND I'LL BE WEARING *YOUR* FACES WHEN I DO IT!
OH MAN, YOU GUYS ARE REALLY BIG.
I HOPE YOU ALL PACKED EXTRA UNDERWEAR FOR THE JOURNEY HOME.
AH... THE RONALDO GIRL... FROM THE LAB. TELL ME, DO YOU...
... RECOGNISE ANYTHING?

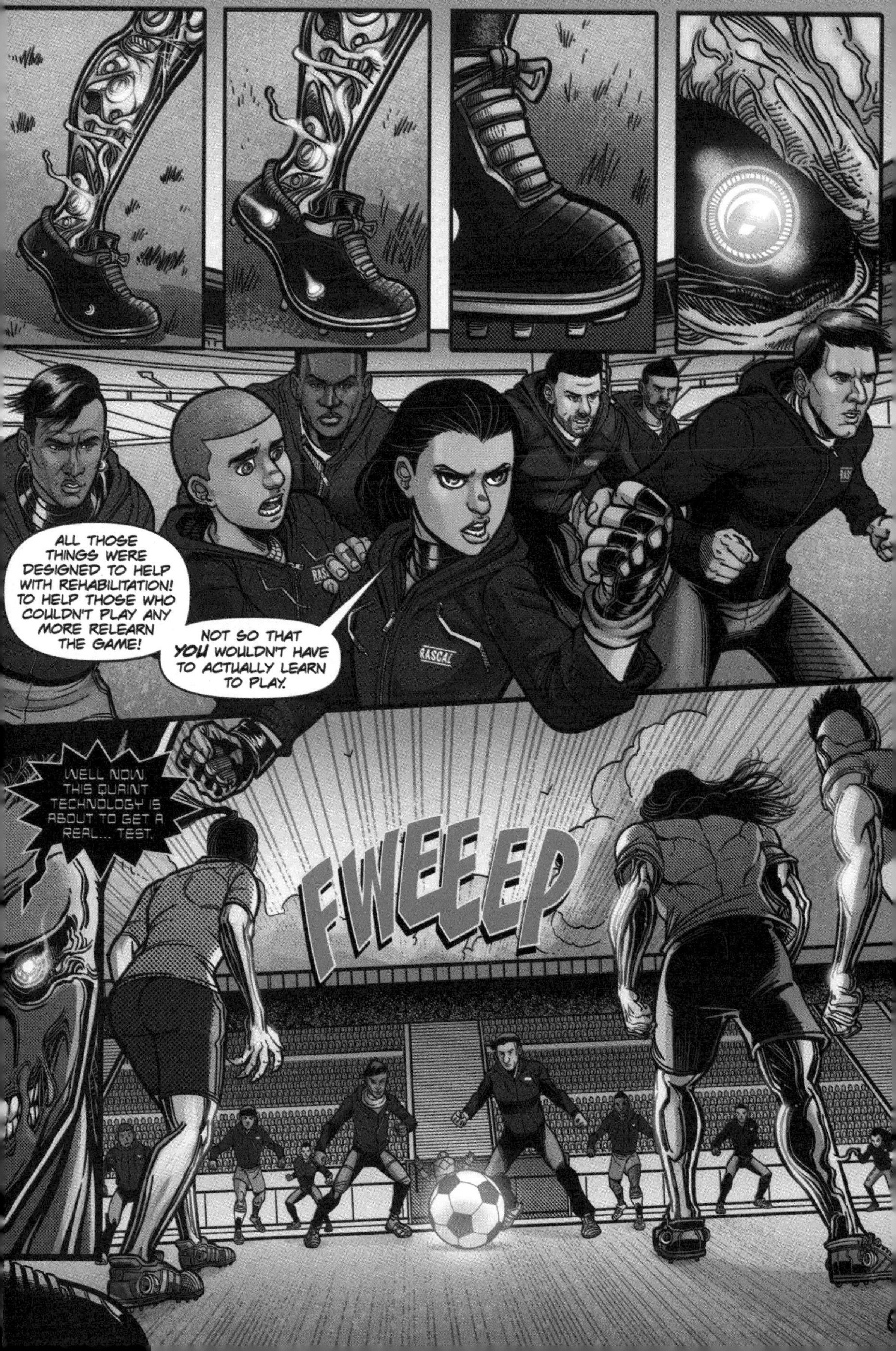
ALL THOSE THINGS WERE DESIGNED TO HELP WITH REHABILITATION! TO HELP THOSE WHO COULDN'T PLAY ANY MORE RELEARN THE GAME!
NOT SO THAT YOU WOULDN'T HAVE TO ACTUALLY LEARN TO PLAY.
RASCAL
WELL NOW, THIS QUAINT TECHNOLOGY IS ABOUT TO GET A REAL... TEST.
FWEEEP

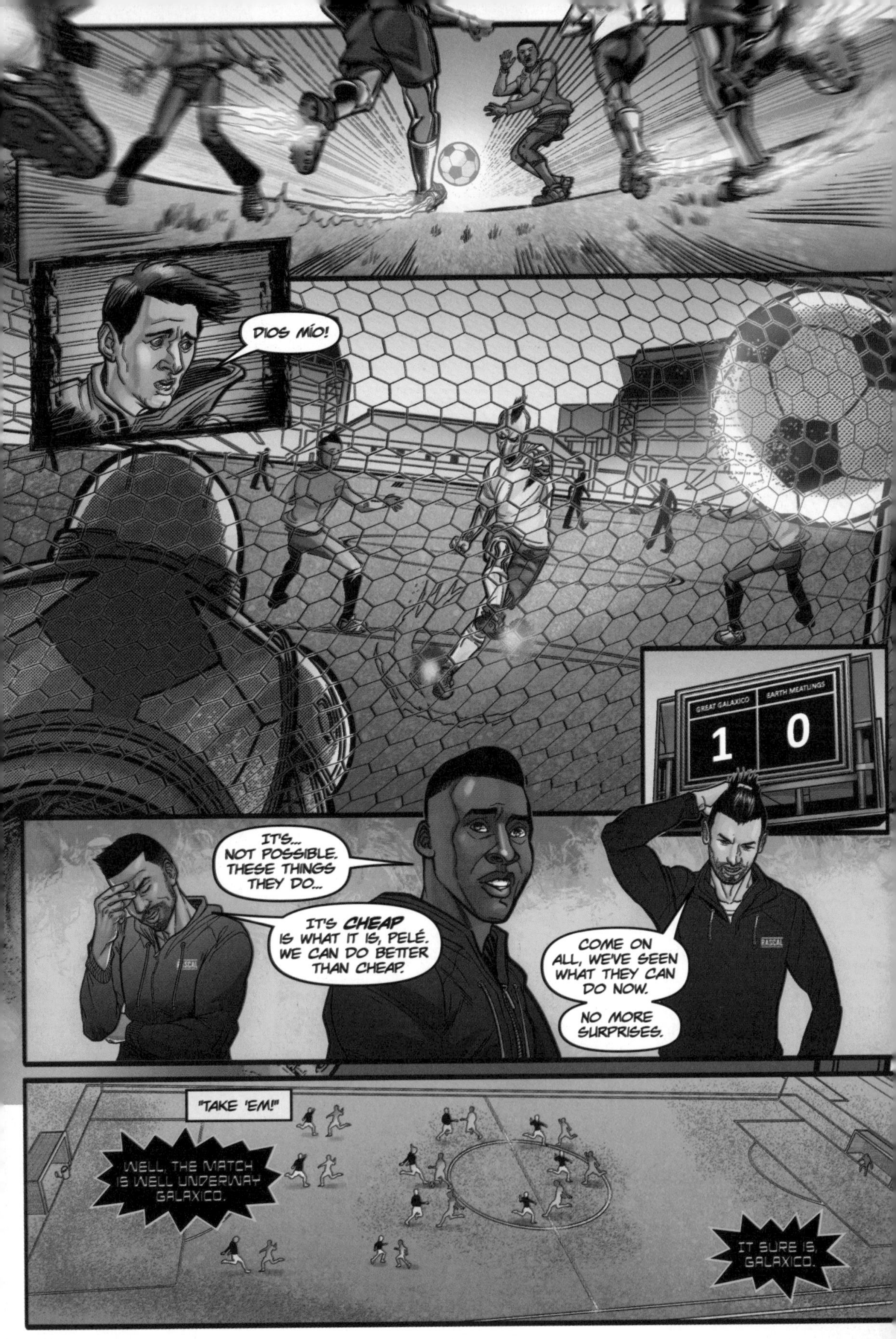
DIOS MÍO!
GREAT GALAXICO
EARTH MEATLINGS
1
0
IT'S... NOT POSSIBLE. THESE THINGS THEY DO...
IT'S CHEAP IS WHAT IT IS, PELÉ. WE CAN DO BETTER THAN CHEAP.
COME ON ALL, WE'VE SEEN WHAT THEY CAN DO NOW.
NO MORE SURPRISES.
RASCAL
"TAKE 'EM!"
WELL, THE MATCH IS WELL UNDERWAY GALAXICO.
IT SURE IS, GALAXICO.

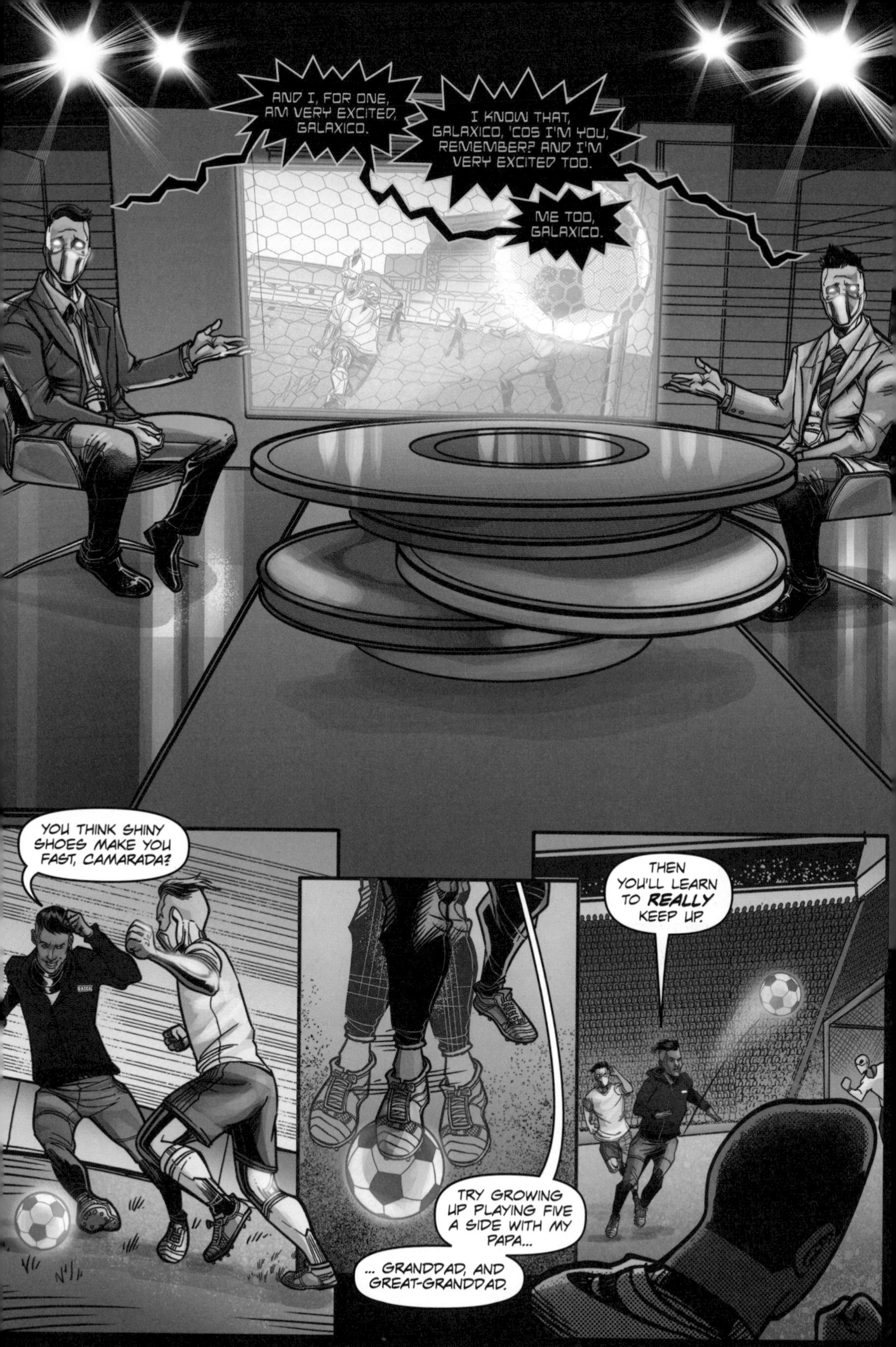
AND I, FOR ONE, AM VERY EXCITED, GALAXICO.
I KNOW THAT, GALAXICO, 'COS I'M YOU, REMEMBER? AND I'M VERY EXCITED TOO.
ME TOO, GALAXICO.
YOU THINK SHINY SHOES MAKE YOU FAST, CAMARADA?
TRY GROWING UP PLAYING FIVE A SIDE WITH MY PAPA...
... GRANDDAD, AND GREAT-GRANDDAD.
THEN YOU'LL LEARN TO *REALLY* KEEP UP.

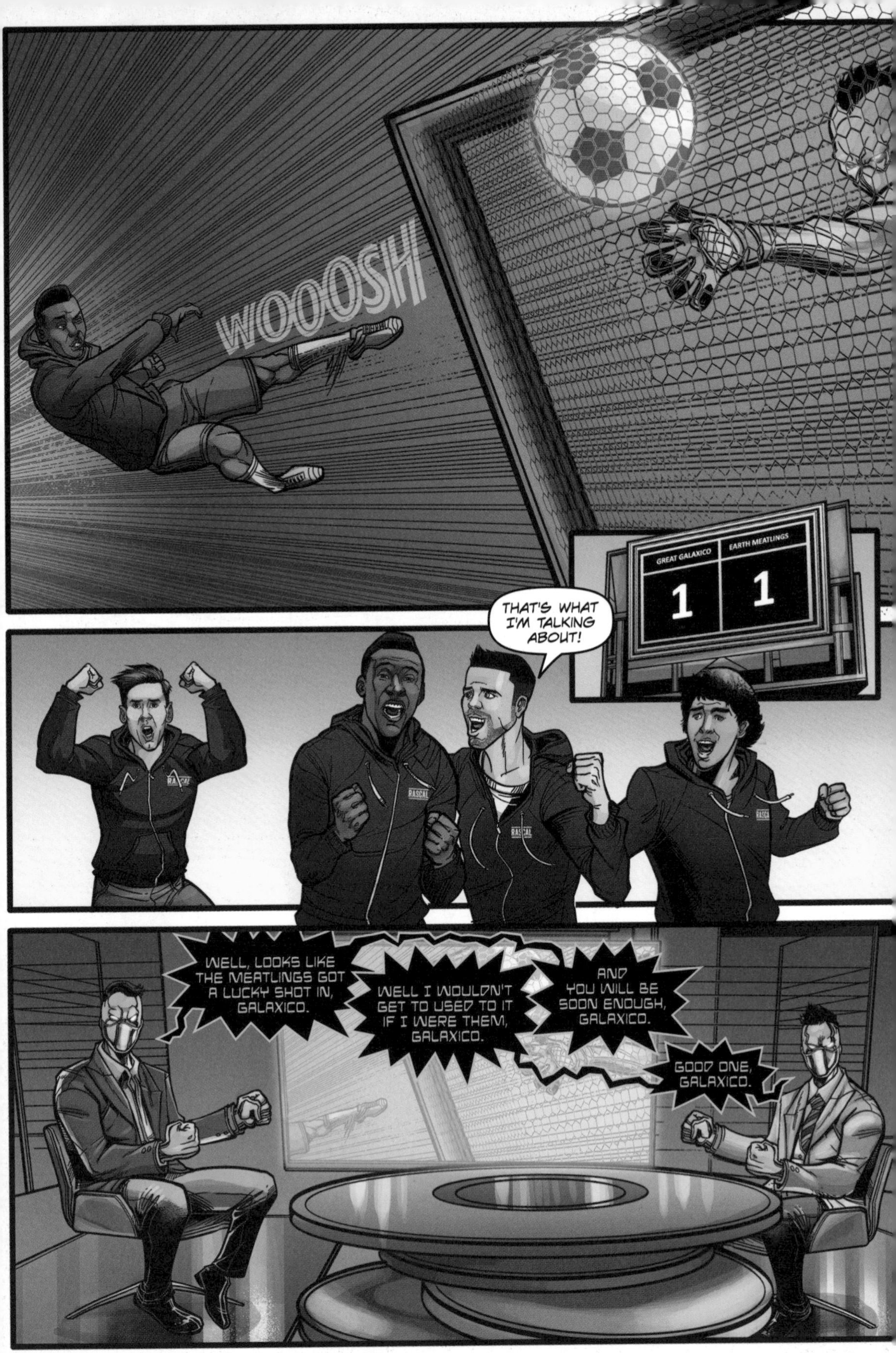
WOOOSH
GREAT GALAXICO
EARTH MEATLINGS
1
1
THAT'S WHAT I'M TALKING ABOUT!
RASCAL
WELL, LOOKS LIKE THE MEATLINGS GOT A LUCKY SHOT IN, GALAXICO.
WELL I WOULDN'T GET TO USED TO IT IF I WERE THEM, GALAXICO.
AND YOU WILL BE SOON ENOUGH, GALAXICO.
GOOD ONE, GALAXICO.

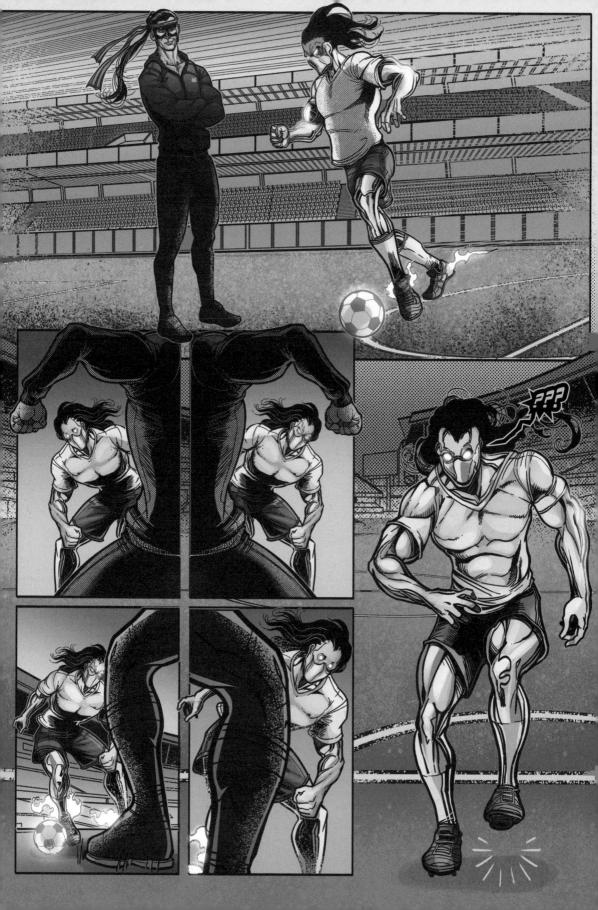

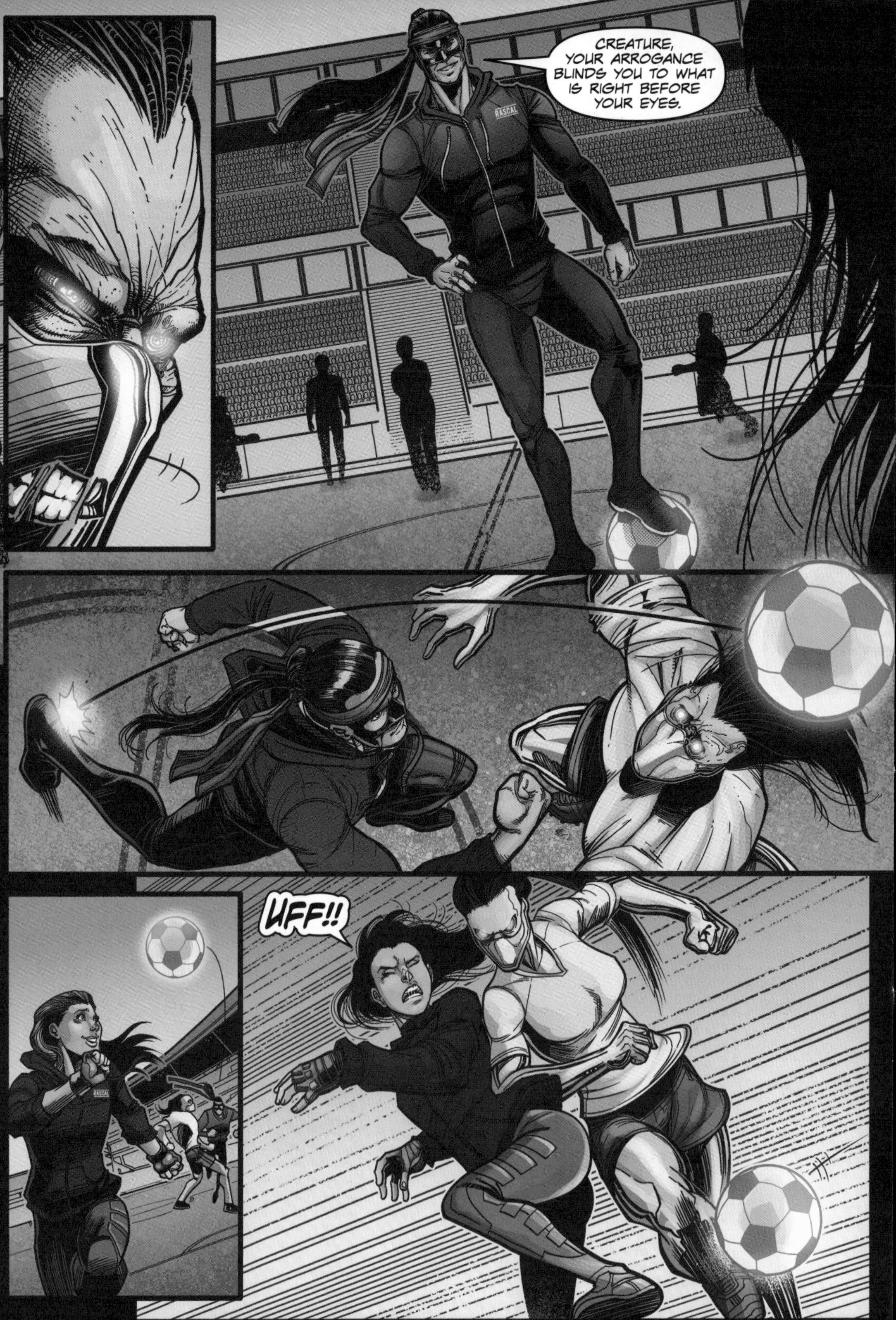

CREATURE, YOUR ARROGANCE BLINDS YOU TO WHAT IS RIGHT BEFORE YOUR EYES.
RASCAL
UFF!!
RASCAL

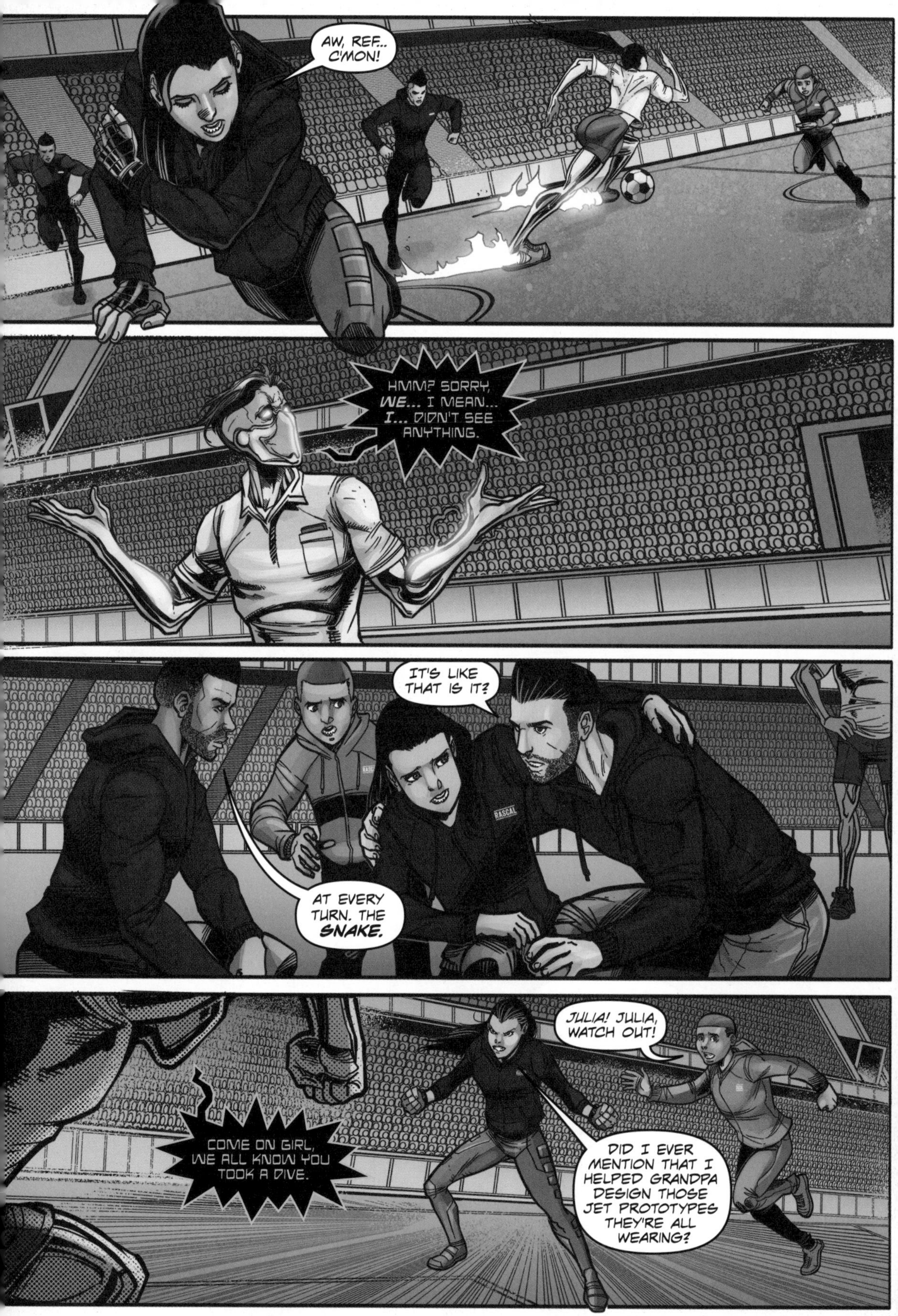
AW, REF... C'MON!
HMM? SORRY, WE... I MEAN... I... DIDN'T SEE ANYTHING.
IT'S LIKE THAT IS IT?
AT EVERY TURN. THE SNAKE.
RASCAL
JULIA! JULIA, WATCH OUT!
COME ON GIRL, WE ALL KNOW YOU TOOK A DIVE.
DID I EVER MENTION THAT I HELPED GRANDPA DESIGN THOSE JET PROTOTYPES THEY'RE ALL WEARING?

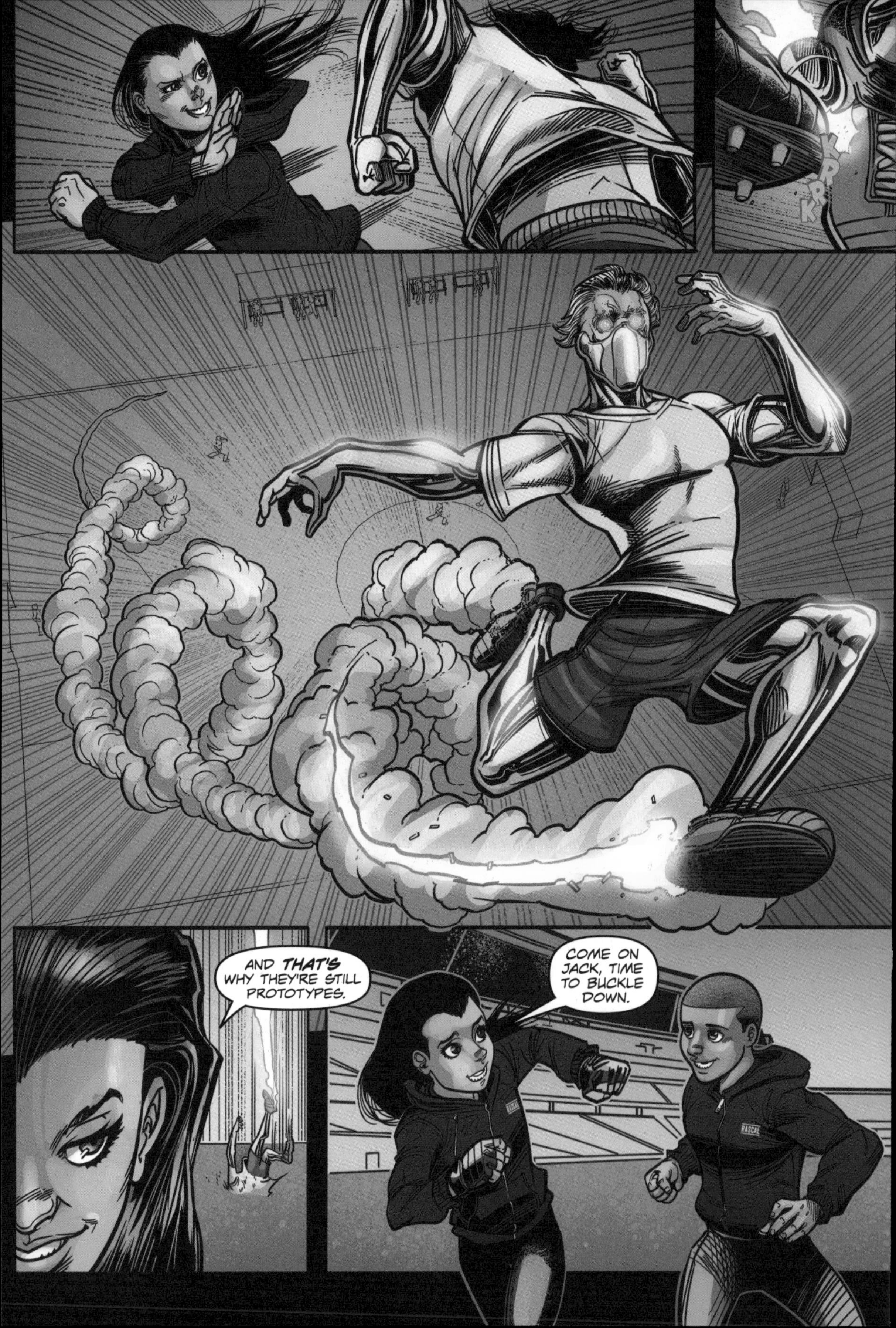
KRRK
AND THAT'S WHY THEY'RE STILL PROTOTYPES.
COME ON JACK, TIME TO BUCKLE DOWN.
RASCAL
RASCAL

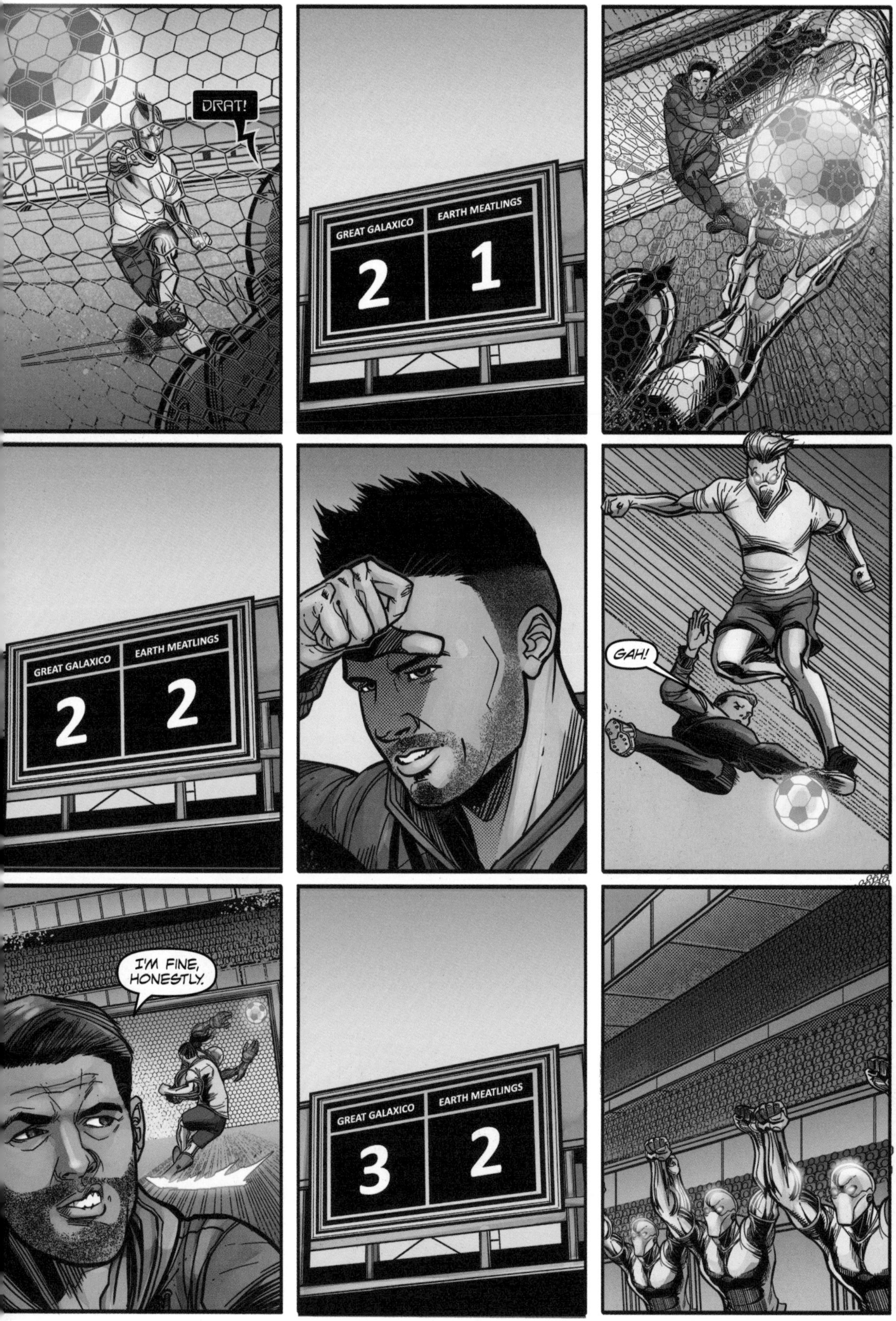
DRAT!
GREAT GALAXICO
EARTH MEATLINGS
2
1
GREAT GALAXICO
EARTH MEATLINGS
2
2
GAH!
I'M FINE, HONESTLY.
GREAT GALAXICO
EARTH MEATLINGS
3
2

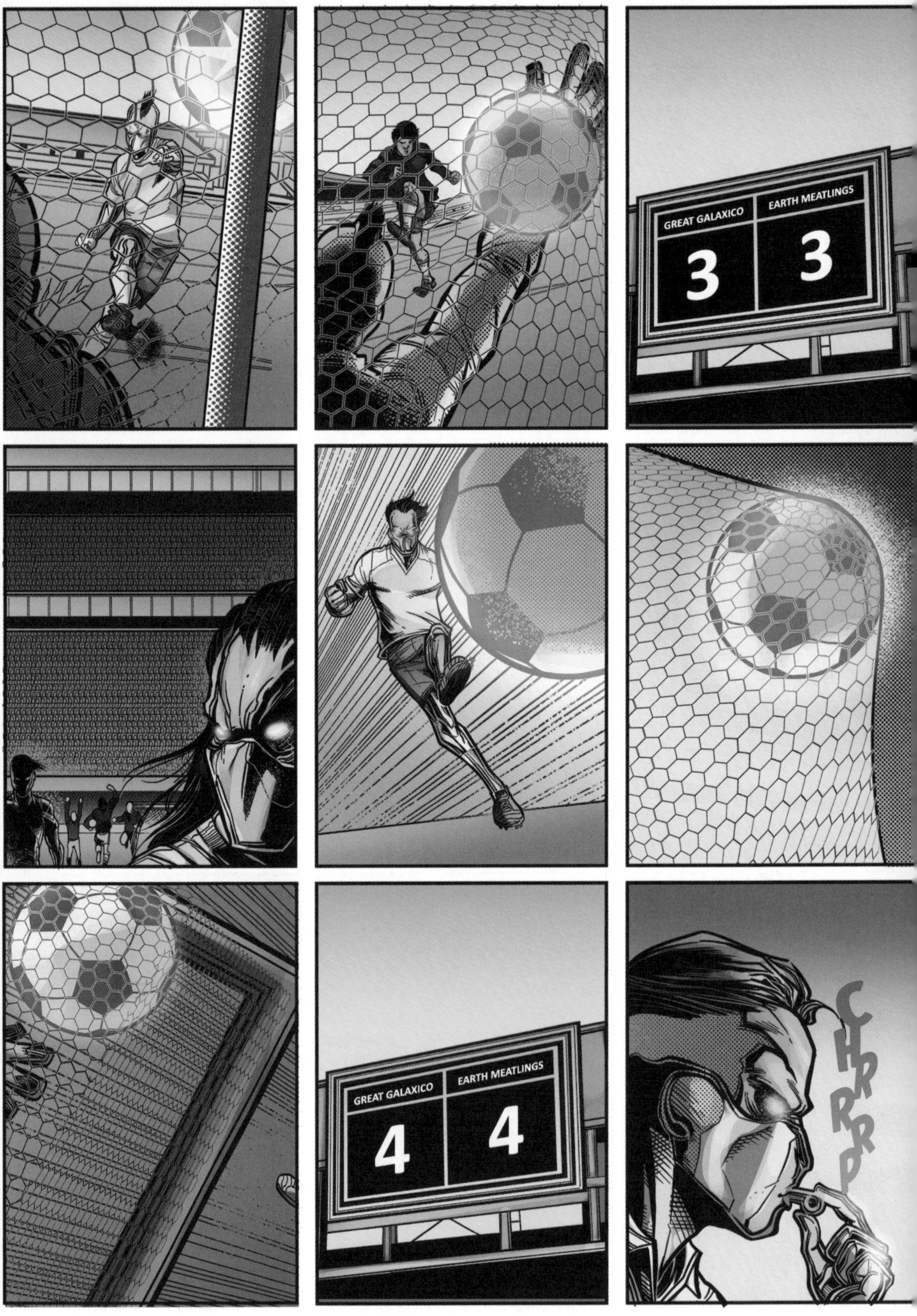
GREAT GALAXICO
EARTH MEATLINGS
3
3
GREAT GALAXICO
EARTH MEATLINGS
4
4
CHRRRP

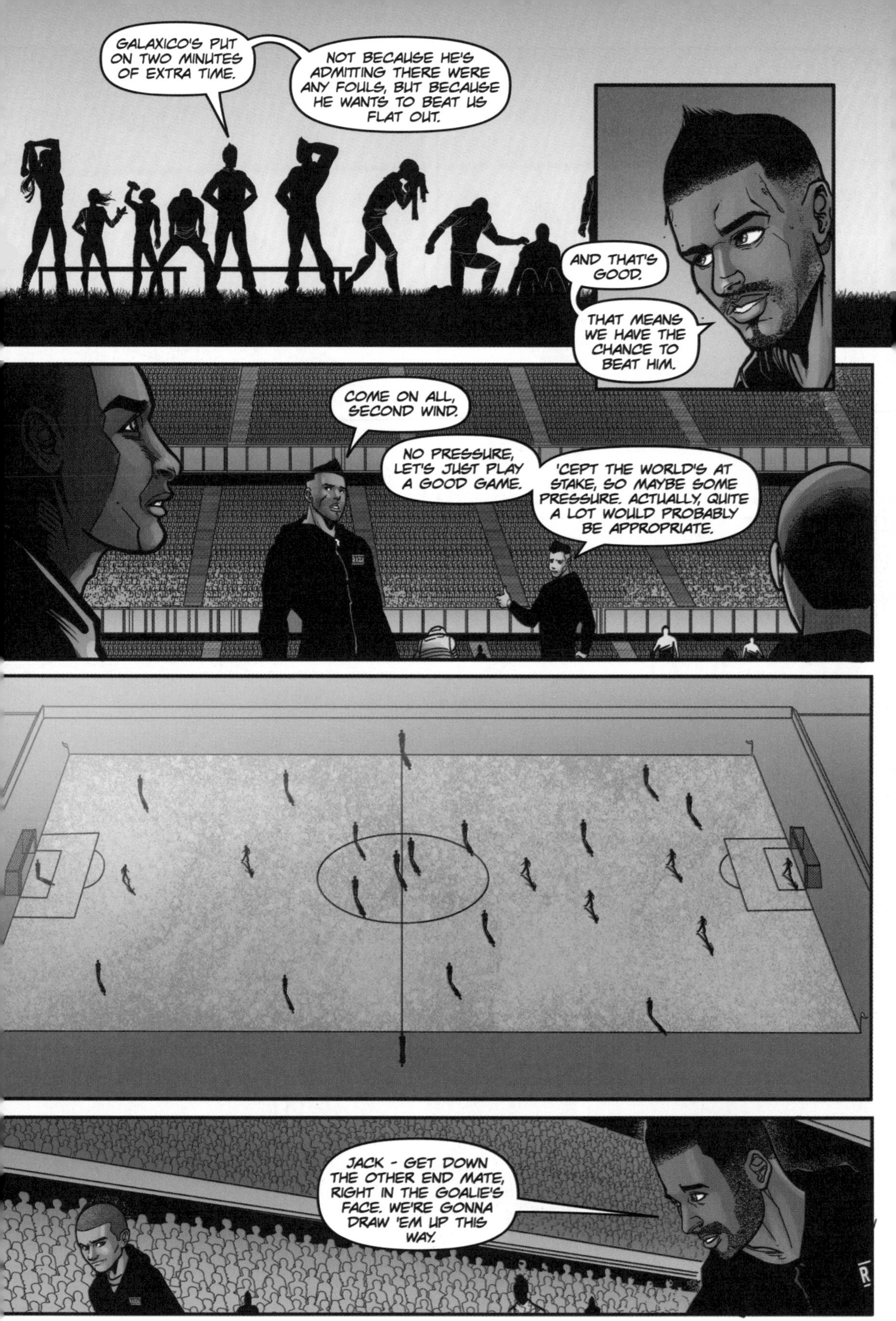
GALAXICO'S PUT ON TWO MINUTES OF EXTRA TIME.
NOT BECAUSE HE'S ADMITTING THERE WERE ANY FOULS, BUT BECAUSE HE WANTS TO BEAT US FLAT OUT.
AND THAT'S GOOD.
THAT MEANS WE HAVE THE CHANCE TO BEAT HIM.
COME ON ALL, SECOND WIND.
NO PRESSURE, LET'S JUST PLAY A GOOD GAME.
'CEPT THE WORLD'S AT STAKE, SO MAYBE SOME PRESSURE. ACTUALLY, QUITE A LOT WOULD PROBABLY BE APPROPRIATE.
JACK - GET DOWN THE OTHER END MATE, RIGHT IN THE GOALIE'S FACE. WE'RE GONNA DRAW 'EM UP THIS WAY.

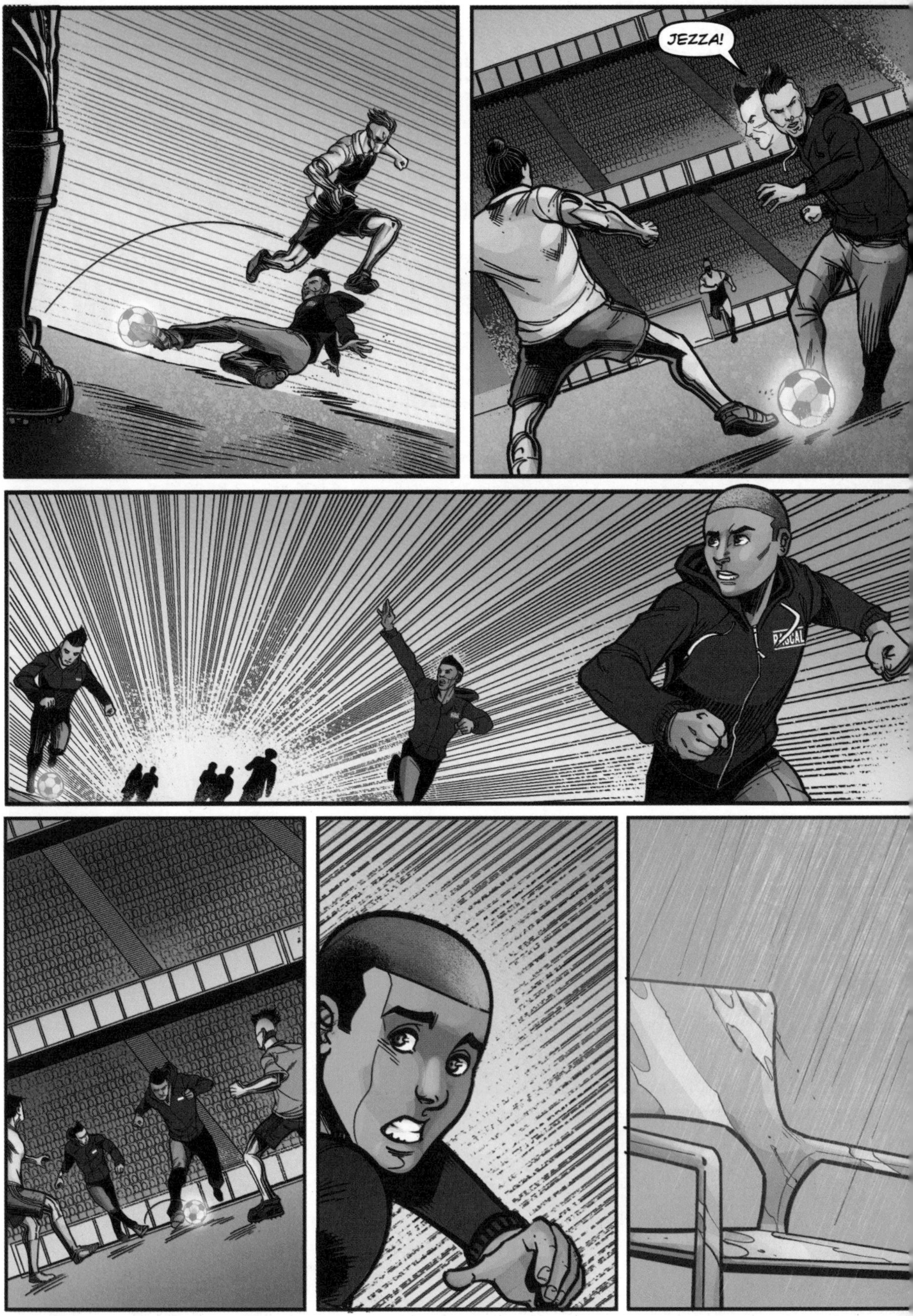
JEZZA!
PASCAL

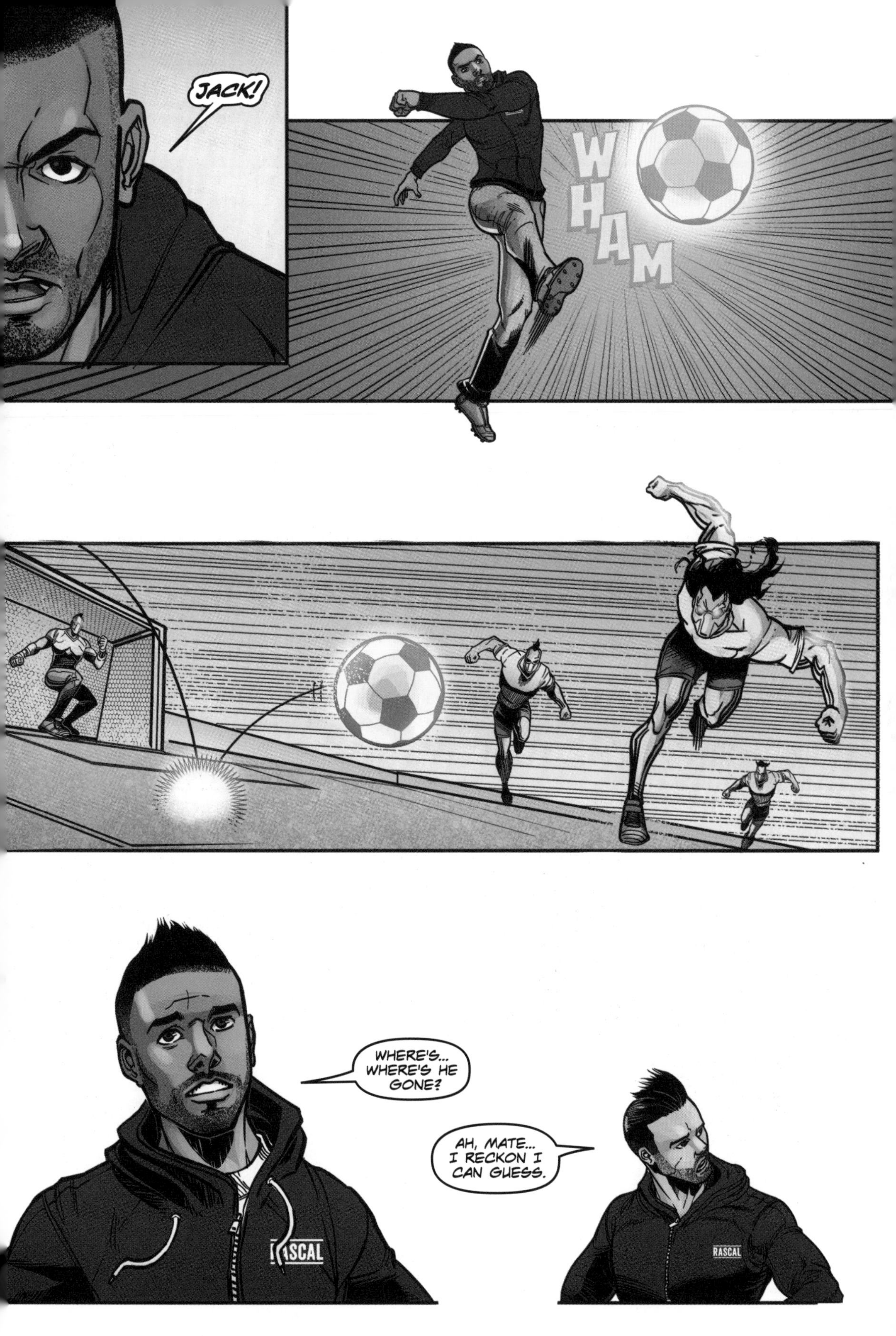
JACK!
WHAM
WHERE'S... WHERE'S HE GONE?
AH, MATE... I RECKON I CAN GUESS.
RASCAL
RASCAL

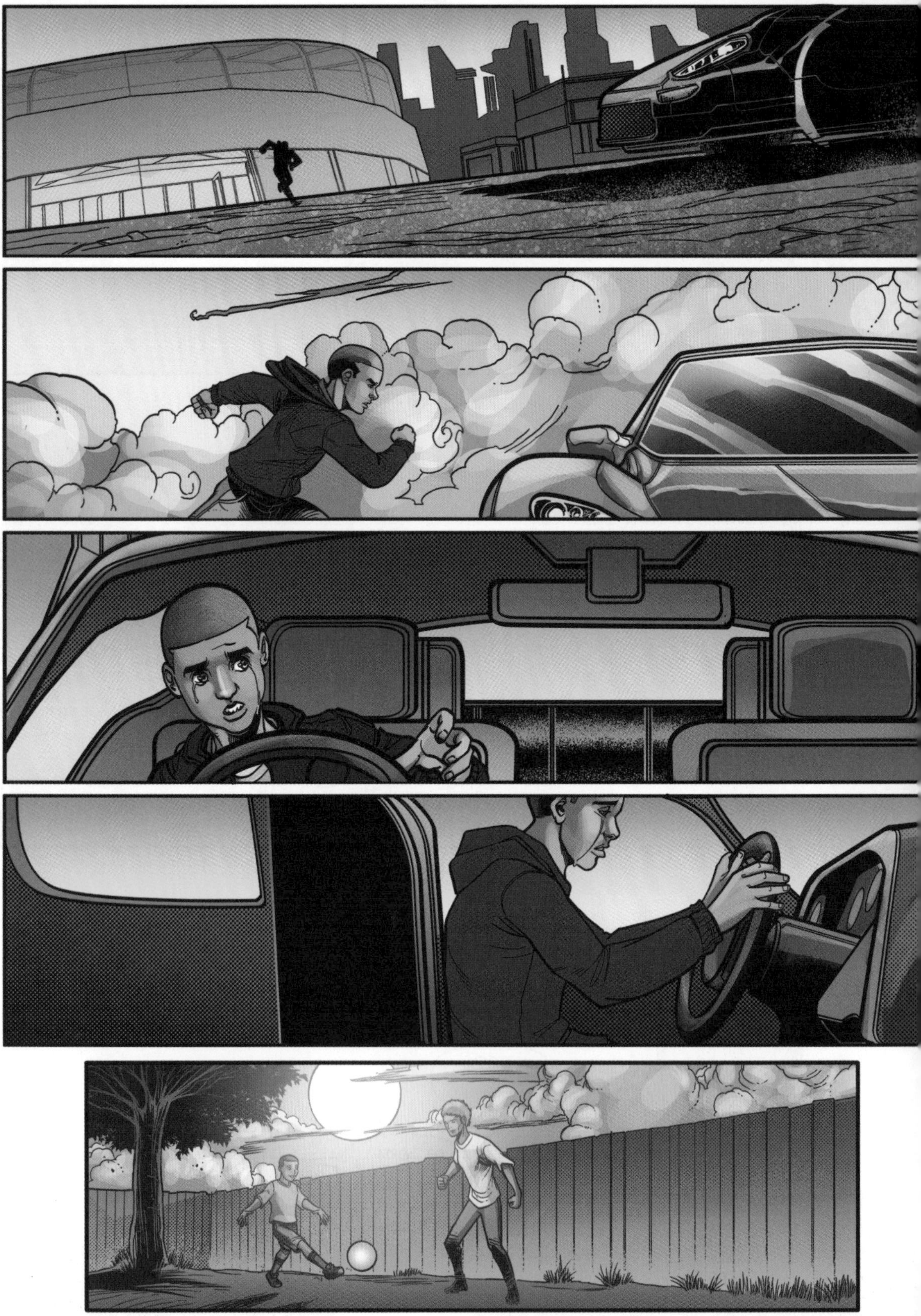

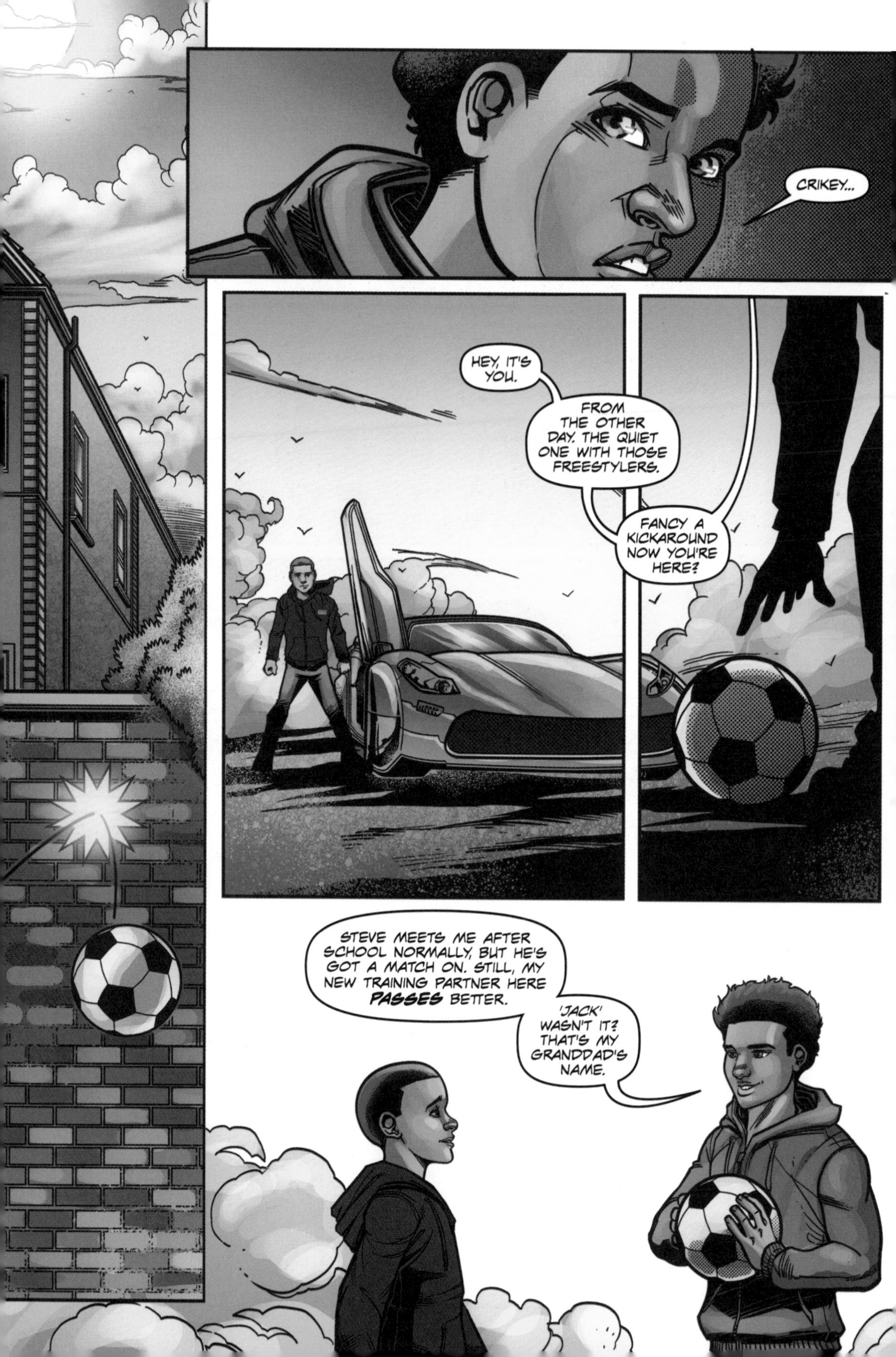
CRIKEY...
HEY, IT'S YOU.
FROM THE OTHER DAY. THE QUIET ONE WITH THOSE FREESTYLERS.
FANCY A KICKAROUND NOW YOU'RE HERE?
STEVE MEETS ME AFTER SCHOOL NORMALLY, BUT HE'S GOT A MATCH ON. STILL, MY NEW TRAINING PARTNER HERE PASSES BETTER.
'JACK' WASN'T IT? THAT'S MY GRANDDAD'S NAME.

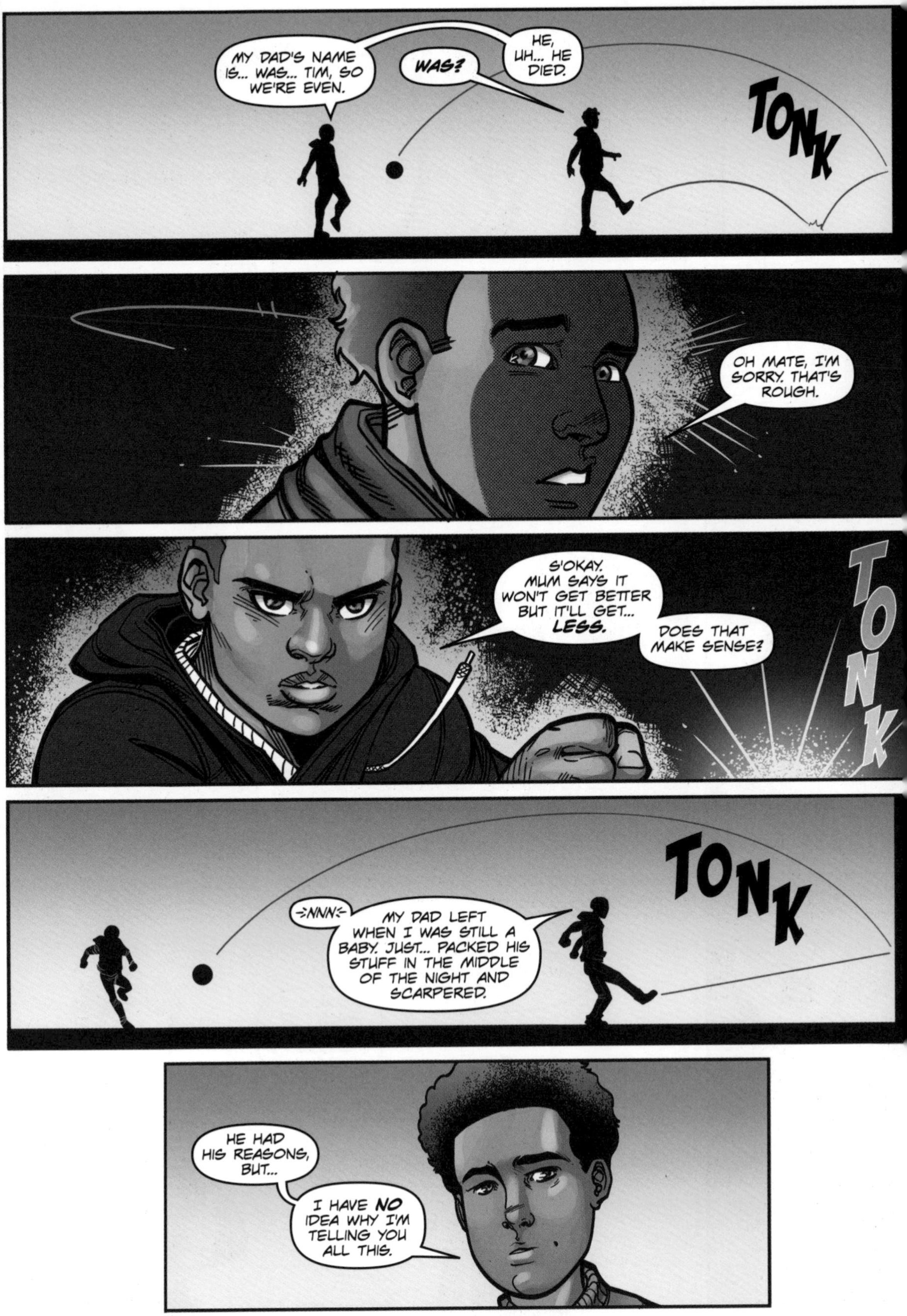
MY DAD'S NAME IS... WAS... TIM, SO WE'RE EVEN.
WAS?
HE, UH... HE DIED.
TONK
OH MATE, I'M SORRY. THAT'S ROUGH.
S'OKAY. MUM SAYS IT WON'T GET BETTER BUT IT'LL GET... LESS.
DOES THAT MAKE SENSE?
TONK
TONK
NNN
MY DAD LEFT WHEN I WAS STILL A BABY. JUST... PACKED HIS STUFF IN THE MIDDLE OF THE NIGHT AND SCARPERED.
HE HAD HIS REASONS, BUT...
I HAVE NO IDEA WHY I'M TELLING YOU ALL THIS.

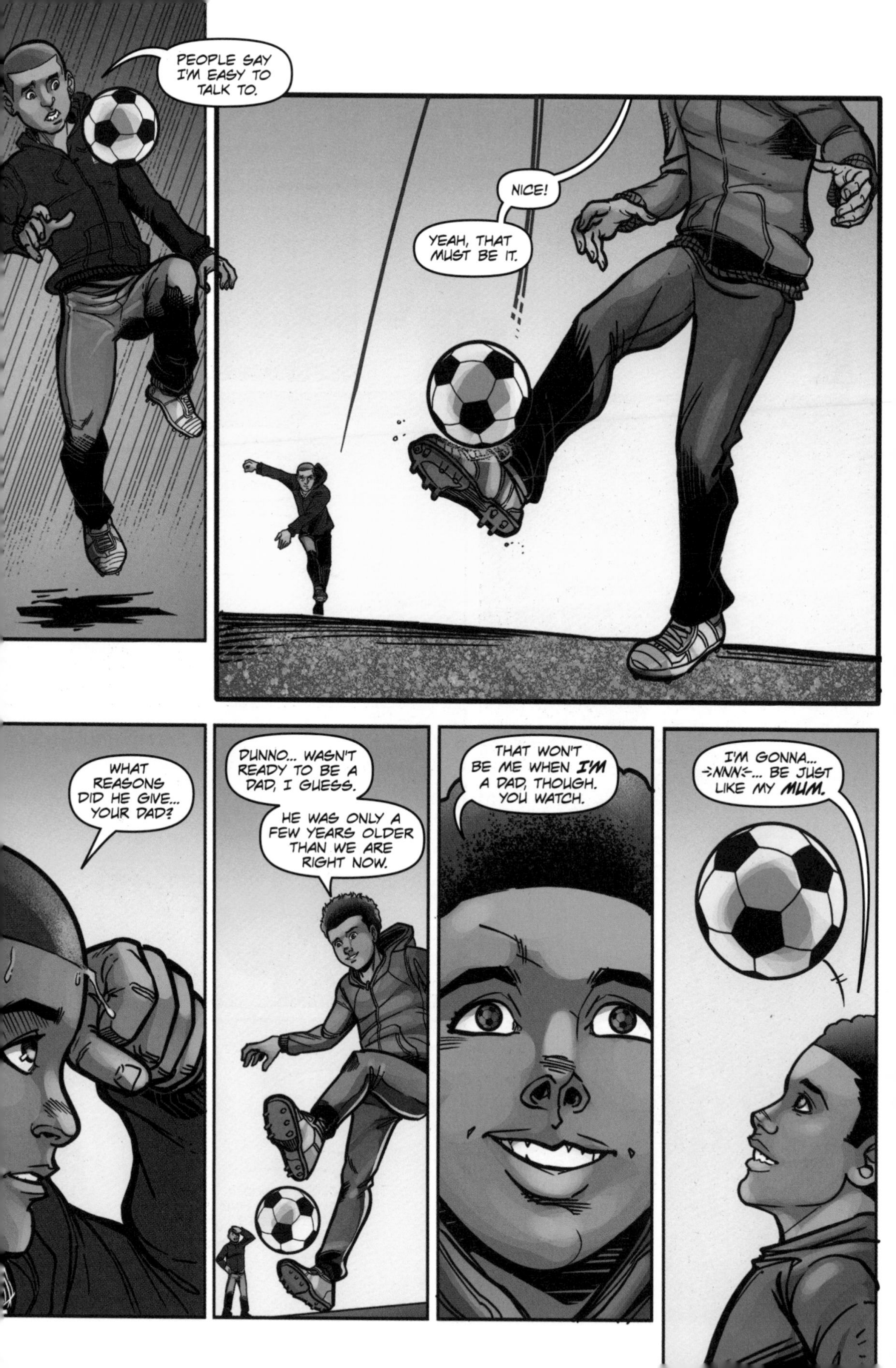

PEOPLE SAY I'M EASY TO TALK TO.
NICE!
YEAH, THAT MUST BE IT.
WHAT REASONS DID HE GIVE... YOUR DAD?
DUNNO... WASN'T READY TO BE A DAD, I GUESS.
HE WAS ONLY A FEW YEARS OLDER THAN WE ARE RIGHT NOW.
THAT WON'T BE ME WHEN I'M A DAD, THOUGH. YOU WATCH.
I'M GONNA... NNN... BE JUST LIKE MY MUM.

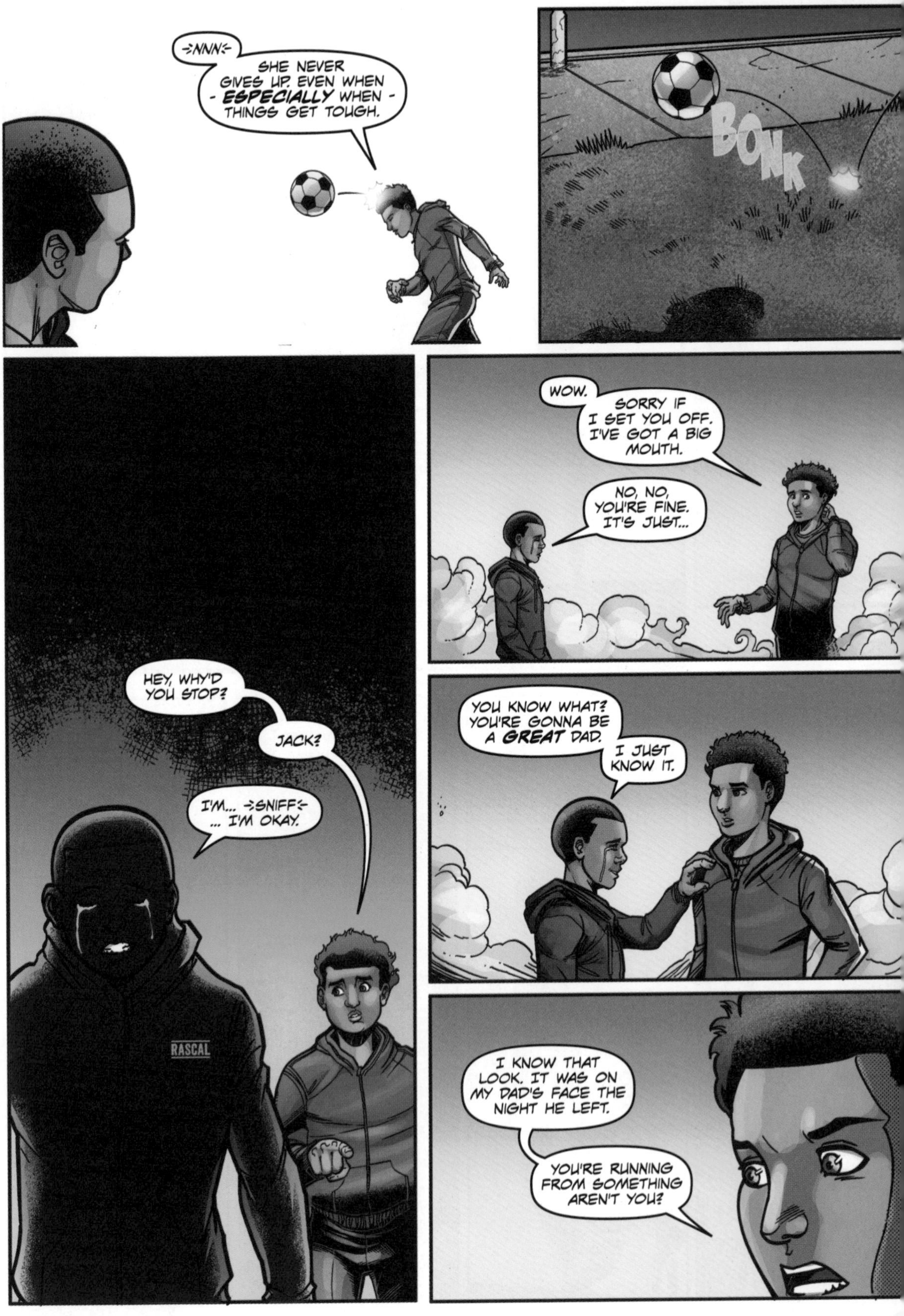
~NNN~
SHE NEVER GIVES UP. EVEN WHEN - ESPECIALLY WHEN - THINGS GET TOUGH.
BONK
HEY, WHY'D YOU STOP?
JACK?
I'M... ~SNIFF~ ... I'M OKAY.
RASCAL
WOW.
SORRY IF I SET YOU OFF. I'VE GOT A BIG MOUTH.
NO, NO, YOU'RE FINE. IT'S JUST...
YOU KNOW WHAT? YOU'RE GONNA BE A GREAT DAD.
I JUST KNOW IT.
I KNOW THAT LOOK. IT WAS ON MY DAD'S FACE THE NIGHT HE LEFT.
YOU'RE RUNNING FROM SOMETHING AREN'T YOU?

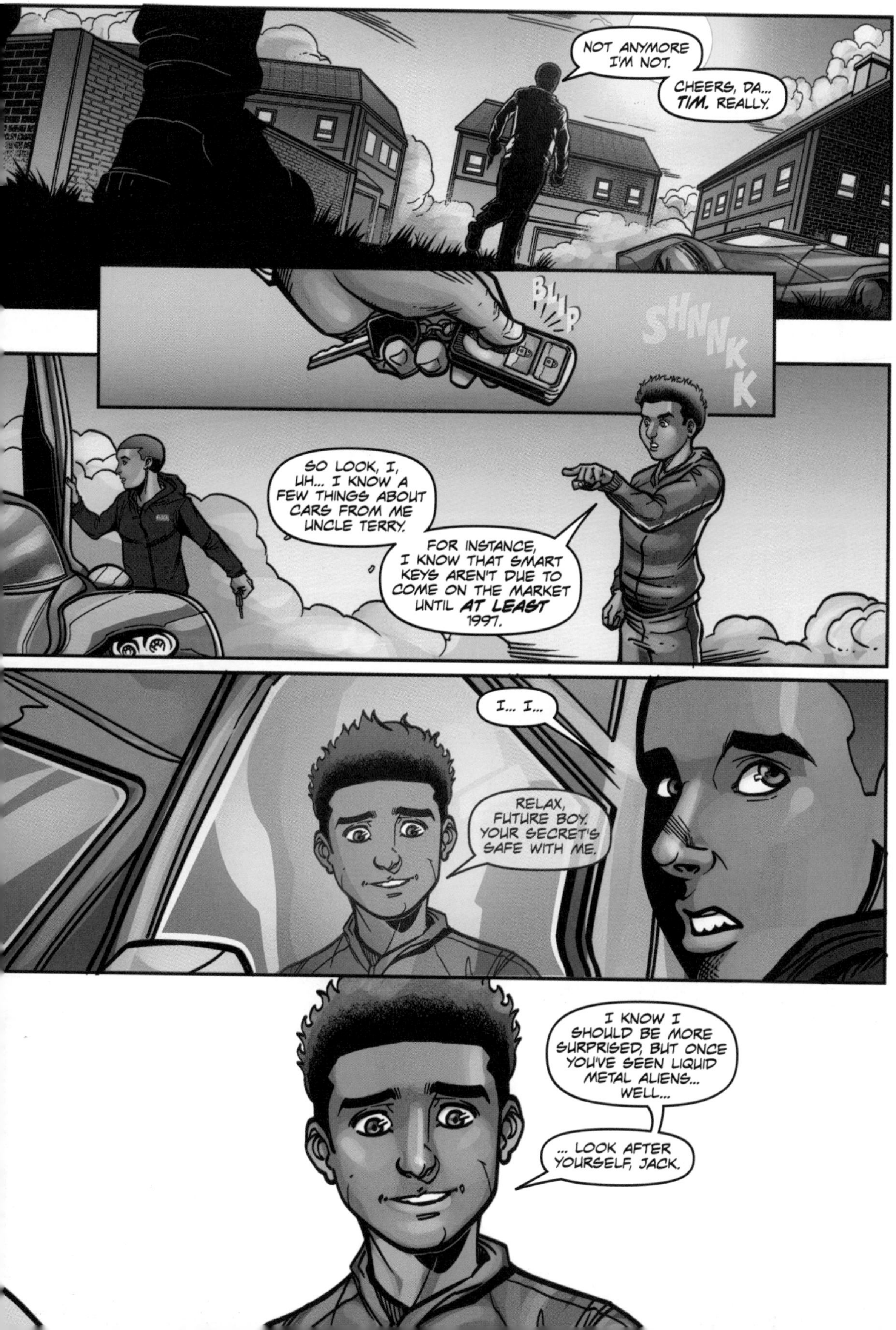

NOT ANYMORE I'M NOT.
CHEERS, DA... TIM. REALLY.
BLIP
SHNNKK
SO LOOK, I, UH... I KNOW A FEW THINGS ABOUT CARS FROM ME UNCLE TERRY.
FOR INSTANCE, I KNOW THAT SMART KEYS AREN'T DUE TO COME ON THE MARKET UNTIL AT LEAST 1997.
I... I...
RELAX, FUTURE BOY. YOUR SECRET'S SAFE WITH ME.
I KNOW I SHOULD BE MORE SURPRISED, BUT ONCE YOU'VE SEEN LIQUID METAL ALIENS... WELL...
... LOOK AFTER YOURSELF, JACK.

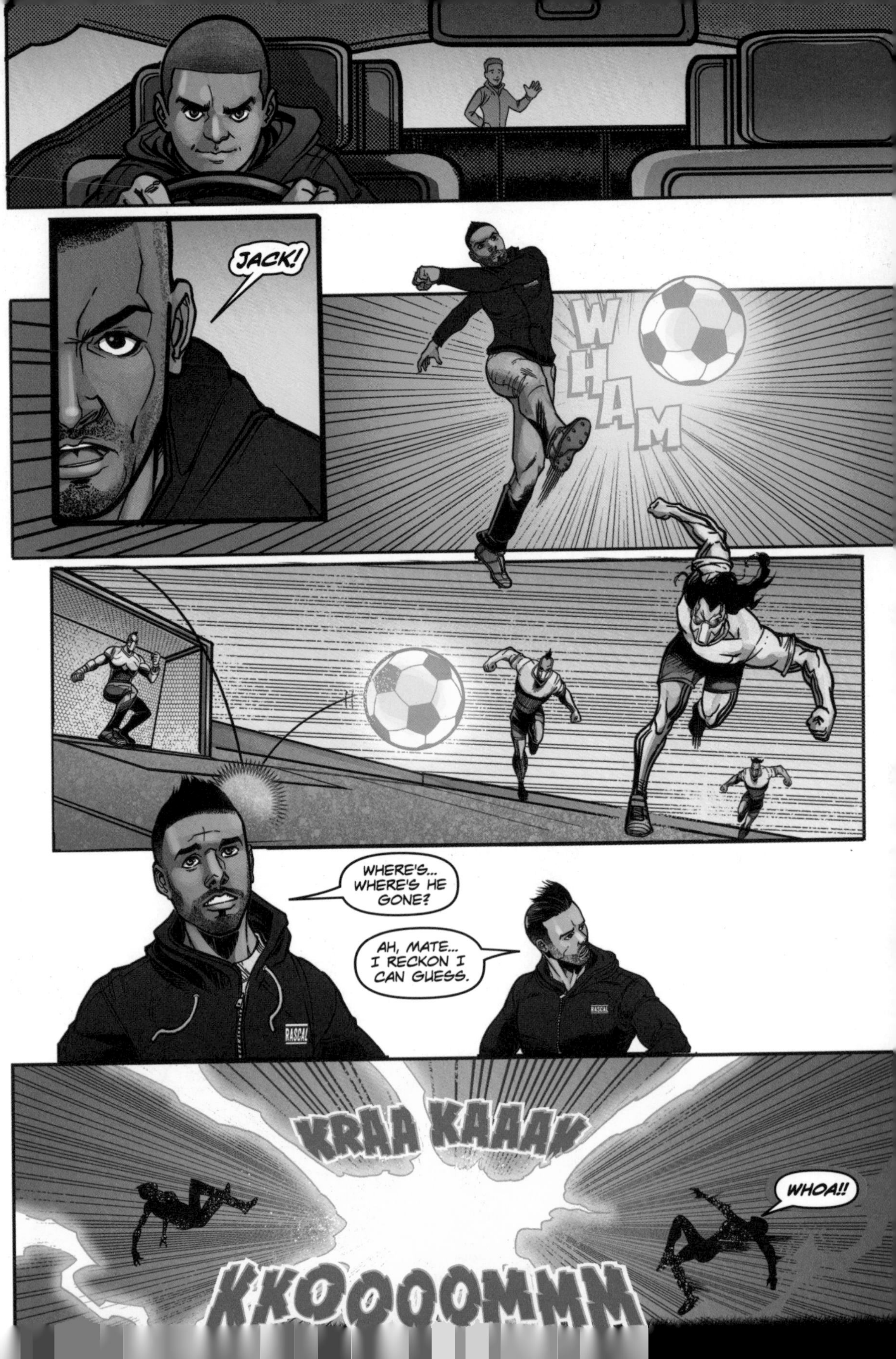
JACK!
WHAM
WHERE'S... WHERE'S HE GONE?
AH, MATE... I RECKON I CAN GUESS.
RASCAL
RASCAL
KRAA KAAAK
WHOA!!
KKOOOOMMM

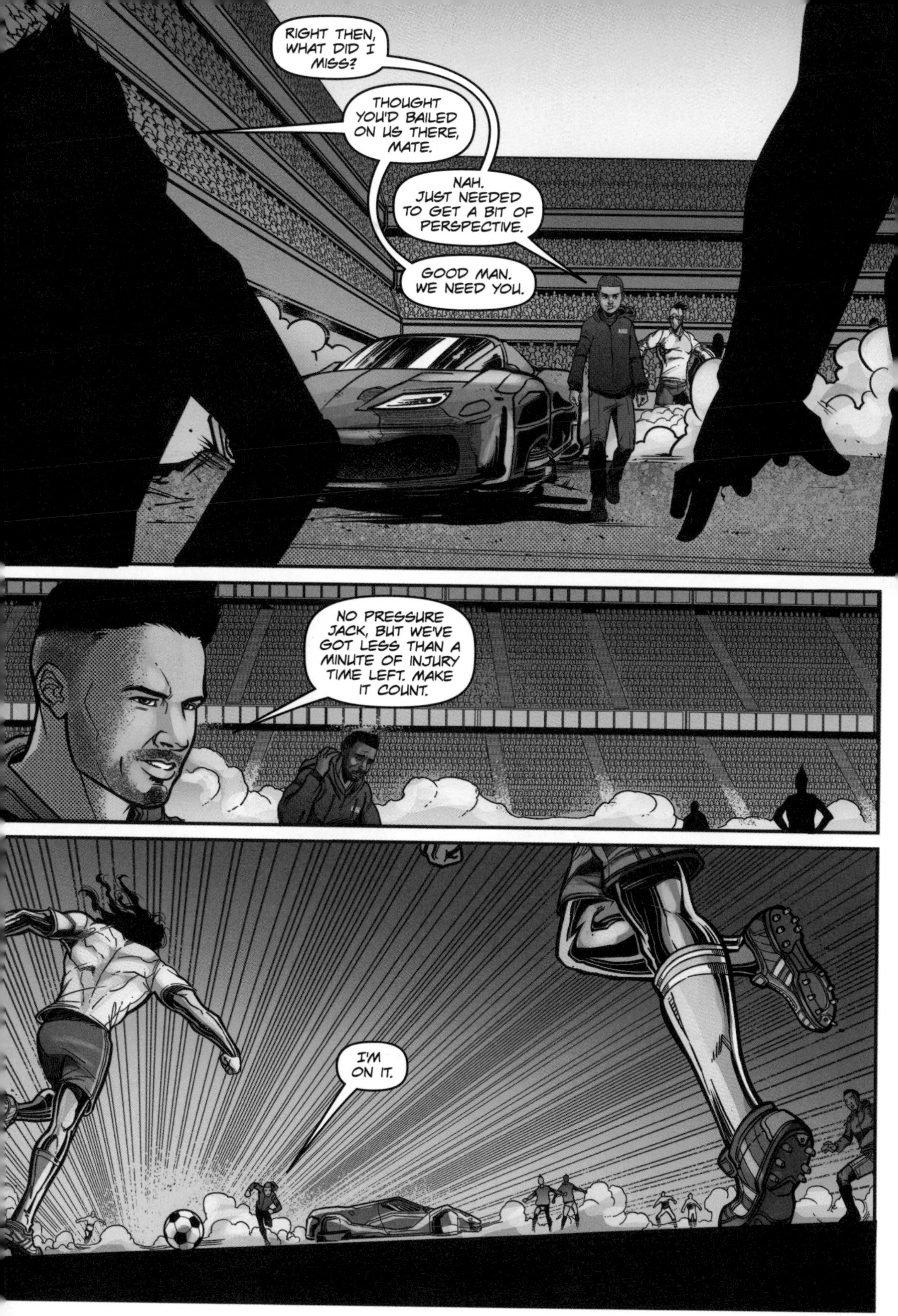
RIGHT THEN, WHAT DID I MISS?
THOUGHT YOU'D BAILED ON US THERE, MATE.
NAH. JUST NEEDED TO GET A BIT OF PERSPECTIVE.
GOOD MAN. WE NEED YOU.
NO PRESSURE JACK, BUT WE'VE GOT LESS THAN A MINUTE OF INJURY TIME LEFT. MAKE IT COUNT.
I'M ON IT.

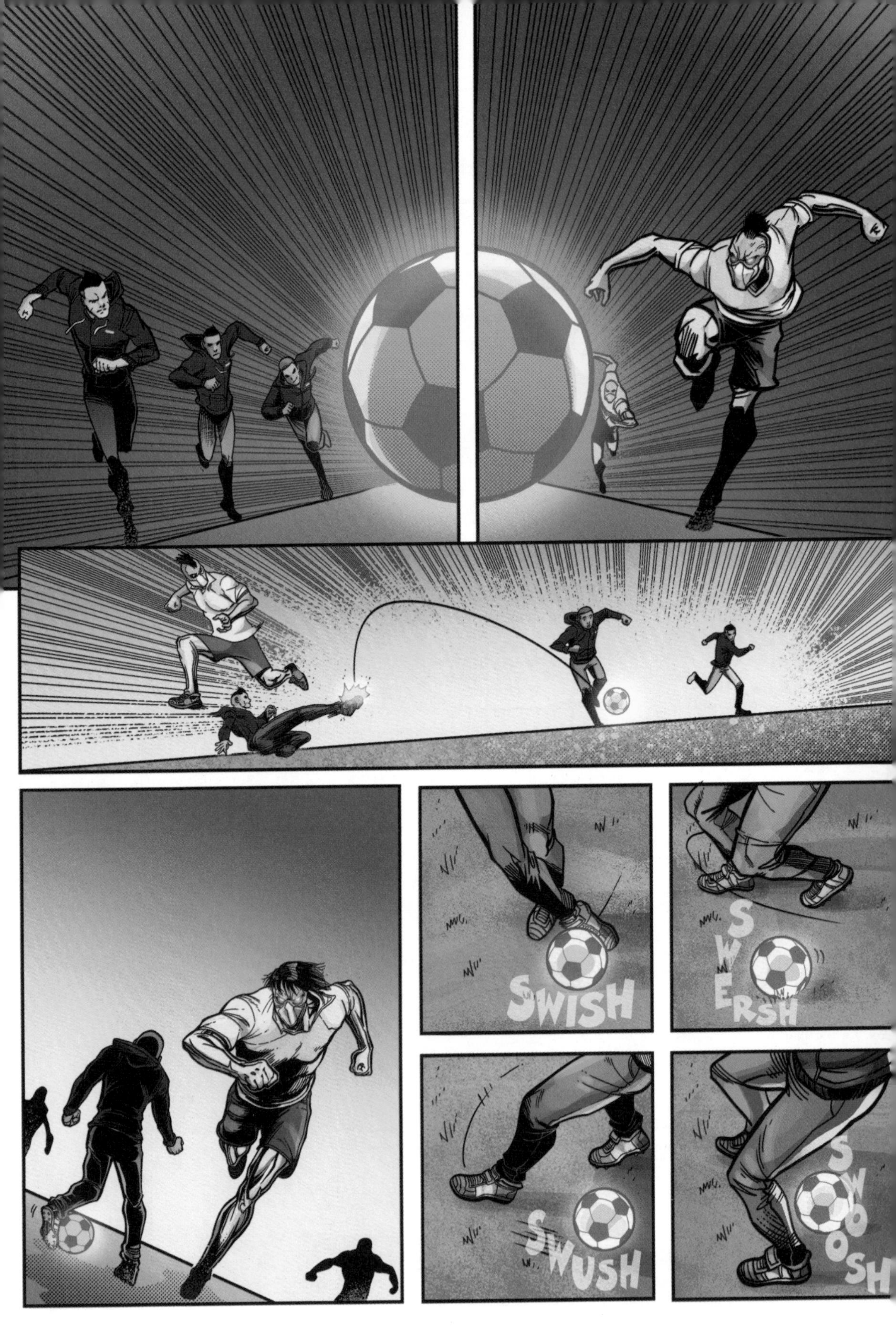
SWISH
SWERSH
SWUSH
SWOOSH

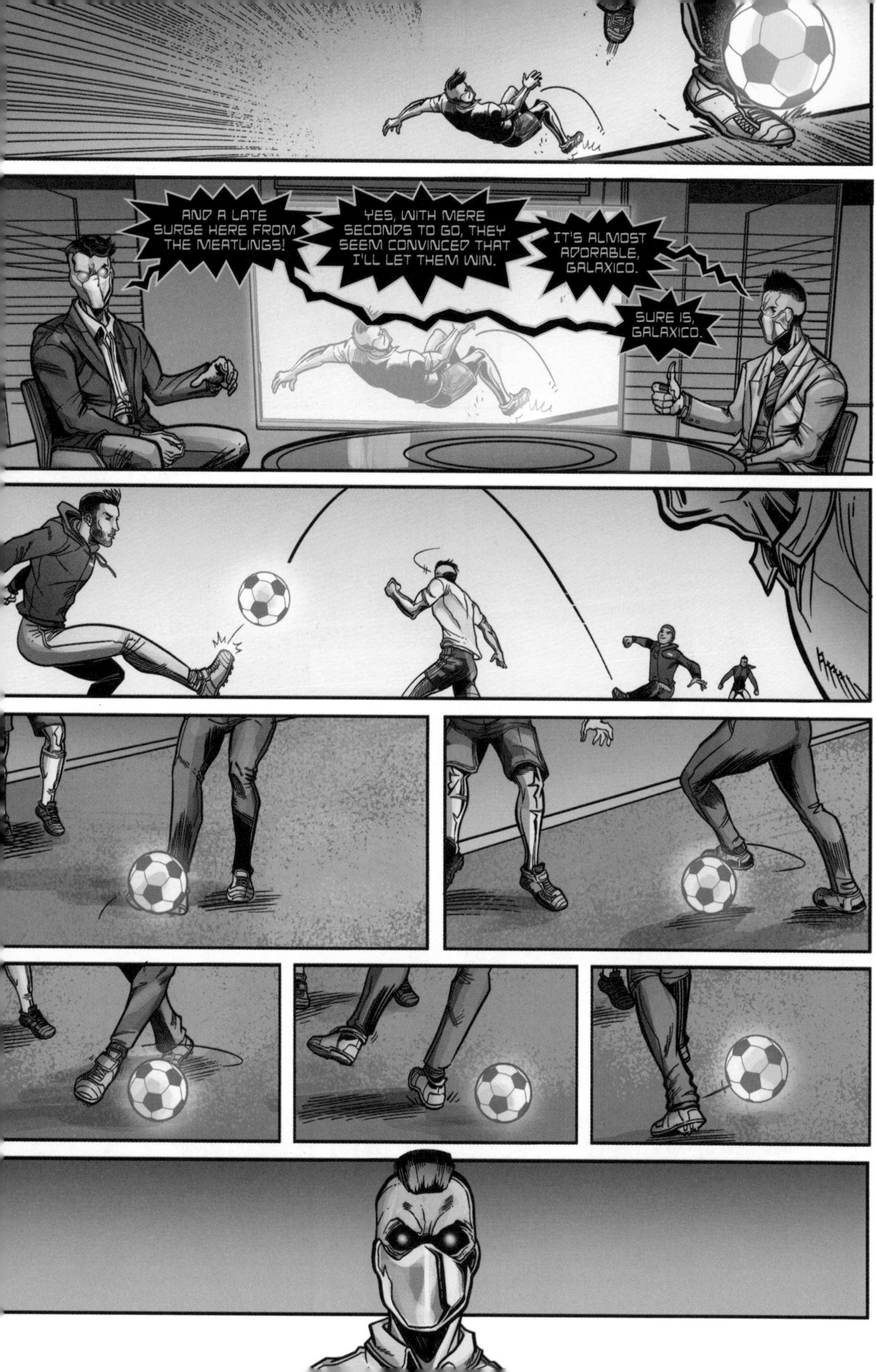
AND A LATE SURGE HERE FROM THE MEATLINGS!
YES, WITH MERE SECONDS TO GO, THEY SEEM CONVINCED THAT I'LL LET THEM WIN.
IT'S ALMOST ADORABLE, GALAXICO.
SURE IS, GALAXICO.

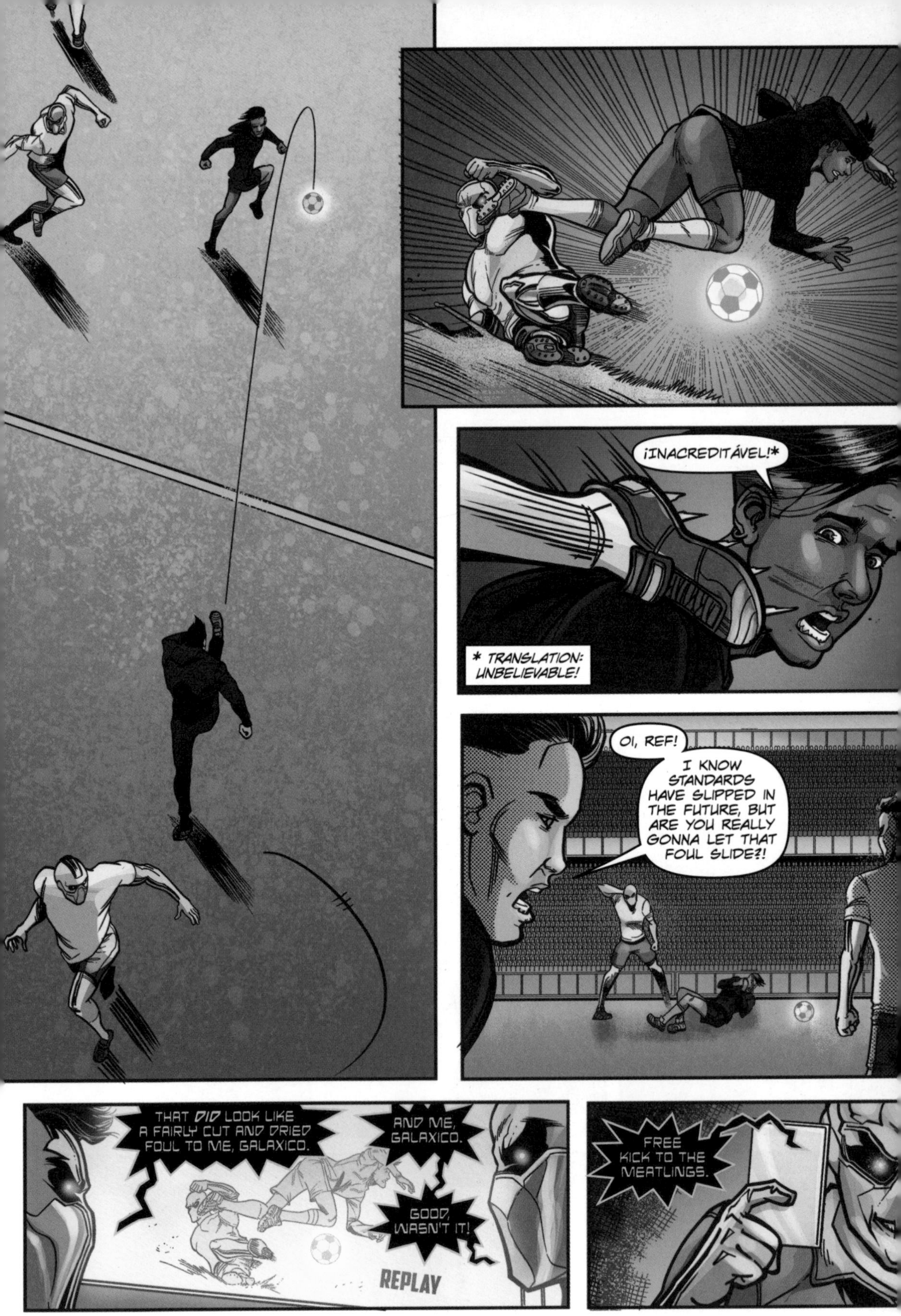
¡INACREDITÁVEL!*
* TRANSLATION: UNBELIEVABLE!
OI, REF!
I KNOW STANDARDS HAVE SLIPPED IN THE FUTURE, BUT ARE YOU REALLY GONNA LET THAT FOUL SLIDE?!
THAT DID LOOK LIKE A FAIRLY CUT AND DRIED FOUL TO ME, GALAXICO.
AND ME, GALAXICO.
GOOD, WASN'T IT!
REPLAY
FREE KICK TO THE MEATLINGS.

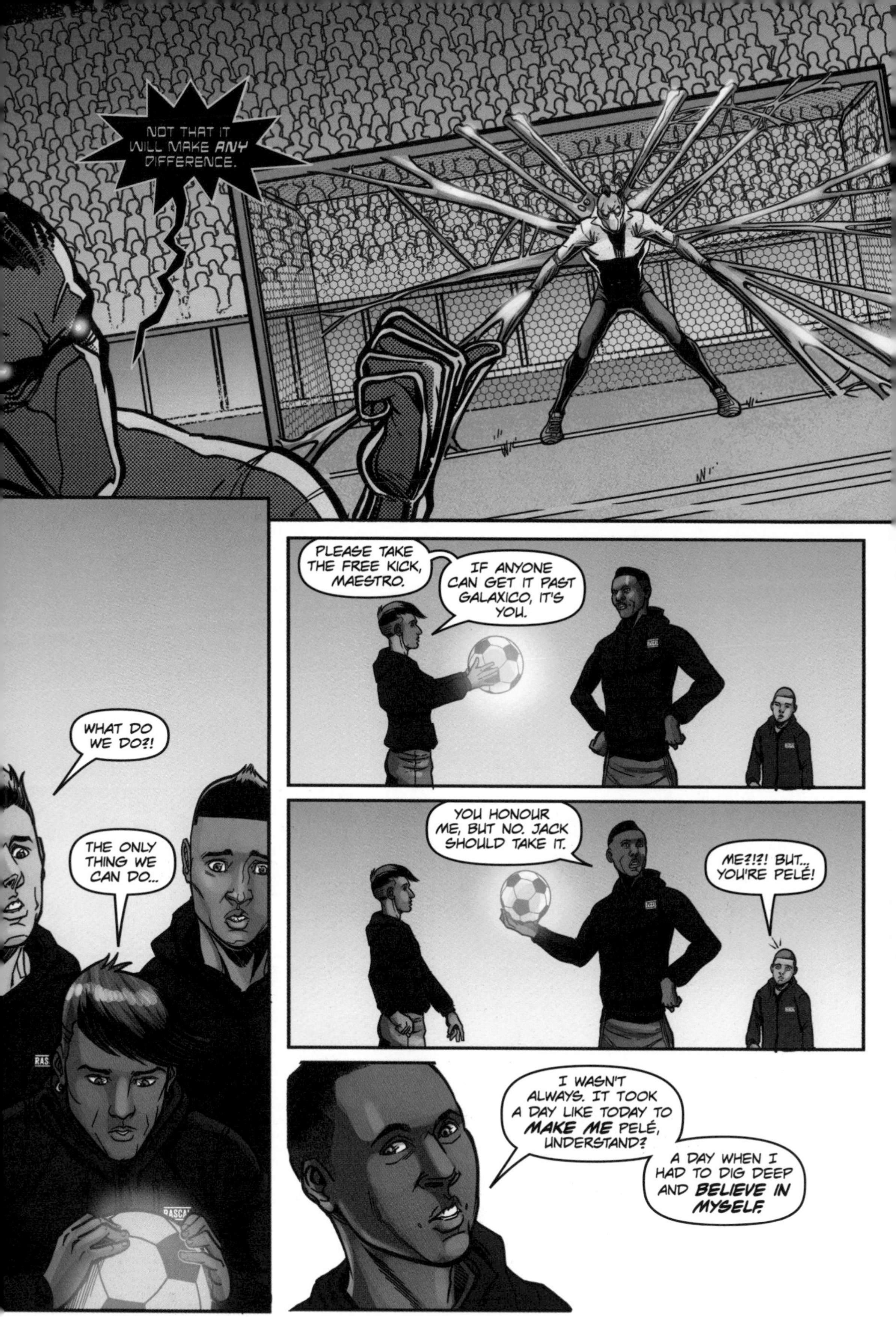
NOT THAT IT WILL MAKE ANY DIFFERENCE.
WHAT DO WE DO?!
THE ONLY THING WE CAN DO...
PLEASE TAKE THE FREE KICK, MAESTRO.
IF ANYONE CAN GET IT PAST GALAXICO, IT'S YOU.
YOU HONOUR ME, BUT NO. JACK SHOULD TAKE IT.
ME?!?! BUT... YOU'RE PELÉ!
I WASN'T ALWAYS. IT TOOK A DAY LIKE TODAY TO MAKE ME PELÉ, UNDERSTAND?
A DAY WHEN I HAD TO DIG DEEP AND BELIEVE IN MYSELF.

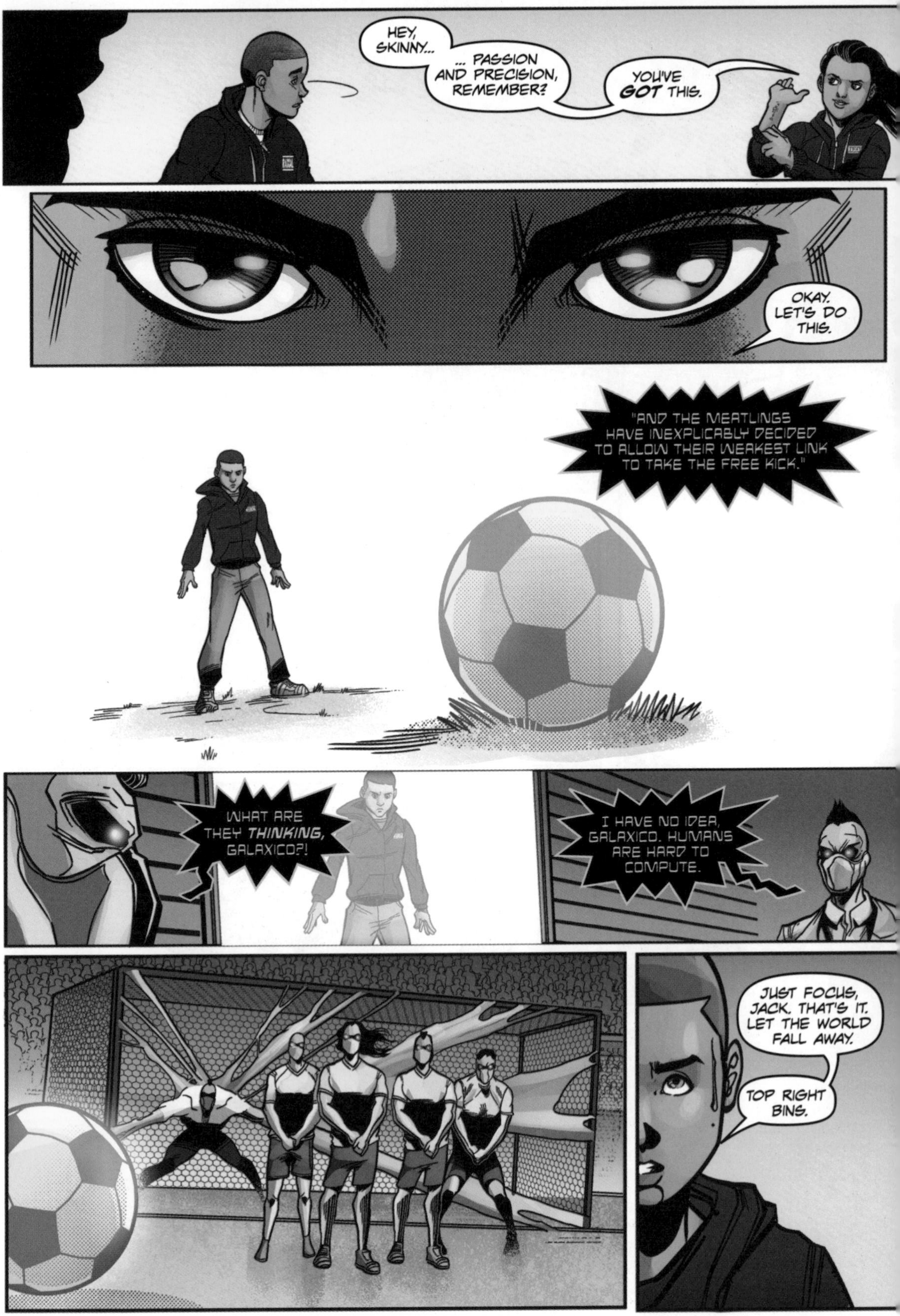
HEY, SKINNY...
... PASSION AND PRECISION, REMEMBER?
YOU'VE *GOT* THIS.
OKAY. LET'S DO THIS.
"AND THE MEATLINGS HAVE INEXPLICABLY DECIDED TO ALLOW THEIR WEAKEST LINK TO TAKE THE FREE KICK."
WHAT ARE THEY *THINKING*, GALAXICO?!
I HAVE NO IDEA, GALAXICO. HUMANS ARE HARD TO COMPUTE.
JUST FOCUS, JACK. THAT'S IT. LET THE WORLD FALL AWAY.
TOP RIGHT BINS.

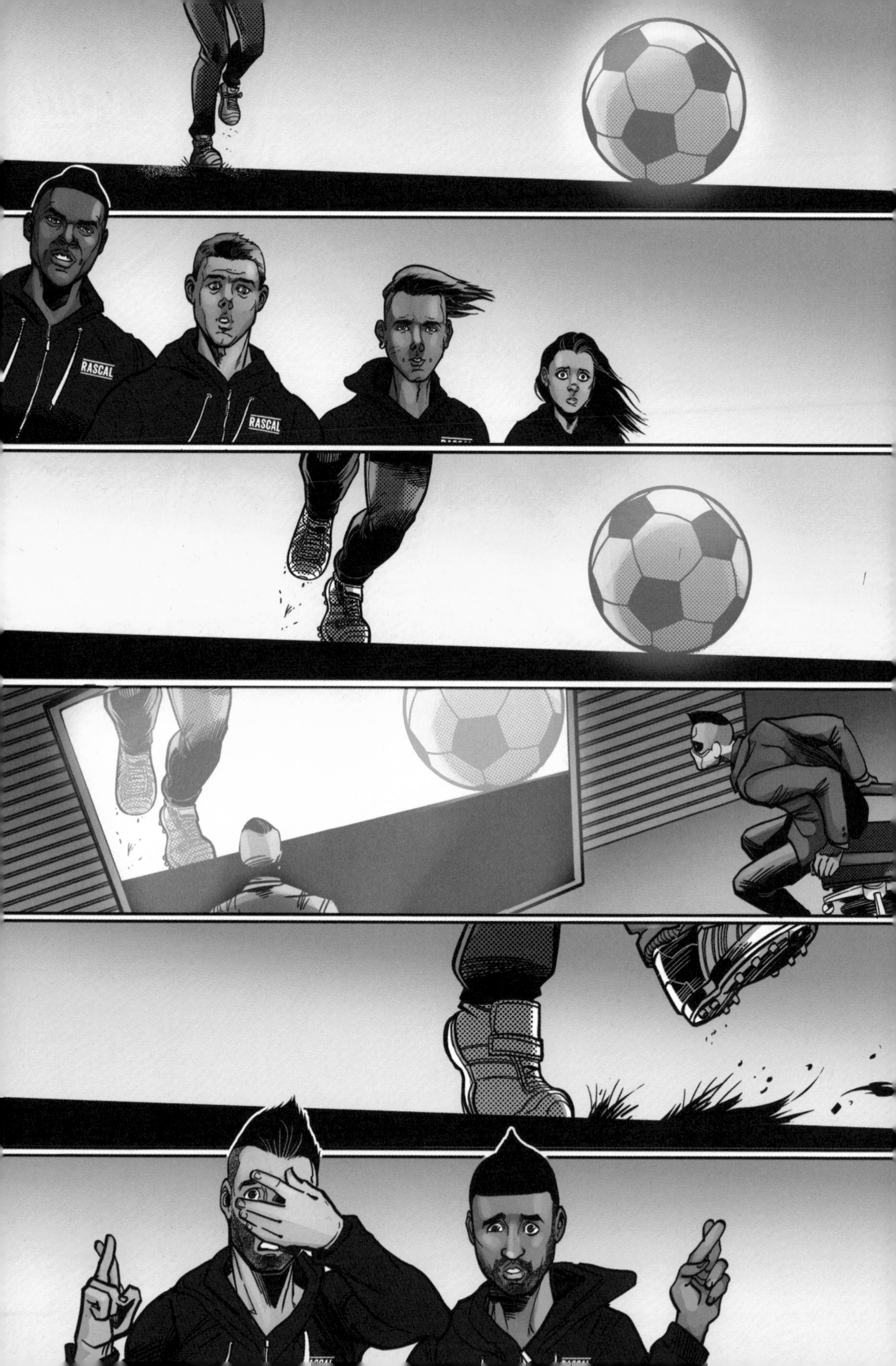
RASCAL
RASCAL

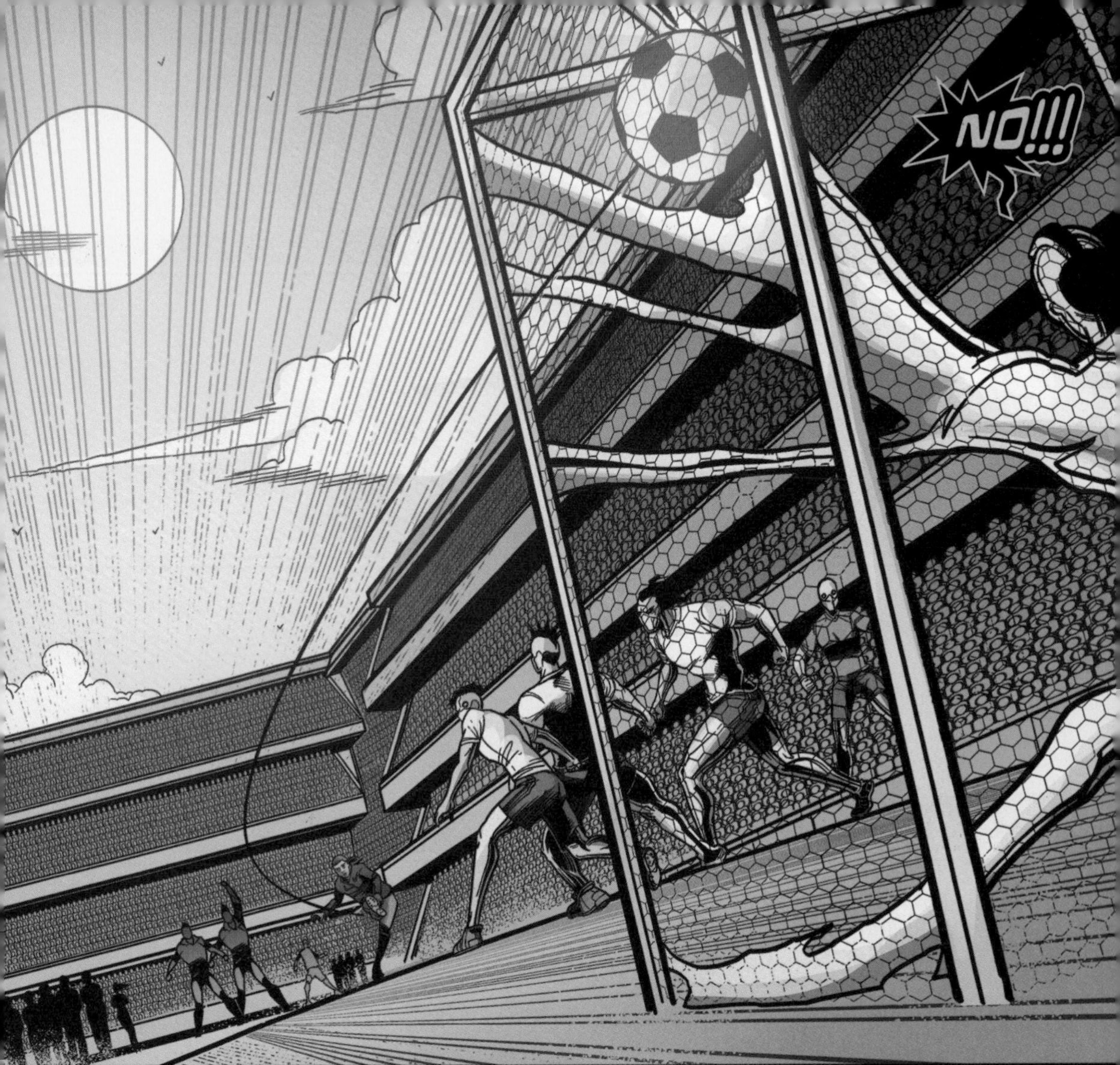
NO!!!

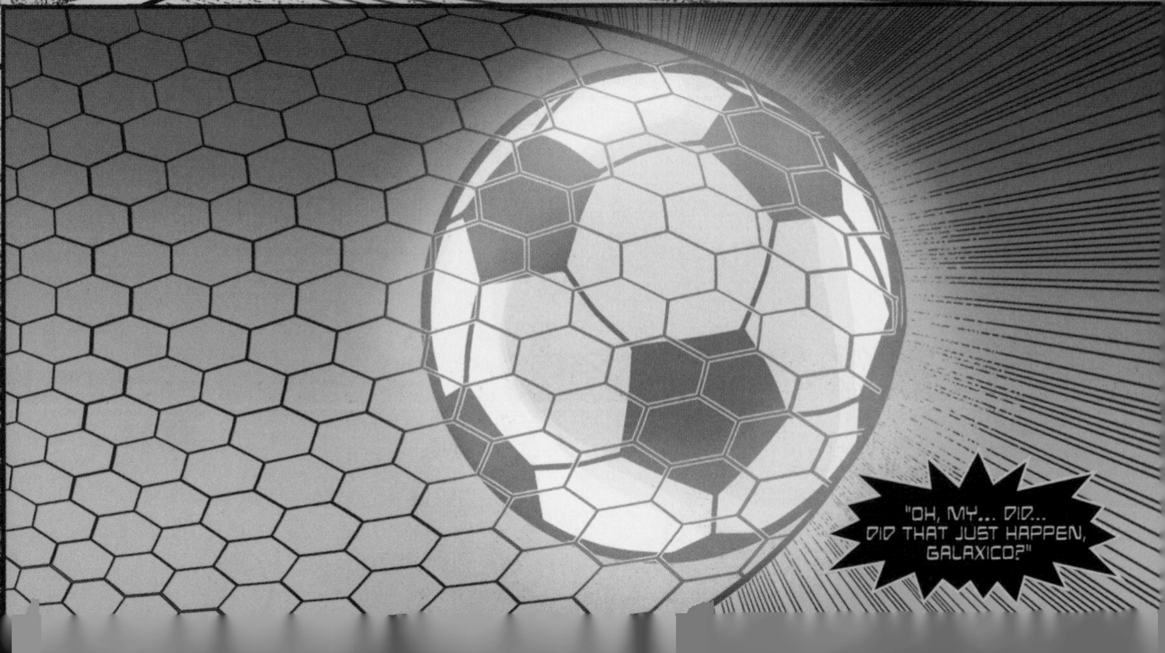
"OH, MY... DID...
DID THAT JUST HAPPEN,
GALAXICO?"

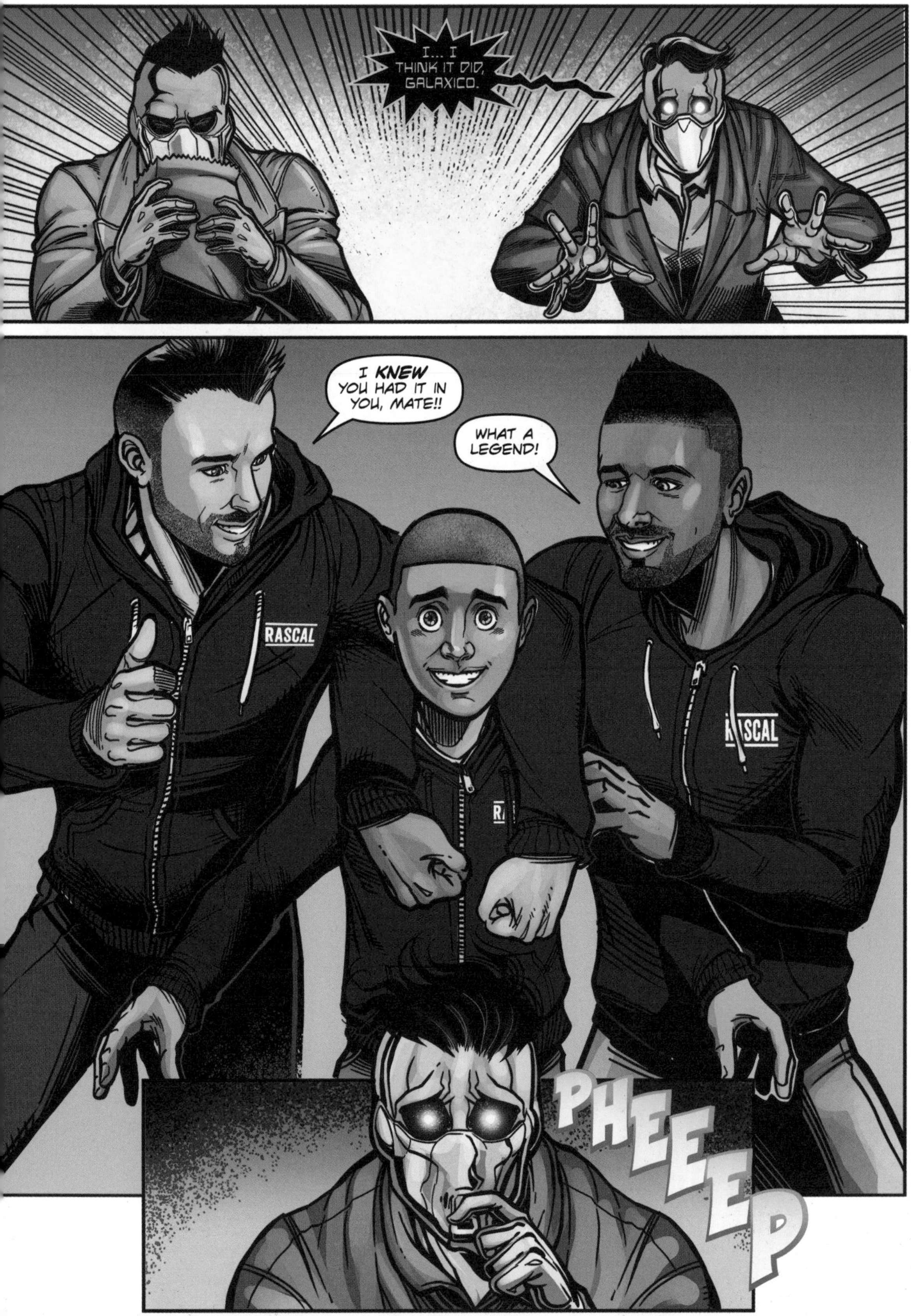
I... I THINK IT DID, GALAXICO.
I KNEW YOU HAD IT IN YOU, MATE!!
WHAT A LEGEND!
RASCAL
RASCAL
PHEEEEP

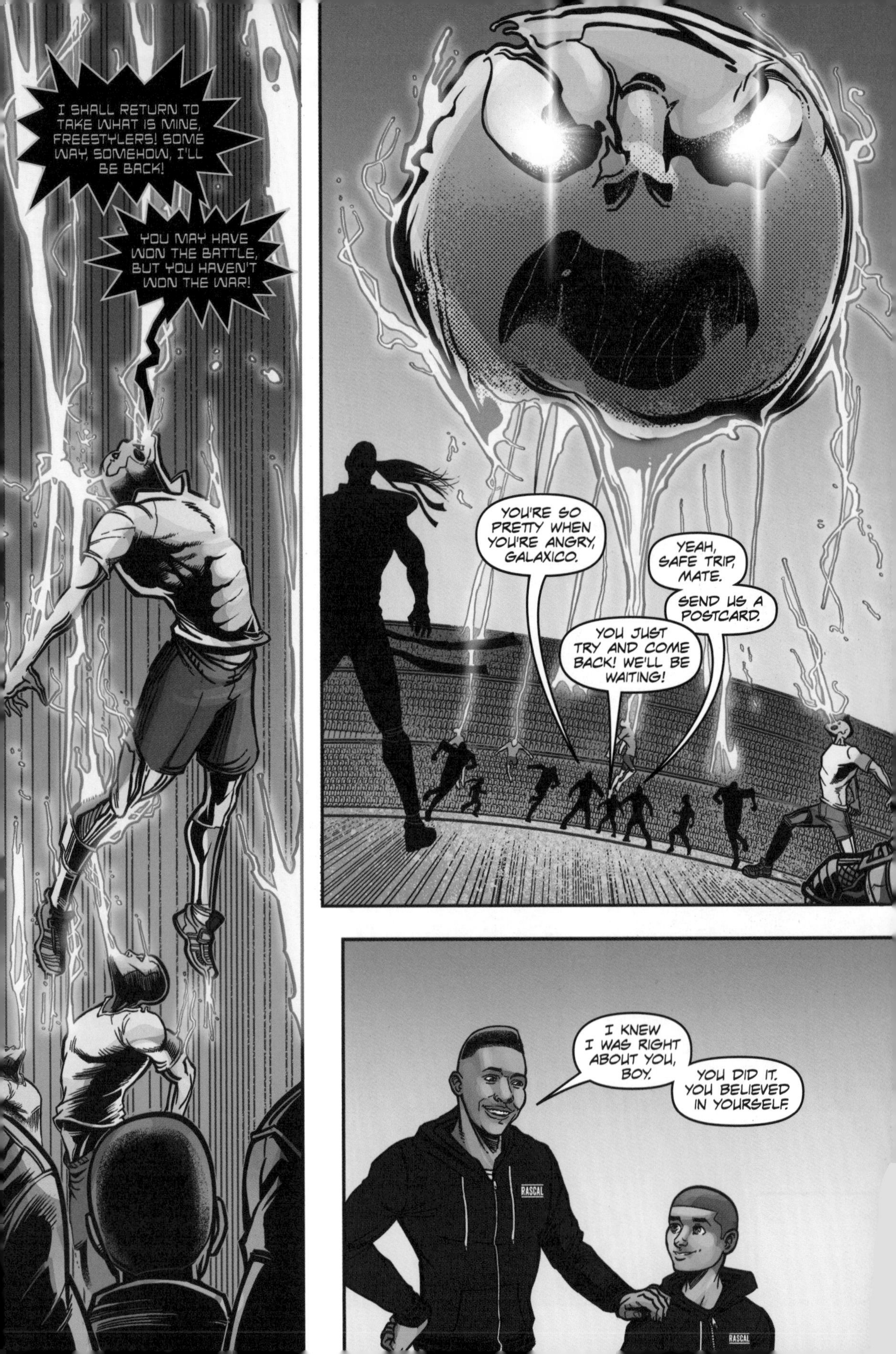
I SHALL RETURN TO TAKE WHAT IS MINE, FREESTYLERS! SOME WAY, SOMEHOW, I'LL BE BACK!
YOU MAY HAVE WON THE BATTLE, BUT YOU HAVEN'T WON THE WAR!
YOU'RE SO PRETTY WHEN YOU'RE ANGRY, GALAXICO.
YEAH, SAFE TRIP, MATE.
SEND US A POSTCARD.
YOU JUST TRY AND COME BACK! WE'LL BE WAITING!
I KNEW I WAS RIGHT ABOUT YOU, BOY.
YOU DID IT. YOU BELIEVED IN YOURSELF.
RASCAL
RASCAL

I'LL BE BAAAAAAAAAACK!!

THANK YOU SO MUCH. THEY TOOK OUR MINDS, OUR... OUR BODIES.

THANK YOU.

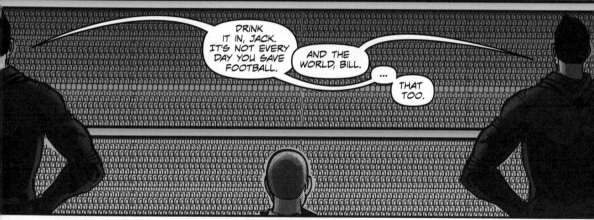

DRINK IT IN, JACK. IT'S NOT EVERY DAY YOU SAVE FOOTBALL.

AND THE WORLD, BILL.

... THAT TOO.

WE'LL BE BACK FOR YOU GUYS SOON, STEVIE G. TIME TO GET JACK HERE HOME FOR HIS TEA.

TAKE YOUR TIME, BOYS.

THAT ONE WAS FOR YOU, DAD.

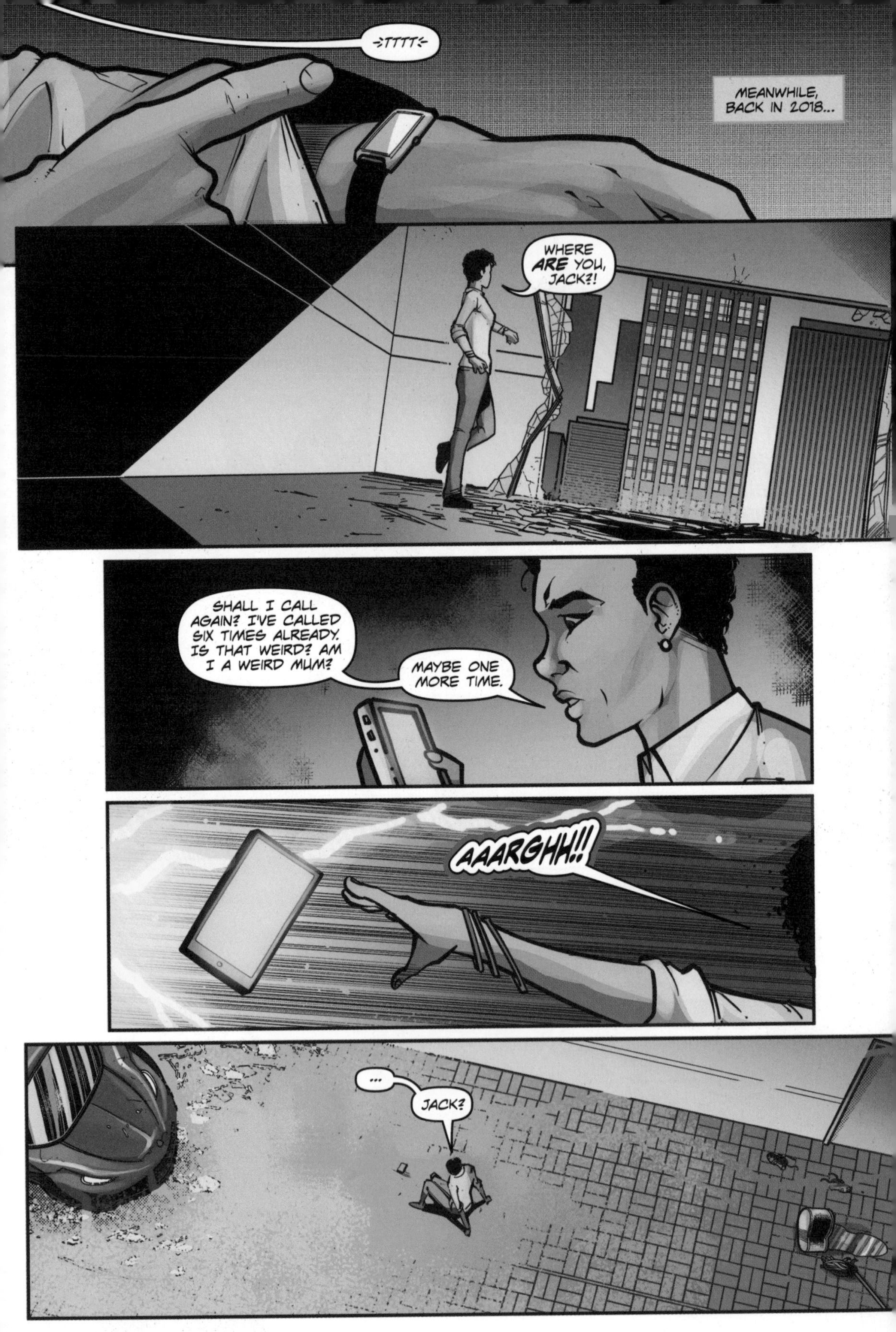

-TTTT-
MEANWHILE, BACK IN 2018...
WHERE ARE YOU, JACK?!
SHALL I CALL AGAIN? I'VE CALLED SIX TIMES ALREADY. IS THAT WEIRD? AM I A WEIRD MUM?
MAYBE ONE MORE TIME.
AAARGHH!!
...
JACK?

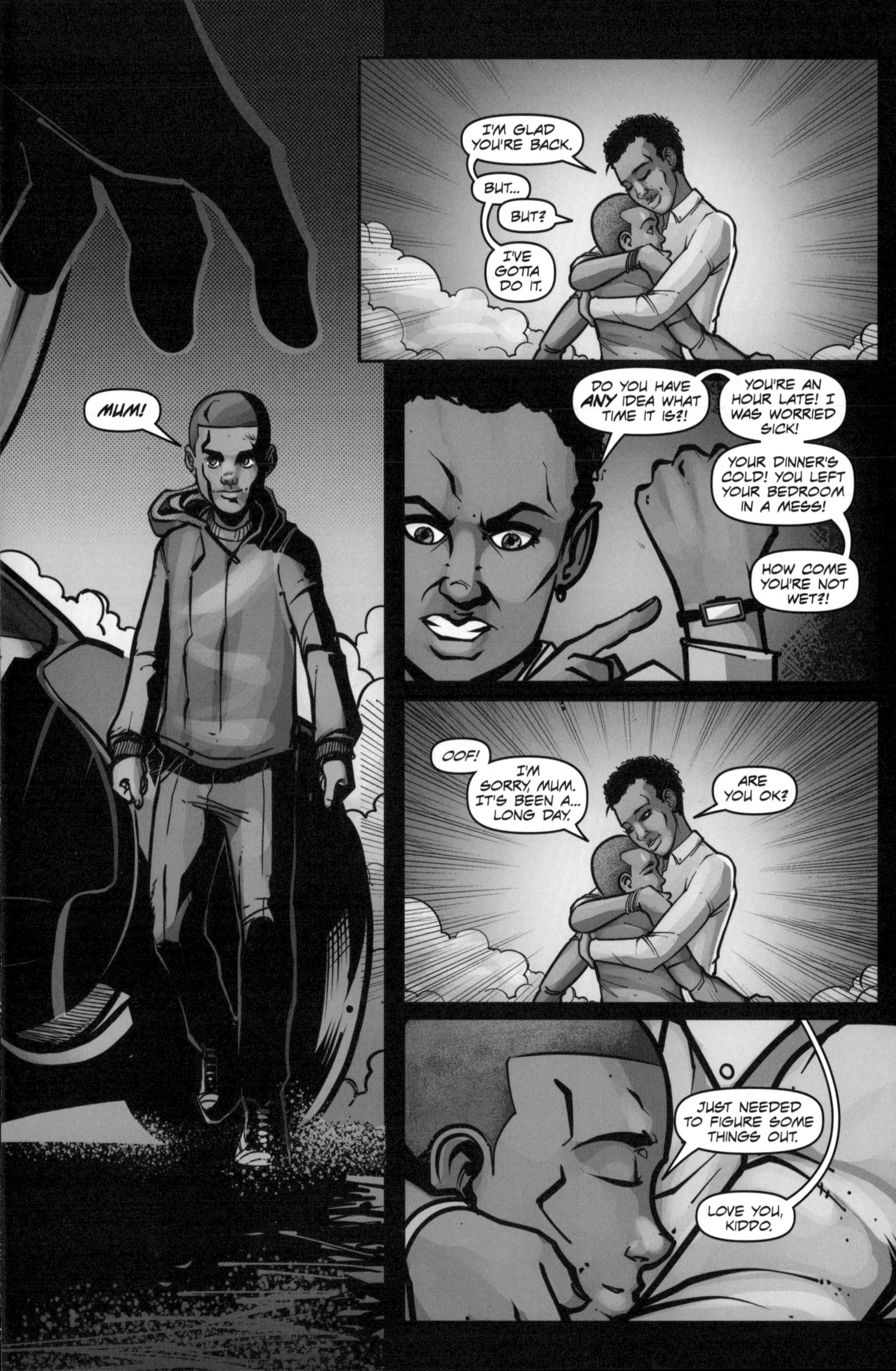
MUM!
I'M GLAD YOU'RE BACK.
BUT...
BUT?
I'VE GOTTA DO IT.
DO YOU HAVE ANY IDEA WHAT TIME IT IS?!
YOU'RE AN HOUR LATE! I WAS WORRIED SICK!
YOUR DINNER'S COLD! YOU LEFT YOUR BEDROOM IN A MESS!
HOW COME YOU'RE NOT WET?!
OOF!
I'M SORRY, MUM. IT'S BEEN A... LONG DAY.
ARE YOU OK?
JUST NEEDED TO FIGURE SOME THINGS OUT.
LOVE YOU, KIDDO.

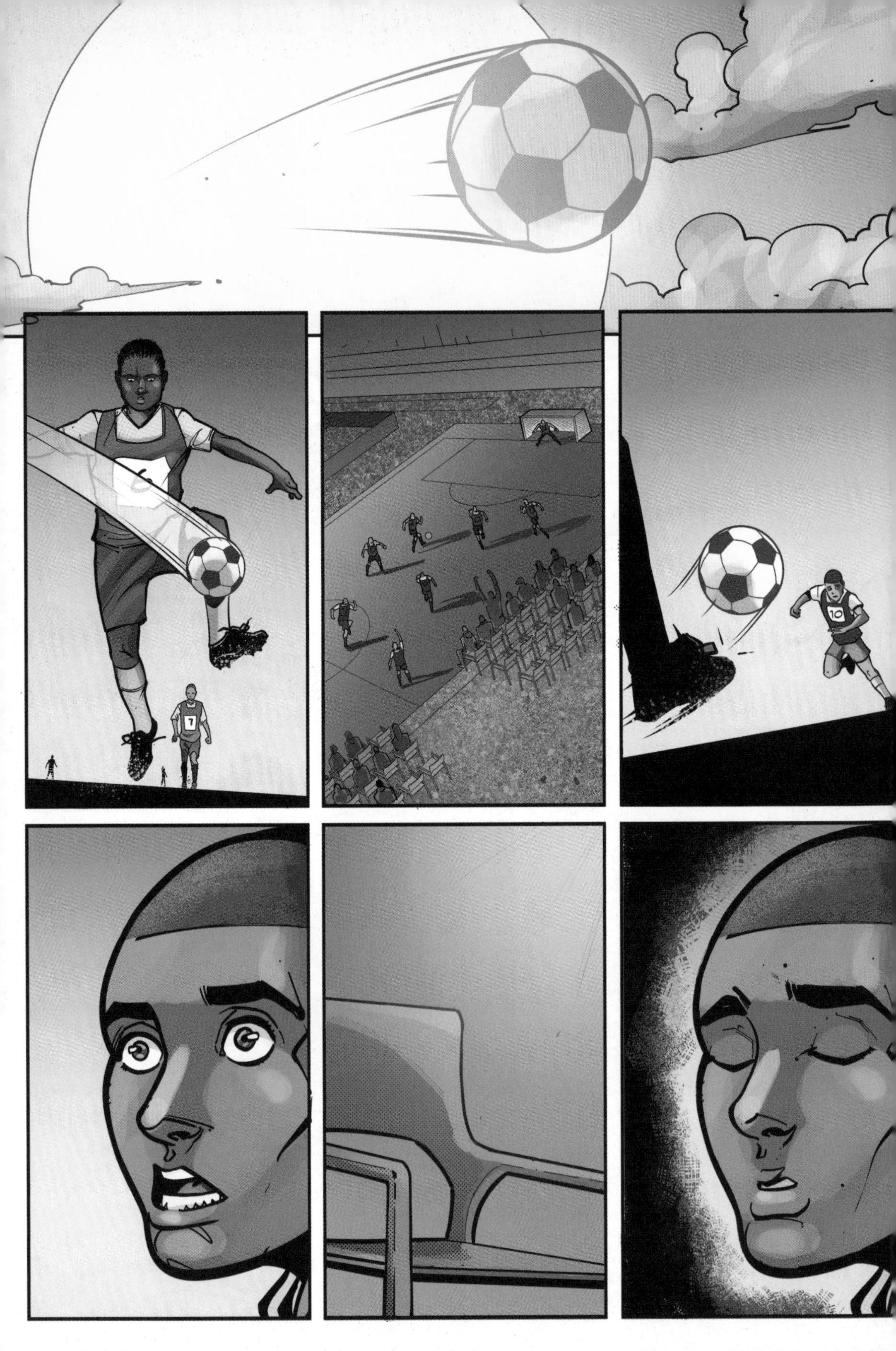

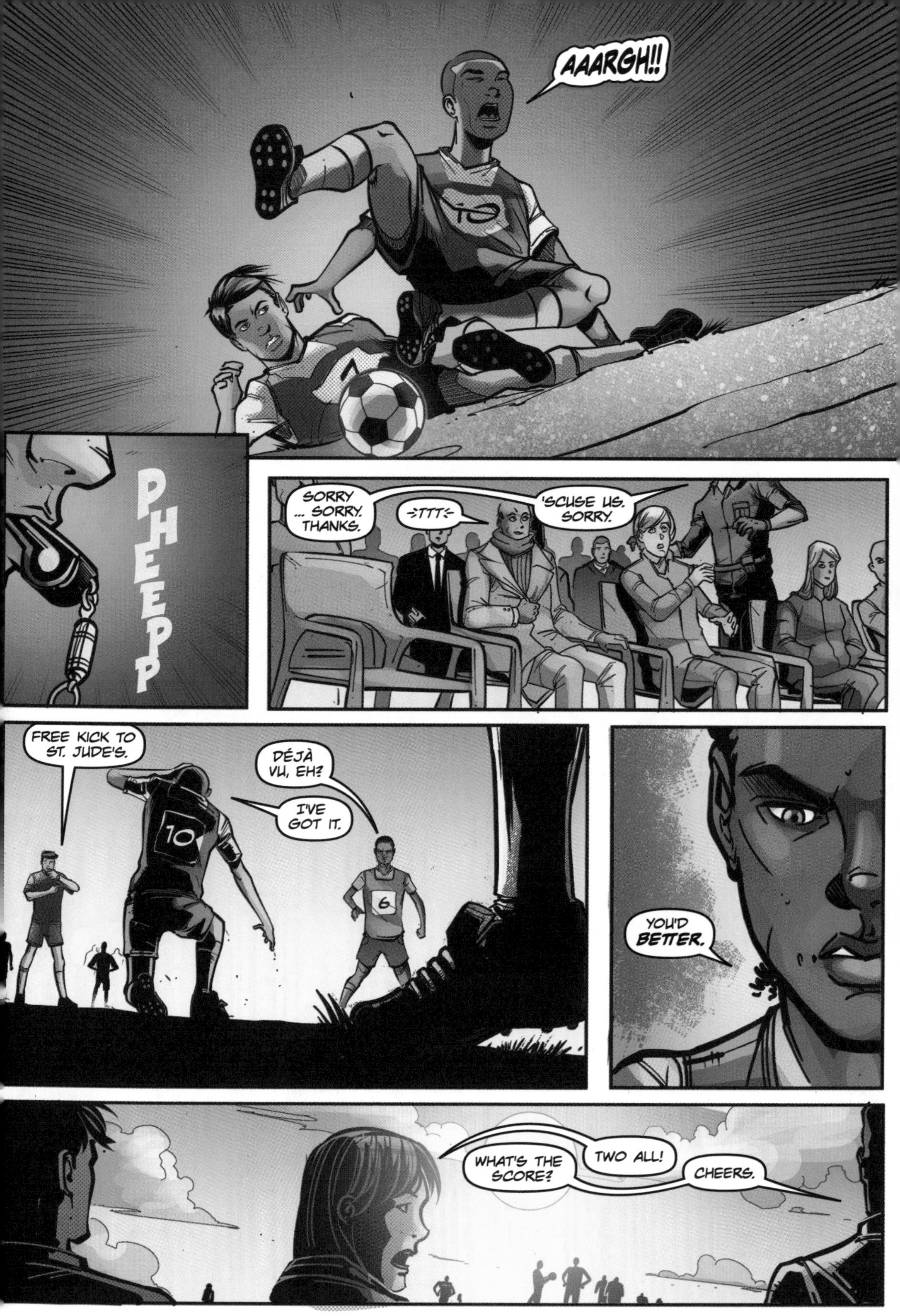
AAARGH!!
PHEEPP
SORRY ... SORRY. THANKS.
-TTT-
'SCUSE US. SORRY.
FREE KICK TO ST. JUDE'S.
DÉJÀ VU, EH?
I'VE GOT IT.
YOU'D BETTER.
WHAT'S THE SCORE?
TWO ALL!
CHEERS.

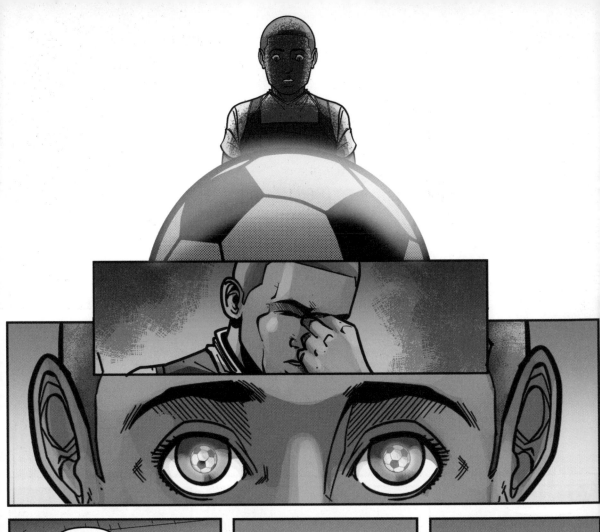

COME ON, JACK... *FOCUS.*

THINK TOP BINS...

COME ON, JACK MATE.

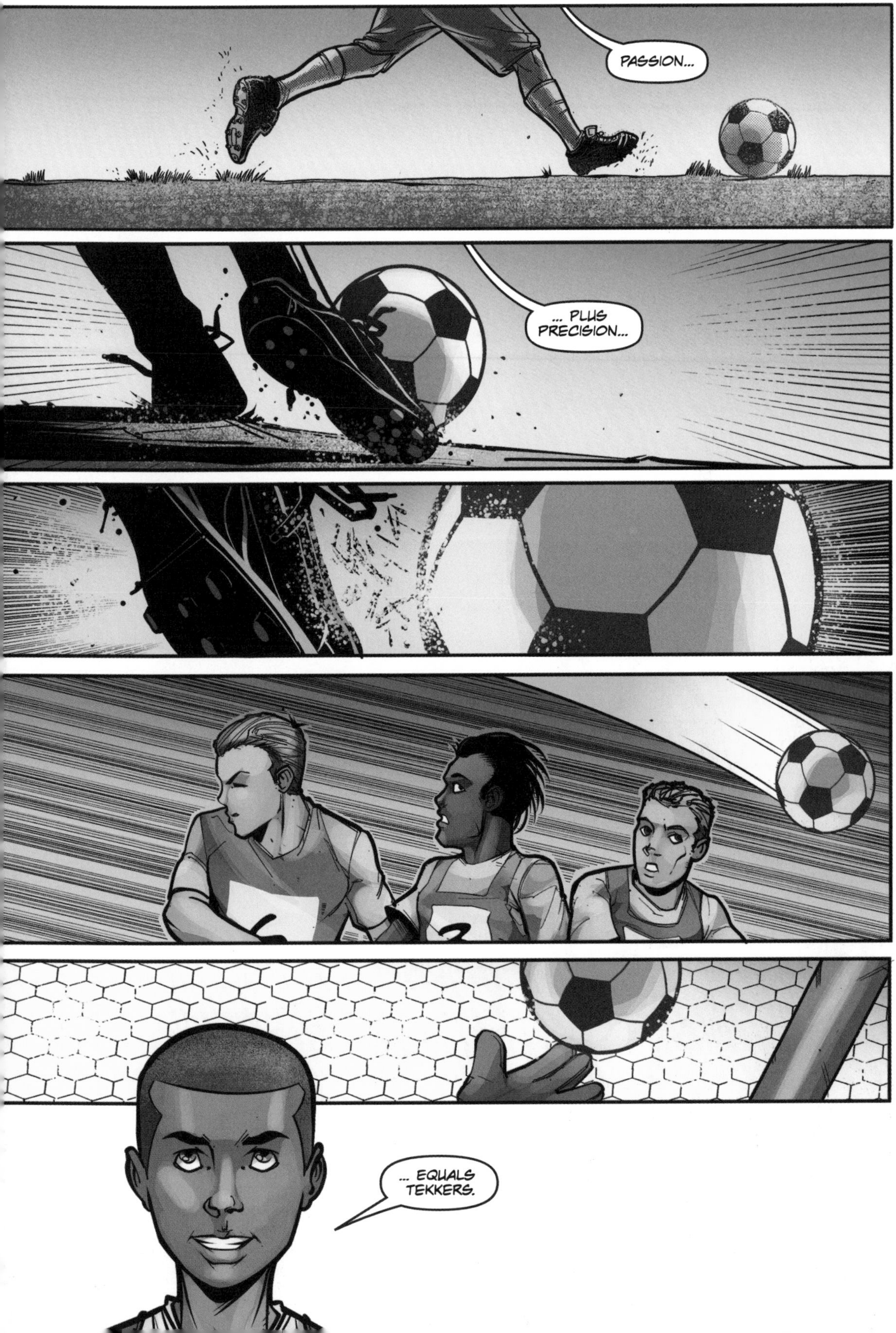
PASSION...
... PLUS PRECISION...
... EQUALS TEKKERS.

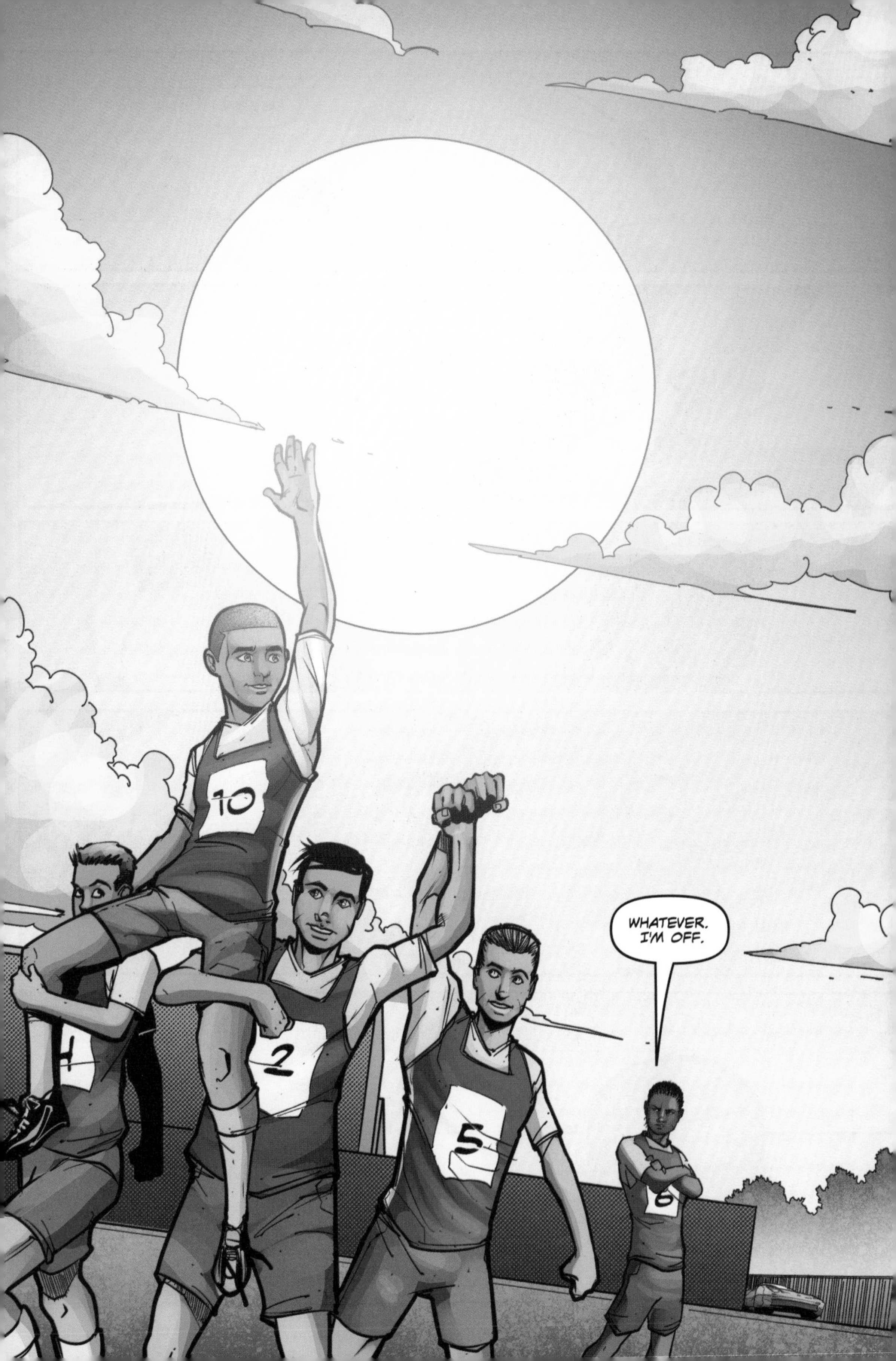
WHATEVER. I'M OFF.

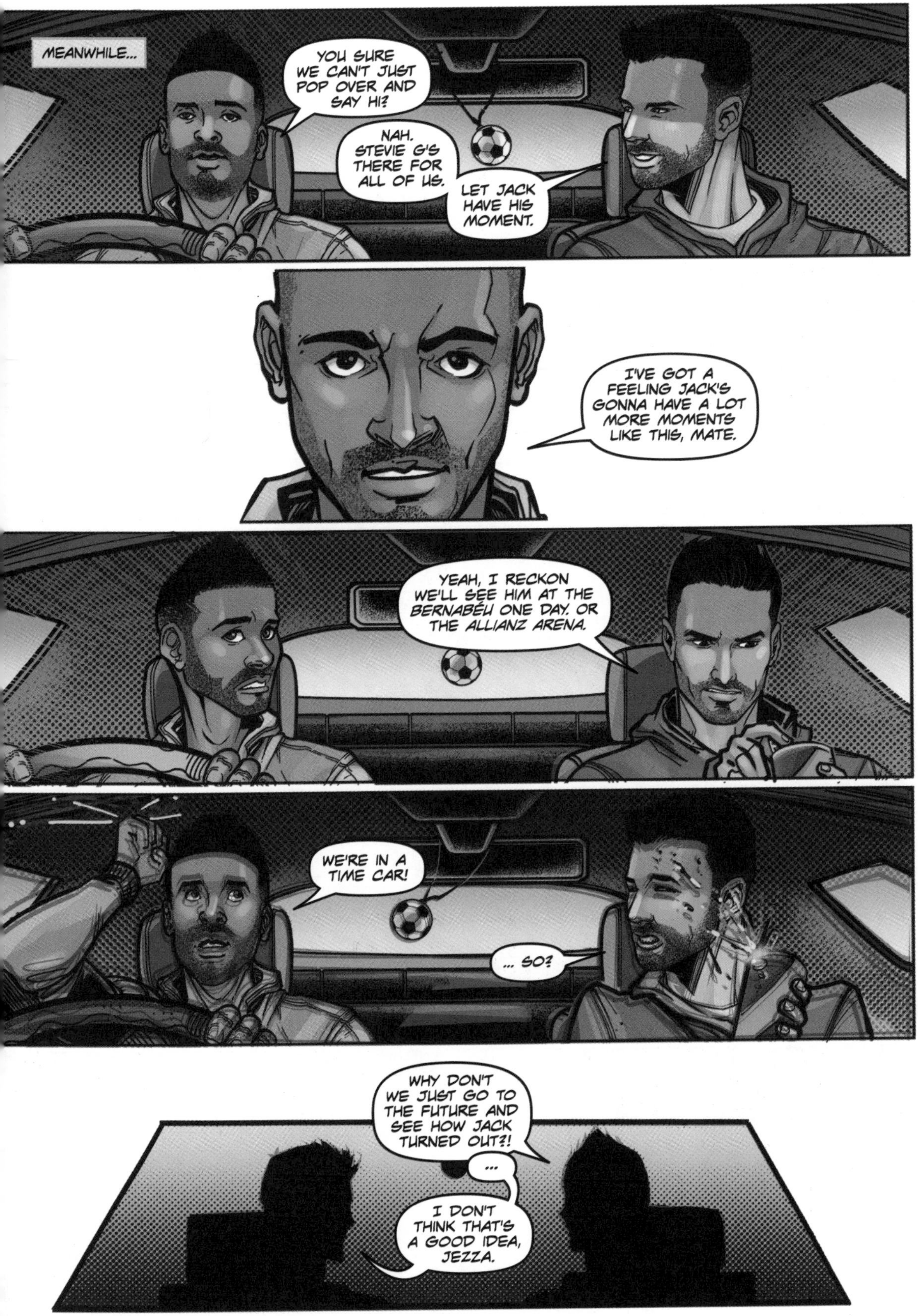
MEANWHILE...
YOU SURE WE CAN'T JUST POP OVER AND SAY HI?
NAH. STEVIE G'S THERE FOR ALL OF US.
LET JACK HAVE HIS MOMENT.
I'VE GOT A FEELING JACK'S GONNA HAVE A LOT MORE MOMENTS LIKE THIS, MATE.
YEAH, I RECKON WE'LL SEE HIM AT THE BERNABÉU ONE DAY. OR THE ALLIANZ ARENA.
WE'RE IN A TIME CAR!
... SO?
WHY DON'T WE JUST GO TO THE FUTURE AND SEE HOW JACK TURNED OUT?!
...
I DON'T THINK THAT'S A GOOD IDEA, JEZZA.

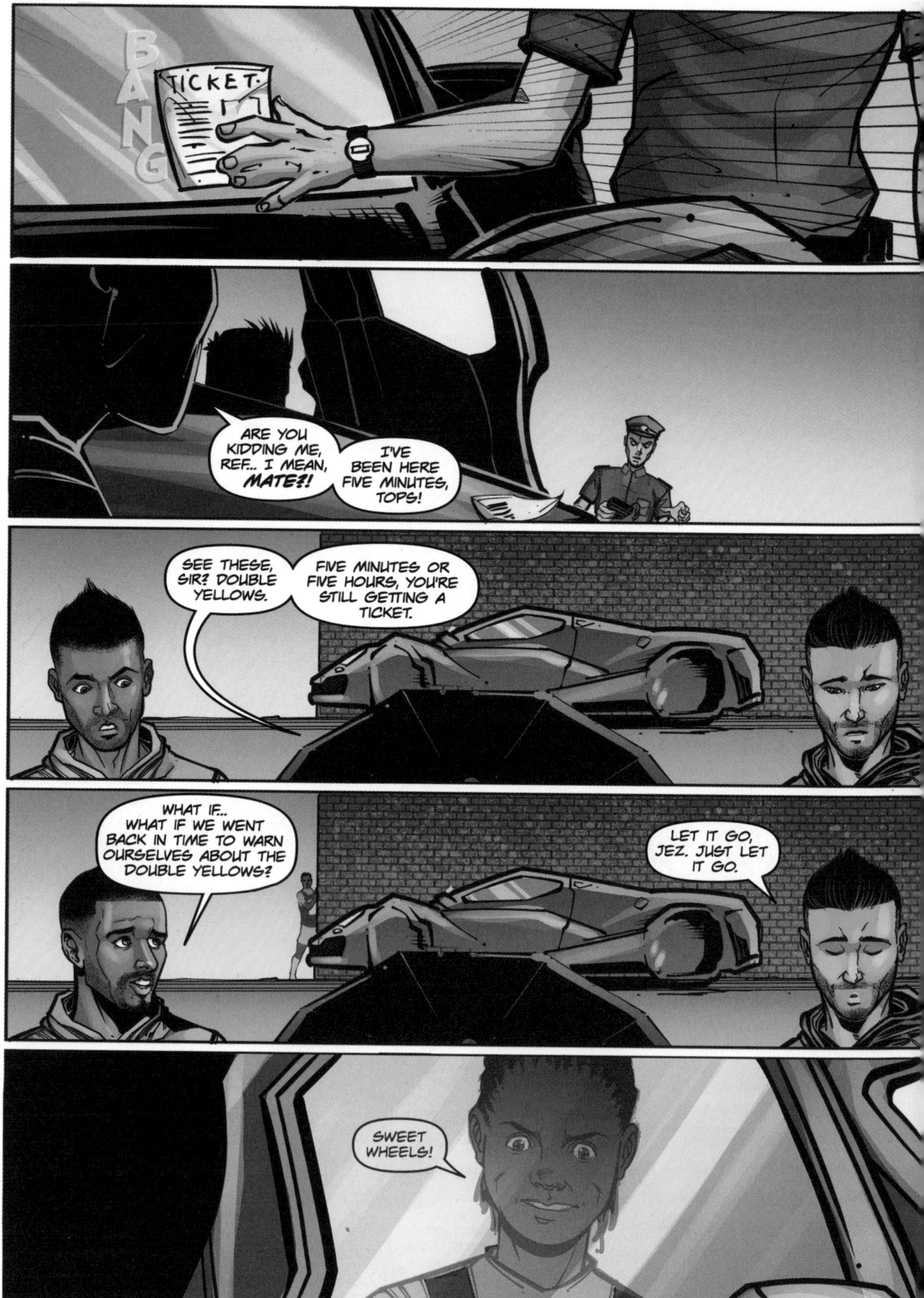
BANG
TICKET
ARE YOU KIDDING ME, REF... I MEAN, MATE?!
I'VE BEEN HERE FIVE MINUTES, TOPS!
SEE THESE, SIR? DOUBLE YELLOWS.
FIVE MINUTES OR FIVE HOURS, YOU'RE STILL GETTING A TICKET.
WHAT IF... WHAT IF WE WENT BACK IN TIME TO WARN OURSELVES ABOUT THE DOUBLE YELLOWS?
LET IT GO, JEZ. JUST LET IT GO.
SWEET WHEELS!

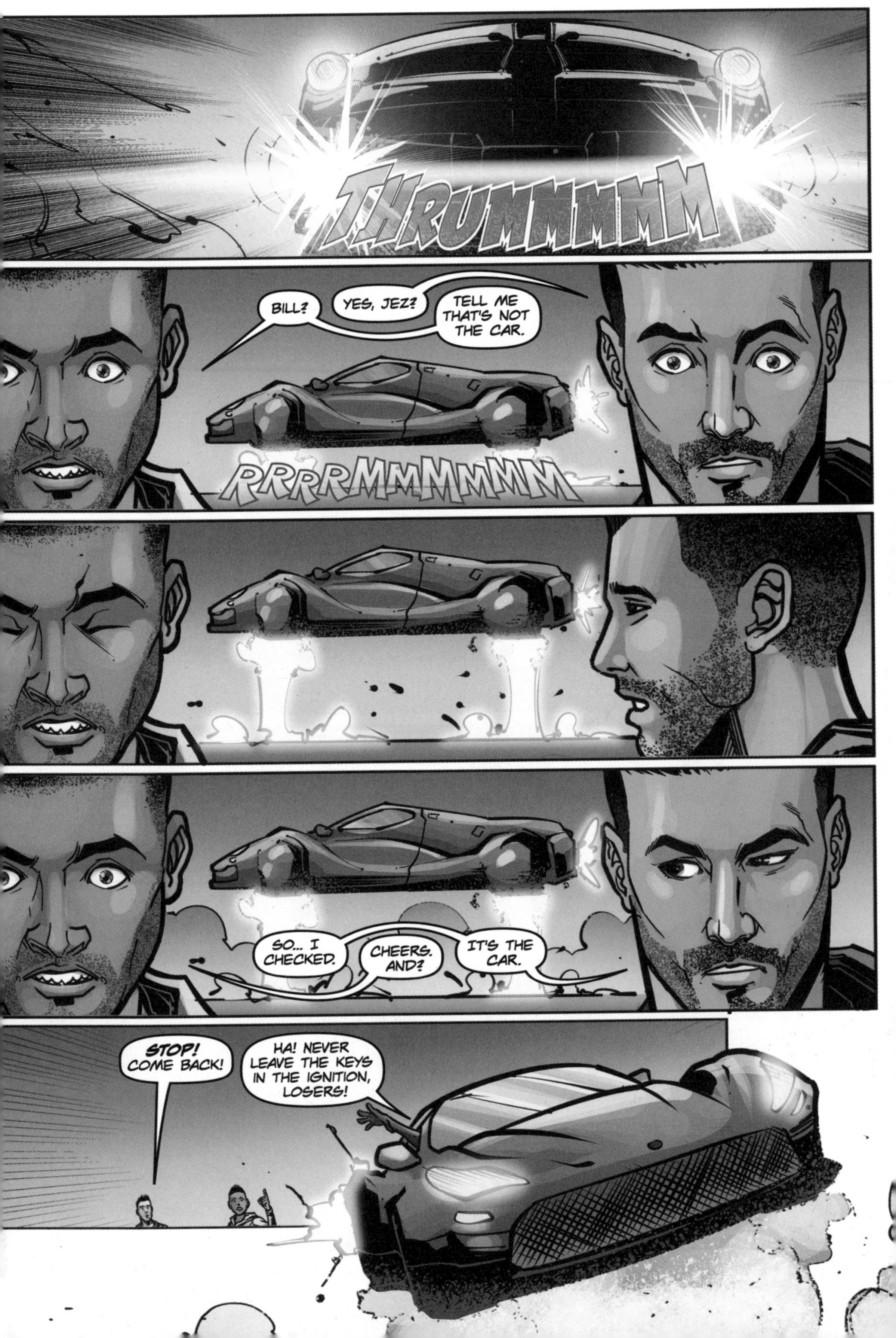
THRUMMMMM
BILL?
YES, JEZ?
TELL ME THAT'S NOT THE CAR.
RRRRMMMMMM
SO... I CHECKED.
CHEERS. AND?
IT'S THE CAR.
STOP! COME BACK!
HA! NEVER LEAVE THE KEYS IN THE IGNITION, LOSERS!

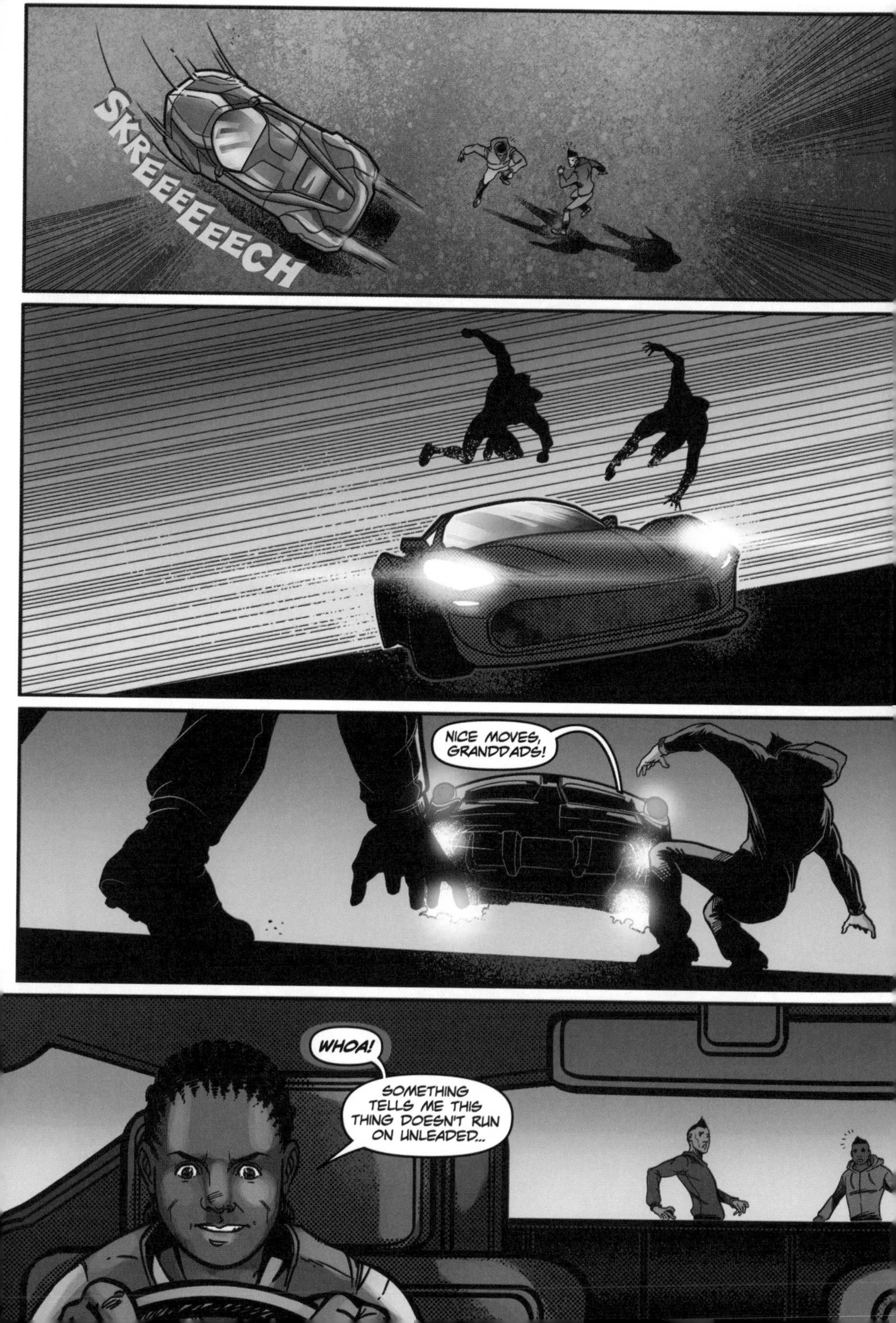
SKREEEEEEECH
NICE MOVES, GRANDDADS!
WHOA!
SOMETHING TELLS ME THIS THING DOESN'T RUN ON UNLEADED...

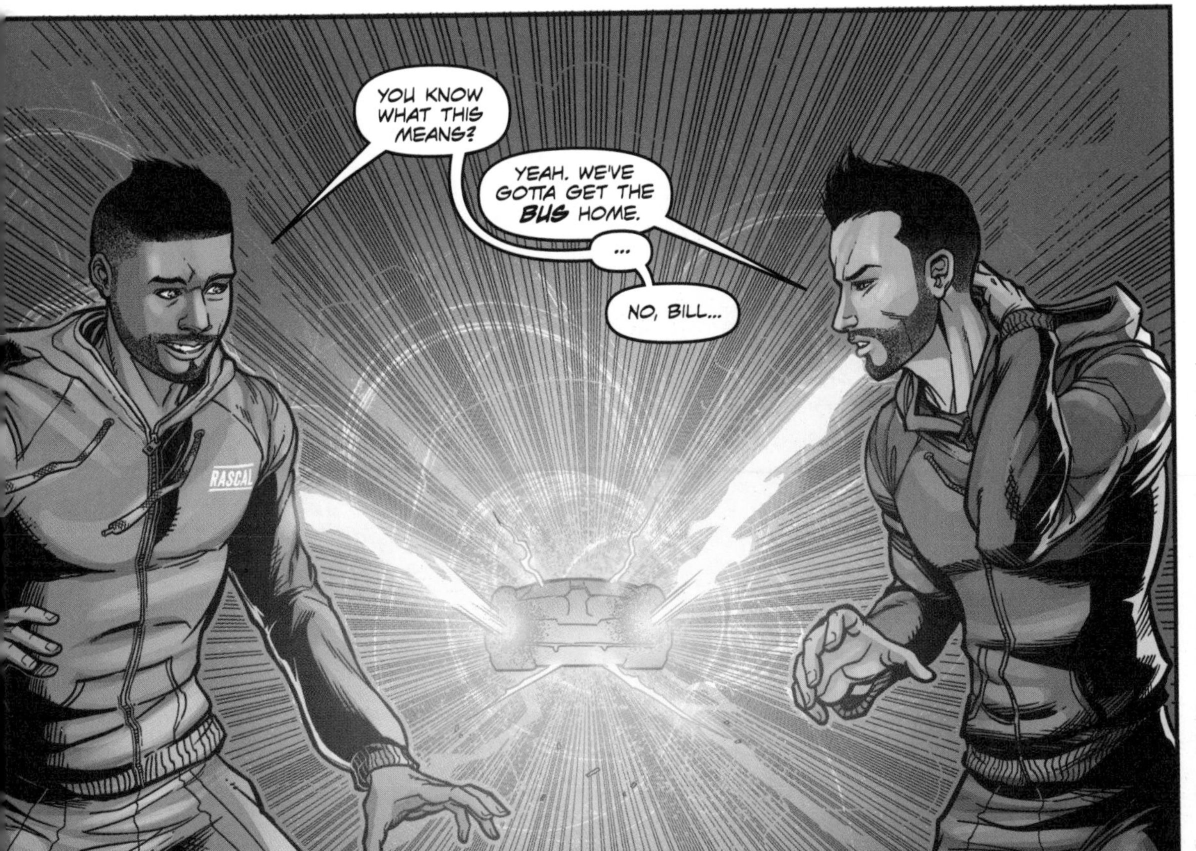
YOU KNOW WHAT THIS MEANS?
YEAH. WE'VE GOTTA GET THE BUS HOME.
...
NO, BILL...
RASCAL

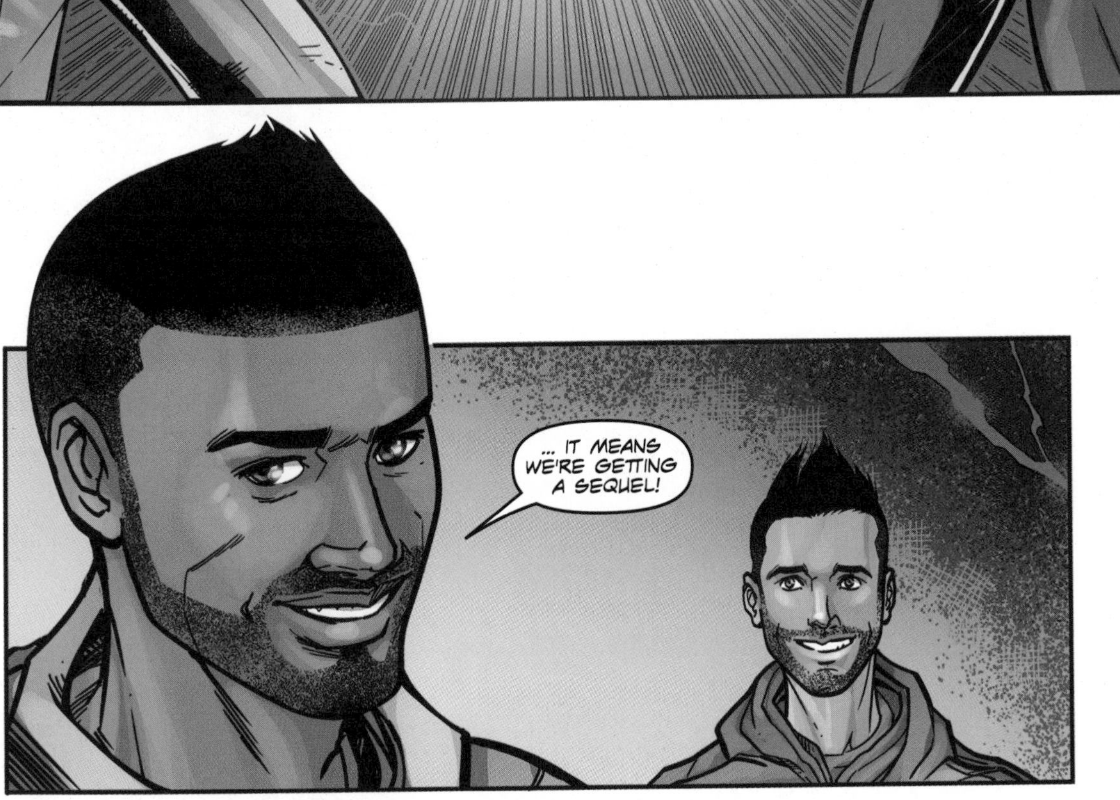
... IT MEANS WE'RE GETTING A SEQUEL!

ACKNOWLEDGEMENTS

Thank you to our families for supporting us, looking out for us and always being there. We've been on some amazing adventures in the past few years and you're all the greatest in the galaxy – much love to you all!

We'd like to say a massive thank you to Amrit Birdi (the Lionel Messi of illustration) and his creative team (the Barcelona of illustration). You're an incredibly talented lot and have shown some supreme pen-Tekkers in the past year or so. Thanks for being so flexible and open-minded with our ideas and for making us look so epic!

Thanks, too, to Dan Watters and Alex Paknadel for writing such a brilliant script. Not only did you get the lingo down, you took our original ideas and turned them into a truly awesome, space-football adventure. Who'da thought ten years ago, when we first started out, that we'd be saving the galaxy and the galaxy's most beautiful game... Cheers Dan and Alex!

Big thanks to our man Sam Bayford and to the awesome team at Blink Publishing, including our editors Joel Simons and Matt Phillips; as well as Nathan Balsom, Perminder Mann, Ben Dunn, Andrew Sauerwine, Lisa Hoare, Lizzie Dorney-Kingdom and Zoe Fawcett.

Lastly, a big shout-out to all you guys – The F2 Family... across the galaxy. We hope you enjoyed this adventure as much as we loved making it. And remember, as Jack showed, nothing is impossible; one day it could be you saving the world... Now get outside and practise your skills!

Love, Peace and inter-galactic Tekkers,

THE F2

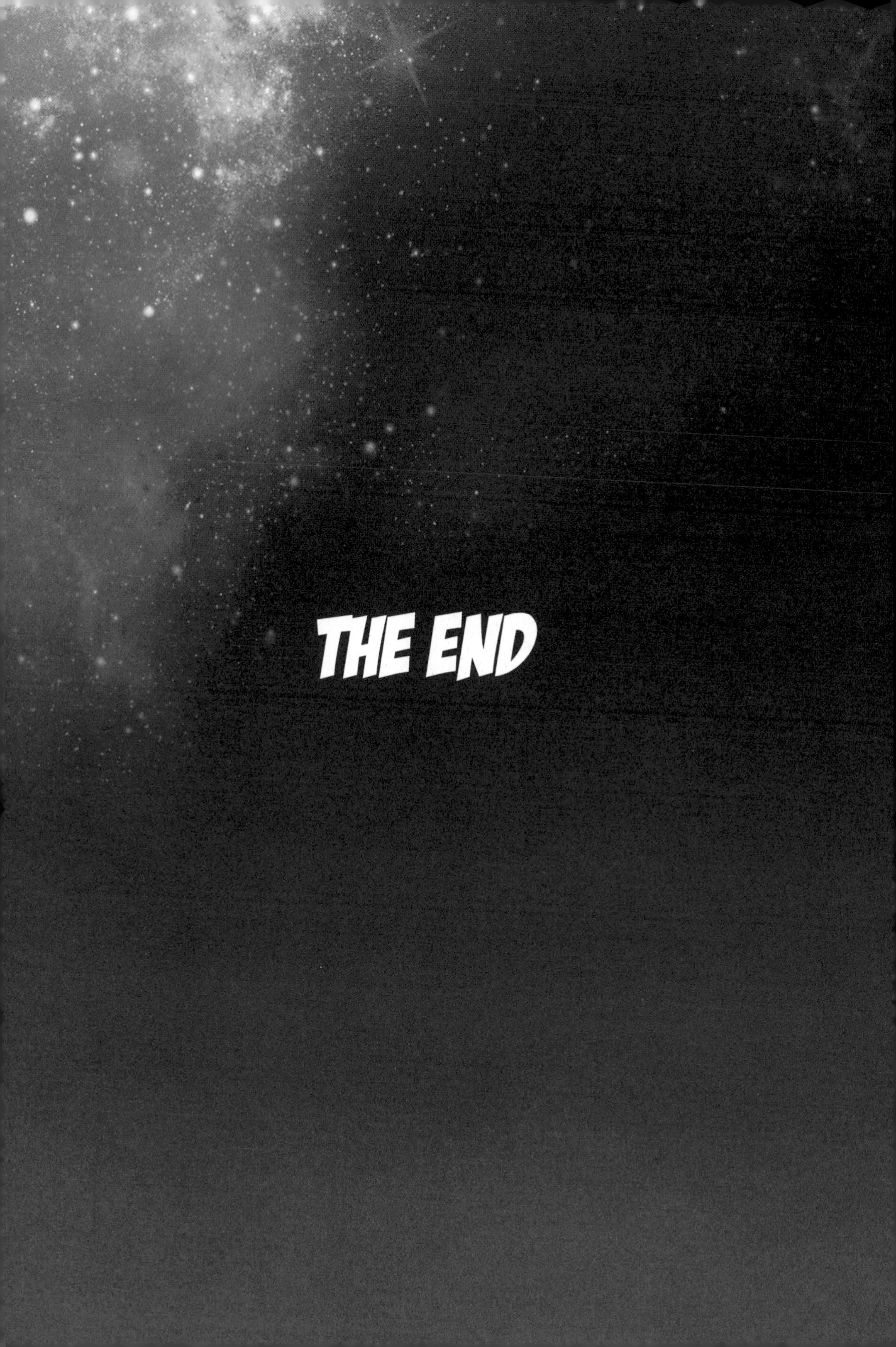
THE END